Private Owens

Paintball Wars Chronicles

Coming soon!

Private Owens
A George Owens Novel

William DeForest Halsted IV

ISBN: 979-8-218-35107-6 (print)

ISBN: 979-8-8693-7491-2 (ebook)

Library of Congress Control Number (LCCN): 2024900238

Book Cover Art by Matthew Halsted

Illustrations by Matthew Halsted and Emeline Halsted

Map Imagery by Nick Budros

First Edition: June 2024 (1.0)

Published by William DeForest Halsted IV

Castro Valley, California.

Contents

Illustrations

To Patricia, my favorite friend-sitter.

Preface
How the Paintball Wars Began

If you have picked up this book and are reading this, you were likely intrigued by what you read on the back — a thirteen-year-old boy who, tired of public school, enlists in the Alamedan paintball Army. Very likely you are wondering what these Paintball Wars are. In one sentence, the Paintball Wars is World War II fought by teenagers with paintball in which the youth populations of different state counties wage war to defeat and conquer each other for territorial bragging rights. But it is really much more.

The Paintball Wars was first conceived around the time I was nine or ten years old as a Nerf war. This quickly transitioned to paintball when my dad explained to me that paint was better because it leaves a mark, making it clear who was hit. From there, I began to create stories of a paintball "war" fought by a handful of kids during a month or two of non-stop action over summer break. This was one of my first attempts at writing a book. However, while such a story was exciting, it wasn't nearly grand enough. As a history buff who loved to study World War II, I wanted something epic.

So I created it. I decided that the kids in each town or county could organize themselves into armies and wage war upon each other on a grand scale, with thousands of soldiers taking part in World War II-style battles. This didn't change civilian governments, but typically you fought for the "nation" (paintball county) "ruling" where you lived. Whoever militarily held the most territory by driving out the other paintball armies had the biggest nation and therefore the biggest bragging rights. And there were only kids, because the Paintball Wars, as I came to call it, was limited to those under eighteen years old. No adults to spoil the independency of the teenagers.

The first real story of this new Paintball Wars was created when I shared this concept with my new friend Adrian. Very quickly it turned into a roleplay scenario in which we each took actions as the commanding generals of two opposing forces. General Halsted of the Alamedan Empire was attempting to make an amphibious invasion of Adrian's island kingdom, which he named Aldemont. We went back and forth with each other, alternately taking actions with our units and creating scenarios that would tip the scale of battle in our favor. This eventually petered out and was left as a draw, but not before I had written half the story of this battle. The Paintball Wars had been established beyond the confines of my own imagination, and the real-character roleplay had been created that would come to define it.

Over time I drew more friends into my social circle of the Paintball Wars. There were varying degrees of interest, but everyone participated, roleplaying and taking actions as their characters and contributing to the dynamic in-game world. I generally represented the Alamedan Empire, but was also the game master, producing some conflicts of interest. However, while everyone worked for his own personal gain, of course, the world was largely story-driven where our imaginations could run wild creating stories, worldbuilding, and lore-building. A good story became more important than our own personal triumphs.

Through this roleplay, an incredibly interesting world developed. We had a group chat for everybody where the game master posted the official happenings, and the players created many private chats to communicate with their allies or connive with their "enemies." During the Coronavirus Pandemic, we discovered Zoom, and used it to meet virtually and hash out what happened in the story, to hold political meetings and to argue, make threats, and play politics, but also to compromise and reach a solution so the story could continue. Nothing half so interesting could have been created without the genuine personalities and schemes of the characters resulting from the real-life human being behind them. An entire world was built and histories written.

Eventually this waned, and presently the roleplay still continues, though not at its former pace. Many of our in-game characters are turning eighteen and aging out of the Paintball Wars. However, the detailed history of some seven-plus game years has already been created and continues to be expanded. Joshua became my Paintball Wars partner, and we two nerds embarked together to write these stories and share them with the world. He and I have put hours and hours into inventing everything from characters to lore to the history of wars and technology of weaponry, and continue to do so. It is truly a passion project. The wealth of potential stories and technical detail that all weave together into the same universe is immense and far from repetitive. Each of us has our own pet project, from our individual nations to our personal military adventures and beyond, but we are both tuned in to the big picture.

One of our main goals in writing about the Paintball Wars is to maintain a level of pseudo-realism. These stories are obviously fiction, but they try to pass themselves off as a potential reality. To this end, nations are typically built from existing locations, like state counties, and almost all locations in the stories really exist and are chosen by scouring Google Earth and other online resources to fit the story or vice versa. The characters sing real songs, play real video games, watch real YouTube channels, and visit real locations. The military technology is based off of World War II for the most part, but invented and adapted with paintball in mind, creating unique weapons and combat doctrine. Yes, this could never happen in real life, and if you fired a paint artillery shell an entire mile, you would probably kill the person you hit. But somewhere reality has to be suspended in order for fiction to exist. It is my belief that these stories are portrayed as entirely plausible, even if unlikely. The Paintball Wars, with a little effort, *could* actually happen. They are fun-and-games war stories for youth, without the death, mutilation, and mental trauma of the real horror that is war. In this spirit of a clean war story, the characters in these stories use mild expressions that we consider to be PG, such as "hell," "blast," and "bastard," while avoiding profanity like the f-word.

That account brings the world of the Paintball Wars to the present day, where this book is. This story itself fits into a wider history of the nations built from counties on the backs of teenage paintball soldiers' sweat and tears. There are parallel stories, prequels, and sequels that have yet to be written — front-line war stories, adventures, espionage, mysteries, grand strategy, technology development, lore and history, other concurrent events and characters — so much background to this book that I couldn't possibly fit it all in, even if I tried. This is the first attempt at producing a complete tale in and of itself, but just one piece of this larger universe of stories, to share with the world. Hopefully, there will be many more novels in the future written by myself and other authors. It would be the realization of a childhood dream come true. With that, I present to you the very first of the Paintball Wars Chronicles.

"Pugna Ut Vincas!"

— William DeForest Halsted IV
December 2023

"The price of greatness is responsibility."
Winston Churchill

"We shall not fail or falter. We shall not weaken or tire. Neither the sudden shock of battle nor the long-drawn trials of vigilance and exertion will wear us down. Give us the tools and we will finish the job."
Winston Churchill

Map Title

Location Name

Road Block

Fortifications

Distance Scale

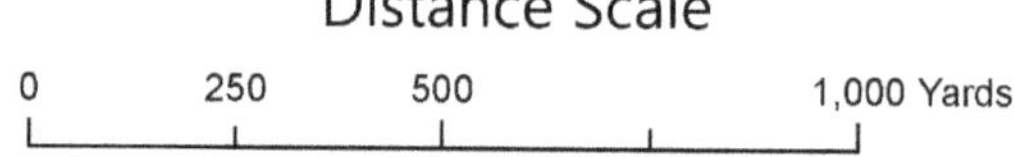

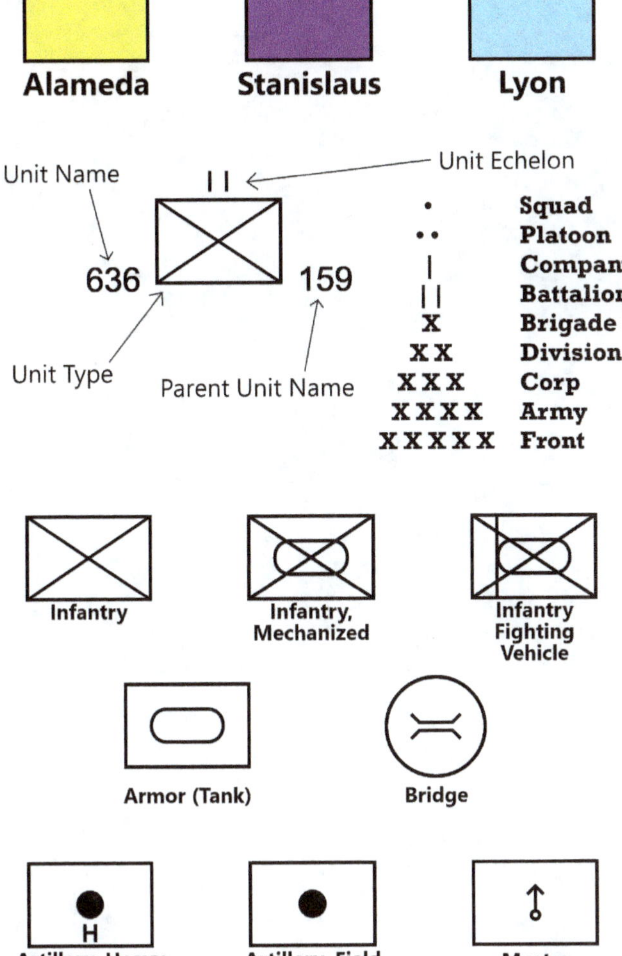

Alameda
Stanislaus
Lyon
Unit Name
Unit Echelon
Unit Type
636
159
Parent Unit Name
Squad
Platoon
Company
Battalion
X   Brigade
X X   Division
X X X   Corp
X X X X   Army
X X X X X   Front
Infantry
Infantry, Mechanized
Infantry Fighting Vehicle
Armor (Tank)
Bridge
Artillery, Heavy
H
Artillery, Field
Mortar

Private Owens

Chapter I

OCTOBER, 5 PBW[1]

BRI-I-ING!

George's head snapped up as the school bell sounded its high-pitch alarm, warning the teachers that they must now release their subjects to the lunch room. His teacher briskly came down the aisles, collecting the assignment she had given her students to work on during the last fifteen minutes of her class period. They fidgeted nervously.

When she arrived at George's desk, she frowned at his uncompleted work. "Young man, this sort of behavior will not help your report card. You had plenty of time to do these problems."

George merely shrugged. He'd got the first three correct, he was sure. Why did he have to do all twenty when he had proved he understood the concept?

Finally his teacher released her students a whole five minutes after the bell. "The bell doesn't dismiss you," she said, "*I* do." Fair enough. But it wasn't like they didn't already have little enough time to eat.

---

1. PBW denotes the epoch (timeline) of the Paintball Wars. 5 PBW is the fifth year of the Paintball Wars.

George meandered after his classmates and arrived at the back of the cafeteria line. When he finally reached the serving bar, he picked up one of the aging plastic trays and faced the woman serving the food. She handed out a small portion of a few different items, just as unappetizing as always and so processed that it looked more like the fare of an astronaut, not the hearty meal a thirteen-year-old boy should have been eating.

He sat down by himself, as usual. Not that he cared; he didn't really have any good friends at school. He ate his food quietly until the shrieking of the school bell cut him off. He had been one of the last to finally get his lunch.

Wolfing down the rest of his meal and competing with the other kids to dispose of his trash and get to his next period, he skipped the bathroom for lack of time, despite the fact that he had to go. Once he had arrived at his class on time, he could ask for a bathroom break, taking as long as he dared before returning to the bondage of his desk.

All these geography facts about what was where, and what city was the capital of which country around the world — why exactly was it so important that he learn them? He would remember just enough of the information to pass the test, and two weeks later have forgotten it all as he crammed his noggin with new facts for the next test.

Oh, yes, and then he'd have to go back over all those forgotten facts again to prepare for his final exam.

Fortunately, his history class was next. Currently, they were still studying the section about World War II. George disliked reading his textbook, but he loved Mr. Mathel's engaging lectures and videos that told the stories of the decades and centuries past, stuff that really happened, the Allies' desperate struggle to liberate Europe from the oppression of Nazi Germany.

History was over all too soon, and after that came English. A week ago, his teacher had passed out their latest essay assignment, which was due in two days. Something about evolution and the origins of man. It was sorta interesting, but really just boring science masquerading as history. George would start working on it tomorrow. It was only a page.

George stamped his feet on the doormat outside his home and entered the refuge. His mom appeared and greeted him with a hug.

"Hello, Honey. How was school?"

"The same," he replied indifferently.

"Well, at least you're home early."

"The school bus was quick today." That was one of the best things that had happened to him all day.

"Well, why don't you get your homework done while I start dinner?" his mom suggested.

"Alright."

George went to his room, unpacked his backpack, and prepared to repeat the school day for two more hours.

After spending about two hours on his homework, he finally decided it was good enough and quit. During that interval, his two little sisters had arrived home from school and were making a ruckus below him. He played World of Warships for a while, then wandered downstairs, feeling brain-dead.

"George," Hannah called, "wanna come play tag outside?"

"Not really," he replied.

"Come on. It'll be fun."

"Mm-mm." He shook his head.

"You *never* want to play with us," Gretel sniffed, and they both ran outside without him.

"Hey, Mom," he asked, "when's dinner?"

"Your dad is working late tonight. He said to eat without him, but I'm going to wait."

"Okay," George said, and disappeared to the living room before he could be given a chore to do. He turned on the television and found that some boring reality wilderness survival show was playing. It was one of those shows where they made it look like the family was working pioneer-style to survive in the wilderness, and it was all very dramatic as they desperately tried to make it through the winter. All the while you knew they were twenty minutes out of town and hired workers to do the construction for them, only getting their hands dirty for the cameras.

This show was boring, so he went back upstairs to his room and pulled up YouTube. His favorite history channel, *Yarnhub*, had a new video! George spent the next fifteen minutes learning about the Royal Navy's failed attempt at sinking the *Tirpitz*, *Bismarck*'s sister ship, using a suicide speedboat attack. Eventually, the warship succumbed to aircraft, however, and one more potential threat to the island's maritime economic lifeline was eliminated. He liked their storytelling and cinematic 3D graphics that showed what happened in detail without showing any gore. It was intense enough without it.

From there he went on to watch a sobering interview with a D-Day veteran who haltingly told of the horrors he had endured for his country. This lead George to an interview with Civil War reenactors, until an hour later he finished watching two videos about how Porsche owns Volkswagen and Volkswagen owns Porsche, and why it used to be legal to mail babies at the post office. Leave it to *Half as Interesting* to come up with such topics. He got up and wandered around his room for a bit and decided to read the news. This was incredibly boring, as usual, so he went back to playing World of Warships. Only, oh, maybe a thousand more battles until he got his Tier VIII aircraft carrier. That would be cool.

Mr. Owens got home very late, as had been common with his job lately, and dinner was a quiet, solemn affair before the exhausted family went to bed. George accomplished nothing else with his day, and he indistinctly felt it, staring numbly at the ceiling, making faces in his mind out of the patterns in the texture until he went to sleep. There was nothing he could think of about tomorrow to look forward to.

The next morning it was rush-rush-rush to cram some food down his throat and meet the school bus. His father had left for work before he even woke up. Between school and Mr. Owens' job, George never did get to see much of him, except on weekends.

The school bus got caught in severe traffic caused by a collision and made up for yesterday's quick trip home by delivering its cargo fifteen minutes behind schedule. Of course, George was excused for being late because it wasn't his fault. However, some of the teachers were less understanding and very flustered at the disturbances to their class schedules. George knew some kids who would drag this all the way to the principal and demand justice, but he didn't really care.

That morning he received his report cards. He had earned a D and a couple B's, but mostly C's. Good. He was passing his classes.

From then on, the morning proceeded as any other dismal school day. George was zoning out in his algebra class as the teacher continued to lecture on imaginary numbers. They weren't difficult at all, and George already knew them as well as he cared to, though he wasn't sure when he would ever use them in his life unless he became a college professor or a rocket scientist. But he was still stuck here, held back by the kids who needed a bit more work to understand the concept.

Bri-i-ing!

The school bell suddenly shrieked again and startled him. It was only halfway through the class period. The students got excited.

"Hey, is there a fire drill?"

"Yay! Do we get to skip class?!"

"Nah, I bet they're just gonna ring the bell until all the teachers go insane and then we'll be free!"

"Quiet, please," said their teacher. "Class, the school is receiving a visitor to give a presentation. I don't know how long they're going to be. Probably too long. Please go quietly to the gym."

George shifted his legs under his desk and got ancient chewing gum all over them.

"Hey, aren't they just gonna come visit our class?" someone asked.

"Oh no," the teacher replied, "instead of doing it the normal way, they have to do it differently. They have to speak to the whole grade at once. And we won't get to study the next very important section in our textbook."

"Hooray!" the class cheered, earning a sour look from the teacher.

Bursting with curiosity and exuberance, the students got up and joined a number of other eighth-grade classes filing down the aisles. It wasn't often that they received a visit from the fire department or the police station, and even George wondered who it could be. It would make the day more interesting than usual.

When he arrived at the gym, he joined the other eighth-graders in sitting on the floor since chairs were in short supply, as always. What he saw was not a firefighter, a policeman, a paramedic, a disabled veteran, or a community service person. Instead, a boy not much older than he was, smartly dressed in a fancy military uniform adorned with officers' trappings, stood stiffly with another boy and girl dressed in much simpler uniforms.

When all of the kids had been assembled and the teachers had settled everyone down, the boy cleared his throat and began to speak. "Boys and girls," he said, "I am Sergeant Nathan Miller of the Alamedan Army. Most of you should know of the Alamedan Empire, whose paintball military has been conquering her foes and expanding her domains."

Indeed, George could remember the great battles that had occurred here as the local paintball forces endeavored and failed to stop the Alamedan invaders. Eventually, Alameda had conquered San Joaquin County and added it as a province to her empire. It had been a while ago, and he had forgotten about it, but every now and then he saw the paintball military en route to somewhere.

"I am here to present to you the honorable pursuit—"

"Hey, what're those things under the white sheets?" a boy interrupted.

"We're not *there* yet," Sergeant Miller replied.

"But I want to know!"

"Now, I am here to present to you the honorable pursuit of enlisting in the Alamedan Army," he went on, ignoring the boy. "We are always in need of new personnel to fuel our ever-expanding Empire. Our new recruits will undergo training at boot camp to prepare them to fight, and then they will be assigned to a unit and sent to a front of the war. Life in the Alamedan Armed Forces is very good. You will be adequately supplied and well-fed."

"You know boot camp has a really bad reputation, right?" someone pointed out.

"Trust me, it's not that bad," he replied. "I survived, and I invite you to come seek your fortune in the Paintball Wars and fight for the glory of your county and the success of her armies. You can help us build our Empire into an even greater nation."

"You know," one boy interrupted, "your empire invaded and conquered our county. Why would I want to join your army and fight for you?"

"Because you're part of the Empire now," Sergeant Miller replied.

"Yes, by force."

A girl wearing an orange baseball hat perched sideways on her head snickered. "Oh yes, the force of a bunch of kids waving guns that shoot blobs of paint and yelling."

"Hey, our army is very serious and a formidable opponent," Sergeant Miller insisted.

"Yeah, so, as I asked, why would I want to fight for you?" the first boy insisted.

"Come help us do what we did to you to everybody else. Like your rival school team from the next county in the annual football playoffs," Sergeant Miller replied solemnly.

"Hey, now, that's not a bad idea!" the boy responded.

"Yes, and this is how you will do it." Sergeant Miller turned to one of his aides, who held up a paintball rifle. "This here," he explained, "is the standard-issue weapon for the Alamedan infantry soldier. Alameda has the finest paintball infantry in all the world."

"Of course you do," a boy commented dryly, "just like everyone else."

Sergeant Miller went on, ignoring him. "If you enlist, you will learn to be one of them. You will carry a gun like this into battle."

"To shoot people with little blobs of paint!" shouted the girl with the orange baseball hat. "It's so dangerous!" Sergeant Miller scowled but ignored the remark.

The students admired the handsome weapon. George looked on complacently, but already this life being advertised here seemed kind of interesting. You were actually taught to do something, and then you did it. Plus, it seemed like it might be exciting.

"Would any of you like to shoot this gun?" Sergeant Miller offered.

Immediately, the teachers expressed their concern. "I think that would be inadvisable. Everyone, we are going to stay right here in the gym."

"I already got this cleared with the principal," Sergeant Miller replied. He turned back to the students. "And if that doesn't interest you..."

One of the aides took the corner of the sheet covering the larger object and whisked it off with dramatic flair. The kids gasped and exclaimed at what they saw. There before them was a paintball machine gun sitting on a small tripod.

"This is a heavy machine gun, such as is used by our army," Sergeant Miller explained. "And this," he continued as his other aide revealed the other covered object next to it, "is a PIAT, which stands for Projector, Infantry, Anti-Tank. It uses a spring to shoot a grenade-like explosive a short distance and is good for taking out tanks, bunkers, anything like that."

"Those things look like Nerf toys!" shouted the girl with the orange baseball hat.

Sergeant Miller glared as the whole room giggled. "These are highly-engineered precision paintball weapons approved by the Alamedan Army!" He paused and composed himself.

"You know, this paintball army looks like it's better funded than our school," another girl observed.

Sergeant Miller grinned at her latest remark. "Why don't we take these weapons outside and you guys can try firing them?"

Eagerly the students hopped to their feet and hurried outside, shouting, George close behind. This was awesome!

"I do not approve of this," repeated one of the teachers.

"The principal gave me permission," Sergeant Miller reminded her, "and we're using training rounds, not live ammo." With that, he proceeded on with his demonstration.

Outside, the aides set up the machine gun with a full tank of paintballs and a small air compressor that connected to it via a black hose.

"Alright," Sergeant Miller said, "who wants to go first?"

"Me!" "Me!" The gun was immediately mobbed by a crowd of eager boys.

"Hey! Hey! Get back!" Sergeant Miller yelled.

"Hay is for horses!" one of the boys retorted.

"One at a *time*! Seriously, if you guys can't cooperate with me I'm gonna take it away." The boys restrained themselves at this threat.

The lucky first operator lay down on the ground as instructed and grasped the spade handles of the gun. An aide turned on the air compressor, which whirred to life. The boy squeezed the butterfly trigger, and with a rapid popping sound a stream of paintballs poured from the barrel.

The grinning boy swept the gun across the field, and then focused his shooting at the soccer nets and basketball hoops, splotching them orange. George found it hard to believe that no one would get detention from this.

The process was repeated by multiple boys after the first one had been forced to end his turn. Three times the aides had to refill the ammunition hopper on the machine gun. George was impressed with how it resembled the Browning .50-caliber machine gun of World War II, the weapon Audie Murphey had used to single-handedly hold off the German army for an hour until he got support.

"Alright, let's look at the PIAT. Nobody touch the machine gun, okay? Okay, to operate the PIAT, you step your foot into this handle on the end. Then you pull back on these side handles to compress the spring until it clicks into place. It's just like loading a crossbow. Then you'll take a shell and push it snugly down the barrel all the way. Now, someone who hasn't shot the machine gun, come shoot the PIAT."

This time a girl was the first to step up. She took the PIAT and knelt down on the ground. She carefully set it against her shoulder as instructed, aimed it, and pressed the trigger.

Unprepared in a steady position for the recoil, she fell backwards, sending the projectile awry and inducing the boys to snicker loudly at her. It bounced off the side of one of the school buildings and activated, spewing paint in jets from nozzles on its side as it spun across the ground.

The crowd was enthralled by this display, and they took turns firing the PIAT. Meanwhile, Sergeant Miller offered up the paintball rifle.

A boy came up and took it. Then he spun around and began shooting at his friends. They yelled and ran to tackle him.

"We need to redesign football!" one of them shouted.

"Hey, that's enough!" Sergeant Miller exclaimed. "You know what? We're just gonna put this away."

At that moment another boy, unsupervised by the aides who had run to help their officer, sent a PIAT shell into the crowd of kids, hitting one in the stomach who fell over with the wind knocked out of him. The projectile began spraying paint and kids ran screaming to get away from it.

Sergeant Miller promptly confiscated all the weapons and ended the trial session. He called the eighth-graders back to order. George had not gotten a chance to shoot any of them, and he was disappointed. But whatever, it didn't really matter.

One of the teachers came up to Sergeant Miller. "Thank you for taking control of the situation. I was worried about this becoming chaos, but you're doing your job. I've heard some bad stories from other school demonstrations. So thank you."

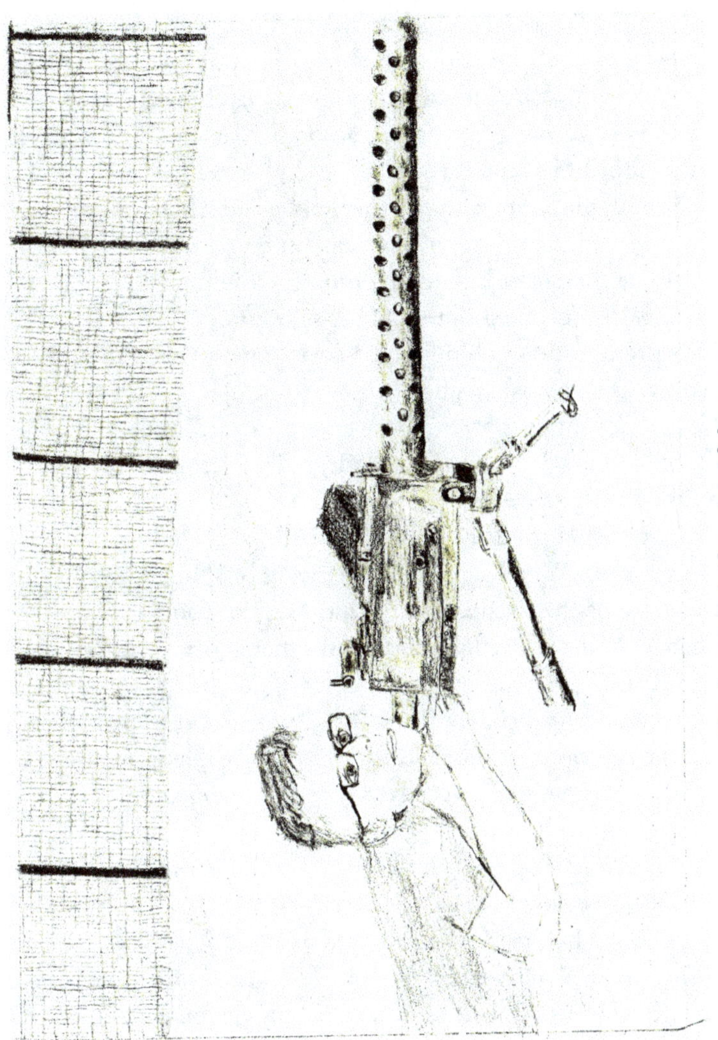

Trying out the machine gun.

"Of course," Sergeant Miller replied. "That was probably Andy you heard about," he said with a grin, then turned back to the kids. "You know," he mused, "I was once watching the army testing a vehicle with a giant nozzle on it that sprayed liquid paint, like the Crocodile flamethrower Churchill tanks from World War Two. Something happened with the piping, and it literally exploded. There was paint flying everywhere, all over everyone. They couldn't turn it off, either. It took about five minutes to empty its paint tank."

"Really?" someone shouted. "That's awesome!"

"It's pretty funny in hindsight. At the time we were all running for cover." The crowd laughed.

"Uh, that sounds *terrible* for the environment," said a girl.

"Don't worry, it's non-toxic biodegradable eco-friendly paint," Sergeant Miller replied.

"Right..." she said skeptically.

"I'm serious. Well," Sergeant Miller went on, "if you wish to use these weapons that we have just demonstrated, you will get plenty of chances in the army, fighting against other paintball powers.

"You can do great things. There is a lot of potential if you enlist. If you show diligence and bravery and skill, you can earn promotions to officer positions in the field. If you prove to be exceptional in training, you can even be selected to train as an officer.

"I urge you to consider my proposition. There are many opportunities. I can tell you from experience that the army is a good place to be. Do you have any questions?"

A girl raised her hand. "How would we do school?"

"There will be provisions for that," Sergeant Miller explained. "We used to have mobile classrooms that taught you condensed versions of regular classes, when you're not fighting on the front lines. The units would rotate in and out of that role. But it's becoming more and more popular to just do online asynchronous classes. You can usually work something out with your teachers because of your unpredictable schedule as a soldier. We'll help you do that. Or you can just bring homework, and check in at school while you're on leave or on your casualty period.

"Schooling in the Alamedan Armed Forces is usually compressed. You learn the important, main material, besides your training as a soldier. None of the chaff; there isn't time for it. Ideally. But you can always just take asynchronous classes online and continue school as usual."

The girl nodded satisfactorily. "Any other questions?" Sergeant Miller asked.

"Yes," said another girl, raising her hand, "how much do we get paid?"

"Um, there's no salary," he replied. "You will be well provided for and taken care of, but you do not get a salary."

"That's sad."

"Well, maybe your parents will give you the money they would normally spend taking care of you while you're off fighting," he suggested.

"Those're some generous parents!" someone exclaimed.

"Yeah, how do you pay for all this anyway?" a boy asked in a skeptical tone.

"A variety of sponsors," Sergeant Miller explained, ignoring the complaints about not getting a salary. "Alameda County provides funding, and other loyal provinces. Rich donors, companies. A little from the military, like the JROTC branches in our area, etc. And parents who don't have to pay for their kids' expenses while they're off fighting will actually donate some of the money to us.

"Anyhow," he resumed, "I have reached the end of my time, but I will have a table set up at the entrance to the school for the rest of the day, and if you are even *slightly* interested in enlisting, *please* come and see me there. Do something, do something exciting and interesting, something *real*. Enlist in the Alamedan Army!"

"Enlist in this fake war!" shouted the girl with the orange baseball hat.

"Thank you," he finished, trying not to grin, "that is all." Sergeant Miller and his aides began putting away their equipment.

"You know, the principal's gonna be so mad when he sees that the schoolyard has been painted," a girl said.

"Oh no," one of her friends replied, "the janitors will be the ones mourning. They'll have to hold a funeral for their mental sanity after they finish all that cleanup job."

"Can you imagine what it looks like after a big battle?" someone asked.

"Yeah," a boy replied curtly, "it takes a good rain to fix it. The Alamedans dropped a lot of bombs and shells on our soldiers that were holed up around my house, where my brother was fighting in the militia. It was so effective that after an hour of that they just kinda walked on through, and there pretty much wasn't any opposition left that had survived without fleeing."

"Wow, that's so cool! I wish I could've seen it," another boy exclaimed.

"It was a mess."

The teachers finished shepherding the kids back inside to continue the day's classes. The rest of the day went as any other for George, but Sergeant Miller's words stayed with him: "Do something, do something exciting and interesting, something *real*." What was he doing now? Nothing like that, it seemed.

Finally, several minutes late by the fast clock on the classroom wall, George left his final class of the day. He was tired and ready to go home and eat his first proper meal of the day. Stopping by his locker, he retrieved his things and headed for the door to catch the bus.

He was about to walk right out the door when he noticed Sergeant Miller and his two aides at a folding table off to the side of the room. A few kids were loitering nearby and looking on with interest, as well as flinging spitballs in the absence of a paintball gun.

A sign on an easel behind the table read, "ENLIST NOW. YOUR COUNTY NEEDS YOU!" The words were accompanied by a proud picture of infantry soldiers standing triumphantly on a paint-soaked battlefield. In the background, defeated enemy soldiers trudged away, looking glum and wearing white shawl-like things over their shoulders.

George was tired, but the words of Sergeant Miller still echoed through his mind: "Do something, do something exciting and interesting, something *real*. Enlist in the Alamedan Army!"

Nah, what could he possibly be missing. He was better off staying here. And anyhow, he was exhausted.

But the poster intrigued him. He idled over to the table. He just wanted to look. The poster was pretty cool, and the weapons were on display. It was like a YouTube video in real life. Another boy moved aside to make room for him.

"How can I help you?" Sergeant Miller asked.

"I'm just looking," he replied.

"Why are you looking?"

"It looks interesting."

"Why does it look interesting?"

"Because it's cool."

"*Why?*"

George looked at Sergeant Miller with annoyance. "Because school is... kinda boring, and this looks like fun. Like, interesting. You actually get to do something."

"Dude, we don't need your life story," the girl aide said. "Just sign up."

"Quiet! *I* do the talking!" Sergeant Miller stood up straight and looked George in the eye.

"The army has just what you need," he began. "You can get out and continue your education while actually doing something. Escape your life as a bondservant to the school system—"

"And become a bondservant to us instead!" the boy aide exclaimed.

"— And seek recognition and promotion on the field of battle," Sergeant Miller went on without stopping. "Learn leadership, diligence, and hard work. Become physically sound. Help Alameda rise to prominence. Accomplish something real.

"That's what the army has to offer," he finished in unison with his grinning aides. He shot them a look, then regally faced George.

George stood and thought. The paintball soldiers looked grand on that poster; they looked successful. The army looked great. But maybe it wasn't so great. It would be a lot of work. At the same time he would be doing something, accomplishing something. Right? And at the same time the whole thing was a sales pitch. You never can trust a salesman.

"How long would I be in the army?" George asked.

"Enlistment terms are three months," Sergeant Miller replied. "After that you can go home or renew for another three. But if you become a casualty your term automatically ends and you can't rejoin for two months."

That was surprising. "Why not?"

The girl aide spoke up: "You're dead, you got killed by paint. You need time to come back to life."

"Er, yes, basically," Sergeant Miller said.

"Hm." George thought for a long minute while Sergeant Miller waited patiently. That wasn't too bad. Only three months, and if he didn't like it he didn't have to come back. I mean, he was already spending his whole life in school. What was there to lose by trying?

Finally he spoke: "I guess, I'll enlist. I'll give it a try and see if it's any better."

Sergeant Miller lost no time in whipping out some papers and firing questions at George while writing rapidly on the documents.

"Name."

"George Owens."

"Age."

"Thirteen."

"Address of residence."

George gave it to him.

"And the branch is army," Sergeant Miller muttered to himself. He wrote a few more miscellaneous things down on the papers and then flipped one around to face George. "Sign here."

George took the pen that was handed to him, looked at the paper, and hesitated for a moment. Hadn't he once heard something about never signing a contract without reading it? Whatever, that was way too much reading. Oh well. He scrawled his name on the line indicated by Sergeant Miller.

"Ha-ha!" the boy aide cackled. "You just signed away your soul!"

"Shoulda read the fine print!" the girl added.

"I told you two to be *quiet*!" Sergeant Miller shouted as he took the documents and put them away in a folder in his briefcase.

Then he composed himself, looked George in the eye, and shook his hand. "Welcome aboard, Mr. Owens. You're in the army now."

And just like that, he was.

Chapter II

Beep-beep-beep-beep!

Beep-beep-beep-beep!

Beep-beep-beep-beep!

Beep-beep-bee—

Clack!

George groaned and rolled over in bed and slept for nine more minutes. Then the alarm clock started up all over again. With a grunt, he pried the covers from himself and tried to focus on the ceiling while that thing continued to yell at him.

"George!" His mom was standing at the doorway. "Get up! You have to leave for school soon. Your sisters are already up."

"Okay," George muttered weakly. His mom left and he sat up groggily. Finally, he dragged himself out of bed and began to get dressed. Who cared whether he got to school on time or not?

It had been a whole week since Sergeant Miller had appeared at school and given that presentation, somehow convincing George to enlist in the Alamedan Army. Since signing up, he had not heard a word from anybody. It was somewhat disappointing, but another disappointment was not that uncommon. Whatever, he didn't care. Not much, anyway. It was probably for the best.

Five minutes behind schedule, George just caught the school bus and rode towards another day of drudgery. Another day of incarceration.

Climbing off the bus, jostled by the other kids, he headed to his first period of the day: chemistry. Oh how he hated chemistry.

Once the class had assembled, his teacher, Mrs. Melbourne, a rather large woman with a muffin top and something resembling a triple chin, began the day's lesson.

"Class, please turn to page 132 in your textbooks, the first heading on the page, 'Calculating Molar Mass from Empirical Formula and Percent Composition.'" She turned to the blackboard and wrote a number of figures on the board. George slouched in his seat.

"Now, remember that molarity is the amount of a substance in a quantity of another substance, measured in grams per mole. We represent this with a capital M. Now who remembers what a mole is?" A girl raised her hand. "Yes, Cassandra?"

"It's this nasty little black creature that digs holes in the ground and eats my garden. I *hate* moles. Oh, it's also what you call a traitor embedded in an organization. I hate them, too."

"Miss Lewis! We are here to *learn*, not to make sarcastic jokes!"

"I'm serious! And also I'm going to be a landscaper, not a chemist."

Now Mrs. Melbourne looked very angry. "You are learning to prepare for your future, to go to university! This is a very important time, Cassandra. Now please sit down." Cassandra quietly obeyed.

"Now," Mrs. Melbourne went on, "a mole, as I hope you remember, also known as Avogadro's number, is this here." She wrote out a rather long string of figures. "Six-point-zero-two-two-one-four times ten to the twenty-third power."

George was not even paying attention. He had no idea what he wanted to be when he grew up, but it definitely wasn't a rocket scientist working for NASA. No, that was too prestigious. Too much effort. And *way* too much textbook reading.

Since he had decided what his career wouldn't be, he didn't want to bother learning things he wouldn't use. None of the adults George knew could tell you anything about molarity because it didn't matter to them, but they were still successful in life.

Which reminded George why he had enlisted in the army. They had made it sound much more productive and useful. Or not so much that, but you were actually doing something. Not wasting your time, hopefully. This was ridiculous; all he wanted to do was do something. He wasn't actually doing anything now. He slouched lower in his seat.

Come lunch time, George sat at his usual table off in the corner of the cafeteria where nobody else ever sat. However, as had been the norm lately, he was joined by Cassandra and a boy named John.

"Heard anything from the army yet?" John asked George.

"Nope."

"When're they gonna contact us? I want to start my adventure. I mean, real war is awful some— most of the time, but this sounds like a lotta fun. You heard anything, Cassie?"

She shook her head. "No. Not yet. I can wait, but I wish they'd hurry up. Aren't you tired of this, living at a desk and, you know, learning molarity? I'm never gonna need to know that."

"I dunno, I just want to do something interesting. Something exciting. Like paintball!"

"You know," commented George, "they like to talk about how useful chemistry is, and how cooks use chemistry all the time. But really, the cook doesn't need to know all that stuff."

"Exactly," said Cassie. "He just needs to know how to cook an egg, not what all the chemical reactions going on in the egg are, or what electrons are in what orbitals and what bonds are being made with them."

"The only people who need to know the actual chemistry are the ones in the food factories trying to produce some processed, adulterated packaged thing," George said. "Like the liquid egg you buy in a bottle. Nasty."

"Exactly. It's like they want you to go become one of those people."

"Waste of time," George muttered. "I'm bored."

"Ditto," replied Cassie with a sigh. "It really just irritates me sometimes. There's so many other things I could be learning, like actual life skills, but instead we're *stuck* here, learning *nothing* useful."

George nodded. Even their life skills class failed to actually influence most of the students. Though it's not like paintball was exactly a useful life skill, either.

"Actually, I prefer my eggs scrambled," John commented.

"Poached," said Cassie. "How 'bout you, George? How do you like your eggs cooked?"

"Well, honestly," he replied, "I don't really care much for eggs anyway." Cassie and John burst out laughing.

"Oh, that's hilarious," she said. "Just hilarious."

George nodded and bit into his pizza. He was positively sure this thing had come out of a box in a freezer not an hour ago. It really didn't taste that great. Army food in the field probably wouldn't be much better, though. After all, it had to last through less-than-comfortable conditions and not require too much preparation in order to eat.

Maybe enlisting hadn't been the best idea. Those conditions wouldn't exactly be any more pleasant for him than for the food. He hoped he wouldn't regret it. But it was only three months. He could last that long, right?

"Guys," George asked, "do you think that, maybe, enlisting wasn't the greatest idea?"

"What d'you mean?" asked Cassie.

"Well, maybe I'm better off just staying where I am. I dunno."

"I think anything is better than staying here," she replied.

"It is pretty boring," John agreed.

"That's the least of my concerns," she said. "Anyway, it's only three months."

"Well, you know, I have some cousins that decided to homeschool," John said. "It seems to work pretty well for them. They complained about all the things you two do."

"Yeah, well, I've already picked my path for the next few months."

Then the school bell rang.

"Rats!" said Cassie. "We've been so busy talking that I haven't had time to finish my food!"

"Whelp," said John, "too bad. So sad." He and George dumped their trays and rushed to use the bathroom before heading to class. Behind them, Cassie followed, trying to cram the remainder of her lunch down her throat.

George hurried from the bathroom and then down a maze of hallways to his geography class. Following that was history, which he enjoyed, and then English. When that was through, he went to pre-algebra, the end of arithmetic and the beginning of math misery for years and years, until he graduated college. And by then he would have to get a job. He wasn't sure which was worse.

Halfway through pre-algebra, the fire alarm went off with a shriek. Students sat bolt upright and looked around excitedly.

"Take cover!" some kid yelled. "The Soviets are launching a nuclear attack!" Everyone dived under their desks with glee.

"Don't be ridiculous," the teacher said. "This is a fire drill. We don't do nuclear drills anymore. The Cold War ended in 1991."

"Aw, man."

"Now all of you," she went on, "get out from under your desks unless you want to burn up with the building. In a real fire you would crawl along the floor so you don't breathe too much smoke, but don't do that now unless you want to get sick."

"Agh, I can't breathe, I'm dying," someone said as they stood up and made contorted faces.

There was a lot of jostling, joking, and fooling around, but George got out of his seat and mundanely filed outside with the other kids. He considered sneaking away and playing hooky for the rest of the day, but that wouldn't be the greatest idea. Too much effort to pull it off, besides.

When the fire drill was over, the teachers herded the kids back inside. This was not done without some difficulty, though George did not contribute to it other than by not moving. Who would be eager for the teachers to resume teaching them again?

A week later on a Saturday afternoon, George was lying on his bed playing video games, as he did every Saturday. More specifically, he was playing *Crossy Road*, one of the most mind-numbing, brain-cell-killing video games in existence.

Downstairs he heard the front door open and close.

"George!" his mom called. "There's a letter for you!"

Huh, that was interesting. George rarely got letters. But whatever, he didn't feel like reading right now. It was probably from the school or something anyway.

Half an hour later, he flattened his chicken beneath a commuter train for the umpteenth time and wandered aimlessly downstairs.

"George, come play tag with us!" his sisters begged. He grunted, and they accepted that as a no and left.

"I put it on the counter," his mom informed him.

"Huh?"

"Your letter."

"Oh, yeah."

"It's on the counter."

George walked over and picked up the ordinary-sized business envelope. It had prepaid postage, and thus was not stamped. He turned it over and looked at the sender: Department of Human Resources, Alamedan Empire.

Suddenly he remembered enlisting a fortnight ago and not hearing anything for two weeks. Now they had finally gotten around to telling him something. He had probably been rejected for being useless. He tore the envelope in half and extracted a few sheets of paper neatly folded inside. Ugh, there was an awful lot to read.

Mr. George Owens,

Thank you for your enlistment in the Alamedan
Army. You have been accepted to the infantry and
will participate in an upcoming training session.
In two weeks' time, you will be expected to report
to the rendezvous location below, where a bus will
take you to a training camp. Boot camp will last
two weeks, then you will be assigned to a unit. The
rest of this document will expound on this. Please
read it in its entirety to ensure you know exactly
what to do and what is expected of you.

So he hadn't been rejected after all. This was interesting. He
would be shipping off to train, and from there go off to fight.
For once he would finally be doing something. It was really
happening now.

He skimmed over the rest of the letter, which was an awful lot
of reading. It informed him of where to meet the bus and what
possessions he could bring. There wouldn't be much room for
personal belongings as an infantry soldier. George was actually
a little bit excited, something that didn't happen all that often.

There was only one catch to his impending fortune: his parents had to sign a release form admitting him to the care and
instruction of the Alamedan Empire. That night he waylaid his
parents after his sisters had gone to bed.

"Mom, I'll do the dishes."

"Why thank you, how thoughtful. What prompted that?"

"Um, well..."

"What'd you do?" his dad asked accusingly.

"I enlisted in the Alamedan Army."

"You *what*?" his mom asked.

"I enlisted. They accepted me. You just need to sign this release form letting me go."

"I don't know if I want you to go."

"It's only three months; then I can come home."

"Three months! You're kidding me. No way."

"Well, hold on," his dad interjected. "You let him go to summer camp."

"That was *one* week. And besides, he hated it."

"We forced him to go. For once the boy actually wants to do something."

"But I don't think I want him going off all by himself with some random other kids to who knows where to fight a paintball war. What could happen?"

"It's like the JROTC program I went through. Might do him some good, put some grit in him. It straightened me out. Got me into the Marines."

"And look what happened to you! You don't know what I went through those two weeks, waiting to hear word, if..." she choked off and didn't finish.

Mr. Owens gently touched her shoulder. "He's not going to war, it's paintball. I think it would do him some good. And if he actually wants to go, let him go. Find out what real work is like. The Paintball Wars isn't like eating chocolate cake, from what I've heard."

"What if he gets hurt?"

"Good, it'll toughen him up. Every boy gets hurt. But I don't think he would get hurt very bad."

"George, do you actually want to go?" his mom asked.

"Yes."

"Why?"

"I dunno. I'm... bored. I want to do something interesting. Actually do something. Instead of just..."

"Just what?"

"Oh I dunno."

"But why?"

"Mom, I don't know."

"*What?*"

Internally George was very frustrated. How did he say it? Words were hard. Finally he got out, "...Doing, nothing."

"See?" his dad said. "Let's take advantage of this unusual George while we can."

Quietly, Mrs. Owens stood there, chewing her lip, thinking. Finally, she spoke in a hushed tone: "Well. We'll think about it, George. Go to bed now. The dishes can wait 'til tomorrow."

"Okay," said George. "G'night."

"Goodnight," his father said. Then he turned, grunted, and limped off to his bedroom.

"Sweet dreams," his mother said and followed after his father. George slowly climbed the stairs and crawled into bed.

George watched as his mom drove away in the family car. She had just dropped him off at the local office of the Alamedan Empire and said goodbye. In his hand he held the signed forms. In his backpack he had homework assigned for while he was on his tour of duty. There was no escaping school, even in the Paintball Wars. So much for that part of his plan. Now he'd have to do school and be a soldier. As if he wasn't busy enough already.

"Hey, George!" He turned and saw John hurrying towards him. "Glad to see you here! Good thing your parents signed those forms."

"Yup. It wasn't difficult to convince them."

"Well, I'm really looking forward to this. It'll be an adventure. Great fun. There's not an experience in the world like this that a thirteen-year-old boy has available to him! C'mon, let's go sign in."

They attached themselves to the back of a line leading to a folding table, at which sat a busy officer. When their turn came, he took their names, signed them in, and took the forms their parents had filled out. In exchange, he handed them a ticket.

"Don't lose it," he said sternly.

"What happens if I do?" John asked mischievously.

The officer scowled. "*Don't*. Next!"

Having finished, they spotted Cassandra rounding the corner and went to greet her.

"Hi guys!" she said.

"Hello! You sign in right over there."

"Okay." She walked over and repeated the same process that the boys had done. Then the trio stood off to the side and watched the rest of the kids. There looked to be about thirty or forty present.

A car door slammed and they saw Mr. Lewis walking towards them. He was carrying a pink backpack that looked rather out of place on him.

"Hi Dad!" Cassie called.

"Hello, Honey," he said. "Here's your stuff."

"Thanks! I forgot my backpack," she explained to the others. "It would have been rather unpleasant to go to boot camp with none of my own things."

"You boys excited?" Mr. Lewis asked.

"Oh yes!" said John. "This'll be great!"

"What about you, George?"

"We'll see," he replied.

"Alright, well, I've gotta get to back to work now. Have a good time, Honey, and stay outta trouble. Don't disobey your commanding officers."

He winked and turned to go, but paused. "And I want you to remember something. What you're going off to do is play a wargame, a simulation of war. And there's nothing wrong with that. I'm sure you'll learn things and it will be a good experience for you. But remember, it is not real war; it is a game. Do not get them mixed up; they have very little in common."

Cassie nodded solemnly. "Bye Dad!" she called, waving as he drove away and tapped his horn a few times in response.

A couple of other boys and another girl were standing around nearby, waiting to see what would happen next.

"Hey," John said to one of them, "why did you enlist?"

"I'm off to seek my fortune in the army," he replied. "It'll be exciting."

"That's what I say! It will be. How 'bout you?" he asked the girl.

"I'm just here 'cause my brother here somehow talked me into it," she said. John chuckled. They all turned to the other boy.

"Why're you here?"

"Oh, I thought I'd try it out for a while," he said. "It's the closest thing I could find to trying a career in the military. When I get out I'll go and find something else to do, like an internship. Experience different things, see what I might want to do someday." They all nodded thoughtfully at his response.

"And what about you?" John asked a sullen-looking boy who was leaning against a wall.

"Hm?" he grunted back.

"Why are you enlisting?"

"I don't want to go home."

"Why not?"

"Home is... not a nice place to be."

"Oh. How come?"

"I don't want to go back."

"But why—" Cassie elbowed John in the ribs and he shut up.

George was surprised by this. He had never considered such a thing. For him, home was a refuge where he could escape after school. A place to escape from life by commanding virtual warships in a virtual world. Or run a virtual chicken endlessly across the widest virtual freeway in the world while trying to not get run over by virtual cars.

They all hung around for a little while longer until several military cargo trucks drove up. The truck beds were covered with canvas, like a pioneer wagon. A soldier opened the back of one and came out.

"All right, everybody load up!" he ordered.

The kids milling around began shuffling towards the trucks. They handed their tickets over to the soldier in the back, who let them in. Inside were a series of benches; nothing of much comfort.

"Some 'bus' this thing is," Cassandra commented as they sat down.

"False advertising," said John.

"Guys, this is what the army does," George said. "Soldiers don't get to live in comfort."

"Oh I know," said John. "It's just funny. And *you* have no sense of humor, *George*." George merely grunted in return.

Ten minutes later, the truck was fully loaded. A rather rough and bumpy forty-five-minute ride after that, the soldier again opened the back of the canopy.

"Everybody out!"

The trio climbed down and found themselves in a paintball military base. From the top of a tall flagstaff flew a red and yellow flag, emblazoned with a star in the top right corner and, in the center, a compass rose wreathed by laurels. A large sign announced that this was a training facility of the Alamedan Armed Forces. A smartly-dressed officer appeared beneath it.

"Welcome to boot camp! You'll spend the next few weeks training here to learn how to become a good soldier, and then you'll be sent to war. Go sign in at the office over there."

The officer promptly disappeared, and the recruits formed a line leading towards the building. Off to the side were a number of kids in uniform, dressed just like Sergeant Miller's assistants that fateful day a whole month ago. They were all lounging about, snickering and grinning at the new kids. Suddenly, one of them began singing and the rest of them joined him in chorus.

> A recruiting sergeant came our way
> From the inn near town at the close of day.
> He said, "My Johnny, you're a fine young man;
> Would you like to march along behind a military band
> With a scarlet coat and a fine cocked hat
> And a musket at your shoulder?"
> The shilling he took and he kissed the book.
> Oh, poor Johnny, *what'll happen to ya?*

The recruiting sergeant marched away
From the inn near town at the break of day.
Johnny came too with half a ring;
He was off to be a soldier to go fighting for the King
In a far-off war in a far-off land,
To face the foreign soldier.
But how will you fare when there's lead in the air?
Oh, poor Johnny, *what'll happen to ya?*

The cheeky group of kids made particular emphasis on the last line of each verse, directing their needling at the queue of recruits waiting to sign in.

"What a lovely introduction to the army," George said dryly. John merely grinned, enjoying the joke they were making at his own expense. Cassie had already stepped up to the window at the office. This line was moving pretty quickly.

"Name." The officer at the desk fired the question at her.

"Cassandra Lewis." He scanned through a document, found her name, and crossed it off the list. Then he fumbled through and wrote on a couple more pieces of paper.

"Very well. Next!"

"Excuse me?" Cassie asked.

"What?" the officer said impatiently.

"Who're all those kids in uniform singing that song?"

"The boot camp staff. Next!"

George and John were quickly signed in, then they followed the directions the staff gave them towards a couple of long buildings. As they walked, the boot camp staff continued singing their song to tease the new recruits.

Alamedan Flag "Rose and Laurels"

Well, the sun rose high on a barren land
Where the thin red line made a military stand.
There was sling shot, chain shot, grape shot too;
Swords and bayonets thrusting through.
Poor Johnny fell but the day was won,
And the King is grateful to ya.
But your soldiering's done and they're sending you home.
Oh, poor Johnny, *what'll happen to ya?*

Well, they said he was a hero and not to grieve
For the two ruined legs and the empty sleeves.
They took him home and they set him down
With a military pension and a medal from the crown;
But you haven't an arm, you haven't a leg,
The enemy nearly slew ya.
You'll have to go out on the streets and beg.
Oh, poor Johnny, *what'll happen to ya?*

"They are not helping to convince me that this was a good idea," said George.

"That's just what I was thinking," agreed Cassie.

"Well, you see, that's real war, just like your dad was saying," said John. "Paintball, fortunately, is not dangerous."

"Hopefully," said George.

"Ugh, you're such a pessimist," John griped. George merely looked at him.

"I mean, they do fire artillery," Cassie pointed out.

"Agh, how bad could it hurt," John said dismissively.

The same officer that previously ordered them to sign in reappeared. "Attention! Thank you. I am Captain Hughes, and I am in charge of this facility. These two buildings here are the barracks. You will be living here with your fellow trainees during boot camp. Boys in that one, and girls in the other."

"Hey," someone said, "I was expecting a five-star glamping experience! Where's the spa?" The crowd snickered at the comment.

"Shut up!" the officer barked. "There will be no snarky back talk, do you hear? You are to do as I tell you.

"Now, after I finish speaking, you are to go inside your respective barrack and choose a bunk. Any bunk. Just put your stuff on it and it's yours. There are plenty of 'em, so I don't want to hear of any squabbling over who gets which one, understand?

"Good. Now this check-in day you have free, and the weekends. The rest of each week is work days. And just so you know, when you're out fighting, you don't get the weekends off." He gestured towards the boot camp staff.

"These are the staff that work at boot camp to run it under the direction of the officers. Their rank is that of an aide, and you will address them with respect to their superior position. You will defer to their orders.

"And finally, I expect good behavior. No fooling around, no stupid pranks or games, and no smart remarks. Discipline will be enforced by whatever means are necessary to ensure you comply with the rules.

"Alright, get to it. If you want to tour the base you may do so. The aides will show you around if you wish."

With that, Captain Hughes turned and marched away. Everyone stood around and looked at each other. The aides stood and smirked, watching them.

"I want the top bunk!" some kid yelled, and everyone rushed into their barracks. George plopped his pack down on a bottom bunk while John took the one above it. Easier to climb into the lower one.

The barrack was a long, narrow building. Two thirds of it had bunks down the sides stacked two high. The last third contained lockers, restroom facilities, and a few tables and chairs. The lockers were numbered and corresponded with the numbers on the bunks.

"Come on, let's go explore," John said. George hesitated. He had homework to do. But that could wait; it was his first day, after all. He followed John outside where they met up with Cassie.

"The facilities here are actually really nice," she said.

"Yeah, I think this place is better funded than our school," John replied.

Cassie laughed. "Just what I was thinking. See, even George is grinning."

"It's true," George said.

"Well let's go explore," John said. He and Cassie started off in a random direction.

"Uh, guys," George said, "how 'bout we get one of the aides to show us around?"

John cocked his head at him. "You really want one of *those* guys showing us around?"

"Yeah, let's have someone show us around." John shrugged and they strolled over to where the aides were casually milling about. The trio stopped and looked around at the crowd. A boy a bit older than them walked over and saluted.

"Vice Chief Aide Davis. But you can call me Jim. Just not while Captain Hughes is around to hear it."

"Vice chief aide?" John asked.

"Yes, I am in charge of the boy aides. We're all divided up by gender so we can operate in the barracks. One of the girls is the chief aide in charge of all of us, and I'm her subordinate for the boys, which is where the vice comes from."

"How sinful," Cassie said.

"Very funny. Alright, shall we start with the mess hall? Right this way." He led them over to a nearby building.

"This here is the kitchen, and then the tables under that canopy are where you guys eat. We officers get to dine in our own building. We get better food, too." George snorted.

"*Oh*, aren't *you* lucky," said Cassie.

"Very much so," Jim replied, grinning. "Officers' privileges."

"Alright, if we go over here we have the administration buildings. There's where you checked in. There's Captain Hughes' office. And there's the brig."

"The brig?" asked George.

"Yes, it's a small jail with a few cells. So don't get in trouble, just saying. Discipline is taken seriously around here. Seriously." He cocked his eyebrows for dramatic effect. Then he led them to another large building nearby. "Over there are some classrooms."

"Uh-oh, George," John said.

"The classrooms are for teaching stuff that doesn't involve being outside, like the structure of the army and lecturing on tactical theory. You know, stuff like that."

"Sounds better than school," George commented.

"And this here is the storehouse and armory."

"Shouldn't an armory be guarded?" asked George.

"It is. The armory is a separate room inside the storehouse. Here, I'll show you."

Jim led them to a side door, produced a key from his pocket, and opened it. They stepped inside what resembled a small warehouse or a Costco store. Shelves equipped with mobile ladders of the kind found in libraries held all sorts of things they might need to use at boot camp.

At the back of the building was another door. An aide with a rifle sat reading a book nearby. She glanced up at them briefly as Jim unlocked the armory door and led them inside.

To their amazement, weaponry and ammunition were everywhere inside. A few large guns of various sizes were parked on the floor while shelving held other smaller arms, from rifles to machine guns to PIATs and other weapons whose names and functions George did not know.

Still other shelves held bulk packages of paintballs or boxes of shells. One entire column of shelves was devoted to propulsion. It contained air compressors and cartridges of compressed gas for the smaller weapons.

"And over here," Jim said, "is our refill station. You're actually looking at the back of it. On the other side of the wall, outside the building, are hoses and such where you can charge air tanks. This room here holds the air compressor and machinery in a muffler.

"And over here are the spare parts for repairing weapons." He gestured to another column of shelves.

"Wow," said John, "this place is neat."

"It is," George and Cassie agreed.

"Yup. You'll be learning how to use the equipment in here while you're at boot camp."

"So we spend two weeks learning how to become soldiers, and then you send us right into battle?" George asked.

"Well," Jim grinned, "yes — but it's not how most people take it. You'll be at the war, but not on the front at first. You'll gain some experience behind the front, guarding supply lines, stuff like that. You'll keep learning then, and *then* you'll eventually be put on the front lines."

"Okay," said George, "that makes a lot more sense."

"Yes. You know, it takes a lot of people just to supply the kids on the front. The reality is that most of the personnel are not on the front, but engaging in some activity in support of the front." George, Cassie, and John all nodded solemnly.

"In real war, that is," Jim added. "In paintball, it's less of an issue, and you can have more guys on the front than in support a lot of the time.

"Well, I think you've seen most of the facility. The rest of boot camp is just kinda open places for training and marching and digging foxholes. You do a lot of marching and digging here."

"Great," George muttered sarcastically.

"Well, it's only two weeks," Cassie said.

"Until you actually go to the war and then you could live in comfort in a tent camp or spend all day walking through the rain carrying your heavy packs and digging in the mud. It varies."

"Maybe this isn't quite everything I thought it was going to be," said John.

"Oh, trust me, it ain't that bad most of the time. We just like to torture the new trainees."

"Yes, we could tell your staff was enjoying that," said Cassie.

Jim grinned. "Ah, yeah, very much so. They're harmless, though. We get away with all sorts of stuff, but the officers have to maintain their formality and be all professional and stern." Jim marched around the room like a stick while doing a cartoon impression of an officer with stiff, protruding lips and a permanent, glaring scowl. They all laughed. "Don't tell on me for making fun of them," Jim said.

"Well, I think that's all of my tour. You can walk around, but stay in sight of the buildings or you might get lost." He ushered them out of the armory, locked it, and did likewise with the storehouse.

"Have a nice day!" he said. "Dinner's in a half-hour. Don't be late. Captain Hughes hates it when people are late." The trio returned his wave and wandered back towards the barracks.

"Wanna explore the rest of the place?" asked John.

"Well, not really," George said. "There's nothing to see."

"Yeah, and I'm hungry," Cassie added.

"Okay, fine," John said. "Let's be the first to the mess hall."

"Yeah, mess 'hall,'" snorted Cassie. "It's a bunch of tables under a tent." The other two chuckled.

When they got there and took a seat, they found that they were not quite the first to arrive, but nearly. They hung out and chatted for a bit.

Then a bugler marched over and played a short tune.

Nothing happened.

Suddenly, Captain Hughes hurried past. They heard him talking loudly at the barracks and saw the aides scurrying about. Shortly the rest of the kids were gathered to eat.

"My apologies," said Captain Hughes, "I forgot to explain eating. When you hear the bugler sound the Mess Call, come eat. So learn that call. There will be others to learn, as well. And do *not* be late to meals. Else you might go hungry."

With that, Captain Hughes disappeared, and the aides carried around pots of stew, which they dished out to the hungry kids. It was not a fancy meal, but it was a good and filling one.

After eating, they went back to their barracks and stood around outside them, chatting. Then the sweet strains of a bugle floated across the base.

"Ah, Taps," John said. "We all know that one."

"Yup," replied Cassie, yawning. "G'night, guys."

"Goodnight," they replied.

The boys went inside and found their bunks. They changed into their pajamas and climbed into bed. This didn't seem so bad after all. George fell asleep listening to the breathing and snoring around him and wondering what tomorrow would bring.

Chapter III

November, 5 PBW

George groggily came to consciousness, hearing a faint bugle call. A few minutes later he was just starting to fall back asleep when suddenly multiple bugles sang out strong through the crisp morning in a lively, bouncy tune.

Listening to it, George sat up. Above him, John continued to sleep like a British soldier playing dead at the Battle of New Orleans. It was pretty early, it felt like, but not as early as in the boot camp horror stories.

Then the door of their barrack opened, and Vice Chief Aide Jim Davis marched in, leading a number of boy aides behind him. He was grinning and singing along with the bugles' rollicking morning call.

> You've got to get up,
> You've got to get up,
> You've got to get up this morning;
> You've got to get up,
> You've got to get up,
> Get up with the bugler's call.
> > The major told the captain;
> > The captain told the sergeant;

> The sergeant told the bugler;
> The bugler told them all.

Marching down the aisle, Jim and his aides roused the boys from their sleep. They were not unkind, though anyone who refused to get up was subjected to the entertainment of the aides, which generally meant getting rolled out of bed smack-dab onto the floor in a bundle of blankets.

The bugles kept repeating their call. Jim ceased singing his lyrics, and his cheeky aides took over with their own.

> I can't get 'em up,
> I can't get 'em up,
> I can't get 'em up this morning;
> I can't get 'em up,
> I can't get 'em up,
> I can't get 'em up at all!
>> And tho' the sun starts peeping,
>> And dawn has started creeping;
>> Those lazy bums keep sleeping;
>> They never hear my call!

Gradually, the whole group of boys was roused, and they began dressing. When the aides had finished singing, one of the boys belted out his own lyrics in return.

> I hate to get up,
> I hate to get up,
> I hate to get up this morning;
> I hate to get up,
> I hate to get up,
> I hate to get up at all.

He paused and scratched his head as the bugles continued blasting away. "I forget the rest," he said.

Jim laughed. "I don't think there is any more for those lyrics," he replied. "You're thinking of 'Oh, How I Hate to Get Up In the Morning.' It's a different song."

One of the aides grinned wickedly and began singing to a different tune as the bugles sounded on. The other aides cackled and joined in.

> Some day I'm going to murder the bugler;
> Some day they're going to find him dead.
> I'll amputate his Reveille, and step upon it heavily,
> And spend the rest of my life in bed.

"Alright," Jim said, chuckling, "that's enough of that. Those poor buglers get enough harassment from y'all.

"Okay, guys," he addressed the trainees, "get dressed and get outside. Anyone who doesn't get up skips breakfast. Captain's orders. When you hear Reveille, you get up!"

"How many different lyrics are there to Reveille?" asked John as he finished dressing.

"A lot," replied Jim. "Now let's get moving! Quit standin' around, you lazy bums!" He was not unkind about it.

"How long are they gonna keep playing that tune?" George asked. "It's starting to get on my nerves."

"This is the first day," Jim explained enthusiastically, "so they're gonna keep playing until everyone has that tune *so* stuck in their heads that you won't be able to forget it *or* sleep through it tomorrow morning!"

"Great," George muttered as he passed outside.

"Unless they blow their lungs out first," said John.

"Oh, yeah," piped up one of the aides, "one of them blew so hard last week he exploded and died. The whole camp threw a party to celebrate."

"Elijah!" Jim rebuked. "Enough, that's not true and you know it. Now get your butt outside with the rest of the boys! Elijah attempted to smother his triumphant smile with moderate success and scurried outside as instructed.

Five minutes later, all of the boy and girl trainees were standing outside yawning and rubbing sleepy eyes. To George, there was a fresh appeal of promise in his first full day. A bit of apprehension as well. He was about to experience the dreaded boot camp.

Finally, the buglers ceased to blow. Weren't they tired before then? They had kept it up for a long time. A girl aide with trappings slightly better than Jim's marched out in front of the group of trainees where everyone could see her.

"Attention!" she shouted. "I am Chief Aide Mallory. I oversee the staff of this facility. If you have any issues, come talk to me. Now, that bugle call you just heard is Reveille. Every morning that call sounds to wake you up. Hopefully you will remember what it sounds like."

"I'll never forget," a girl muttered.

"No sarcasm!" The chief aide glanced at her watch. "Now, in just a minute here..." Shortly the bugles played a short, bouncy melody. They again played it repeatedly. "That," shouted Chief Aide Mallory, "is the Assembly. When you hear that, you are to assemble outside your barrack, right here, for role call and inspection."

"What's inspection?" a girl asked.

"We'll get to that later. Learn this bugle call."

"How many do we have to learn?" George asked.

"There are eight bugle calls that we use on base: Assembly of Buglers, Reveille, Assembly, Mess Call, Drill Call, Recall, Tattoo, and Taps; but you are only required to learn the last seven. The Assembly of Buglers just calls the other buglers together to sound one of the important calls for the rest of us."

"That's an awful lot," someone said. George silently agreed. And since bugles could only play five notes in one key, they were probably all very similar. Well, at least Reveille was pretty distinctive, and so was Taps. Maybe it would be fine.

"Well too bad!" Chief Aide Mallory replied. "You don't get a choice."

She proceeded to take roll call of her girls while Jim, the vice chief aide, took roll call of his boys and reported to her. Everyone was found to be present.

Then she sent some of her aides scurrying off on a task. Several minutes later they drove up in a small ATV with a bed like a pickup truck.

"Okay, everyone," the chief aide said as the buglers stopped their Assembly call, "time for your uniforms. Form a line, please."

The kids did as instructed. When George's turn came, he was quickly measured and handed a bundle of clothes. He got a thick pair of olive drab trousers; a leather belt; a heavy-duty, khaki-colored button-up shirt; and a darker olive drab trench coat with a sand-colored inner lining. Both shades of olive drab were a sort of greenish brown, with the trousers having more brown and the trench coat tinted a stronger green. It looked like it would do a good job of providing general concealment in most terrains.

"Go inside your barracks and put your uniforms on," they were ordered. "In the army, this is what you will wear. It is only different from our uniforms by the color. It's not complete, but you will receive your full complement of gear after you pass training."

George found the new clothes to be a bit stiff, but not uncomfortable. They were very well-made of thick, durable material. The trench coat fell halfway down his thigh towards his knees and contained skirt flaps that could be buttoned back so they hung behind his legs and out of the way.

George came back outside, feeling much more official. Now he looked like a real soldier. Next, he had his feet measured and was given ankle-length combat boots. They chafed a little, being not yet broken in. That was unpleasant, but hopefully it would pass soon enough.

Then the bugles began in chorus again, playing a bouncy tune that rose and fell. Again, it was repeated.

"That's the Mess Call you learned yesterday," their chief aide informed them. "Time for breakfast." George frowned. It reminded him too much of Reveille. Hopefully, he would be able to keep them all straight.

Breakfast was a simple but rich meal of eggs and bread and bacon. George was impressed, but still, in the field they probably wouldn't eat so well. When the meal was over, the bugles sounded a slower but still bouncy tune. They all seemed to be bouncy! There was no way he was going to be able to tell them all apart.

"Drill Call!" Captain Hughes informed them. "Time to start work! We will begin in the classrooms." With that he disappeared in their direction and the aides rounded the trainees up to follow him.

The classrooms looked very much like any school's classrooms, but they were nice. George took a seat at one of the desks. An officer stood at the front of the room, watching and waiting, until they were all seated.

"This place is definitely way better funded that our school," Cassie whispered.

"Welcome to boot camp," said the officer at the front of the room. "I'm Sergeant, and I'll be doing most of the classroom teaching. Our first day here you will be learning about the army you have chosen to join."

"Excuse me?" a girl asked.

"Yes?"

"What's your name?"

"Sergeant."

"No, your name, not your rank."

The officer smiled. "They're both Sergeant."

"Your last name is literally Sergeant?" a boy exclaimed.

"Yes, as is my rank. So people just call me Sergeant." The whole class guffawed loudly.

"Now, on to the lesson." Sergeant gestured to some charts on the wall. "The Alamedan Armed Forces are the collective military units and resources under the government of the Alamedan Empire. You won't be studying the politics at boot camp, so we'll suffice to say that the Emperor has final say in everything unless the Parliament of consuls elected by the Empire's provinces overrules him with a three-fourths majority in that thing.

"Anyhow, the ground forces of the military are organized into field armies, and each is, of course, commanded by a general.

"Now, all of the Empire's military are devoted to different theaters, or areas, of operations. Each area is called a front, and commanded by a field marshal, who is in charge of all of the resources sent to that theater of the war. He can have any number of units in his front, depending on what high command sends him; he's just the officer overseeing all the operations there.

"Currently Alameda has three fronts — North, East, and South — as we expand out from the West Coast. We have four field armies; one each in the North and South Fronts, and two in the East Front.

"Now, you're in the army, so that's what we'll be focusing on. In standard condition, each field army has about 164,000 infantry soldiers, plus other personnel.

"Each army is divided into four corps, and each corp has four divisions, which is one of the larger strategic units. The truth is that divisions and corps can be shuffled around among higher echelons as needed, so this isn't always exact. But below that, each division has four brigades, and each brigade has four battalions. This is usually consistent.

"Battalions are the basis of maneuvering and allotting forces to major battlefield objectives. Because of their composition, they are the smallest fully-self-sufficient unit that can conduct sustained operations in the field and fight alone, much like a mini army.

"Battalions have four infantry companies, plus other attached companies, such as a heavy weapons support company or a supply company to deliver supplies in the field, which is why they are self-sustaining. Companies are the basis of minor strategic objectives that progress towards the brigades' major objective, with 164 soldiers, capable of taking and defending individual battlefield positions. For instance, a brigade might be tasked to take a town, and its companies would attack important strategic positions encroaching upon the town so as to secure control of it.

"Each infantry company has four platoons, and finally, each platoon has four squads of ten soldiers each, one of which is the corporal who leads the squad. That's the smallest unit."

Sergeant looked around the room. George felt dazed, like when his science teacher had explained all of the molarity calculations in thirty seconds.

"Be glad I didn't give you all the officers too," Sergeant said. "Now you don't need to memorize all that, but you do need to understand the general structure of the army and how it all works. Your barracks have books with all of this information and everything else." Ugh, great, more reading. But at least he didn't have to memorize it.

"Now that concludes our lecture here," Sergeant said. "Any questions?"

Cassandra raised her hand. "What is the difference between tactics and strategy?"

"Excellent question. Broadly speaking, strategy is *what* to fight for, what locations, such as hills or towns, are important to capture to secure your position, weaken the enemy's position, and exert effective control over the area you are fighting for. Strategy involves long-term decisions about where to best spend your limited resources. You could win all the wrong battles and lose the war because your enemy controls supply lines, roads, high ground, and urban areas.

"Tactics, on the other hand, involve short-term decisions based on the immediate situation and task in front of you — the routes by which you approach a house, the combined arms method you use, the artillery you call in, the maneuvers you make to secure your objective. Tactics is *how* you go about obtaining control over the positions you conclude to be of strategic importance.

"As an example, Germany's strategy in World War II was to control the Atlantic and prevent merchant shipping from reaching England, thereby starving her into submission. The wolfpack was a tactic used by German U-boats to obtain that control over the strategic objective, the Atlantic, by sinking merchant convoys. Of course, everything I mentioned is scalable. The strategic locations could be considered the tactics by which you complete your strategy of controlling an entire region. Sub-strategy, if you will.

"Alright, any more questions?" There were none. "Class is dismissed."

The trainees were all ordered back outside and taken around to an open field by the storehouse and armory. Captain Hughes appeared again.

"That guy is uncanny," George said. "He just 'appears.'"

"Now that you know about the army, you will begin learning your weapons," Captain Hughes said. "The aides are distributing paintball rifles, your standard arm. Drill Sergeant Hayes will instruct you."

Captain Hughes turned and was gone. In his place appeared a sober, stern-looking boy of sixteen or seventeen. The fact that he already had a prominent mustache made him even more imposing. He stood silently and stared as if at nothing.

The aides handed out rifles and ammunition to all of the recruits. George took his with interest. It looked like a cross between an M1 Garand, an M16, and a paintball gun. It was chunky and hefty, but not heavy or clunky. Drill Sergeant Hayes took one and demonstrated its operation to them.

"This gun is semiautomatic," said Drill Sergeant Hayes in a sharp, clear tone that everyone could hear, "which means it will fire every time you pull the trigger. It's powered by a cartridge of compressed gas that screws in here." He held the rifle up and pointed to the screw port at the front end of the stock. The gas cartridge, a cylinder with a screw top, attached there and became an extension of the stock. His movements were quick and stiff. "They are smaller to make them easier to carry, which means you will go through several a day during heavy fighting.

"Near the bolt is a gauge. When the gauge drops to this red line, you *must* change your cartridge, or the gun could jam. Up to that point, performance should be consistent. You should change your gas cartridge every time you reload your hopper. They are designed to last one full load, and no more. Get a fresh one every morning if you've used it at all, and change it after every battle. Don't reload your hopper without changing your cartridge, and pay attention to that gauge. Part of the gear you're going to get is a bandoleer that carries spare gas cartridges for your rifle. They are small enough to not be inconvenient when prone."

"To load the gun, get one of these plastic tubes, called a pod, snap open the top, and pour the paintballs into the hopper." As he spoke, Drill Sergeant Hayes loaded his rifle. "From the factory, the pods contain paintballs in cornstarch. The barrel is slightly larger than the projectile, meaning the cornstarch coats the paintball and allows it to fly smoothly down the barrel. It goes farther, too, though it's not accurate at that range."

"Wait, that makes the gun not accurate?" George asked.

"No, at the extra range it's not accurate, but it's just as accurate at regular ranges."

George nodded. "What's the point then?"

"Longer range is better. At the very least it unnerves the enemy, even if you can't hit them." George nodded. That made sense. Drill Sergeant Hayes added, "These gun barrels are rifled, which makes the gun work like a rifled musket, firing a roundball.

"Now," he continued, "at your side on your belt you will carry a bayonet in a sheath. The bayonet has a foam blade that soaks up liquid paint, and squeezes it out when you stab someone. It attaches to a mount below the muzzle of your rifle, or it can be held by the handle as a short sword.

"The sheath is lined with foam and filled with liquid paint. You will keep a bottle of liquid paint in your pack for refills. When the bayonet runs out or goes dry, just put it back in the sheath. We're not gonna use bayonets right now, but you need to understand them."

George clumsily put the rifle to his shoulder for the first time and pulled the trigger, feeling the gun lightly press back into him and hearing it pop as the paintball was ejected. It flew through the air, almost too fast to see, and splatted against the ground, leaving an orange smear on the dirt. George grinned; this was actually fun. He practiced with his rifle for a while longer under the instruction of Drill Sergeant Hayes, who corrected his posture.

"Set your body up so your bones support the gun and not your muscles," he said. "Left elbow on your hipbone; right elbow in the air, straight out from your side and parallel to the ground. If you're left-handed, reverse it. Lock in your posture. Keep the rifle snug against your shoulder and rest your cheek on the stock. That is basic standing position. You'll learn more about positions later."

George was also made to repeatedly change his gas cartridge and reload his hopper so the actions would become familiar. They were kind of tricky at first, but gradually he became less clumsy. Screwing a cartridge on and off was tricky because the rifle barrel prevented him from getting his hand all the way around the cylinder.

"Hold the rifle straight," Drill Sergeant Hayes said. "Do not cant it to the side. You see this in movies a lot, and it's wrong. If you do, the sights will not work properly, and you won't hit what you're aiming at."

Eventually, the bugles blew the Mess Call. "Alright," said Drill Sergeant Hayes, "take your rifles and put them on your bunks. Always keep your rifle with you in the field. At all times. It is your lifeline. Never leave it lying around. Never go anywhere without it."

After they had eaten lunch, the trainees were ordered back into the classrooms where they found Sergeant waiting for them again. "Hello, guys," he said when they were all seated, "it's time to learn the rules of paintball warfare."

George looked up, surprised. "Rules?" he asked. "What rules?"

"The rules by which we fight. There have to be rules for this to work. I mean, it's paintball, it wouldn't work without rules."

Cassie raised her hand. "What makes everyone follow the rules?"

"The Secret Society. They run the paintball warfare all over the world. They make and enforce the rules. You break 'em, you get punished. It's your honor and duty to follow the rules, and most people do, simply because those that don't are kicked out.

"Or worse," he added ominously. "Understand?" The class nodded solemnly.

"How would they know if I cheated?" Cassie persisted.

Sergeant looked her straight in the eye. "They know everything," he said in a hushed, icy tone that made George shiver as if with dread. "Everything," he whispered, letting the words sink in.

"They sound like a lovely organization," Cassie said dryly.

"There's conspiracy theories about them galore, but really, none of this would work without the Society," Sergeant replied.

"What conspiracy theories?" a boy asked excitedly.

"Nothing of importance. You'll learn them from the grapevine sooner or later.

"Okay, so the rules are very simple," Sergeant resumed his lecture. "When you get paint on the trunk of your body, you're dead. Not your head or limbs, but the trunk of your body only. Any paint there at all, by any means, even if it happened by accident or you did it to yourself, and you're a casualty.

"At all times you *must* carry a white casualty shawl with you. No exceptions. We carry ours in a small pouch on our belt. If you're hit, drop *everything*, do *nothing*, and put it on. You're dead, so act like it, and don't talk to anyone. People can loot you, too."

"Can they loot your underwear?" John asked.

"Uh, no... You can only loot equipment, not personal items. Besides, that would be inappropriate. "

"If you're supposed to act dead, do you just lie there?" Cassie asked.

"No," Sergeant explained. "You find your way to the nearest Society outpost where they'll process you as a casualty and then ship you home. See, they're a nice organization and important to this entire game working.

"Now to help demonstrate this, I have an assistant today. This is Mr. John Doe." Sergeant gestured to the dummy at the front of the classroom. The trainees chuckled.

Sergeant took a paintbrush out and smeared paint on Mr. Doe's arm, head, and leg. "That does not kill him. Or his neck, either." Sergeant added paint to the dummy's neck. "He's still alive.

"However," Sergeant said as he put a blob of paint on the dummy's hip, "this does. Now he's dead." He knocked the dummy over with a crash, and everyone laughed. George wished Sergeant would come teach at his school. He might even make chemistry enjoyable.

"Now, after two months," Sergeant continued, "you get to come back to life and come fight again." He stood the dummy back up. "Of course, once you reach the rank of captain and higher, the casualty periods start getting longer."

"Why is that?"

"Higher-ranking officers are more valuable targets, hence the extra reward if you take them out. Now, there is no such thing as injuries. If you get shot in the leg, you do not have to hop around on one foot. You're either fully alive or all dead."

"Aw, man!" someone said. "What about mostly dead? Not all dead, just mostly."

"That's stupid," Sergeant said. "What good is that distinction?"

"Well, that's where medics come in. Miracle Max to cure you!"

"You know, that would be kinda cool, but, sorry, doesn't work that way. Now no more smartness, okay? You better be glad I'm not Captain Hughes. But I can report you to him." Sergeant raised an eyebrow at the boy, who looked away and remained mute. Sergeant grinned. "Besides, everyone just fights to the death. It's paintball, so there's no reason to surrender, really."

"Can you surrender?" Cassie asked.

"Yes, but if you become a POW you'll spend three months in a jail instead of two on casualty leave, although you can escape early. You can also choose to just go home, but then you're out for four months and you can't escape. So don't surrender; no reason to.

"Alright, that's the end of this session," he finished. "Time to drill with your weapons and do target practice."

"Why do you keep sending us back and forth between here and there?" John asked.

"Exercise," Sergeant said with a smirk. "Oh don't worry, it'll get more realistic soon."

George spent the rest of the day practicing with his rifle and getting the hang of it. He competed with John and Cassie to see who had the best marksmanship. So far John was in the lead, hitting the practice dummy more often than the other two. He also blew through the most ammunition, spamming the trigger.

"That is not a good habit to get into," Jim said.

"Why not?"

"Uh, because you get in an intense battle, and then presto, you're out of ammo. There are times for that, but not here."

"Hey, at least I'm getting the best score."

"Not on average you aren't. And just wait until we get out the motorized dummy that runs around while you shoot at it."

"What, that's a thing?"

The next morning, George and John were roused from their slumber by Reveille, and shortly Jim entered, singing that they had to get up this morning.

After breakfast, Drill Sergeant Hayes demonstrated how to salute properly. "When you report for roll call, you will also report for inspection, where you will salute and hold your posture while your commanding officer examines your uniforms. You will be instructed in this procedure tomorrow morning."

George clacked his heels together and saluted as demonstrated. Jim walked among the boys, and when he got to George he corrected his posture. "Be a man and stand up straight. Square shoulders."

George was pleased at the moment with where he was. So far this was proving to be interesting. He was learning some useful skills that would serve him soon. Hopefully. But another disappointment wouldn't surprise him.

"Alright," Drill Sergeant Hayes said, "time to march." The aides began distributing backpacks. George took his and nearly dropped it. He staggered as he pulled the backpack onto his shoulders.

"These things weigh a ton!" Cassie exclaimed.

"Marching is simple!" Drill Sergeant Hayes went on. "Pick your knees up and put your feet down flat, so you don't wear yourself out. Now we're going on a march. You will be carrying these backpacks the entire way, understand? No shirking your load."

An ATV drove up, and Drill Sergeant Hayes sat down in the rear-facing back seat. The driver slowly steered the vehicle out towards the open ground and rumbled along at a brisk walking pace.

"Follow me!" Drill Sergeant Hayes ordered, bouncing around in his seat as the ATV jolted on the rough terrain. "March, guys!"

George strode to the front of the line behind the ATV and set off, lugging his pack. This was his first march, his first chance to accomplish something, to prove himself.

They walked for an hour under the blazing sun. George sweated. He was thirsty. His shoulders ached from the heavy pack he was carrying. His feet chafed against his new boots and grew sore from walking.

Another hour had passed when Drill Sergeant Hayes called a halt and told the kids to rest and drink some water. George plopped down where he was. John joined him.

"This," John panted, "is nothing like PE class."

George was too busy guzzling water to answer. "What's in these packs?" he wondered after he had put his canteen away. They both opened them, like many of the others were doing. They stared at the contents.

"Sand," George said. "Bags of wet sand. We've been carrying around *sand* this whole time."

John shook his head. "I guess it makes sense. They're gonna toughen us up."

"That's stupid. Why would we be carrying around *sand*? Completely pointless. I thought there wouldn't be any of this."

"Because it's heavy, that's why. This is an adventure, alright."

"Alright, break's over!" Drill Sergeant Hayes yelled. "Get back on your feet!"

"Sir?" someone asked.

"What?!"

"Why are we carrying sand? It's pointless."

"You are carrying sand because you have to get used to carrying weight! You'll often have a lot to carry in the field, or much farther to go. Of course we're not giving you real supplies to carry. That would be a waste. Now suck it up and move! In two weeks you'll be doing the real thing."

George trudged forward again, but the ATV picked up its pace and moved quicker.

"Keep up!" Drill Sergeant Hayes ordered.

George didn't know if he could keep up. He couldn't remember ever doing anything like this before. Bit by bit he fell from the front to the back of the line. He saw Cassie, grim and determined, head down and sweating. John tried to look confident.

"George!" Jim shouted from the ATV following behind them. "You're falling behind! You have to keep going."

"My feet hurt."

"You'll fail."

"Whatever."

"George, why did you join the army just to fail?"

"I wanted to do something interesting. But I can't if my feet hurt. Besides, we're carrying *sand*. Waste of time. We could be doing more important stuff."

"You *are* doing something real! It just takes effort. Anything takes effort. The better it is, the more effort it takes. You have to follow through with it. Now get your butt back up there and keep moving. There aren't any breaks unless the commander orders them. Keep going, George, you have to do it. Don't be a pessimist."

George said nothing. He just stood there for a moment. Then with a grunt he caught back up to the end of the line.

"If I were you," Jim warned, "I'd not be the last one."

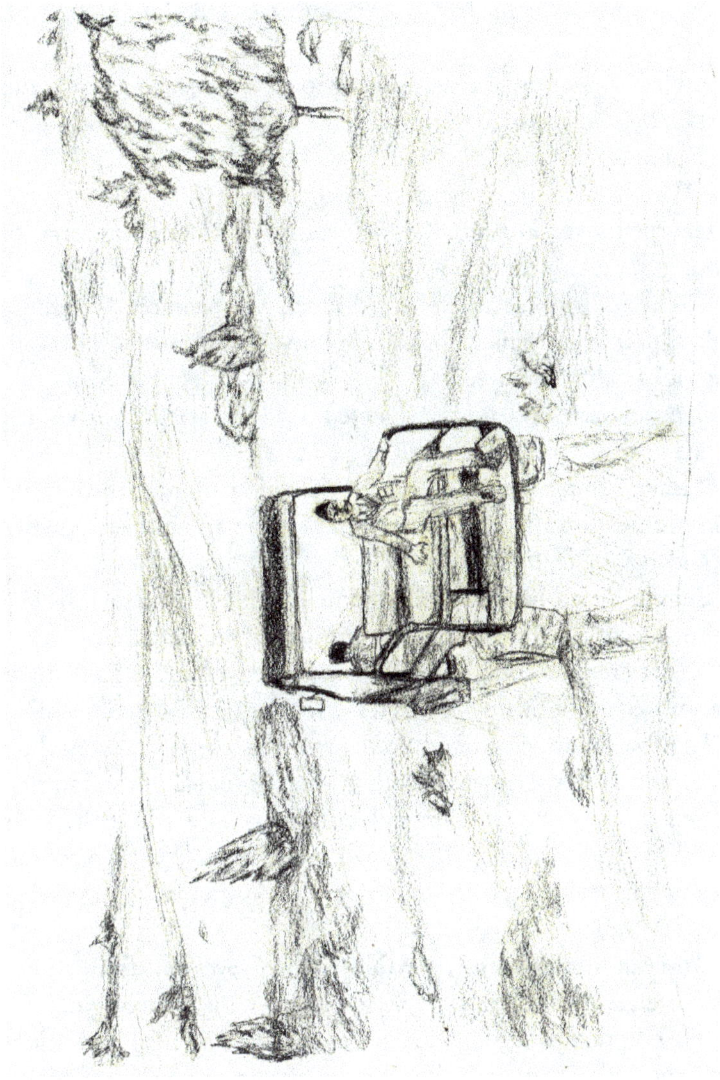

"Follow me!"

"Who cares if I come last," George griped. "I did it." Jim held his peace.

After hours more of marching, or so it seemed, and a few water breaks, the sun was high in the sky. The leading ATV stopped moving again.

"We're here!" Drill Sergeant Hayes declared.

George looked around. "Here" was merely a random scrap of ground in the middle of nowhere.

"We're going to eat lunch," the drill sergeant went on. "There are rations in that last vehicle for you. But first, I want the five of you in the back to come up here!"

George gulped and did as instructed. Two other boys and two girls joined him. They faced the drill sergeant.

"Slackers don't cut it!" he said. "We expect more than the bare minimum around here. While the rest of your comrades eat, you five will be digging foxholes."

George closed his eyes for a moment, then looked at Jim. His expression said, "I told you so," yet he looked sympathetic.

"What are you doing?" Drill Sergeant Hayes said. "You'd have already been shot by now if this was a real battle. Move your ass!"

The five delinquents removed their entrenching tools from their packs, a sort of dual shovel-pick that could be folded up, and started digging. The ground was hard and scrubby, making it difficult. After twenty minutes George had scraped a shallow hole in the ground. Meanwhile, the others who had not been in the back were eating their field rations.

"You call that a foxhole?" Drill Sergeant Hayes confronted him. "You need at *least* eighteen inches to lie down in. Keep digging!

"Foxholes are your individual protection in the field," he lectured everyone. "They can easily be scraped with any tool, and vastly increase the difficulty in hitting you. They are the solution whenever you are sitting in one place."

Finally, George satisfied the drill sergeant's demands and received his meal. Everyone else had finished eating and they were also ordered to dig foxholes, which they did. Everyone sat in his own foxhole for about an hour before being ordered to march back to the base.

George was the very last to arrive, completely exhausted. The sun was already setting, and dinner was a lethargic affair. When the Tattoo sounded, signaling that it was time to prepare for bed, everyone went straight to his own barrack.

George crawled into bed without changing his dirty clothes. When the buglers sounded Taps, the last call of the day, he was already fast asleep and never heard it.

Chapter IV

The next morning George woke up hard, struggling to reach consciousness while his brain phased back and forth like a drunkard in a movie, unable to fully boot up. He was still exhausted from yesterday, and his body ached. Jim came in, singing along with Reveille, but George ignored him, and the singing faded from his conscience.

Suddenly, he jolted awake. "Hey!" an aide was shouting at him. "You've been reported absent for role call and are to report to the captain immediately so he can cook you for breakfast!" Rather nervously, even though he knew the boy was being facetious, George got up to the sound of the Mess Call and walked outside, rubbing his stiff shoulders.

At Captain Hughes' office, he found several other kids also there. He himself was clearly the last to arrive since Captain Hughes ceased reading whatever papers he was holding. Why did it seem like officers were always shuffling papers?

Captain Hughes cleared his throat in a laborious, ominous manner. "I understand that you are all tired and sore after yesterday. But I know for a fact that two of you did not go to sleep in a reasonable amount of time. That is your own fault.

"Furthermore, sleeping in is not allowed. You're not the only ones tired around here, but you selfishly thought only of yourself. That is not acceptable. You must pull your weight with the rest of your comrades. They rely on you. If you don't do your share, then someone else has to do it for you. You're *stealing* from that person and letting the team down!

"Now, while everyone else eats breakfast, you guys will be digging foxholes." Oh no, not another march on an empty stomach. He had to be kidding. What on Earth. George mentally groaned.

"Don't we get to eat?" asked a girl.

"No. You will have to wait for lunch. Now follow me." He led them outside his office. "I want you to go right over there and dig some foxholes. Dig good ones that will serve their purpose." He sent them off, and they trudged over, pulled out their entrenching tools, and started digging. It was some comfort that they had no taskmaster forcing them to work hard.

"Here," a small boy said, "I've got some jerky." He divvied it up, and everyone gratefully accepted a piece.

George dug a shallow hole in the ground and sat down in it. Why did they have to pick on him? He had been legitimately tired, going to bed when he should have and not staying up late. And now he was being punished with all the people who had stayed up past bedtime. Around him, the others dug farther.

"That's not deep enough," a girl said. He looked at her, annoyed. "Captain Hughes wants them to be deeper," she said. "You're gonna get us all in trouble again."

George sat there grumpily for a long minute. There wasn't even anyone shooting at them. Who cared. "Come on!" the girl said. "We're already finished." George huffed out an exasperated breath. Fine, whatever. He got up and continued digging until his foxhole was about as deep as the others. They all sat there until Captain Hughes marched out to them again.

"Those are decent," he said. "Now go join the rest of the trainees in front of your barracks."

In a few minutes, Drill Sergeant Hates appeared and addressed them. "Now, you are going to learn the basics of some other infantry weapons. Most likely you won't be using them much, but you need to understand them in case you have to."

Drill Sergeant Hayes first picked up a PIAT. George was already familiar with the crossbow-like mechanism, but he had never operated one himself. The handles were surprisingly difficult to draw back. Some of the girls had to lie down on their backs and use their leg muscles to cock the thing, but fortunately George was just strong enough to do it standing up.

The rear sight on the PIAT was a simple metal stud. The front sight, which folded down when not being used, was a large metal circle that contained three pins for close, medium, and long range. George estimated the distance to the target, lined the rear sight up with the center pin, and scored a near miss. Not bad for his first shot.

After getting familiar with the PIAT, George learned machine gun operation. There were different types, but he practiced on a heavy one like Sergeant Miller had used at school. They all worked similarly, with compressed gas propulsion connected somehow. This one had a mini air compressor charging a tank that connected to the gun via a short black hose.

Finally, Drill Sergeant Hayes got out the BAPR rifle. "BAPR stands for Browning Automatic Paintball Rifle, named after the American weapon from World War II," he explained. "However, we call it the BAR like the real weapon, because it's easier to pronounce. Every squad has one dedicated BAR gunner, so you all need to be familiar with this. It's basically a light machine gun slash assault rifle."

The BAR rifle only had about ten seconds of sustained fire before it had to be reloaded and its gas cartridge changed, a somewhat lengthy process, and its rate of fire wasn't as high as a proper machine gun. Even so, it still was a valuable asset to the infantry, providing automatic firepower forward on the assault and into close quarters or confined spaces where actual machine guns were not so useful.

George was pleased with these new skills. Now he would be able to make use of all the legendary firepower that Alameda's infantry attacked with, if he ever found himself needing to operate one of these weapons.

After the BAR rifle, George learned about the grenades Alamedan soldiers carried into battle. He was somewhat surprised by how small they were, easily fitting into his hand. A pin was pulled to release the handle, which was held in place by his hand gripping the grenade. Once he let go of the handle, allowing it to fly off, he had five seconds to throw the grenade before liquid paint sprayed from nozzles, much like the PIAT shell that fateful day at school. He was told that, internally, it functioned just like a spray can of paint.

Next morning's small arms training came with more instruction on the various shooting positions, just as they had been promised. First, Drill Sergeant Hayes went over standing position again. George had this one, he knew. Maybe it was harder to hit anything from standing position, but he had the posture down. He stopped paying so much attention since he already knew it.

"Alright, next is kneeling position," Drill Sergeant Hayes went on. "So, stand straight, like this. Then lower yourself down onto your right knee. If you're left-handed, it's your left knee. Turn your right foot sideways and sit on it. Sit back and brace your butt against your foot, with your other foot flat against the ground. Then prop your left elbow on your left knee, tuck your right elbow into your side, and you're in your firing position." Drill Sergeant Hayes took a shot, squarely striking the target.

That didn't look too difficult. George went down on his knee, flattened his foot, and tried to sit back without falling over backwards. Agh, that actually hurt. He wasn't used to bending in that way. He strained to pull himself into the proper position, but it was so uncomfortable and he was taking too long. His foot felt like it was being twisted off his leg. He hadn't even acquired his target yet in his sights, and he felt like he would fall over backwards any moment now. This was a stupid position.

"A lot of you are having trouble," Drill Sergeant Hayes said. "That is because you spend all day sitting around, staring at a screen, and you don't move. It'll come easier over time, and as you practice quickly getting into the position, and you get into shape.

"In the meantime, though, you'll have to adapt. If you can't get into that position quickly, then do not try it in a battle. Just get down, steady yourself, and get off a shot."

George proceeded to modify his position so he was kneeling like a knight being knighted. From there he was able to shoot relatively comfortably, even though he had to hold his butt up off the ground. Drill Sergeant Hayes said it wasn't as good of a posture, less stable and with his left elbow unsupported, but who cared, it was good enough.

"Crouching position is better," Drill Sergeant Hayes went on. "Squat down and brace your elbows on your knees to get a stable firing platform. It's quick and easy to acquire and get out of."

George got back to his feet and experimented until he found the right crouch position. Now that was a low-profile shooting position he liked. He tried running, dropping to a crouch, bracing his rifle, and shooting, then running on again. It worked pretty well.

"Alright, enough of that," Drill Sergeant Hayes said. "Prone positions. That means lying down. It's not that complicated — just lie down and brace yourself on the ground. You should have no floating contact points. Elbows down, hold the gun up to eye level."

George copied the drill sergeant and lay down on his stomach. He steadied his rifle before him and peered through the sight. Pulling the trigger, he hit the target. Nice! This was a good position.

"Now while you're prone," Drill Sergeant Hayes went on, "you move by walking on your elbows. Keep your muzzle out of the dirt or you'll jam your gun."

Copying the drill sergeant again, George cradled his rifle in his arms perpendicular to his body and crawled forward, walking on his elbows. It wasn't very comfortable. Dirt smeared all over him. His left elbow bruised itself on an unseen rock. How did Drill Sergeant Hayes move so quickly?

"When you're on the battlefield, you'll want to choose your position wisely," Captain Hughes went on. Standing works for everything. Kneeling is a good way to reduce your profile without compromising on speed. If you can't kneel, crouch. Some veterans prefer crouching over kneeling anyway. Prone is an excellent position when there is ground cover or when you can lie hull down behind a hill or ridge. It's slower to get out of, though, if you have to move. And some weapons have components underneath that make them impossible to use prone.

Prone position.

"Now if there is anything you could brace yourself on to help steady your shot, do it. Modify your position to make use of that support. That is called a jackass position. If you're standing and you rest your gun on a wall or tree, that is jackass standing position. If you're kneeling and you use a log, that's jackass kneeling. If you're lying in a foxhole and propped up over the edge, that's jackass prone."

"Why're they called jackass positions?" Cassie asked.

"I do not know, but that's what they're called. Use them. It is of no credit to you if you make a hard shot offhand when you could have braced yourself on something. You will make a better soldier if you always take advantage of every opportunity to improve your performance."

"Did you say offhand?" Cassie asked. "What's that?"

"It's like standing position, but you haven't had time to properly situate your posture. Basically it's potshot position. We're at the end of our time right now, but each barrack has a small library. One of the books we have is *The Art of the Rifle*. It will tell you everything you need to know about marksmanship, with positions, including offhand, pictures, everything. I highly recommend you read it."

That evening, George went to his barrack's library and quickly found the book. There weren't very many to choose from. He flipped it open and looked at the pictures. Obviously, that was standing and that one was kneeling. But there was also a lot of small text. He had enough schoolwork reading to do already.

One day after lunch, George was ordered back into the classroom where everyone once again greeted Sergeant. He had become a favorite, along with Jim.

"Hi, guys, been a few days. Well, today we are going to give you a brief overview of infantry tactics, both offensive and defensive. Throughout the rest of boot camp we'll go into more detail, but for now we're going to spend today covering the basics." George was intrigued. This is what he would be doing.

Sergeant turned to the blackboard. It was covered with charts and graphs, illustrating the composition of army units, different weapons and their abilities, and sample theoretical missions and positions in the field.

"We'll start this lecture by saying that Alamedan warfare doctrine can be summed up as firepower and infantry. Firepower and infantry are the two main assets we synergize in our tactics and strategy to win battles.

"Alamedan weaponry design focuses on flinging as much paint as possible. Our artillery and air force are less precision and more mass paint and carpet bombings preceding the infantry, who themselves are equipped with plenty of ability to throw a lot of paint.

"Firepower is a critical feature of our military. All of our technology primarily focuses on means of delivering that firepower, whether it be via bomber, warship, artillery, or paratrooper.

"Infantry is the other half of our doctrine. Nothing makes up for good infantry. *Nothing*. In paintball, you can never obliterate an enemy with purely firepower, which means that, in the end, the infantry have to go in and finish the job. And because it's paintball, the concern is efficient use of the infantry, not sparing them at all costs by using bombs and such.

"When attacking, always precede an attack with firepower if possible. Not so the enemy immediately knows to prepare, but rather to pin them during an advance. Creeping artillery barrages are a crucial tactic here since they can also help screen the infantry as they go forward.

"The idea is to pack a heavy punch and rain fire and brimstone ahead of an attack to annihilate the enemy or pin them down while the infantry get close. Remember, nothing makes up for masses of good, solid, well-trained infantry. Well, not in a mass so they're easy to hit, just a lot of them.

"When you attack, hit hard. Attrition is something to be avoided if possible. An attack can be a swift punch or a methodical advance, but always hit hard and keep hitting with lots of infantry if conditions are favorable.

"Never send infantry in without cover or suppression fire. Rather than waste soldiers that way, prepare your position as a defensive standpoint and wait for reinforcements if you can.

"When advancing, always take the route that provides the most cover. Even if it is the longest route, it is almost always better to use cover instead of charging across open ground. Also make good use of foxholes.

"And I seriously want to stress this one. You've been practicing a lot of foxholes for a reason. If you find yourself sitting somewhere and not moving, for whatever reason, *dig a foxhole*! If you are in a foxhole, then you are thrice as difficult to hit and *four* times as difficult to roust from your position, and infinitely harder to even see in the first place. And if they can't see you they can't shoot you, eh?"

A trainee raised his hand.

"Yes?"

"Can I ask how you calculated those probabilities?"

"I didn't, I made them up to make a point."

"Uh, how much of the rest of what we're hearing did you also make up?"

"None of it. That was the only part."

"Ri-ight..."

"Anyhow, I'm serious about the digging foxholes thing. It marks the difference between a good soldier and an average soldier. Seriously, a foxhole is likely the most useful hole you'll ever dig in the ground."

Sergeant proceeded to explain a little bit more about these principles while George listened, fascinated, although the boy in front of him seemed to be falling asleep. Then Sergeant put up a couple of other visual aids and changed the subject.

"Alright, a very brief discussion of defensive fortifications. Now I don't mean foxholes. Those are field defenses, personal cover. I mean the more elaborate fortifications an army uses to defend a prepared position.

"Now, when people think about fortifying an area to prepare for a siege or something, for some reason the first thing they want to do is dig trenches all around it. That and build bunkers everywhere. But you don't want to do this.

"Trenches have their usefulness, but for the most part, they require a lot of effort to make, a lot of upkeep to maintain, and a lot of soldiers to man them. Plus, unless you build an elaborate system of support trenches, once the enemy punctures a hole in your trench line, well, now it's useless and they can drive right through it.

"So don't dig long trench lines. And if you don't believe me, go read about World War I." George nodded to himself. He knew what Sergeant was talking about. Technology had advanced greatly, but the tactics had not. He liked how sensible Alameda was. "Instead," Sergeant continued, "our defensive doctrine is that of defense-in-depth using mutually-supporting isolated strongpoints. We call this DIDUMSIS. Also known as hedgehog defense, but the acronym is more fun, right?

"I mentioned bunkers previously. Bunkers are a great defensive mechanism, though they also tend to be a death trap if you get overrun. Really they are for building a more permanent defense, like a defensive line along your border, when you can put a lot of effort into it. For field defenses in a campaign that you will just leave behind soon, dugouts are better.

"Basically, you construct a bunch of individual mini fortresses. You *can* use some trenches in these, as well as ramparts and bunkers made by digging into the earth and building around the opening you create. Nests and gun pits are also important features. Basically, make lots of dugouts and then add other stuff if you can." As Sergeant talked, he plugged Lego bricks together to illustrate the design features he was talking about.

"These strongpoints are placed within range of each other, dotted across the landscape, and staggered in multiple rows." Sergeant took a piece of chalk and illustrated this on the blackboard. "Thus, an advancing enemy can go between them and get shredded by our firepower, or try to take them one by one, a costly approach. And if they get one, they come under fire from the others.

"This works especially well if each strongpoint has an open back protected by the front of another strongpoint. You can even fall back out of them if necessary, without being trapped. The enemy will have a very hard time trying to penetrate your line. These types of defenses are also easier to set up quickly in the field. Trenches take a lotta work.

"In fact, in the Pacific in World War II, the Japanese defended their islands with bunkers that had a closed front and open sides. Each side covered the front of another bunker. The US Marines found it very unnerving to not be able to shoot at an enemy in front of them. They had to do a lot of flanking.

"Just be careful about mechanized attacks that whip through unopposed. Obstacles are useful to break up an attack. Ideally they would stop vehicles but not provide cover for infantry, like the anti-tank wall on Omaha Beach that gave the Americans a place to shelter and then attack the German bunkers.

"You can arrange these defenses with false weak points where it looks like the enemy could have the best chance of going through, then mass your firepower there for an unpleasant surprise. This is a great way to guide vehicles towards your anti-tank weapons by providing a way around the obstacles. But don't overdo it, or it might just backfire." George nodded again. Even Napoleon used enticing "weak" points to occupy the enemy while he pursued his own objective.

"Also note the strengths of individual weapons," Sergeant continued. "Artillery is good for both the offensive and the defensive; for you infantry that means mortars and man-packed guns you can take with you when attacking or use in defense. Just remember that adequate range is needed for supporting an attack.

"Machine guns are more useful on the defense than the offense simply because they're good at sitting in place and spewing paint. They are still valuable in an attack, of course, but must be used carefully and they can't lead an assault. They work well as suppressive fire while infantry are moving forward, dragged along with the advance, or area denial. Lighter guns are better for this movement, too.

"BAR rifles are mainly offensive assault weapons. They are great for leading an attack. Also, use them in short bursts if possible so you don't blow through all your ammo. They can still be used defensively, but machine guns are better suited to such a role unless you're in a city or somewhere that limits how much ground a machine gun can cover. BAR rifles are great in close quarters and more adaptable to the situation.

"And remember, nothing makes up for good infantry. Infantry can go anywhere and tackle any job, offensive or defensive or counteroffensive or whatever. Infantry are the key to success. You are the single most important weapon in the entire armed forces."

George like the sound of that. He would really matter here. He was one of the most important people in all of Alameda.

"*Pugna Ut Vincas*[1]," Sergeant said. "Fight to Win. That is the motto of the army, chosen by General Halsted when he organized our first field army. That is *your* motto. Whatever battle you find yourself in, no matter how desperate, or how easy — fight it with your might, fight it to win. Live by that. *Pugna Ut Vincas.*"

"*Pugna Ut Vincas*," George repeated to himself.

George's first week at boot camp was very consistent. Each day consisted of training with his weapons, target practice, bayonet drills, the various shooting positions, learning tactical theory in classroom lectures, going on marches, and digging in the hard ground. In fact, George spent a lot of time digging. After he was proficient at foxholes, he was taught how to dig dugouts, which were like foxholes but bigger and shaped differently and with the dirt thrown up for

---

1. Pronounced "POON-ya oot VEEN-kas."

a rampart — a larger defensive fortification and not just personal cover.

He also learned about trenches, how to keep them from collapsing on their occupants, and how to design supporting trench systems. Digging an actual trench system large enough to adequately defend what seemed like a small area was a tremendous amount of work. It occupied a good portion of two whole days' training.

George had little free time to spend. Almost every hour of his day was planned for him. He was so busy and so tired from the hard work that he had no time to get to his schoolwork. But that was okay. He was doing important things, like becoming a good soldier.

Almost before he knew it, the weekend had arrived and George finally got to rest. His body was still not used to the effort demanded of it by the training regimen. He was also glad to have free time to lie around and play games. Briefly, he touched upon the homework that he had put off for so long, but it was the weekend. You didn't do school on the weekend.

Compared to the week, Saturday and Sunday seemed to drag by. When Monday came, training resumed in full and George thought no more of his homework. That morning, Drill Sergeant Hayes called the trainees together at their usual time for small arms practice.

"You have all been doing very well at the target range, so now you are going to participate in a war game. You will be divided into two teams on opposite sides of the facility. There will be a flag mounted on a small weight in the middle. The first team to get it back to their base wins."

Cassie raised her hand. "Yes?" Drill Sergeant Hayes asked.

"How do we do that without killing each other?"

"The paint you have been using is orange. That is training paint. Combat paint is some shade of red or pink. Orange doesn't make you a casualty except in this game.

"These are the rules of this game. Each team has a base marked off by ropes. This is your safe zone. You cannot be eliminated while you are standing in your base. If you are hit and eliminated, you get a maximum of two respawns. You have to wait two minutes to respawn. The third time you are eliminated, you're out for good. The first team to get the flag back to their base wins."

"Oh, so it's War Thunder IRL," someone commented.

George was excited. Time to actually fight a battle! He got in line with all the other recruits. Several aides had set up a table and were equipping the trainees for the game. When George's turn came, one of the aides tied a red cloth around his left arm, just below the shoulder, and gave him an ammunition pod and gas cartridge.

"You get one load for the whole game. It has to last you through all your respawns. When you're out of ammo, you're out of the game," the aide told him. "Red base is on that side."

George headed that way and found that stakes had been used to mark off a rectangle with rope. A large red flag had been driven into the ground inside the base. Behind the base was another table staffed by aides. Jim waved at him from the table and George waved back. His teammates were busy electing officers and trying to organize units.

"George, come join me!" Cassie called. "I've been elected sergeant!"

"Sure," he replied, and attached himself to her unit.

"Okay, guys," she explained, "we're going to providing cover fire for Zachary's unit while they rush to grab the flag."

"I want to get the flag!" someone complained.

"Then go with him." There was a good deal of shuffling, and shortly Cassie found herself leading a very small group of trainees while Zachary had amassed a mob of followers, all excited to be the hero to grab the flag, bring it back to base, and win the game. George stayed put with Cassie. If they were all going to fight over the glory, they could have it. He was staying out of it.

"Alright, guys," Jim said, "remember — two respawns, no ammo refills, and if you're hit, drop the flag and get out of the way." He glanced at his watch. "Okay, we start in five minutes. If you're not ready by then, too bad."

"So where's the flag going to be?" Cassie asked.

Jim grinned. "You'll have to find it." Cassie frowned, and he added, "It's not hard, we didn't hide it."

George waited. Everyone shuffled and fidgeted, but didn't say much. "One minute," Jim informed them.

"Team Red, yeah!" Zachary, a boy of fourteen, said, pumping his fist in the air. Many of their teammates joined him in chanting, "Team Red! Team Red! Team Red!" until Jim cut them off.

"Alright, get ready!" he put a whistle in his mouth. "Do not leave the base until I blow," he said around the whistle. He held up his hand and counted down with his fingers. Five. Four. Three. Two. One. *Shriek!* Jim blew hard on his whistle, and George thought he heard another whistle blowing at the opposite end of the facility.

"Let's go!" Zachary yelled and charged forward, his horde of minions following behind.

"Team Red! Team Red! Team Red!" "Red Devils!" "Scorching Red Hot Sauce!" the trainees yelled.

Cassie promptly took off too, and George ran after her. They could hear Team Blue's shouting in the distance. George ran around the building in front of their base, glanced around, and immediately saw the orange flag standing in the center of the facility, surrounded by open ground.

As Zachary's unit barreled straight for the flag and Cassie's unit moved up behind them, George saw Team Blue divided into multiple smaller groups spreading out and moving around. Immediately, guns began firing and George could feel the adrenaline start to flow. Man, that felt good.

He bounded forward to engage the enemy, forgetting about the group he was a part of. Raising his rifle, he took shots as he ran. Team Blue in their small groups was not charging the flag, but rather moving around it, raining paint upon the horde of Team Red around the flag.

"If you're hit, get outta the way and back to base!" Sergeant yelled. He and Captain Hughes were refereeing from the sides.

George and some of his teammates were moving to oppose one of Team Blue's units. George dropped to a crouch and fired, missing.

One of his opponents fired back. George felt something hit him in the stomach and jumped. It felt like he had been stabbed through his shirt with a needle. Smarting, he rubbed his stinging belly with his hand.

Feeling something smear, he held up his hand and saw orange paint. He had been hit by a paintball. They really hurt *that* much?

"Get back to your base and respawn!" Sergeant shouted at him. George remembered the rules and followed many of his teammates back. He turned to look as he heard cheering, and saw a girl with a red armband holding the flag and streaking to follow him.

However, team blue had worked their way around the arena and cut off her escape rout. She was hit multiple times and left the flag sitting on the ground.

George reported to Jim, who gave him a towel to wipe the paint off and set a kitchen timer for two minutes.

"When it rings you can go," he said, making notes on a log sheet.

George waited impatiently as both teams fought over the flag. It moved very little from its new spot. Finally, his timer rang and without waiting he was off, throwing himself back in the battle, flinging continuous paintballs at Team Blue as they hid behind buildings and sniped at the Reds.

Again, he jumped as something stung him, this time on his back. He was going to have to get used to that. Running back to base, he checked his hopper and found it was empty. Ah, man. He wouldn't get to use his last respawn.

George reported to Jim, then went back to watch the game. Everyone was cheering for his team. Team Red fought hard, but Team Blue had early on gotten a better position, and now Team Red was running out of respawns after refusing to give up their costly strategy.

Finally, team blue charged in one grand assault. John seized the flag and was shot. Another boy took it from him, dropped his gun, and ran for his life while his teammates held off their opponents. The runner disappeared behind a building where Team Blue's base was, and George knew he had lost.

"Congratulations to Team Blue," said Drill Sergeant Hayes. "As you can see, they better employed small unit tactics, and used firepower to neutralize the local numerical superiority of Team Red going for the flag. Frontal assaults without supporting fire are costly. Flanking is better."

"What's our reward?" asked John.

"Bragging rights," replied Drill Sergeant Hayes.

"That's it?"

"Yes. We're going on another march now. Get your packs and get moving!"

Week two contained many more exercises like this — war games with varying missions and objectives, obstacle courses, and a cover course where George had to cross the distance quickly and avoid being seen. Many of these were fun, although George felt that some of the games didn't seem like realistic combat simulations. He did not distinguish himself in anything, but he completed them all. What more could be asked?

In addition, the regular training regimen of weapons drilling, marching, digging, and classroom lectures continued. The days were even more packed and strenuous. It seemed to increase in intensity as the weekend drew closer.

Finally it came, and George was grateful for another break. He really should do some schoolwork. He hadn't hardly done any this entire time. But it was the weekend, and Sunday was his last day. And seriously, the weekend was supposed to be a break from school.

Sunday morning, George lined up outside his barrack with the other trainees, faced Jim, and saluted. Drill Sergeant Hayes walked down the line with a notebook. Then he nodded satisfactorily and left.

After breakfast, Captain Hughes appeared and addressed the trainees. "I would like to congratulate you all," he began, "on passing boot camp. There have been no failures. I am very pleased with you all. Every one of you has earned the rank of private."

George was elated and thrilled. He had persevered through two whole weeks of boot camp. He had completed a training course, passed it, and was now going to actually do the job. He was going to be a soldier in the army.

"A few of you did very well and will get a corporalcy," Captain Hughes went on. He called out the names of the five lucky kids. George was slightly envious. But private was good enough. He had succeeded.

That night, George, John, and Cassie got together to hold a small celebration. John had somehow obtained a bag of Hershey's Kisses, which were passed around and devoured. They eagerly talked of what was to come for them all.

It was George's last night at boot camp. Tomorrow he would be sent to an army base and join a unit. As he fell asleep in his barrack for the last time, he listened to Jim singing softly along with the bugles as they played Taps.

> Day is done. Gone the sun
> From the lake, from the hill,
> From the sky.
> All is well. Safely rest;
> God is nigh.

Chapter V

Reveille's bouncy call woke George the next morning. He dressed and hurried outside for inspection. From there it was on to an exceptionally nice breakfast. When that was finished, Captain Hughes came out. George was excited for this day.

"I would like to commend you all once again on your hard work and perseverance. You have succeeded in your efforts. I hope you will continue your success in the name of Alameda."

A round of applause occurred for the trainees and the staff. George swelled with pride and satisfaction in his accomplishment. He had completed his training, and now he could move on to something greater.

"I have assignments for you all," the captain went on. "There will be some more buses arriving to take you to join your new units."

"Uh, buses?" someone asked. "You mean cattle trucks?"

"Do you want a demerit?" Captain Hughes asked sternly. The boy did not answer. "I didn't think so.

"Alright, you guys can go round up your things. Keep your uniforms, but leave the equipment. You'll be getting a few more items to complete your gear. We load up in an hour. Do whatever you want with it, just get ready to go."

George and John packed up their personal belongings and looked around at what had been their home for the last two intense weeks. Then they headed outside.

Cassie took much longer to join them, but when she did they strolled around the base, reviewing it. Someone had filled in the foxholes that George and a few other recruits had been forced to dig for sleeping in that day, but not the ones they had been forced to dig the second time he had slept in.

Then they heard a lonely bugle sounding Recall.

"I guess that's the signal that it's time to go," Cassie said.

Just as expected, several "cattle trucks" had arrived, and each had a soldier standing by the bed with a clipboard, shouting names. Cassie's name was heard from one direction, but another boy called for John and George.

"Well, I guess we're going our separate ways," Cassie said. "See ya, guys!"

"Good luck!" John called. He and George climbed into their designated vehicle.

After another bumpy ride that seemed to last an awfully long time, they climbed down and found themselves in a military base. This one was not like boot camp, however; it was vast and busy. Vehicles and soldiers were everywhere.

The new privates were ordered to check in at an office that required them to walk inside a large building complex. A desk sergeant took their names and, instead of shuffling through papers, consulted his computer. Then he printed out some pages, stapled them together, and handed them to the boys.

"You guys are both assigned to the 636th Infantry Battalion, which has been put into reserve to rest and replace its casualties. These papers contain everything you need to know."

"Cool, we'll be together," said John.

"No, sorry, you're in different companies. Now, here are your IDs," he said, handing them small wallets that flipped open like a police badge and held a card inside that designated their rank, unit, and other information. "Head right down that hallway and show them to one of the officers."

"Hey, can we drive with this?" John asked.

The desk sergeant looked at him. "No. You can't. Next!"

George thanked him and followed John. Time for his soldier gear! They walked into what looked like a gym, reminding him of school, where an officer greeted them and checked their IDs.

"What is this, a bar?" John joked.

"Alright," the officer said, ignoring him, "here is the rest of your gear. This is your helmet." George took it and examined the plastic "steel pot" shell, interior liner, chin straps, and camouflage netting around the outside. It looked pretty much like the M1 helmet the American troops wore during World War II. He knocked on it with his knuckles. It looked like the same plastic hard hats were made of. Sturdy stuff.

Next the officer gave them bandoleers for carrying gas cartridges for their rifles. Suspenders were provided to help hold their pants up and provide places to carry extra ammunition. They were also given large army backpacks and other gear, such as a bedroll strapped below the pack.

"There are a few things in the pack, like a tarp, but it's mostly empty. You'll fill it with what you need in the field, and often you won't carry it into action, just from camp to camp. It's rather heavy and unwieldy, but it will carry all your field rations, ammunition, grenades, etc. Everything you could possibly need. These packs are awesome."

"I see," said George. A practical, utilitarian tool. It made sense.

"Trust me," the officer went on. "I was there at the siege of Fort Ross in Sonoma County. They saved us."

"The siege of Fort Ross?" George inquired. "What was that?"

"We were a single company that camped in the historic blockhouse overnight during winter. It was freezing cold, and we had nothing but what we carried in our packs. They weren't the same ones, but they were about the same size. We were part of a forward group in an offensive that didn't start well.

"We did manage to do some improvement work on the fort, but we were besieged there by a large enemy force. This was back in the beginning, before air forces and tanks really started being used, and we didn't have any radios with us. Or cellphones." John rolled his eyes, but George was paying close attention to the story.

"They counterattacked our advance," the officer continued, "cut us off, and threw up lines around the blockhouse, figuring on starving us out. But no, sir, we held out on meager rations and ammunition for two weeks, fighting off repeated attacks after they got sick of waiting.

"But we held out for *two weeks* using *nothing* but what we carried in our packs. The supplies was quite different back then, too. You guys have so much technology at your disposal now. Two weeks, until General Halsted fought a division through and relieved us."

"Wow, you fought in Halsted's First Army?" John asked. Even he knew about Alameda's legendary general.

"I sure did."

George was impressed. Here was a veteran who had been in the wars a long time. He had experience and stories to tell. "How'd you end up here, then?" George asked.

"Oh, I dunno. Just — did. I don't have that long until I turn eighteen and then age out of paintball. Retire."

"Age out?"

"Yeah. Once you turn eighteen you can't be in the Paintball Wars anymore. No adults. Everyone, officers too, is under eighteen."

"That's actually really cool."

"Yeah. Anyhow, the blockhouse was little more than four walls around a few buildings, but back then there weren't really any mortars or planes, so we were pretty safe. A while back, actually, there was a rebellion over there, and after getting their butts kicked by the local troops the rebels retreated to Fort Ross. But the Empire sent in ground-attack planes over the walls, and everyone who couldn't fit in the buildings was, you know, 'killed,' and then our guys just walked right on into the fort and stormed the overcrowded buildings with grenades.

"But yeah, I fought with the First Army through Solano and Napa and Yolo...

"Anyhow, enough reminiscing. Those were some great battles. Under your backpack you'll wear these pod packs, which strap onto your lower back. Your ammunition pods for reloading your hopper go in these sleeves for easy access. There's more sleeves on your backpack, but when you leave that behind you'll use the pod pack. It's smaller and more comfortable and doesn't get in the way. Fits under your backpack where the bottom is cut back, so you can wear both. That is something we didn't have back at the blockhouse. Notice the pod sleeves on your belt and suspenders, just in case.

"Okay, I've got work to do," he said. George cocked his head. Wasn't he working now? "That's all your stuff; now go report to your barracks," the officer said. George and John picked up their stuff and left the building.

"Thanks, have fun giving the next set of kids a history lesson, Gramps!" John called back.

"That's rude," George said, "he's amazing."

"Ah, I bet he didn't hear me anyway. Besides, he talks like a World War II veteran."

"He's living history." George glanced through his papers. So many pages. "Barrack B15 is where I'll be."

John looked at his own documents. "B17." Lucky John, he had the name of a famous bomber from World War II. There had to have been a B-15 bomber, of course, but it wasn't famous enough for George to know anything about it, and that was saying something.

"Well, I guess I'll see you... later," George said.

"Good luck!" John said. "I bet I'll win a battle before you."

"Maybe," George shrugged.

After approximately half an hour of searching, he finally found his barrack. In front of it sat a pompous-looking officer at a desk, and George walked over to him. The officer was probably about sixteen years old.

"Are you with B Company?" the officer asked.

"Um, well, I don't really know."

"What do you *mean* you *don't know*? It tells you on your documents. Do you *privates* ever pay attention to what you're told?"

Confused, George tried to look through those documents that he had not bothered to read. There were an awful lot of pages to skim through. "I can't find it," he finally said.

With a grunt of irritation, the officer snatched them from him and found the correct page. "Right there in front of you," he said, waving the papers in George's face. George saw that he was indeed assigned to B Company. "I am Captain Ogden, Philip Ogden, of B Company, 636th Battalion," the officer said. "Welcome to my force. Go find a bunk."

George obeyed and walked inside. He was immediately surprised by the size of the building. The aisle was wider than the one at boot camp, the building was longer with a larger common area at the end, and the bunks were stacked three high.

George found an empty second bunk halfway down the room and climbed up to it. It didn't really look like he could sit all the way up without banging his head on the bunk above. Setting his pack on the mattress, he climbed back down the ladder to the boy reading a comic book on the bunk below his own.

"Hey, how many people are in here?" he asked. The boy looked up casually.

"Each barrack sleeps a company, which is 164."

"Huh." George looked around him. More boys were trickling into the barracks. "So, can you tell me more about, well..." he trailed off, not sure what to say.

"Us, and now you?" the boy asked.

"Yeah."

"Well, we're the 636th Infantry Battalion, and we were pulled out of action a few weeks ago to rest and replace our casualties, and soon we'll be on the march again."

"Marching where?"

"East, generally. Towards Nevada. Just conquering whoever's in front of us, expanding the Empire." The boy spoke with one eye on George while the other continued to read his comic book. Presently, he turned the page.

"Hey, Bernie!" another boy said, lugging in his pack. "Did you just get back or have you been here the whole time?"

"Hello, Jack," Bernie replied. "Nope, I've been here the whole time."

"Have you *ever* become a casualty, or do you just have this magic force field that deflects all paint onto everyone else around you?"

"A few times."

Jack snorted. "Uh-huh, 'a few.'" Bernie merely shrugged and continued reading his comic book.

"Magic force field that deflects paint onto everyone else?" George asked, confused.

"Oh, yeah," Jack said, plopping his pack down on a bunk, "I'm telling you, Bernie went forward with a squad of soldiers, and crossing an open field they were totally nailed by enfilade fire. They all got splattered, but then Bernie comes up off the ground after they stop shooting and walks back into cover without being hit. And that's not the first time he has somehow been the only survivor."

George nodded, impressed. Here was another experienced veteran.

After living in the barracks for a week, George returned from breakfast one morning to discover that his unit was being ordered to pack up. This was of slight concern. He still hadn't gotten much of his homework done, even though he'd had time. Whatever, nothing he could do about it now.

Getting his things together, George obeyed the officers shouting that B Company was to load up in these trucks. To his surprise, he found that there were quite a few girls in B Company. Bernie casually explained that they were the rest of the soldiers, but of course bunked in their own barracks, G15.

"So, were there actually a hundred and sixty-four people in our barrack?" George asked.

"Nope."

George could not see what was going on outside, but he thought he could hear lots of other engines as they rumbled along. This was his longest trip in one of these less-than-comfortable transports yet.

"It's getting hot in here," a girl complained. "There's too many people in here, and I'm *sure* that boy is not wearing deodorant."

"This ain't no beauty parlor," Jack replied, "this is the army. Get used to it."

"But you stink," she whined.

He scooted up closer to her. "Doesn't it smell nice?"

"Eww, gross! Get away from me, you barbarian! Why couldn't they send the boys in their own truck?"

"Sally, that's enough!" a girl in an officer's uniform said. She was George's platoon sergeant. "And Jack, quit annoying her. We're *all* gonna stink after we've been in the field for a little while, but we do not need to start fights over it."

"We should tie Sally to the roof and make her ride up there," Jack suggested to no avail.

The ride went on and on. And on. George's butt was sore from sitting on the hard benches. What were they, driving all the way to Nevada?

Finally, the truck rumbled to a stop. Sergeant Ivy got up and ordered everyone outside, while the other trucks were doing likewise.

George looked around to find that they were on the outskirts of a suburb in what appeared to be a military base in the field. Tents were pitched everywhere, surrounded by vehicles and equipment.

After the battalion had been organized, orders were transmitted down from its commander, Colonel Hoffman. The captains maneuvered their companies onto a main road. George's 636th Battalion had several support companies attached to it, including machine guns and light field artillery.

"Attention!" Captain Ogden barked at his troops. "A heavy artillery battery will be proceeding forward under the guard and escort of our battalion. B Company, under *my* command, shall be preceding her in the vanguard, to make sure everything is safe and guard against attacks." A boy raised his hand. "What is it?" Captain Ogden asked, annoyed.

"Our transports left."

"You will *walk*!" Captain Ogden responded. "You are privates, and your job is to march and fight. I lead you so you know what to do and don't screw everything up."

With officers shouting orders, the soldiers of the 636th Battalion got moving. George and his company walked ahead. He watched a heavy artillery battery behind them, which was a fascinating sight.

Medium-sized trucks towed the largest paintball artillery guns George had ever seen. There were some twenty of them. The trucks had large air compressors in their beds, and they were stacked full of shells anywhere one could fit. Each gun's five-man crew rode on the truck. Behind this procession came a dozen more box trucks, some of them pulling trailers, which George surmised to be supply vehicles hauling extra ammunition and probably other stuff as well.

The scene was quiet and peaceful as they marched along, the trucks rumbling onward, pulling their heavy guns behind them. It was so serene it made George begin to wonder.

"Hey," he asked a boy next to him, "aren't we, like, behind the front lines?"

"Yeah, I think so."

"Then, uh, why are we guarding this gun battery if there are no enemy around?"

"I dunno."

"Maybe they are worried about an attack from the air," a girl offered.

"Oh yeah, a bunch of infantry can really defend against airplanes," another boy retorted.

George shrugged, and shifted his pack on his shoulder. Nobody said anything after that. They merely walked on, periodically sipping from their canteens.

When the sun was high in the sky, the column was ordered off to the side of the road for lunch. George plopped down on the ground, grateful for the rest. He had grown much more used to long marches over the past few weeks, but still, they were tiring, and he was glad to ease his shoulders from their heavy burden.

Looking back, he could see the line of trucks pulled over and parked on the side of the road. Behind them, infantry stretched out farther than he could see. He knew that that line was over six hundred kids that formed his battalion.

Army field rations were nothing special, but they sufficed and filled you up, and he had discovered that they really weren't bad at all. He opened a one-meal package that contained tinned beef with plenty of fat for durable energy, some regular biscuits, cheese, a granola bar, and dried fruit for dessert. He used the biscuits, the beef, and the cheese to make a sandwich, and decided to save the granola bar in case he wanted a snack later.

While he ate, another military column passed him by on the road. It was much shorter, containing only a half-dozen or so supply trucks preceded by a single patrol car built out of a dune buggy for an escort. They moved at a rapid pace without infantry on foot, much faster than his own unit.

Only half an hour had elapsed before Captain Ogden ordered his troops to pack up and resume their march. Ten minutes later, the column had gotten underway again.

"You know," George heard one boy comment to another, "Ogden made a big deal out of saying that we *privates* have to walk, but yet he's on foot too, right at the front."

"Go figure," was the reply.

After another hour they passed three trucks going in the opposite direction. Boys and girls wearing white shawls, casualties from the fighting up ahead, were hitching rides. Piled in the beds of the trucks were heaps of plastic and foam pieces and other scrap.

"What's all that?" George asked Bernie, who happened to be walking near him.

"Used shells," Bernie explained.

"Used shells?" George was confused.

"When the artillery fire their shells, the pieces are picked up to be reused."

"Oh, okay," George said. "That's cool." He shifted his pack on his tired shoulders.

A while later, George grew even more weary and was not going as strong as he had been. He needed a break. Maybe this was a less extreme march, but it was awfully long. Many of the other soldiers were also beginning to drag.

"Keep it up!" Ivy shouted at them. Other sergeants were likewise "encouraging" their troops. "Come on, guys, you can't be tired yet!"

Up ahead, Captain Ogden was not quite so nice. "Move it, you laggards! You're holding the artillery up!" To his credit, he demonstrated what he demanded.

The day dragged on, though, seeming very long, and George was nearly spent. When were they going to stop?! Finally, somebody ordered a thirty-minute rest. He had already eaten his spare granola bar and been glad he had saved it, but now he was out of food.

Soon they were on the march again, although they were going slower despite efforts by the officers to pick the pace up. George felt like he was doing the best he could. The very best. You couldn't get more out of yourself than that, so if that's what they wanted, then he wasn't good enough.

What seemed like ages later, B Company was finally ordered off the road onto a large field dotted with trees and a couple nearby houses. George could see several vehicles parked around a couple dozen olive drab tents scattered across the landscape.

The heavy artillery parked their trucks and guns, and everyone set to work preparing camp for the night. Pup tents and the tarps carried in each soldier's pack were joined together to make larger tents that could sleep half a dozen. Bedrolls were unstrapped and laid out inside. The area shortly became covered with a multitude of tents.

Some of the soldiers cooked beans and rice on camp stoves while the rest sat around campfires built from scavenged deadfall. Dinner was a very simple meal, but beans and rice are always filling, even if not the most appetizing. Not to mention they are cheap and easy to store. George enjoyed it.

Sooner than later, Tattoo was sounded by B Company's bugler, and not long after, snuggled in his bedroll, George heard the quiet, sweet strains of Taps. Exhausted, he fell hard asleep quickly, crowded in his tent with five other boys, two of whom were carrying on a whispered conversation in the corner. It was his first ever day and night in the field. It was a milestone for him.

The next morning George was roused from his slumber by the ever-familiar and obnoxiously-repetitive Reveille.

"Reveille," someone said, "everybody's favorite tune."

"Ravioli."

"Oh, that sounds good. Now I'm hungry."

The thought of food made George's stomach rumble, despite his hearty dinner last night. Breakfast was eaten cold and quick, camp was broken, and by seven-thirty they were on the march again.

After marching until nearly noon with only one quick rest, the column was ordered off the road. Signs of recent combat were evident. They were clearly not far behind the front lines. George wondered what was going on.

The heavy artillery battery carefully positioned their guns and unhitched them from their trucks. Then the gun crews set to work in a flurry of activity, setting out shells in neat stacks, connecting hoses, and firing up air compressors as their officers shouted orders. George watched their scripted routine with interest. As they worked they sang:

> Praise the Lord and pass the ammunition.
> Can't afford to be a politician.
> Praise the Lord and pass the ammunition,
> And we'll all stay free.

The 636th Battalion was immediately divided into multiple work details by Ogden's shouting. Platoons were sent off on patrol to reconnoiter the area and establish security. Some were ordered to walk around and throw dirt over any hazardous puddles of paint on the ground. A few were given the task of cooking lunch.

George found himself assigned to pick up pieces of shells and grenades and other discarded equipment for shipment back to… wherever they took them. Now he got to see the operation up close, actually do it. This was a useful thing to be doing, and he knew exactly what benefit would come of his efforts.

He trudged around, gathering anything he could find — pods, gear, gas cartridges, paint bottles, paintball packs, pieces of grenades and shells, rifles and other weaponry — and adding it to the growing heap of plastic, being careful not to get paint on himself. All the while, the rumbling of the air compressors muffled the shouting of the gun crews, who were manhandling their ordinance into precise positions and aiming them.

Boom! The first shot rang out from one of the guns only twenty yards away, startling George. Firmly anchored by stakes driven into the ground, it did not recoil. The other guns fired in sequence, and a rapid bombardment began against something somewhere far away.

George stopped his work and watched in fascination as the gun crews labored under the direction of their officers. Each person had a job. Some loaded shells, others aimed and fired, while still others messed with the air compressors and valves and switches. One kid was pouring gasoline from a gas can into an air compressor's fuel tank.

The battery's radio operator was listening into his headset and re-laying information to the officers, who then messed with their guns. The whole operation was conducted with extraordinary precision and efficiency. George wondered where their shells were falling.

"Hey, Owens!" his Corporal James barked. "Quit standin' around! You've got a job to do!"

"Praise the Lord and pass the ammunition."

Grudgingly, George slowly got back to work. By the time the salvage crews had cleared the area of everything they could find, the artillery bombardment had ceased and there was nothing left to watch. The patrols had returned to report on their position and surroundings, and lunch was ready, so the bugler sounded the Mess Call, and they all convened and ate.

As soon as this was finished, the 636th Battalion was ordered back to work. They marched away through the wooded, hilly terrain until they came to an old dirt road badly in need of repair.

"Lemme guess," Jack said. "We're going to be repairing this road!"

"Why don't they just use the main highways?" George asked. "Why make us fix a road they don't need?"

"Well," Bernie replied, "there may not be a pressing *need*, but there's rarely not a use for something like this."

"Isn't road-building fun?" Ella asked.

"Alright!" Captain Ogden shouted. "I want this road here in useful shape for supply trucks. It's a more direct and secluded route towards the front. Now this guy here is Sergeant O'Connell of the Army Field Engineers, and he will be running this construction."

Engineer Sergeant O'Connell nodded. Then he carefully studied the road up and down as far as he could see, scratching his chin intently like a movie detective. George judged him to be about sixteen years old by the peach fuzz on his face.

"Okay," he said slowly, "5th and 6th Platoons, I want you to clear all the branches, the brush, and pull out all the plants and pile all the rocks to the side." There was a pause while everyone looked at him.

"Alright!" Ivy told her platoon. "Let's get to work." Sergeant Liam was also ordering his troops into action.

"7th and 8th Platoons," Engineer Sergeant O'Connell continued, "come with me." He turned and walked off to where the road disappeared out of sight with some eighty workers following behind him.

The eighty workers left behind looked at the work confronting them. The veterans promptly set to it, but George and the greener recruits dragged their feet.

"Get to work *now!*" Captain Ogden barked. "I'll be back to check on you." With a final glare across the work party, he followed where the rest of his company had gone with Engineer Sergeant O'Connell.

It was hot, and they were also working in the heat of the day. George's hair was damp, and sweat trickled down the back of his neck. Everyone had shed their coats, but their thick shirts weren't exactly tropical clothing. He followed the example of his squad's corporal in hauling the debris off the old road and piling it to the side.

"Owens!" Corporal James snapped. "Quit lollygaggin' and do the job!" George grimaced and moved a little faster. This reminded him too much of yard work.

When Engineer Sergeant O'Connell returned, he was satisfied with their progress. Captain Ogden had not come back to check on them as he had said he would. At least not yet.

Walking up and down the road, O'Connell instructed the soldiers in the next step, filling in the ruts and potholes and strategically placing rocks to support sections of the road that were washed out as they built them back. He explained how he wanted the road to peak in the middle and slope gently outwards to shed water into a ditch they dug along the side.

"Man, this has gotta be like the best road in California," Jack said.

Then Engineer Sergeant O'Connell rushed back out of sight to check on the other work party. The sergeants immediately ordered a rest. George flopped down and wiped the sweat from his brow. When O'Connell came hurrying back, everyone scrambled back to work. He never even noticed.

Engineer Sergeant O'Connell spent the next hour and a half running, breathless and harried, back and forth between the two groups and supervising their construction work. Multiple times he ordered parts to be redone until they met his standards. The biggest difficulties were in getting an evenly-graded surface with the basic tools they were using.

Having completed the first section of the road, B Company was shifted forward to start the process all over again on the next part. George was tired. His arms ached. How much longer were they gonna be here?

"Pick it up!" Ogden shouted. "I want this road finished before dark. Nobody gets dinner until it's done, understand?!"

He got his wish, and finally B Company packed up and headed back to camp, their task complete. A soldier ran up to meet Captain Ogden, and then ran to talk to the radio operator.

George observed that one of the supply trucks attached to the heavy artillery battery had stacked its shells neatly on the ground. A work party was loading up the last few pieces of the pile George had helped to accumulate yesterday. A few minutes later, the truck's headlights faded into the distance as it drove away.

Even though George was tired, the unpleasant, weary work of road-building had given way to a pleasant sense of accomplishment. He hoped it would now be put to good use. His effort had paid off and a satisfying tangible accomplishment had been achieved. Petty high school homework seemed like child's play compared to this.

Just then the Mess Call sounded, and several hundred ravenous kids made a mad dash to get their dinner. Officers immediately enforced discipline with much shouting and ordered everyone into line.

As George waited for his turn, two transports full of troops drove by on both ends of a short column containing a handful of smaller artillery guns towed by ATVs and one accompanying supply ATV that was like a mini pickup truck pulling a trailer. They turned off the main road and bounced towards the one George had just worked to repair. He felt a surge of pride that made his arms not ache so much.

Getting his bowl of steaming stew, he found a seat by one of the small campfires. Everyone ate silently, except for the sound of slurping hot liquid. When George had gotten his second bowl and the edge of hunger had been abated, the kids began to chat.

"X Corp is making steady progress towards Reno," a boy commented through a mouthful of stew. "Heard the colonel talking to some of his staff."

"Where are they?" another boy asked eagerly.

"Dunno. They noticed me and yelled to get back to work 'fore I could hear the rest."

"What of our IX Corp?" someone asked.

"We seem to be pushing on," a girl said. "I mean, we're moving. At least us here."

"I heard the Fourth Army is doing alright," her companion stated, "but the Southern Front is pretty bogged down."

"And the First Army?"

"Humph," she snorted, "the First Army is always accomplishing something."

Conversation continued as bits of such gossip and rumors were passed around. "I wish they would give us news instead of making us filter illicit gossip out of the grapevine," one boy said.

Finally, they heard the Tattoo. With little complaint, everyone got up and shuffled towards their tents. George was surprised by how appealing sleep was after a day of hard physical labor.

Not long later in bed, George heard the bugler sound Taps. Halfway through the tune, however, he was interrupted by shouting. George sat up with the rest of his tentmates and listened to the growing commotion outside. He couldn't see what was going on, which was somewhat unnerving.

At the first report of a heavy artillery gun opening fire, everyone sprang up and dashed outside. The wary veterans, who apparently had experience in things like this, grabbed their guns and came out of the tent like they were expecting to find enemy soldiers in the middle of their camp.

George flung aside his sleeping bag and dashed outside to see what was going on. The artillery gunners had leapt into action while the radio operator shouted seemingly random numbers at them. Evidently, those numbers meant something, for the crew responded instantly. They were working full speed to the roar of air compressors as the pile of shells on the ground rapidly diminished and was replaced by scattered piles of spent cartridges. It was truly an impressive sight; these were definitely experienced veteran gun crews.

"What's going on?!" Captain Ogden yelled, dashing out of his tent. He stopped and looked around. "What are you idiots doing? We're not under attack!"

"Sir, we thought we were," a soldier replied.

"Go back to bed," Ogden yelled, "before I court-martial you for crying wolf!" He was completely ignored as cautious veterans decided to assure themselves that the sentries were doing their job properly. George scratched his head. How were they crying wolf?

"I mean it!" Ogden continued. "Go *back to bed*!"

Eventually, snuggled into his bedroll a little while later, George fell soundly asleep listening to the thunder of the bombardment.

Chapter VI

WHEN GEORGE AWOKE THE next morning upon hearing Reveille, the artillery battery was no longer shooting. In fact, after getting up, the gunners had begun packing. George knew that they would be moving again.

Sure enough, as soon as breakfast was over, the 636th Battalion broke camp and was quickly on the march. As they passed over the road that George had helped to repair, he straightened his shoulders in pride.

Progress on the road was slower than usual. Being an outback road, it was not quite as nice as the main highways, but still, the column moved on.

Leaving that road, they walked on using other roads and trails for about an hour until they entered a residential area. A sign welcomed them to the town of Pine Grove.

Here the column stopped to take a break in a large open space next to Route 88. George whipped open his backpack and extracted another field ration.

"Hey, look," Jack said, "it's a burger joint to-go."

"Ooh!" said Ella. "I want a burger. What about you, Bernie?"

"They'll never let you leave the battalion," he replied.

"Are you *sure*?" Jack asked. "C'mon, man, you gotta try."

"Me?" asked Bernie. "I ain't the one that wanted a burger."

"But you're good at this," Ella implored.

With a sigh, Bernie got up and strolled away. A good ten minutes later, George saw him meandering back from the truck that served as the battalion's mobile field headquarters.

"Alright," he said casually, "they said I may get some burgers."

Immediately, there was a cheer from the crowd and pretty soon a couple hundred kids were all clamoring for a burger. Myriads of toppings were shouted out.

"You're all getting the same thing," Bernie informed them, and strolled away. The clamoring abruptly fell silent. A minute later he was back.

"Okay, if you want one, give me seven dollars in cash." This resulted in a number of kids turning away. "Sorry, guys, but the colonel refused to pay for the burgers," he explained. George parted with a few bills he had. A cheeseburger sounded great. Pretty soon Bernie walked off again with a small fortune in cash. Boy, everyone really trusted him.

A half-hour later he came back, carrying two bags and accompanied by waiters carrying more bags. The eager soldiers formed a line and they each received a burger handed to them.

"There are more on the way," Bernie informed them.

The burger joint simply could not cook that many burgers so fast, but they were pumping them out as quickly as they could. This naturally took a while, and battalion command wanted to be moving again.

"I knew we shouldn't have agreed to this!" Captain Ogden yelled. "We should be moving by now!"

Eventually, the burger joint finished delivering the burgers and was very pleased with their income. By then, however, other salesmen had noticed the somewhat-familiar mass of bored army kids marching to somewhere and set about selling them things.

"Get in line!" Captain Ogden roared at them. Other officers were doing likewise. So far George had not seen his colonel even once.

Still munching on his burger, George set off walking with his company, leading the column. Jack came dashing up with an ice cream cone.

"You lucky rat," Ella muttered. Bernie merely shook his head. He had not even bought a burger for himself.

As George left the small town of Pine Grove, he could see other small combat units moving through the town. However, they were not creeping along as if expecting an attack.

In addition, paint was splattered everywhere. It looked like there had been an intense battle. Pieces of shells, grenades, and other equipment were scattered around all over the place. Some of the other troops were gathering them up and stacking them in piles.

Commuters honked their horns irately as the 636th Battalion's hundreds of marching persons blocked the roads.

"Look at all the sheeple," Jack said.

"Follow the leader," Ella added.

"Ba-a-a, ba-a-a," they said together at the impatient drivers.

Overhead a dozen planes roared by. Emblazoned proudly on their wings was the Rose and Laurels of the Alamedan Empire. George watched as they flew on to somewhere up ahead.

Suddenly, a kid came running up past them to Captain Ogden marching at the front. The trucks behind them were pulling off to the side of the road.

Instantly upon stopping, the gunners leapt out of their vehicles and got to work. George and his comrades were left standing and watching as the routine began all over again.

A boom sounded off in the distance. Everyone stopped and perked up. The boom was followed by more. There was definite fighting going on nearby.

"It's a battle!" Jack said.

"We're the advance guard, we should get to go to the front!" Ella said.

"Be careful what you wish for," someone replied.

"Aw, I ain't been in a fight since I last got killed," Jack complained. He and Ella promptly burst out laughing. "I've come back to life!" he yelled.

"Can you believe them?" commented a boy with glasses who was much too mature and serious for his age, shaking his head.

"Hey!" Captain Ogden ordered. "We're moving forward! Now pay attention! Do not go rushing off without me. I must be there to command you. But we're going to make sure that counterattack does not affect the battery."

B Company was rather excited and went quickly forward with Captain Ogden. The veterans discarded their packs in a pile, and George noticed and eagerly disposed of his own. He was excited for his first battle and was swept along with the other 163 soldiers.

"Stay with me!" Captain Ogden ordered. "Do *not* scatter!"

"Why is he so concerned about that?" George asked James.

"A few reasons," James muttered, not offering to elaborate. George shrugged and moved forward.

The veterans moved forward steadily with their guns at the ready. They did not run or go slowly, and carefully paid attention to their surroundings.

In contrast, the excited green recruits who had never fought a battle before dashed in spurts across the terrain, holding their rifles to their shoulders and swinging the things in circles as they looked for enemy soldiers.

George was somewhere in between, but he mostly followed his corporal, watching and trying to learn from his example. James was yelling at his squad to stay together.

Moving forward to the opening volley of their heavy artillery battery, they heard increased sounds of combat and engines roaring. The crackle of semiautomatic rifles joined the ripping of machine guns firing in bursts and the booms of larger weapons. The humming of air compressors was continual.

George looked far ahead and actually saw the fighting taking place. A mortar team was crouched in the bushes, firing its weapon at an enemy light machine gun in some other bushes. The near-miss prompted the gun's crew to withdraw.

"Hey, stay with me!" James told his squad. "You don't go running off by yourself. We're to work together."

With a wave of his hand, James led them off to the side, and George thought he saw him sneering in Captain Ogden's general direction where he could be seen shouting at his soldiers. George followed. Ivy and the rest of their platoon were somewhere nearby.

George passed a small two-door ATV pickup truck toppled into a ditch on the side of the road. It had been fitted with a small cannon, but was now covered in paint. A couple of enemy soldiers wearing dirty white casualty shawls were eating and talking a few yards away from it.

James halted behind a tree, holding his arm up as a signal for his squad to stop. "There's a couple of people hiding in the brush right over there on the side of that trail," he loudly whispered. "Move out, and come around, but they might be our own guys, so don't get trigger-happy."

George crept forward, his rifle ready. He peeled his eyes, trying to process all his senses at once until his head spun, but he couldn't see what James was talking about until a boy raised his hand in recognition through the brush, putting a finger to his lips.

He was wearing an Alamedan uniform and manning a light anti-tank gun. The weapon and its crew were so well-camouflaged that they were nearly invisible.

Dropping into the bushes, George watched and waited. The rest of his squad likewise hid themselves while the anti-tank gunners scanned their surroundings carefully. They did not seem to have an air compressor with their gun.

Then an engine rumbled ahead of them and out of sight, locking George's attention. An enemy fighting vehicle rounded the corner and came into view. From out of sight, someone threw a grenade at it and missed. The vehicle stopped, sending machine gun fire spurting toward whatever had attacked it.

A few seconds later it rumbled on. The anti-tank gunner took aim. Then his comrade made a rapid hand gesture.

Bang!

The anti-tank gun jolted backwards as it fired. A shell struck the vehicle on the windshield with a crack, splattering it with paint as pieces of plastic flew like shrapnel in every direction. Immediately the driver stepped on the gas and shot forward erratically while the two anti-tank gunners frantically ejected their spent cartridge and slammed another round into the breech.

Bang!

The next shot entered perfectly into the vehicle through the side, where the attack opening was per the Society's rules. George and his comrades cheered as the driver, with a faceful of paint, lost control and rammed into a tree, bringing his vehicle to a halt with a crumpled nose.

The machine gunner on top, however, turned his weapon and sprayed paintballs in the direction that the shot had come from. George did a belly flop on the dirt with the rest of his squad, but the anti-tank gun's camouflage and gun shield protected its crew.

Bang!

A third shell scored a nice hit on the stationary vehicle, soaking the machine gunner with paint. Another cheer erupted from the 22nd Squad.

Three enemy soldiers wearing white casualty shawls and covered in paint, including the machine gunner, climbed out of their vehicle and glared at the anti-tank gunners as they walked off. Then two more unpainted soldiers made a break down the road for safety and escaped.

Ah, man, they had gotten away! George was excited to see these proceedings. It was a bit nerve-racking, but this was his first witness of battle, and if those Alamedan gunners hadn't smoked their enemy then he was blind. They would win the war for sure, and he was going to help do it.

The gunner that had been loading the weapon got up from where he was crouching behind the gun shield and walked over to Corporal James.

"Can you go forward and scout around the bend so we can set up in another position?"

James nodded and signaled with his arm. The 22nd Squad moved forward on both sides of the road.

"Don't go much farther than the bend," he instructed. "Just see that it will be safe for the gunners to prepare another ambush."

Behind them, the two boys had taken the camouflage netting off of their gun and were wheeling it forward by the tails of its split-rail mounting.

George walked forward and stepped around the bend in the road. There wasn't anything in sight. His comrades likewise assured the gun crew that they were safe to proceed.

About this time the airplanes that had passed them by earlier were coming back. Shortly, another flight of bombers also headed for the front.

The gun crew wheeled their anti-tank gun just past the bend in the road, turned off to the side, and moved away some dozen yards. After a few moments' deliberation, they nestled the gun into a gap between two bushes.

Next, they threw the camouflage netting over it and added some branches from the two bushes on either side to the existing foliage. Carefully arranging it so that only the gun barrel protruded, they smeared mud on the exposed metal and decided their concealment complete. George was impressed by how they had become nearly invisible. He could look right at them and not see a thing if he didn't know they were already there.

A couple of George's squad members walked up carrying several cases of anti-tank ammunition, which the gun crew hid behind the bushes. Showing their thanks with brisk salutes, the two boys settled down behind the bushes, checked the plants stuck in the camouflage netting on their helmets, and made themselves comfortable with a snack for a long wait.

Corporal James waved his squad to follow him back. George was disappointed; he wanted to stay and see what was going to happen. Nevertheless, he obeyed his officer.

When they returned from their impromptu scouting mission, they found B Company standing around and not doing much. There were no other soldiers of either side in sight, no sound of battle, and the artillery they were escorting had stopped shooting.

"Where were you?" Ivy hissed at James as she came running up to them.

"Off scouting."

"You're supposed to tell me," she said, "so I know where all of my platoon is."

"Sorry," James apologized. "I just didn't want the Ogre to notice."

Ivy sighed. "Yeah, I know."

"We came across one of our anti-tank guns and helped 'em. They took out an enemy vehicle."

"Nice!"

"Hey, who's the Ogre?" George interrupted.

"Uh... never mind," James and Ivy both replied. George shrugged.

In just a little while, B Company was recalled back to the heavy artillery battery. George saw that the other troops had thrown up some simple earthworks all along the front of their position. The machine guns and light field artillery attached to the 636th Battalion had positioned themselves in these fortifications.

A group of kids came running up to them. "How was it?" "You guys defeated their counterattack!" "Nice job!"

"Oh, we did?" James replied, feigning surprise. "Yay, we're heroes," he finished flatly. The group eyed him skeptically.

"We didn't fight," explained Bernie.

"Well we found an anti-tank gun and destroyed an enemy tank," Jack enthused.

"Wow, awesome!"

"Yeah, that's not quite what happened," James said, "but okay."

B Company had hardly returned from its peremptory advance before being ordered off on the march again. The soldiers were told to bring their packs this time.

"What's going on?" George asked Ivy when she had returned from briefing with their captain.

"D Company under Captain Spotorno is being left behind to guard the heavy artillery battery. The rest of us are going to make ourselves useful fortifying captured enemy positions."

"Um, so, this means more digging?"

"Oh, but don't you just *love* digging?" she teased. George snorted.

Marching a short distance, they went over the edge of a ridge and descended the steep hillside into a valley. In the bottom of this valley ran the North Fork Mokelumne River, which marked the border between Amador County, where they were, and Calaveras County next-door.

The entire area was littered with the signs of a recent battle. Paint and shell fragments were everywhere, and dozens of casualties wearing white shawls were leaving the field.

As George came down to the bottom of the canyon, he saw an army field engineer company building several bridges across the river under heavy fire from the enemy-occupied heights above. George and his fellows too came under sporadic fire as they moved forward. This made him slightly jittery. No one had ever shot at him before in combat, but the adrenaline was invigorating.

The first thing they did was dig foxholes for cover, but as enemy fire was very light, George scraped a shallow hole and called it good. The field engineers were taking the worst of it.

The sound of heavy artillery joined in with the sounds of immediate battle, and George surmised that it was the battery he had been escorting. The shells landed atop the ridge opposing them, and enemy fire became erratic and scattered. It did not, however, cease entirely.

"What are we doing here?" George asked.

"I don't know," Ivy replied. "I have a feeling we are not supposed to be here, unless we are to ford the river and assault up the hill."

"Us?" George said, and then ducked as a shell exploded to his left. "You said we were only going to fortify captured area. Instead we're sitting in the dirt hiding from enemy fire."

Ivy shrugged. "Maybe it's all a mistake. But improve your foxholes into dugouts," she ordered.

This annoyed George. Why wasn't his foxhole good enough? It held him just fine. Dugouts were excessive. Begrudgingly, he scraped his hole a little bigger and threw the dirt up in front, not bothering to shape it into a proper rampart. There was no need for that. This was plenty good enough. It wasn't like they were being attacked; just shot at, and very little anyway.

Ten minutes later, George's company began withdrawing from its position. George's platoon was the last to leave. Simultaneously, another unit of dirty soldiers was occupying its position, including the filthiest girls he had ever seen. The girls George was used to were ultra-concerned about hygiene. Dirty boys, on the other hand, were nothing unusual.

Three girls crowded into the "dugout" George had made and began digging it deeper, but enemy fire was becoming more and more concentrated at them. A shell landed right in front of their position and showered them with paint.

George stared. If he had made that "dugout" properly, that wouldn't have happened. But nobody had noticed, and besides, if that shell had been angled just a little bit higher, it wouldn't have made a difference anyway. How was he supposed to know that would happen? It wasn't his fault. Good thing he wasn't the one in that dugout. He turned away from the scene.

When Ivy gave the signal, he got up and ran for the trees on the side of the hill. Everyone scrambled as fast as he could to get to the top. Right as they reached it, George heard lots of shouting.

He turned around and watched as the Alamedan soldiers below him arose and ran forward. Many of them waded right through the river. Others, especially the light field artillery and machine guns, crossed over the bridges.

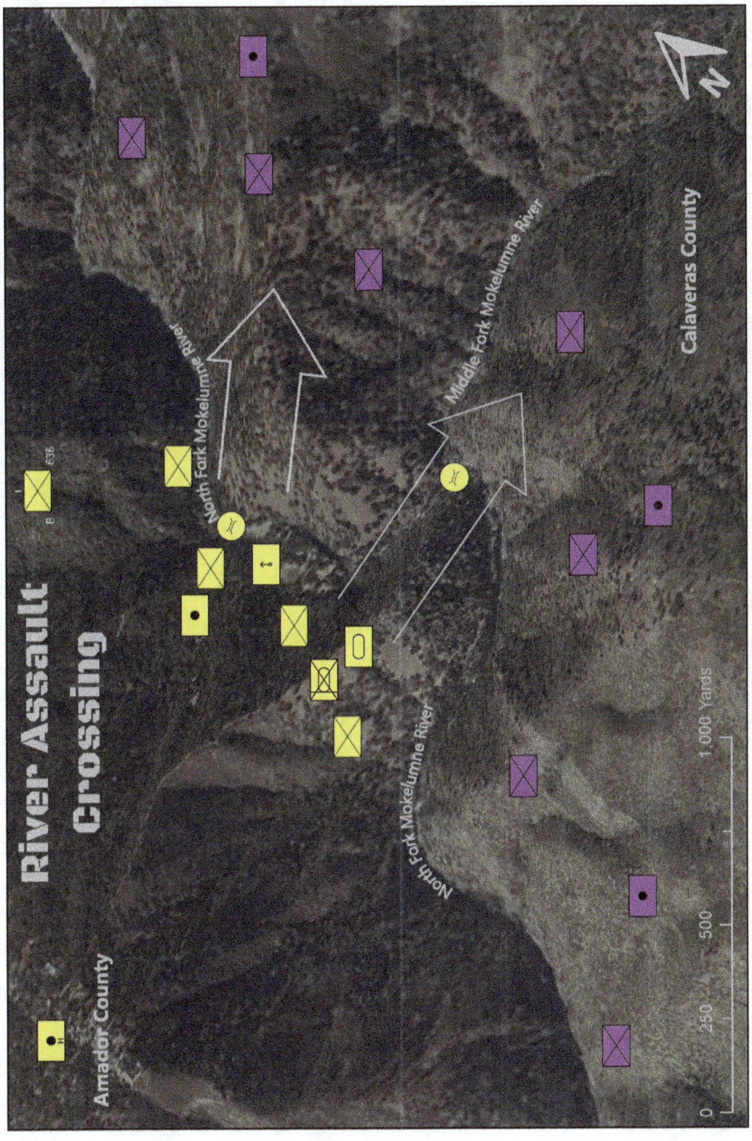

River Assault Crossing
Amador County
Calaveras County
North Fork Mokelumne River
Middle Fork Mokelumne River
North Fork Mokelumne River
B 636
N
0
250
500
1,000 Yards

To the south, a ridge that ran down into the riverbed provided a good place to cross vehicles. A stream of tanks and infantry fighting vehicles was pouring across at full speed as infantry crossed on foot on both sides.

From down in the bottom of the canyon mortars were firing, while other guns atop the Alamedan side of the canyon added the weight of their fire onto the opposing lines. The fact that their ridge was higher than the one the enemy held provided them with a distinct advantage.

Individual Alamedan ground-attack aircraft flew along the enemy position at low altitude, raining bombs on anything that appealed to them. Another spotting plane for the artillery buzzed circles overhead.

Enemy forces atop the opposing ridge attempted to fight back as best as they were able. Shells, canister shot, and machine gun and rifle fire from dugouts and foxholes met the advance like a sandstorm. George watched displeased as Alamedan infantry were repeatedly hit.

"Owens, come on!" Corporal James called to him.

George pried himself from the sight and hurried to catch up with the rest of his company. They moved west, clearing some unmanned roadblocks left by the enemy so their vehicles could pass through, then returned to battalion headquarters.

George noticed that his squad was short a person. Various other kids were discussing the absence of a few others.

"I saw him sprayed by a shell," one boy said. "He put his shawl on and left."

The sergeants briefly took a roll call and tallied the figures. Ivy came back from the conference with Captain Ogden and shrugged. "We lost four," she said. "Not bad."

"For no reason," James complained. "What exactly were we doing? There's no way we were supposed to dig some earthworks for some other kids to get into and then charge from, all under enemy fire. That is stupid."

"Well..." Ivy said. "Maybe Captain Ogden made a mistake..." James laughed scornfully and walked away. George listened, confused.

The infantry of the 636th Battalion rested, but the heavy artillery continued to fire. Working in tandem with their radio operator, the gunners never rested. Shells were relayed to the guns and spent casings tossed to the side where a rotating work detail of soldiers loaded them into one of the empty supply trucks. George watched as the guns ate up their ammunition at an incredible rate.

As the day drew to a close, a more permanent camp was set up, and dinner was cooked. The soldiers did odd jobs here and there. George found himself assigned to unload ammunition from the supply trucks. Several supply trucks joined their unit with more ammunition for the heavy artillery, while the truck bearing the spent casings departed, going away from the front lines.

The sound of the battle going on not far away continued without diminishing, even though only the larger weapons were audible from that distance. George wondered how his fellow soldiers of the IX Corp were doing. He sincerely hoped they were successfully attacking. Other than the three he had gotten killed. But seriously, how was he supposed to know?

Dinner was once again rice and beans, the army's favorite staples for troops on the march. Everyone was a little tired of rice and beans, but the veterans ate it without complaint. Sally, on the other hand, was abandoned by herself after the other kids around her campfire got tired of her crankiness. She almost looked lonely. But then again, it was her own fault.

"Anybody heard any news on the attack going on over there?" a boy around George's meager campfire asked.

"Yeah, like, literally right over there," someone replied. "You could go look."

The boy rolled his eyes. "Well, nobody's heard nothing?" he confirmed. "Well, then, I'm gonna ask around and see if I can learn anything."

"Yes, and then come share it with us," a girl asked eagerly.

After he had left, another boy cleared his throat. "I did hear some more news about X Corp's progress towards our north," he said. "I'm with D Company," he explained, "and I kinda hung around headquarters and eavesdropped as best I could."

"Well, out with it!" someone exclaimed.

"You know the penalties for that if you get caught," an older girl reprimanded.

"C'mon, Sis, I've never been caught yet. They ain't gonna catch me. Well, X Corp is making steady progress towards Reno. Lieutenant General Doyle pulled a feint with his strongest mechanized division, and then used a weak unit to bash through the enemy line. They totally retreated pell mell. I mean, supply issues for us meant they were able to close the gap in their line, but the mechanized division put the pressure on hot and they are still retreating."

"What supply issues?" a girl asked.

"I think they, like, ran out of ammunition."

"How do they *run out* of ammunition?" someone asked. "That was bad planning."

"So, unlikely they actually ran out," a boy named Lou spoke up, "but they ran low, and if they broke through enemy lines then it's understandable they couldn't resupply. I went through a similar experience, but we were forced to fight a battle with bayonets and liquid paint against guns. Extremely costly, and in the end we lost."

"Wow," someone said. "How many years have you been in the Alamedan military?"

"Well," Lou replied, "I fought with Concord, a long-gone faction from Contra Costa County for a few months, and only a year ago joined the Alamedan Army — I mean, they defeated and killed me — but I've spent most of it fighting."

"You go pretty far back," George said, impressed. More living history.

"Yup."

About then the boy that had gone off in search of information returned with a smug grin. He snickered. "Well, two kids are being hauled off for discipline, but I got the scoop from them before that. They snuck off to go see how the battle was going."

"Oh brother," his sister muttered.

"Well, all along the river there were a total of three different assaults, and we saw one of them. I think two were successful, one just barely, and the other one failed pretty badly because the enemy was just too-well-entrenched."

"Ugh, that sucks," someone said. "Well, good thing the other two were successful."

"Yup, that was a fairly major natural obstacle. If we can just keep our toeholds like on D-Day then we can win."

"Well, is there any news from anywhere else?" someone asked.

"Not that I know of. I mean, the wars go on."

"Anyone else know anything?"

"Well I heard that General Marley of the Fourth Army was assassinated—"

"He wasn't assassinated, he was hit by lucky artillery fire during a visit to the front," a boy interrupted.

"No, the Society sent assassins to silence him because he criticized their latest rule change."

"Rubbish, Drew, you can't believe all that gossip."

"I wouldn't put it past them. They're a bunch of power-hungry adults trying to get control of our teenage world."

"Are there really adults in the Society?" George asked.

"Don't ask questions or they'll black-bag you," Drew told him.

"Drew, you're a tin-foil nutcase," said the skeptical boy. "Society assassins schmassins." He snorted. Right then they all heard the battalion's bugler sounding Tattoo.

"It's a little early for that," someone commented.

"You know what that means," Lou replied.

"What?"

"They plan to get us up and going bright and early tomorrow morning."

"Ugh, great...."

"So I recommend getting to sleep. Don't stay up and whisper. You'll regret it."

He got up and went to his tent. Pretty soon everyone had followed suit, and George heard the bugle sounding Taps. Not long later, he was sound asleep.

Next morning George was awakened by Reveille and rolled out of bed feeling refreshed and ready for his day. Glancing at his watch, he saw that it was five-thirty in the morning.

"Break camp and prepare to march!" Captain Ogden ordered once everyone was up.

George helped to take down the tents and load the other camp implements onto one of the trucks of their supply platoon. Then the bugler blew Mess Call, and they sat down to beans and beef and eggs and bread.

"This is better than our school lunches," he said. It even reminded him of home cooking a little.

Jack took a slice of bread and piled his beans and beef on top. He grinned and held it up for everyone to see.

"Know what this is?" he asked.

"An open-face sandwich?" someone guessed tentatively.

"Nope," he replied, grinning. "Stool on a shingle, the classic breakfast of a soldier on the front lines."

"Eugh, gross," Sally said, "I'm eating. That's so uncouth. Can we please not talk about excrement at breakfast?"

"You know," a scholarly boy wearing glasses pointed out, "technically S.O.S. is chipped beef in a white cream sauce on toast, which that is not."

"Say what?" Jack replied.

"That's not exactly the correct ingredients."

"Um," one of the veterans spoke up, "any stewy thing that you cook in a pot and eat on a slice of bread is stool on a shingle as far as I care. Better if it's actually brown, though, like this is."

"Yes, thank you very much," Jack replied through a giant mouthful of stool on a shingle.

"Don't talk with food in your mouth," Sally said.

The offender rolled his eyes. "I never thought poop could taste so good," he remarked through his mouthful of food.

"Would you all stop talking about eating excrement?" Sally whined. "It's *so gross*. And don't chew with your mouths open, I don't want to listen to that."

The annoyed kids stared at her for a minute. Then they all took a slice of bread, heaped their stew on it, and proceeded to chew loudly with their mouths open and talk through their breakfast. Sally glared at them, verging on tears, then got up, took her food, and walked off to sit somewhere else, brushing a bit of dirt off of her trousers.

"You have to wonder," the veteran mused, "why someone like her would want to join the army."

"I bet somebody glamorized it enough to suck her in."

"I bet her parents dumped her in here to get rid of her," Jack suggested.

When breakfast was over, the last few things were cleared away and the meal equipment loaded into the mess truck. The 636th Battalion got underway, marching down Route 88. George and B Company led the way.

They walked on the shoulder off of the road, however many could fit abreast at a time. Plenty of rubberneckers slowed down to look at them, and plenty of cranks blew their horns at the traffic this caused.

Captain Ogden, the company commander who never seemed to tire of walking, kept them going at a brisk pace. In just over an hour they arrived at the town of Pioneer. They did not stop for a moment, though, but pushed right on through, going hard.

"Is he trying to do a Truscott Trot?" George panted to Bernie. Bernie merely shrugged.

In another hour they entered the town of Buckhorn. Here Captain Ogden finally called a halt, and the exhausted troops plopped down on the ground wherever they could to rest.

The rest of the battalion shortly arrived behind them, along with all of their support companies. The 636th Battalion had three support companies attached: a field artillery company with twenty guns; a weapons company with mortar, machine gun, and anti-tank gun platoons; and a supply company. The latter's trucks, containing ammunition, food, and other necessities for use in the field, were the last to arrive.

At the same time, George watched various dirty, weary-looking kids heading the opposite direction that he had come. Some trudged while others seemed beaten, but most walked proudly upright and looked pleased.

Pretty soon everyone was congregated in a mass of hundreds of young people. The captains, who had disappeared, came out and called their companies to attention and told their sergeants to come forward.

"Those soldiers you saw leaving," Captain Ogden informed them, "were of several depleted units that are being withdrawn to rest and replenish their manpower. We're going to be taking their place."

Captain Ogden then briefed his sergeants, Liam, Jackson, Emma, and Ivy, on the operation they would soon be embarking on. The privates crowded around to listen.

The attack was to be a forced crossing of the North Fork Mokelumne River at Tiger Creek Reservoir, which was essentially a portion of the river that had been widened by the installation of a dam. There would be three separate crossings with supporting fire and attacks from remaining paratrooper forces that had been dropped behind the river two days ago.

George's B Company under Captain Ogden would attempt to take the dam. They would cross the North Fork Mokelumne River below the dam at a ford where the water level was shallow and attempt to take the dam itself with direct attack and boat assaults across Tiger Creek Reservoir.

Meanwhile, C Company under Captain Westfall would cross via boat from the peninsula that protruded into the middle bend of

Tiger Creek Reservoir, which was shaped like the basic drawing of a flying bird made from two curves in middle school art class. Captain Spotorno would lead D Company in crossing by boat where Mill Creek emptied into the reservoir. A Company would remain in reserve, ready to cross wherever support was most needed.

A small attempt to cross here previously had been thwarted, but the area was now lightly defended and a force was moving north against it from the other side of the river. The 636th Battalion was considered sufficient for the operation. Other elements of the 159th Brigade would be moving in behind the battalion's advance and attacking in conjunction with it.

Finally, Captain Ogden told the troops to prepare for action. They deposited their heavy packs with the supply company, taking a small amount of food in their pockets. George, following the example of the veterans, crammed ammunition everywhere he could, hanging it from his outfit. He also received several grenades and discovered that his pod pack had some pockets that could hold more than just pods.

"Um, aren't we supposed to spend some time behind the front lines learning before we actually fight?" he asked.

"We did," replied Bernie.

"Yes, but shouldn't it have been longer?" Bernie merely shrugged and made no reply.

"Alright, guys," Ivy said. "Remember everything the captain said?"

"I could barely hear him," James retorted.

"Well, follow my lead. I know exactly what we're gonna do."

"Move out!" Captain Ogden ordered. "Let's go! March, now!"

George took a deep breath, checked his gear for the umpteenth time, and walked towards his first battle.

Chapter VII

As B Company moved forward, armed and ready for the attack, George felt a little nervous. For all he knew, he would be the first to get shot and would go home as nothing more than a casualty. Then he really would have accomplished nothing.

That was unlikely, though, and even if it did happen, he would be back. If he wanted to come back. He hadn't actually done any fighting himself yet. Maybe he wouldn't want to come back.

And he had already accomplished getting those other soldiers killed with his lousy dugout. Agh! Why did that bother him so much? It's not like he could have predicted that shell would land *right* there in that *exact* spot.

Shaking these thoughts from his head, he considered what he was about to do. Would he be fording the North Fork Mokelumne River below the dam, would he be crossing on the dam, or would he be ferried over the reservoir via boat above the dam? Only Ivy knew that.

B Company was being accompanied by two platoons of field artillery, which were light, man-portable guns. They also had a single platoon of machine guns with them.

As B Company came over the crest of the ridge and began descending through the trees towards the bottom of the canyon, George could see the dam below. To his left, Sergeant Liam's 6 Platoon was dragging inflatable rubber boats, oars, and small motors.

Following Ivy, George headed down the hill, keeping near trees for cover as they approached the ford below the dam. The enemy across the river had picked up on their presence and opened fire, but it was puny compared to what George had witnessed the day before.

Captain Ogden was proceeding in the middle of his company, shouting orders. Gradually the 5th Platoon became separated from him as he directed the dam and boat force.

Ivy had stopped moving and was looking up at the sky as if searching for something.

"Waiting for our artillery and air support?" Corporal James asked.

"Yes. It's supposed to be here by now, and I don't want to cross without it, but we have to hold this flank. We might have to go anyway."

"That would be stupid. We'll get murdered," James retorted.

"Orders are orders. And they need support."

"Stupid orders."

"We have to go eventually."

"I know."

After another minute's deliberation, Ivy once more proceeded forward. Fortunately, the dam was drawing most of the enemy fire. In a few more minutes, the 5th Platoon began digging foxholes under the trees near the bottom of the hill for extra protection as shells finally began falling on the far bank.

He could see the enemy soldiers across the river. Some of them finally decided to shoot at his platoon, but the small quantity of fire, the shelling, and their cover minimized the effect. He couldn't see much around him down in his foxhole, anyway. In a way he was glad that he had been forced to dig foxholes so often at boot camp. He felt safe in his. Unless it was a false sense of security that would make things worse for him.

The two field artillery platoons wheeled their guns into place behind trees and bushes. The gunners dug dugouts big enough for them and their weapons, carefully piling the earth up in front to create a shield. The machine-gunners did likewise.

From these positions, they began firing at the enemy. Defending artillery on the far bank engaged them in counter-battery fire, drawing all their attention away from the infantry.

Ivy stuck her head up and looked around. The rest of their company was congregating around the dam, while the remainder of the field artillery company fired across it.

Then the first boat launched from the shore, followed by another and then another, little black specks on the water. Ivy looked around. Still there were no airplanes.

"Alright, we have to support their attack," she said to Corporal James. Then she rose up from her foxhole holding her rifle.

"Charge!" she yelled, and did so.

Finally, it was time! George scrambled to his feet and bounded the last of the way down the slope. Then he splashed into the river, hopping across rocks and fallen logs. To his right, Bernie was wading knee-deep through the cold water.

George did not look up, but ran as fast as he could, which wasn't very fast considering the terrain. The North Fork Mokelumne River was about eighty feet wide at this point, and the ominous distance he had yet to go loomed out before him.

Paintballs peppered the rocks around him as machine gunners fired at George. A shell ricocheted off a log and splashed into the water, which contained much of its paint spray. The pink smear was quickly swept away by the gurgling current.

Only halfway across, George slipped on a wet granite boulder and fell face-first into the water with a splash, bruising his left side on a rock. As he tried to regain his footing, he slipped and fell again, ducking behind a snag of logs to hide from the machine guns.

He stopped, suddenly tired and unwilling to press on. One hundred yards upstream to his left, the water poured from the dam in white billows. Kids were running across the top, mere dots against the green hills in the background. He was bruised and wet, half-submerged in cold water, hiding from enemy fire. Why had he joined the army?

Then, behind him, machine-gun fire caught one of his platoon mates, who slipped and fell with a splash and landed hard on a rock, crying out in pain. George remembered that there was the rest of B Company depending on them for support. Depending on *him* to not give up and bail on everyone. Captain Hughes' words echoed in his ears.

Gritting his teeth, George grabbed his rifle and clambered up from behind his cover, wet and cold and dirty, determined to get to the other side of that river. Crawling over the rocks and logs as his wet pants chafed at his skin, he pressed on.

In less than a minute he leapt onto the dry sand of the riverbank at the back of his unit. Enemy machine gunners were putting on their casualty shawls as their infantry retreated uphill. Climbing up after them was much more difficult than going down.

The 5th Platoon swung left, running from tree to tree while they dueled with the enemy. George fired wildly at every movement ahead of him.

The attack across the top of the dam had been stopped in its tracks, and George now saw that the end held by the enemy had been turned into a veritable fortress. Dugouts and earthworks were built up into the hillside, and the position was a roaring nest of paintballs and shells directed both at the dam and the boats crossing the reservoir above it.

Ivy waved and shouted at her platoon to climb up the hill and circle around behind the position. George clambered up the side and knelt behind a tree as the machine gunners who had followed them across the river dragged their heavy weapons up the steep slope.

The enemy fortification was ill-suited to anything but defending against an attack across the dam, and George was basically safe sitting higher up above it, raining paintballs on the hapless infantry below. Still, though, it was not a meager threat, but George was having a great time.

At this moment a plane engine was heard and the Alamedan bombers arrived very late. Noticing the enemy position, they rained much of their cargo down in its general direction, completely oblivious to George's platoon, who scattered from the onslaught.

After a minute, when they were sure the planes had gone, they crept back and peered down the hill to find that the bombers had been very effective. Ivy organized a grenade toss volley which was followed by a bayonet assault. In about thirty seconds every weapon was silenced, and the pinned soldiers on the dam finished crossing.

Meanwhile, the rest of B Company's three assault platoons were arriving in boats. They found almost no opposition on the riverbank, and in short order everyone else had crossed over the dam.

As B Company quickly scaled to the top of the hill, George was pleasantly surprised by how easy this was. They knocked out one more light field gun nest and chased away a few remaining soldiers. Besides that, there was nothing. He was starting to dry off, too.

Captain Ogden quickly gathered his company together and drove them rapidly along the top of the ridge towards the rest of the battalion. "Let's go!" he yelled.

"Wait, Captain," the light field artillery and machine gun officers said, "we need to establish ourselves on top of the ridge in case they counterattack."

"Move it! You're under my command and we're going this way!" Ogden replied. The gunners shrugged at each other and hurried after the infantry.

George ran along after his commander, not even concerned about the possibility of enemy soldiers. They had kicked butt. He saw C Company climbing up the hill as their boats returned back across the reservoir. Not a shot was fired at their advance.

"Quick-march, faster!" Captain Ogden yelled at his company as he verbally whipped them along. George ran to keep up as C Company came scrambling after them under the prodding of Captain Westfall.

As George neared the northern end of Tiger Creek Reservoir, a peninsula on his side of the water shaped like the end of a dog's bone was the landing site of D Company's boats. As they disembarked and ran up the shallow slope here, they ran into a stiff concentration of enemy soldiers who put up a furious defense.

"Get to the high point over there!" Captain Ogden ordered. "Run, now!" Not far behind them, Captain Westfall was giving his troops the same order.

"What are we doing?" Corporal James panted to Sergeant Ivy. "D Company needs support! Hey, Captain Ogden! We should be helping D Company!"

"Shut up and do as I say!"

"But sir, they—"

"We're *not* and that's final!" James did not continue the argument.

B and C Companies raced for the high point on the ridge that overlooked the whole area while D Company was driven back to the water's edge.

"They're about to be pushed right back into the water," Ivy muttered under her breath. George was confused. What was going wrong? If D Company really needed support, why weren't they helping?

About this point George noticed Captain Sanders' A Company crossing all at once using C and D Company's boats from about the middle of the reservoir.

Landing on the side of the peninsula, A Company swiftly struck the enemy in the flank. D Company was able to rebound as the enemy reeled to face A Company. Shortly they were scattering back up the hill to get to friendly units.

"See that?" Ivy told James. "Sanders just saved D Company. That was close."

B Company arrived at Captain Ogden's destination and George hit the ground, exhausted. Captain Ogden himself was sucking in large breaths, but stood tall. C Company caught up to them.

"I got here first," Ogden sneered at Westfall.

"Humph!" Westfall retorted. "I advanced the quickest once we hit the shore."

"That's because you had no resistance! *I* took a whole fortress guarding the end of the dam by storm!"

Ivy suddenly burst out coughing. James looked wryly at her. After a few more minutes of this argument, A and D Companies caught up.

"I was here first," Captain Ogden quickly told them.

"Cheater," Westfall muttered.

"You *idiots*!" Sanders burst out at them. "What the *hell* did you two think you were doing?! D Company was almost wiped from the face of the earth!"

"I broke through enemy lines the quickest, taking a whole fortress by storm, and took the highest position that commands the whole battlefield, and the enemy retreated," Captain Ogden said. "Clearly *I* have accomplished the most."

"*I* advanced the quickest once I landed on shore!" Wesftall interjected.

"Yeah, and I came back from near defeat to rout a large enemy force," Spotorno added.

"Oh, so it's this stupid political game," Sanders sneered. "Who *cares* who did what. And furthermore — *I, I, I* — you mean *we*, or rather your *soldiers* who did what *you ordered* them to. Your games nearly cost us a whole company in casualties down there! A hundred and sixty men!"

"It's not my fault Spotorno's incompetent," Westfall said indifferently.

"I am not incompetent!" Spotorno yelled back.

"Enough!" Sanders snapped. "Furthermore, you all want to sit here on this tiny little treeless knoll of absolutely no tactical value simply because it's the highest position instead of securing this bank. Actually, you wanna know who's incompetent? It's Colonel Hoffman who hasn't court-martialed you three yet."

"I'm gonna report you to him for that," Ogden threatened. "Then see who gets court-martialed."

"Go right ahead," Sanders shot back. "Your word against mine."

"Yeah, when's he gonna cross with us?" Spotorno asked.

"I don't know," Sanders muttered. "Well, look, we gotta do something. Let's spread out along the ridge."

"*I'm* staying right *here*," Westfall replied with a haughty look at Ogden, who glared right back.

"Well now that I've taken it I'll go and win the battle," he retorted. "You can stay behind and do nothing."

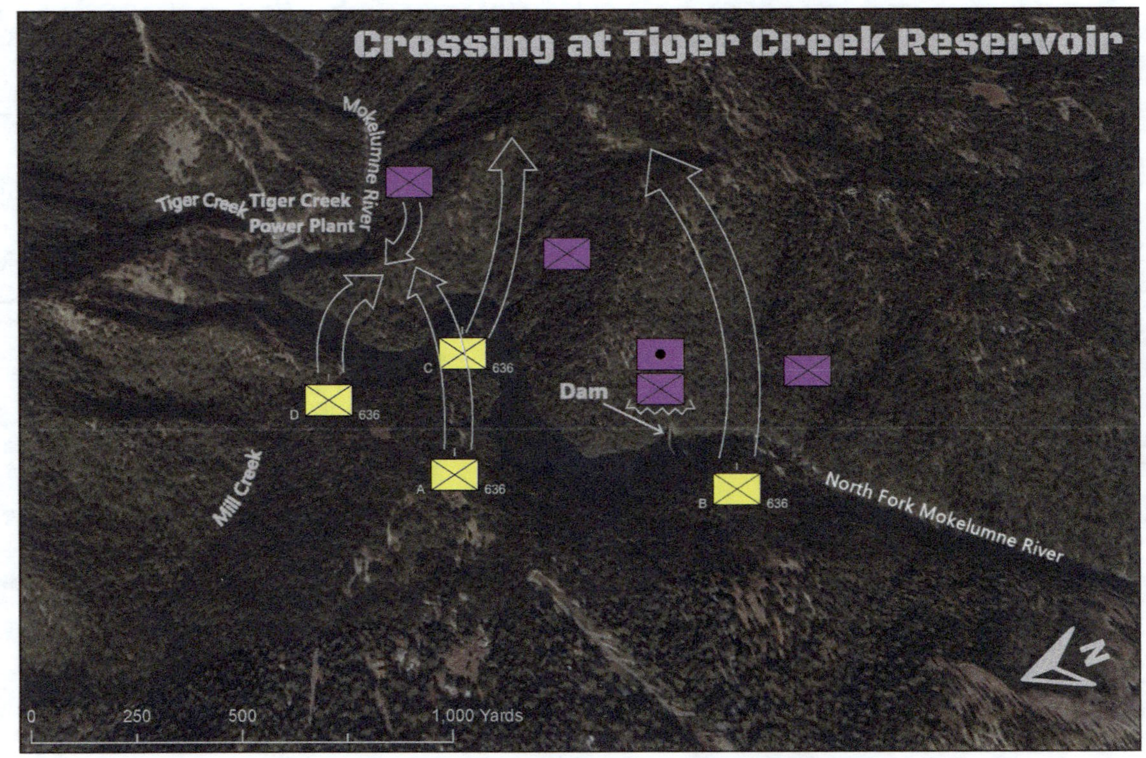
Crossing at Tiger Creek Reservoir
Mokelumne River
Tiger Creek Tiger Creek Power Plant
C 636
D 636
Dam
A 636
B 636
Mill Creek
North Fork Mokelumne River
N
0
250
500
1,000 Yards

Suddenly, a soldier came running up, out of breath and panting. "Captain Ogden, the Stanislausi are reoccupying the hill overlooking the dam."

"Blast it!" Ogden exclaimed.

"I thought you successfully took that," Spotorno said. "Guess you forgot to *secure* it."

"Shut up," Ogden muttered.

"I told you!" Sanders exclaimed.

"Hah, who's the winner now?" Westfall jeered.

"You know what, why don't you two go chase them off," Sanders suggested. Ogden and Westfall looked at each other. "Come on, let's move it! And hey, radio operator, please call in for more forces to cross the river and ask where our air force has disappeared to." George raised his eyebrows in surprise. Sanders was so much nicer to his inferiors.

Reluctantly, B and C Companies marched back along the ridge towards the dam. George was about midway in the advance and very confused. Wasn't Alameda supposed to be professional? Shortly after, he heard firing up ahead. The Alamedans moved forward quickly, driving back the Stanislausi before them with a wide flanking maneuver. In a few minutes the firing stopped.

George was elated. They had crossed the river, taken the hillside, and defeated the enemy counterattack; and he had helped do it.

"It was only twenty or thirty of 'em, and they fled pretty quickly," someone said. "We lost one or two."

"You know, I'd like to know where a counterattack is," asked a boy who held his rifle like a natural part of his body.

"Uh, that was one."

"That wasn't a counterattack, that was a few kids. Normally, we'd have been counterattacked by now, and we're not, and that bothers me."

"Well, we need to stop sitting here and advance."

"Yeah, when some more units cross to support us."

Over the next half-hour various units began arriving. George watched as a platoon of armed patrol cars crossed over the dam and two more infantry battalions finally arrived on the scene. Supply trucks crossed as well.

"So what's the news on our air support?" Ivy asked Captain Ogden.

"X Corp is engaged in a *tremendous* fight trying to encircle Reno and they've sucked up most of our air support," Ogden replied with a hint of dismissive sarcasm and irritation.

"Oh, great," James said, "so we have to fight with little aerial cover? I mean, what about our doctrine?"

Ogden snorted disdainfully. "As I heard, they're bombing Interstate 80, which they failed to cut off by land and is a lifeline that the enemy are shoving supplies and reinforcements into Reno through. Humph, if *I* was in command of the X Corp *I'd* have taken it already."

James turned around and rolled his eyes where Ogden couldn't see. George grinned, and Ivy mysteriously began coughing. Ogden was kinda funny.

George and the rest of the 636th Battalion waited for nearly an hour before Colonel Hoffman crossed with his headquarters and staff, and the unit was able to proceed. During that interval, George had the chance to rest, drink water, and eat a field ration. He was in a good mood and ready to chase down the enemy who refused to show themselves and counterattack. The cowards.

The terrain before them, as he could see it from the top of the ridge, was hilly and wooded, rising and falling. The light forest was scattered with clearings here and there.

"Alright, get up, let's go!" Captain Ogden told his troops.

George hurriedly packed up his things and followed as his unit began marching. The ground was covered in brush and deadfall, and B Company walked slowly down a slope to the bottom of a dip in the terrain.

From there they crossed a dirt road and hiked up a larger slope. Behind B Company came elements of H Company hauling their light field artillery guns and ammunition.

As George climbed over a large fallen tree, he suddenly heard shouting and the pop of rifle fire. Rolling backwards, he landed roughly on the ground behind the log, scratching himself painfully on the branches sticking out of its side.

Rubbing his hurt leg, he put his head up to see Stanislausi soldiers coming over the crest of the hill, running from tree to tree. He got to his knees behind the log, leveled his rifle over the top, and began shooting.

Around him soldiers were taking cover behind trees or hitting the dirt. George fired wildly at the enemy, and hit one of the boys! He stumbled back and sat down, grumpily putting on his casualty shawl. George pumped his fist. He had got one! His first kill!

Then there were enemy soldiers at his log, shooting over at him. He shot one point-blank in the chest and fell back from the log as paintballs whizzed around him.

The rest of his unit was also falling back from the determined counterattack. Alamedan machine gunners strafed the enemy with paintballs and the light artillery gunners lobbed shells at them.

Not wanting to retreat, but not wanting to be left behind, either, George returned all the way across the road that ran along the low point in the terrain and stopped behind a tree in the woods on the far side. There they finally stopped the counterattack, using the open space of the road as a killing ground void of any cover. The two sides sniped at each other from across the no-man's land.

George glanced up at the trees and suddenly had the brilliant idea of climbing one to shoot from an elevated position. Selecting a sturdy-looking pine and slinging his gun on his back, he grabbed for one of the lower branches and pulled himself up. They were covered in sticky sap.

He wiped his hands on his clothes and made it to about thirty feet high before deciding that was far enough. This was exciting, even if he was now sticky from sap. Eugh, that was really annoying. It was getting all over his rifle, too.

George swung a leg over one of the thicker branches and sat astride it, facing out towards the road, partially sheltered from the front by other branches. From here he looked down on a girl with bright blond hair that stood out like a sore thumb among the bushes.

Pointing his rifle, he rapidly pulled the trigger, dropping paintballs all around her and causing her to run for cover, but sadly not hitting her. Then he abruptly ran out of ammunition and struggled to reload his hopper and cartridge while sitting astride the branch.

Clearly, he was not the only one who had decided to climb a tree, as both friend and foe were doing likewise. After repeated attempts, George finally shot a young boy in a tree across the dirt road.

As this was going on, the enemy had dragged some large artillery pieces to the crest of the hill they had just retaken and began firing salvos at the Alamedan infantry. The heavy shot penetrated the trees and began inflicting numerous casualties. The Alamedans started to fall back even further.

As the situation continued to deteriorate, two Alamedan light bombers appeared in the sky above, flew right on past, and bombed some target up ahead. They turned around and flew back overhead, before banking about to circle above. Then one of them came down and made a pass, bombing the heavy artillery, followed closely by the other.

This attack seemed to be extremely successful. It coincided with the sound of engines approaching, and George saw several patrol cars drive up. They fired right into the enemy on the side of the road.

George heard the officers shouting to their men to charge, and he began climbing down from his tree as soldiers ran beneath him, shouting. The light field artillery and machine gunners fired in support.

He finally reached the ground and started moving at the back of the assault. One of the enemy's heavy artillery guns was still firing, but only the one.

The Alamedans fought their way from tree to tree back up the hill against stubborn resistance, using their BAR rifles to saturate the enemy with firepower. Near the top of the hill, opposition finally broke and they captured all but two of the heavy artillery guns.

The enemy disappeared to reorganize, giving the Alamedans a few minutes to prepare.

"Get those field guns up here!" Captain Ogden shouted. "And the machine guns! And radio back to headquarters and ask if they'll give us the mortar platoon!"

The radio operator put his headphones on and began pushing buttons and spinning dials on his radio. Meanwhile, the gunners were hauling their field guns up the hill.

"George, over here," Ivy told him. She was organizing her platoon. "I expect Captain Ogden to order us forward again once our support gets in place," she said. "He never waits much."

"Captain Ogden, the colonel refuses to send you the mortar platoon," informed the radioman.

"Why not?!"

"Uh…" he spoke something into his headset. "He says he already gave them to Fred."

"That goody-two-shoes," Ogden snorted. "Why can't he take them away from him and give them to me?"

The radio operator sighed and repeated the request. "He doesn't feel like it."

"Humph." Captain Ogden grumbled to himself for a minute before rousing his soldiers into action. "Alright, move out!"

B Company launched forward and began moving at a rapid pace along the top of the hill. George could see a farm below him in a clearing. The patrol cars were advancing tentatively across it while infantry scurried about, taking cover behind them. The enemy was putting up a staunch resistance.

Then George saw a horse and rider gallop out of the trees. Behind her came over a dozen more. George watched, confused. What were they doing? And what were they carrying? And wait, they were kids wearing Stanislausi uniforms and carrying short paintball guns.

As the horses galloped past the infantry from a distance, their riders turned sideways in their saddles and began shooting, somehow not using the reins. George's jaw dropped. Cavalry? Mounted snipers? That was a thing?

"At the double! Move it!" Ogden shouted at him.

"Sir," Ivy said, "we can't advance too far ahead of the battalion."

"Shut up and do as I say!"

George ran along a ridge in the terrain that extended out from the hill. Both sides dropped steeply away and a road ran along the top.

Suddenly, there was movement to the side and they were attacked by a group of infantry. Then more infantry came at them from their other side and front. B Company fell back as George ran from tree to tree, wildly firing at everything that moved. People were shouting everywhere over the sound of the rifle fire.

"Blast it!" said Ivy. "We're completely outflanked and they're getting around in our rear."

"Hold steady and push on!" Captain Ogden said. "Keep going!"

B Company rallied and pressed onward, skirmishing with the infantry that harassed them from all sides. The cavalry kept their distance and never stopped moving. George tried repeatedly to hit them, but their horses were too fast and agile, and even when he managed to hit the horse itself the rider did nothing. Apparently, horses couldn't be killed.

The Stanislausi cavalry were amazingly accurate, too, considering that they were shooting from the back of a moving animal. One of the riders hit George in the arm, ruining the shot he was trying to take. It stung very strongly as he rubbed it, grimacing, and convinced him he was no match for those guys. Better to just avoid them.

The situation seemed chaotic with friend and foe running everywhere. George felt overwhelmed, constantly looking everywhere around him, his head whirling as he tried to process everything that was going on as those cavalry soldiers sniped at him.

He ran around a thick tree to escape one's sniping and found himself face-to-face with a large, strong boy. Both of them were startled and slow to react, but George yanked his rifle up first and shot him in the chest multiple times. He stumbled back and fell on his butt, wincing from the stings.

George paused, breathing hard, and scrutinized the fellow to make sure he was really a casualty. The boy looked very deflated and began rummaging through his knapsack, looking for his casualty shawl.

Hearing Ivy shouting somewhere to his left, he ran on, exchanging potshots with a girl running a parallel course. Not paying attention to where she was going, she ran right into a BAR gunner who took care of her.

To George's right, he was shot at by three soldiers and hit the ground behind a small log. Getting to his knees, he returned their fire, and abruptly emptied his hopper. He reached for his pod pack, felt along it, rapidly checked his suspenders, started getting nervous, reached for his backpack, and remembered he didn't have it. He had plumb used up all of his ammunition. Blast it!

Hearing footsteps, he popped his head up to see the three kids charging him. George wheeled around and ran pell-mell for his life, dodging around trees. A paintball broke on a tree next to him, staining its bark a pinkish red. This was not what he had planned on doing in the army. What would he do now?

Then he saw an enemy soldier who had become a casualty. His equipment was piled on the ground next to where he was sitting and putting his casualty shawl on. Remembering that Sergeant had told them they could loot casualties, George ran up and took his ammunition. The boy merely watched with one eyebrow cocked, looking extremely smug.

Relieved, George poured the paintballs into his hopper and closed the hatch. Throwing away his gas cartridge and getting another from his bandoleer, he was ready for action.

George leaned around a tree with his rifle, aimed it at a boy crouched behind a bush about thirty yards away, and pulled the trigger. It clicked, but nothing happened. Confused, he tried again, but still nothing happened. The smug grin of that boy he had killed returned to mind. What did he know that George didn't?

Taking off the hopper, George examined the breech, which was full of paint. He could not get it out. His rifle was thoroughly jammed, and he had no clue why. Double blast it!

Great, now he was caught in the middle of a battle and his rifle wouldn't fire. That left him with only his bayonet, rather a disadvantage. He was supposed to be an infantryman of overwhelming firepower.

Slinging his rifle on his back, he took the bayonet out of its sheath, grasping it by the handle that both mounted it to his gun and made it usable as a short sword. He tested it with a finger; it was wet with paint and ready to go. Then he carefully wiped the finger on his pants.

George promptly hid behind a tree as an enemy soldier threw a grenade in his direction. It landed nicely behind a bush where two Alamedan soldiers were crouching, spraying paint into the air and all over them. The enemy soldier ran past the tree where George was hiding to attack Ivy — there! He'd finally found his platoon!

George stuck his bayonet out in front of the boy as he ran by. He collided squarely with the blade and did a belly flop on the ground. George couldn't help laughing. The boy rolled over and looked at him, annoyed.

"Seriously?" he said. "What is this, the Middle Ages?"

"Hey, you're a casualty, you can't talk!" George reminded him.

"Oh, whatever," he said with a grunt as he got to his knees and pulled out his casualty shawl. "Gotta hand it to you, though."

George grinned, pleased. He had done it after all, even without Alameda's legendary firepower. He had done the hard thing! The boy nodded and turned to walk away, but paused.

"And hey, thanks," he said.

George was confused. "What?"

"I've been wanting to go home."

"Oh. Well, couldn't you, ah, just, you know — shoot yourself?"

The boy looked horrified. "That's bad sportsmanship! And besides, I'd be dead for an awfully long time. I do want to come back."

George nodded. "Well, good luck. Where do you live?"

"Lodi."

"Wait, but, that's the same county I live in. Alameda owns that."

"Yeah, so? I fought with San Joaquin county, and when they were defeated I went and joined Tuolumne. I ain't gonna fight for no invader!"

"But, we're in Calaveras County, not Tuolumne."

"Calaveras is basically part of Tuolumne."

"Oh! I didn't know that. Wait, but I thought we were fighting Stanislaus?"

"Tuolumne joined Stanislaus..."

"Oh. I didn't know they could do that."

The boy looked at George like there was something not quite right about him. "Did they teach you nothing about politics?"

"Um... no, not really?"

The boy shook his head. "Another reason not to join Alameda." Then he grinned. "Wanna switch sides?"

"You can do that?"

"Sure. There's no rule against it."

"Well, no."

"Alright then. Adiós! And thanks again!" With that, he strolled away and left George standing there.

"You're welcome!" At which point George realized the fighting had left him behind. Guessing that his company had pulled back, he ran in that direction, and shortly encountered the firefight again.

George spent most of the battle hiding from enemy infantry and those super annoying cavalry snipers, and throwing the occasional grenade. He got one grenade hit, but was unable to repeat his success with the bayonet against the San Joaquinan-Tuolumnite-Stanislausi boy. Man, politics was just weird. He was somewhat glad they hadn't tried to teach him much about it.

Eventually, the battle ceased, but B Company was nearly all the way back down the hill that they had fought all their way up.

"George!" Ivy said. George whirled around and ran over. "Are you incapable of staying with your unit?"

"What?" he complained. "It was chaos everywhere."

"Only for you people who got excited and ran off into the fight," she said.

"Oh. Well, sorry," he replied.

"Try to pay a little more attention, please."

"Okay."

Then Corporal James walked up. "Yeah, my entire squad just kinda ran off and left me," he said. "And George, I saw you, with your rifle on your back, running around with your bayonet like a sword, hiding behind everything. Can I ask what the hell you were doing?"

"My gun is jammed."

"How'd you do that?"

"I dunno. I ran out of ammunition, so I took some from a casualty, and then my gun wouldn't shoot."

"Which side was this casualty on?" Ivy interjected.

"He was an enemy."

Ivy held her head in her hands. "George, they use larger-caliber ammo than we do."

"Well how was I supposed to know that?"

"Never mind, just come over here and I'll show you how to clean it." George followed her over to a pile of equipment on the ground.

"So, ah, why're we back down here?" he asked.

Ivy sighed. "Because Captain Ogden, seeking the success and the glory, advanced too far ahead of the rest of our battalion. So they flanked us and drove us back down here, and then they turned and took the farm over there back right after... whichever company took it. I've lost track at this point."

"Why did they stop attacking us?"

Here Ivy grinned. "Because the casualty count was kinda lopsided in our favor."

"Oh." That at least was a good thing. Quickly, he tallied up his kills: three. Maybe he should keep a log like a sniper, or make notches on his rifle like they do in *Hopalong Cassidy,* a show he didn't really care for but had seen plenty of since his dad had grown up watching it.

"And hey," he asked, "why do they have cavalry?"

"Why not? They're pretty good at what they do, aren't they," Ivy said wryly.

"Why don't we have cavalry, then?"

"We do, but mostly vehicles. They do vehicles less."

"Can horses become casualties?"

"No. You have to hit the rider. Which I'm sure you already guessed," she finished with a grin. "Alright, look, here we go." She proceeded to show him how to clean his rifle out using a gun-cleaning kit, and had everything working in short order. "You should have one of these in your pack."

George nodded. "Okay, what now?"

"We're gonna regroup and then make another push to take the ground back," she said. "So get ready for more of that, and don't waste so much ammo next time."

George did as he was told. This was a little... ridiculous? He was rather annoyed that he would have to do what he had just done all over again. It felt like public school too much.

Chapter VIII

"Forward!" cried Captain Ogden. "Retake that hill!" George sighed and began walking forward with his unit to do the same job all over again. This time they crossed the road without resistance. The Stanislausi were dug in at the top.

Machine gun fire ripped down the slope as the Alamedans scrambled forward. Behind them, their field artillery gunners returned fire. George figured that they must have gone through a lot of ammunition by now.

The Stanislausi had not had very much time to prepare, and they merely occupied hastily-prepared dugouts and foxholes. The cavalry were also positioned up the hill. The wreckage of their heavy artillery lay nearby where the Alamedans had left it after ensuring the guns would be of no more use to the enemy.

George darted from his tree as a machine-gunner swept his aim away. Quickly he brought it back, but George was already flat against the back of another tree.

He looked around and tried to analyze the situation like a military man. Fortunately, there were not very many machine guns, so their fire was targeted and unable to rake the whole slope. This provided crucial seconds for him to dart farther up the hill.

Such tactics worked to reduce casualties, but progress was painstakingly slow and all the impatient soldiers wouldn't last long. George, trying to improve upon what he had done last time, was glad to still be standing. He stood behind his tree, content to stay there until he had a very good opportunity to advance. He didn't want to spoil his successes so far by getting himself killed.

"Owens, catch up!" Corporal James yelled at him from up ahead. Ugh. Pushy leadership again. George dashed pell-mell to the rest of his unit as paintballs flew past him much too close for comfort.

"Soldiers, quit dilly-dallying and charge!" yelled Captain Ogden from the bottom of the hill.

"You heard him!" Sergeant Liam shouted. "Get 'em, boys!" Immediately, there was a surge forward. George's legs were tired, but he ran too.

"Get 'em!" Ivy yelled.

As George ran forward, a nest dug into the ground loomed up in front of him. A boy with a grim expression on his face was hunched over a machine gun, firing to George's right.

Holding his rifle against his hip like they did in the movies, George fired as he ran and shot the boy, who let go of his weapon. The noise of battle was loud and confusing.

Suddenly, a dozen Alamedans ran in sideways from the flank and hit the Stanislausi line from the end, routing through three dugouts in quick order. George and his unit, having penetrated the thin line, turned right and drove down it, shooting point-blank into each dugout.

George saw two of his own platoon shot in the action, but then Ivy was yelling at them to keep going, and he headed forward along the ridge. The enemy soldiers were falling back before them, but an advancing firefight continued. The cavalry would charge them indirectly, showering paintballs, then turn and withdraw to regroup and charge again. Here and there a lucky shot from a small arm or field artillery gun hit one of the riders, but wearing them down was slow, costly attrition.

George ran to another tree. He had spent most of today running from tree to tree. Firing around it as the rest of his squad did likewise, they convinced several enemy soldiers to retreat. Immediately, Corporal James rushed forward, shouting, "Come on!" and George followed.

Then a tall boy whirled around, raised his rifle to his shoulder, and took a single potshot at them before turning and dashing away. A volley of rifle fire followed him unsuccessfully.

"Guys..." Corporal James said. George turned and saw the single potshot on his stomach. His officer had been shot!

Setting down his rifle, James drew his casualty shawl out of his belt pouch and put it on. Then he walked away without saying a word.

George's squad looked at each other.

"Well, let's go," George finally said, and they all began moving forward, going back along the ridge for the second time.

"I'm hungry," someone complained. "We never ate lunch."

George had not realized how hungry he himself was because of all the adrenaline in his system. It was getting late, and they had been fighting all day.

"Keep going!" Ivy said. "Once we get this ridge secured then we can stop and eat."

George peeked around his tree for the umpteenth time that day and fired a few shots before darting forward. His unit advanced at a slow jog as the Stanislausi defenders melted away.

Then three horsemen galloped through the trees and bore down on them, firing. George jumped for cover and shot back, watching his paintballs fly harmlessly around the cavalry trooper he was aiming at. Trying to estimate lead on them from such an awkward angle was impossible. Meanwhile, that same trooper, steady in his saddle despite the bouncing of his horse, was firing off shots at what seemed like one-and-a-half-second intervals.

About twenty yards ahead of the Alamedans, the riders veered off, refusing to get close enough so George could actually hit them. Somehow they steered their horses with ease despite the fact that both hands were working their guns. One of the foremost Alamedans was hit by their accurate barrage.

George watched as a BAR gunner behind a tree drew a bead on one of the Stanislausi cavalry troopers. She swept her gun to the right, leading him as he turned away from his charge, and pulled the trigger, holding it down and emptying her entire hopper.

A stream of paintballs cut through the air and intercepted their target. The trooper abruptly lowered his gun, brought his horse to a stop, and pulled his casualty shawl from a saddlebag. The BAR gunner ducked down to reload. George cheered at her as only two of the three troopers galloped back the way they had come.

"Forward!" Ivy urged them, and George resumed advancing with his unit. In a few more minutes, they once more held the ridge.

"Alright, halt," Ivy called. She carefully looked around. There were no Stanislausi in sight. "We'll eat here." She called out names. "You four have sentry duty."

George plopped down on the dirt road and took a long swig from his canteen. Then he dug through his pockets for the food he had placed there earlier.

"Aren't we supposed to be linking up with some paratroopers?" someone asked.

"We are," Ivy replied, "but I don't know where they are. The captain does."

Someone snorted. "Ogden'd be much more interested in which objective brings him glory than relieving those paratroopers."

"Why wouldn't that bring him glory?" someone else pointed out.

"How long have they been behind enemy lines?" George asked.

"At least two days now, I think," Ivy replied.

"How long can they last?" He figured that such elite soldiers had to be able to hold out for a good while.

She shrugged. "Depends on how long their supplies last. And whether or not they can obtain more, like via airdrops or local supermarkets."

Jack suddenly burst out laughing. "Imagine being a cashier at a supermarket and these dirty kids in army uniforms come walkin' in carrying their weapons and say, 'Hey, we gotta feed an army. Like, literally. Can we buy all your rotisserie chickens?'"

"'Go rotisserie yourself!'" Ella piped up. "That's what they'd say if they didn't favor Alameda."

A stream of paintballs intercepted the trooper.

"Well, they want the money," Bernie said.

"They sure do love the business," George said, "just like that burger place in—" he broke off suddenly, looking slightly alarmed.

"What is it?" Jack asked nonchalantly. "You look like you've just seen a ghost."

"Um, our sentry just walked away wearing his casualty shawl."

Ivy's head shot up. "What?" she asked, looking around. "Jonathan, Gabriel, are you there? Lucy?"

"Sorry, can't talk," Lucy called back as she walked away. "I'm dead."

"Okay, everybody up," Ivy ordered tersely.

George shoved his remaining food into his pockets and scrambled to his feet, clutching his rifle. Everyone else stared tensely around. The sun was very low in the sky now.

Bernie, however, casually took a grenade from his belt; pulled the pin; released the handle, allowing it to fly off while he waited for a second; and tossed it down the side of the ridge where it landed nicely behind a large bush. The explosion was followed by a shout and angry muttering as two paint-splattered teenagers rolled out from their hiding spot.

"Withdraw, now!" Ivy barked in a low voice. "This ridge is a death trap!"

Immediately, following her lead, the Alamedans scurried back the way they had come. That was when all hell broke loose and a ruined ambush charged up and over the sides of the ridge.

George dashed off the road for the nearest tree as paintballs flew after him, faced about, and returned their fire. The Stanislausi were dragging a heavy machine gun up to fire along the top of the ridge, and George decided his tree was too small to adequately provide cover from such a large quantity of paint.

Running away, he promptly encountered Jack and Ella flat on their stomachs behind a bush with evil grins on their faces.

"Hey, George!" Jack whispered. "Why don't we give 'em a taste of their own medicine?"

George knelt down beside him. "You want to ambush them?"

"In a minute or so they'll have to drag that thing forward again if they plan to keep using it."

"And when they do..." Ella trailed off in an evil cackle. Grinning, George joined them, lying prone behind the bush.

About thirty seconds later, someone shouted at the gunners to bring their weapon forward and they promptly removed the camouflaged netting that looked like one of the local bushes. One of the kids bundled it up in his arms as two more dragged the heavy weapon on its squat tripod down the road. Behind them came two ammunition bearers wearing large backpacks and carrying additional duffel bags, as well as several accompanying riflemen.

George, Jack, and Ella waited gleefully behind their bush, excitement building, as the overeager machine-gun crew came closer and closer. Ella was her squad's BAR gunner, and she checked to make sure her weapon was ready.

The unsuspecting enemy came closer and closer. They were forty yards off. Then only thirty yards away. George fidgeted with impatience. He wanted to shoot them! Now they were only twenty yards distant. Jack readied a grenade for use by pulling the pin.

Then he leapt to his feet and threw it wildly. His overenthusiastic aim was a little off, and it landed too far to the left of the target, missing everyone with its paint spray.

Startled and surprised, the Stanislausi soldiers dropped what they were carrying and looked wildly around, swinging their rifles and shooting blindly as George and Ella opened fire. The BAR rifle spewed a deadly stream of paintballs before the enemy had time to react. Ten seconds later they all stood there, dripping paint and looking rather stunned.

Jack and Ella high-fived jubilantly, then ducked as paintballs flew over their heads.

"Where'd they come from?" George asked as enemy infantry materialized up over the sides of the ridge.

"Quick, run!" Jack said, more like he was playing a video game than actually running for his life. The three of them sped off down the road with over a dozen Stanislausi hot on their tail, firing from the hip as they ran.

"Maybe that wasn't such a good idea," George panted.

"Ain't this fun?" Jack laughed.

"I don't know if we're gonna make it!"

"We do seem to be left behind by the rest of our platoon," Ella commented.

"And it's getting dark!" George glanced back over his shoulder and sped up as paintballs thudded into the dirt road at his feet.

Suddenly, Bernie arose from behind a large bush on the side of the road with his rifle already against his shoulder and coolly gunned down the five leading enemy soldiers. The rest dived for cover, and George, Jack, and Ella rushed to Bernie's side and found a place to hole up.

"How'd you do that?" George asked. Bernie merely shrugged.

"See, remember what I told you about him?" Jack reminded George. George nodded. Bernie was incredible.

"They were running almost straight at me, so it wasn't very difficult," Bernie explained, and fired a few shots at the remaining Stanislausi, who were trying to move forward. The other three added the weight of their guns as well.

"Ella, you pin them with your BAR while we fall back," Bernie said. "Then we'll cover you while you join us." Ella nodded.

"Hold on, gotta reload," Jack said. He and Ella both paused to refill their hoppers and swap out their cartridges while George and Bernie kept watch. Ella had spent her entire load on that gun crew.

When they were finished, Ella fired bursts from her automatic rifle as the other three crawled away through the bushes. Then they kept the enemy pinned down with semiautomatic potshots as Ella crawled to join them.

The Stanislausi were already bringing up reinforcements, including a couple of mortar tubes, but by that time the fugitives had already slipped off into the gathering dusk and there was no attempt at pursuit.

George grinned. He had come out on top despite the swingy nature of this battle, and now he knew why the casualty count was in Alameda's favor.

Finally, the quartet found where B Company had made camp at the top of the hill they had twice charged and finally taken that day. Tents had been erected and dinner was cooking.

"Where were you guys!" Ivy yelled at them. "I'd given you up for dead! George, are you incapable of staying with your unit?"

"Oh, we asked him to join us," Jack said. "'S'not his fault."

Ivy sighed. "And what were you two doing?"

"Oh, we ambushed a heavy machine gun, killed all the crew, and then got chased a ways."

"And then Bernie killed half-a-dozen more enemy, and then they stopped chasing us," Ella added.

Ivy stared at them. "Bernie, is that true?"

"Yup," he simply replied.

Ivy shook her head. "Alright, then, I forgive you. This time. Even though they just replaced the crew if you didn't destroy the gun," she added severely.

"Great," said Jack, "'cause I'm hungry."

"Are you ever not hungry?" Ella asked, and they both giggled.

"There's food over there," Ivy told them.

"Great!" Jack said. "I'm ready for some more delicious stool on a shingle."

"Mm, yummy stool," Ella said. George and Bernie followed them over to the nearest camp stove while Ivy rolled her eyes and walked away, grinning.

As George drew near to the campfire where dinner was being served, he heard whining.

"This food is so gross," Sally complained.

"I beg your pardon!" the boy who had done the cooking said, rather indignantly. "Everyone else seems to like it."

"Well, *tolerate* it might be a better word," volunteered one of the others.

The cook scowled at him. "Then maybe you can just not eat."

"It's so slimy and," Sally continued, "and… yucky."

"Okay, then, go hungry," the cook said, "I don't care. *I* like it."

"And this place, it's so dirty," she went on, ignoring him. "I mean, we're living in *tents*. And I haven't showered in a week. And that boy smells like he hasn't showered in a month!"

"I do have a name, you know," Jack commented through a mouthful of stool on a shingle.

Sally merely ignored him. "This is child abuse! I mean—" she broke off abruptly. One of the veterans was reclined back with his eyes shut, smiling blissfully while holding up his hand and rubbing his thumb and forefinger together.

"Uh, *what* are you doing?" she asked him.

"Oh, can't you hear it?" he replied. "It's the world's smallest violin playing 'My Heart Bleeds for You.'" This was met with loud guffaws and jeers from the other kids.

"*Well*," spluttered Sally, "that's, that's — you're a jerk!" she said and ran off while the others cackled and snickered at her.

Next morning the company was roused by a duet between the bugler's "Ravioli" and Captain Ogden's mouth. The only difference between the two was that the bugler actually sounded musical in a nice way, while Captain Ogden sounded like a hoarse ogre.

George noticed a lone aircraft fly by overhead. It wore the Alamedan rose and laurels, but was much smaller than a bomber. It seemed to be flying a pattern across the front that brought it in and out of sight. He concluded that it was a surveillance craft. He was getting to know the army pretty well already. Wait, except that was the air force, not the army.

Breakfast was served out as everyone gathered their gear together and replenished their ammunition and grenades. This morning the troops were served eggs on toast.

"We just got a delivery of eggs by one of the supply trucks," explained the cook as George commented excitedly on the change of menu, even if he wasn't a huge fan of eggs. It was fresh food, after all. Off by herself, Sally was picking at her meal unappreciatively.

Suddenly, the company bugler began to play a tune that George was not familiar with. Heads snapped up in attention, but George was confused.

"What's that?" he asked Bernie.

"Charge."

"We're— charging? Huh?"

"It's used to warn of an attack."

"An attack?!" George leapt to his feet and grabbed his rifle.

That was when they heard Captain Ogden. "A large enemy force was sighted moving our direction, about thirty minutes away, with tanks and artillery! Prepare our positions for a defense!"

"Tanks and artillery?" George said.

"I knew it!" declared one of the veterans. "It's the first major counterattack since we crossed the river." The boy ran off to prepare.

When setting up camp the night before, a few dugouts had been rudimentarily constructed as picket positions. Now the squads were hastily assigned work details to improve these defenses.

"You!" Captain Ogden shouted at one of his officers. "Harvest wood from these trees. And you, start digging more dugouts. Stagger them, and emplace the machine guns and field artillery. Do not dig a trench line!"

"George, forget your breakfast!" Ivy told him. "Now— ugh, I forgot. 22nd Squad, get over there and dig a dugout behind those trees."

George slung his rifle over his shoulder and got his entrenching tool from his pack. Folding open the shovel, he joined his comrades in digging a hole. The excess dirt was piled in front, between the trees, using sticks and branches to make a sort of wall.

George was not the only one making this dugout, but he recalled the one he had half-assed a few days ago. This time it could be his own hide instead of those three girls. He wasn't going to make the same mistake again.

Rapidly, B Company was turning its hill into a nest of mini fortresses. Logs just too big to easily step over were dragged so that they obstructed the path any attack would have to take. A machine gun crew arrived at the dugout George had helped construct, kicked a firing notch in the rampart, and placed their weapon snugly inside, surrounded by extra ammunition. George hoped they would be safe there. Unlike those other soldiers...

No sooner had they accomplished this then the gunner opened fire with a long burst of paintballs. Figures in the distance scrambled and shot back. George quickly dove into a nearby dugout with half a dozen other soldiers. He hoped whoever had dug this one had done a good job, for his own sake. It went both ways.

The enemy recon troops fell back and the firing stopped. Cautiously, George peered over the rampart in front of him.

"And this," said one of the girls with him, "is where the artillery starts. Those were spotters. We'd better put a tent over us."

Sure enough, a shell landed on the edge of the hill and exploded with a spray of paint. A few more intermittent single rounds homed in on the target, and the bombardment began with gusto.

George lay in the dirt, listening to the whistle of shells overhead. Then one struck the tent over them, causing it to collapse. He lay still, but nothing happened.

One of the other soldiers scooted out from underneath it and peered over. "Guys, it's a dud," she said. "It didn't go off. Here, help me move it." One of the boys joined her, and they both gingerly hefted it aside as the others erected the tent again. "That was lucky," she said.

The shelling lasted for barely ten minutes before it stopped. Immediately, the veteran girl threw off the tent and brought her rifle up to bear as the world erupted into flying paint and the Stanislausi attack surged forward the instant the shells had stopped.

Right in the front came three tanks that rolled up over the crest of the hill, with infantry sheltering behind them. Impervious to the forward fire, they trundled onward, blazing away with their cannons and machine guns.

George set his sights on a strong-looking young man who emerged from behind one of the tanks with some compatriots and began hefting one of the logs out of the vehicles' way. Clearly, he was not the only Alamedan with the same idea, as the whole party was peppered with pink polka dots for their bravery.

Two of the tanks were held up by the obstacles, but a third broke through and drove right between the Alamedan dugouts, blasting their occupants point-blank with massive firepower as they cowered under their cover. Setting down her rifle, the veteran girl took a grenade in each hand.

"Quick, pull the pins!" she said. George reached over and yanked one out as another boy did likewise to the other one. Then, screaming, "*Pugna Ut Vincas!*" she charged the giant beast.

"Brave, but suicidal," commented one of the boys.

"How do you know?" George asked. "She just might survive. Maybe." He was rooting for her.

"I've seen this before, oh-so many times. Brave kid charges tank. Brave kid takes out driver. Gunner takes out brave kid. Everyone else then storms the immobilized vehicle and takes out gunner."

"Well that sucks," said one of the other girls.

"Uh, maybe she wants to go home," added a boy.

"At least her sacrifice wasn't in vain," George said as he distractedly reloaded his hopper and cartridge.

"Seriously, you guys, how can you talk like this in the middle of a battle?!" said a boy wearing large glasses with sweat dripping off the tip of his nose.

"Woo-hoo!" shouted a girl. "She did it!"

The driver and his companion tumbled out of their vehicle, splattered with liquid paint from the grenade. The intrepid girl could not climb inside the vehicle lest she get in the paint she had just gotten all over it, so she jumped back several feet, very much exposed and in the open.

The gunner on top swung his dual machine gun around as the girl flung her second grenade. It bounced into his open-topped turret.

He pulled his trigger as the grenade exploded with a whoosh and soaked him with liquid paint. The intrepid Alamedan girl tumbled over backwards, caught full-on in the chest by a ferocious barrage of paintballs.

George cheered as she stood up triumphantly to put her casualty shawl on, pumping her fist in the air. Then he turned back to the battle facing him, ducking, dodging, and firing over and through his cover. Enemy infantry lay all over the field before him in any cover they could obtain. Casualties were walking away wearing their white shawls.

Suddenly, a shell impacted the ground not two feet away from his position. He and the others with him dived back into their hole as it exploded. Pieces of plastic and foam flew overhead as the pressure of the liquid paint inside forced the light structure of the artillery shell apart.

George sat up and brushed the paint from his helmet. One kid next to him had been thoroughly soaked, and several others were hit in the non-casualty areas. They all hurriedly mixed dirt into the liquid paint on the ground lest it should get on the trunks of their bodies.

A second of the three tanks had broken through their line and was currently directing its cannon shells at the Alamedan field artillery positions. George fired at the gunner in his closed turret, but could not get a paintball through the narrow firing slit that ran all the way around it.

He turned back as two very small boys crawled up in front of his dugout and fired. George hit the dirt. A girl next to him was too slow and got shot.

Rolling onto his back, George aimed his rifle up and rapidly pulled the trigger, sending paintballs into one of the small boy's midriff as he climbed into their dugout. Hit, he fell in on top of the Alamedans as his companion ran away.

Elbowing aside the pint-sized Stanislausi, George sat up and fired at the other fleeing kid, missing such a small, moving target. The vigor of the assault seemed to have worn off, and the last operational

Stanislausi tank was reversing back the way it had come, both gunners killed.

Upon seeing their last heavy weaponry fleeing, the remaining infantry broke off and ran. A few final skirmishes were finished, a captured dugout retaken at bayonet point, and the last enemy non-casualty disappeared through the trees.

George climbed up out of his dugout and looked around. Cautious, dazed soldiers slowly, quietly emerged from their cover and looked around at the mess. Paint was everywhere, as were shell and grenade pieces, discarded equipment, and the two "destroyed" tanks, which Alameda would clean up and add to her arsenal. Or maybe trade or sell them back to the Stanislausi.

B Company had taken rather heavy casualties in the battle, but they had survived and defeated the enemy and gotten some free tanks. George joined a line of kids to get more ammunition. The first to complete this were rounded up into picket duty. George was ravenous and wolfed down some snack food.

"George, over here!" Ivy waved him over to where she was rallying her platoon.

"Where's Bernie?" he asked Jack. "I don't see him. Was he killed?"

"Nah, I bet he's here somewhere. Bernie... just — doesn't die."

"That was quite the battle!" Ella said, bouncing over.

"You know what? You two should be more likely to become casualties with your recklessness," Ivy said, "but somehow you never do either."

"Oh, you haven't been my sergeant for my entire career," Jack replied. "Someday I'll get a platoon of my own.

Ivy snorted. "That'll be the day. They'd better have your luck or you'll be the only one of 'em left. I pity them."

"You just wait until Colonel Hoffman replaces the Ogre with me!"

Ivy shuddered. "I think I'd have a mental breakdown." Jack cackled and rubbed his hands together evilly.

"I'd be your co-captain," Ella added.

"I don't think I could ever recover from *that*," said Ivy, "but fortunately, there is only one captain to a company."

"We do everything together," said Jack.

"Yes, that's part of what makes you two so terrifying. When I can see one of you or both of you, it's alright. But when *both* of you are *missing...*"

"Bernie!" George shouted. Everyone whirled around. "You made it!"

"I was starting to doubt," said Ivy.

"'Oh ye of little faith,'" he replied.

"Where were you?"

"Nature called me over to that tree over there."

"Tha-anks, I really needed to know that."

"It was a very nice tree."

"You asked," George reminded her.

"How many people did you get today?" Jack asked Bernie.

"Only three."

Jack snorted. "'*Only* three.'"

"Wait, you were in the back," said Ella.

"They circled almost all the way around us in a pincer move."

"Wow. What of... the... company that was to our right?" asked George.

"C Company," said Ivy. "Dunno. I guess they were overrun or pushed back."

"So what now?" George asked.

"Well, ideally we wait until we receive reports on the situation at large, and orders. Maybe reinforcements. But knowing Captain Ogden..."

"He'll be attacking any minute now," finished Bernie.

"Exactly what I'm afraid of."

It took fifteen minutes for this prediction to be realized, when Ogden rallied up his unit to advance. He had conducted some brief, but by no means thorough, scouting. The enemy were all the way across the ridge at the flat part on its other end. Supposedly.

"Alright, let's go," Ivy said.

This time, instead of marching along the dirt road in the center of the ridge, the troops stayed to both sides of the steep slope. It was rougher going, but at least they wouldn't be ambushed. They didn't encounter any enemies, however.

Upon reaching the other side, they spotted and engaged Stanislausi pickets. These enemy soldiers looked about as bedraggled as they were, and put up a weak resistance.

Per Captain Ogden's shouting, Ivy led them forward, pushing hard, and her platoon skirted the edge of the enemy camp, coming at them from the flank.

Once they got past the outskirts, however, they ran into much more determined opponents. George's squad got pinned down by what looked like the same machine gun whose crew he had helped destroy the day before. Sure enough, it was back in service. Cavalry troopers were also appearing, and now they were separated from the rest of their platoon.

"Come on, guys!" he said. "Let's fall back and skirt around behind and see if we can find a weak spot."

Following his lead, they crawled back through the bushes and trees until they could crouch. Discreetly moving to their right, they circled around to where the fighting was lighter.

Encountering a half-dozen Stanislausi troops, George ducked to the ground and fired, missing. Scooting sideways, he jumped forward to the next tree. A girl next to him was shot, but he paused behind his cover and successfully avenged her.

The squad's BAR gunner moved forward and opened up, striking down one more kid who was in the act of throwing a grenade. He dropped it and it went off, killing the kid next to him. The other three ducked down, firing erratically over their heads.

"Get 'em!" yelled George. Immediately, his squad bounded forward. Two of the enemy were gunned down, and the third was shot as he fled.

"Nice job!" George said. "Alright, quietly, now. Go slow." He thought they could do it. They were doing it so far.

Creeping forward, he saw another machine-gun nest that wasn't doing anything, just sitting there, waiting. Fortunately, they were looking the wrong way. He held up his hand and halted the squad. Taking out a grenade, he watched the others do likewise. They all pulled their pins.

George held up three fingers. This was awesome. Those machine gunners had no idea what was coming! Oh, the thrill of infiltration.

Eyes locked on George. He dropped one finger. Then he dropped another. Taking a deep breath, he clenched his fist, then flung his grenade.

Everyone tossed in roughly the same three seconds. As the grenades bounced and spun through the nest, the Stanislausi gunners tumbled backwards, streaked with paint.

The Alamedans high-fived enthusiastically while the Stanislausi rather glumly got their casualty shawls on. They stood up to leave.

"Hey," George stopped them. "Go that way." He pointed away from their advance.

The officer looked at him a moment. "Alright," he said. George nodded. "Pretty good job, there," the officer complimented him.

"Thanks. Alright, guys, let's go." They all began moving forward again.

Between the trees in the distance, they saw moving figures. Lacking the distinctive Alamedan green trench coats, they were definitely Stanislausi. George waved his comrades onward, and they slunk forward between the trees.

Then a faint rumbling reached their ears, grew louder, and a very small wheeled tankette rolled into view, sporting a triple-barrel heavy machine gun in its little turret. They all froze. Accompanying it came a large body of enemy troops armed with several heavy weapons. At the very back pranced at least a dozen horses. The whole group was moving rapidly in their direction.

"Take cover!" someone hissed, and everyone got down on the ground and hid among the trees and bushes. This was way more than they were prepared to deal with.

They lay silently in the bushes, their green trench coats and darker trousers blending into the surrounding foliage as the enemy column passed by. George breathed a sigh of relief that they had not been spotted.

Suddenly, he heard the boy lying to his right draw in a sharp breath. Glancing at him, George was horrified to discover that he was holding in a sneeze. He reached over and clamped his hand on the boy's shoulder. They locked eyes, George begging and ordering all at once, and the boy desperately trying not to sneeze.

Achoo! Achoo! The quiet sound of marching feet, the tankette's engine, and the merry clip-clop of hooves was shattered by two explosions. Not only did he sneeze, and twice at that, but he had an extremely loud sneeze, like a trumpet. Great. Just great.

Immediately, the Stanislausi column jolted to halt and the soldiers, pointing, looked in the direction that the sound had come from.

"Who's there?!" a stern-looking officer barked.

"Right there!" someone said. "I see something moving in the bushes!"

"It's those blasted Alamedans!" another shouted.

"Tally Ho!"

Meanwhile, George was making split-second decisions in his head. They were in for it now, and they had just one chance.

"Charge!" he screamed, leaping to his feet and running forward, firing wildly. Desperate, his comrades flung themselves after him. The enemy, surprised, scattered to get into suitable positions from which to conduct a firefight.

Then George whirled around and dashed away as fast as he could. "Come on, guys, run! Get outta here!" They wasted no time in following.

Their feint had worked, buying them precious seconds to make their escape. Immediately, the tankette's heavy machine gun sent a torrent of paintballs splattering into the trees around them. George did not look back; he only ran.

Finally, panting, he came to a stop. The enemy had broken off their pursuit of such a small force and returned to their original mission. George took stock of his comrades. They were all there, every single one of them, dropping on the ground to rest.

"Whew," he panted. "That was a close one."

"You're telling me. George, that was some quick thinking there. You saved our hides."

George shook his head. "Wasn't much."

"Hey, guys," said one of the boys. "While we were lying in the dirt, I found this." He held up a rusty old keychain with a pendant hanging from it. "Someone's lucky charm. It's got the initials 'J. H.' on it. Everyone gathered around to look.

"Wow."

"Neat!"

"I wonder what they stand for?"

"That's cool," George said. "Well, guys, let's get back to the group. I wish we had a radio to tell them what's coming."

Chapter IX

Following the sounds of the battle, George's squad rejoined the main body of Alamedan troops. He looked around, but couldn't find Ivy and the rest of his platoon.

"Come on!" Forgetting about the rest of their unit, his squad engaged the enemy at a distance. They had a job to do. George maneuvered from tree to tree, dodging the mortar rounds that came his way.

"Blast those mortars!" someone said. "Where are they coming from?"

"I see one over there," someone else replied.

"George, let's put an end to those."

"Alright," he replied, "lead the way."

"Well, uh, why don't you do it."

"I'm not a corporal any more than you are. I mean, we never did replace James."

"Well we've been following you."

George glanced around at everyone and shrugged. "Okay, let's go. You and the BAR gunner, pin them from the front. The rest of us, let's go around."

Checking his automatic rifle which could be a bit finicky at times, the BAR gunner and his accompanying rifleman moved towards a mortar that was set up in a foxhole they had found behind a tree and a large bush. George and the rest of his squad circled around to the side.

Spotting them, the mortar team lobbed a round towards the BAR gunner and his rifleman, who dodged a few yards away behind a tree. Then they dashed forward and again sought cover as the gunner dropped another mortar down the tube.

As he reached for yet another one, the rifleman fired potshots, causing him to duck. A few seconds later he got the mortar in, but the BAR rifle opened up and pinned the team to the dirt.

George decided it was time to advance, and he rushed forward with his squad, shooting at them from the flanks. They took out one of the riflemen who was with the mortar team, but that was when an enemy infantry squad appeared on their own flank and began shooting at them.

The Alamedans stopped and engaged this new threat, and their BAR gunner, who had to stop firing to conserve ammo, vigorously shot at the Stanislausi, who seemed a bit apathetic.

"Hey, look out!" one of his comrades yelled, pointing. George turned to see that the mortar team had rotated their tube to aim at them.

Turning to flee for cover, he tripped over an exposed root and did a belly flop on the ground. He cringed, waiting for the explosion, but it never came. Instead, he heard *"Pugna Ut Vincas!"*

Getting to his knees, he saw the mortar team scattering to a headlong charge by the BAR gunner and his rifleman, who fired from the hip as he ran. George started to cheer up until he saw that they had taken their tube with them and wasted no time in setting it back up farther up the hill.

"Drat them!" George muttered and began moving sideways as he saw the Stanislausi trying to sneak around behind him.

The Alamedans responded by keeping in front of them. Next, however, the Stanislausi left half their group in front of the Alamedans while the rest tried to circle around. George, seeing their plan, pulled his squad back until they were facing both groups.

The two opponents continued dancing circles around each other while the Alamedans dodged mortar rounds from the mortar team up the hill. For ten whole minutes this went on with no casualties.

"What the hell!" someone griped. "How much ammunition do they have?"

"Apparently an awful lot."

Then shouts were heard, and George saw more Alamedan infantry arriving on the other side of the Stanislausi with a field artillery crew. This forced the Stanislausi to withdraw to get in front of the Alamedans.

"This is annoying," George said.

"What is?" asked one of the newcomers.

"Uh, never mind."

The Stanislausi, now rather outnumbered, retreated up the hill a ways to where their mortar team was. George promptly began going after them.

"Wait!" someone called. He looked back. "Let the artillery get that mortar first."

The mortar team had clearly gotten the same idea as it was now lobbing rounds at the gun, killing one of its crew. Unfazed, however, the Alamedans carefully aimed their weapon and sent a shell sailing right over their heads. The Stanislausi ducked and stayed down while it detonated too far back, then came up to lob another mortar.

"Come on!" George yelled at the artillery gunners. "Hurry!"

He was answered by another boom. A shell flew straight and true, knocking the mortar tube over and spraying paint onto everyone nearby. The Alamedans cheered and rushed forward to take care of the infantry.

The Stanislausi, however, had had enough. Grabbing the tube, they turned and dashed away.

"Blast them!" exploded the boy who had first suggested attacking the mortar team in the first place.

"Oh well," George said. He looked around. "Now what?"

"Um, we were just getting here," said one of the artillery gunners, "but everyone else seemed to be withdrawing."

"Really?"

"Yes."

"Well, let's go find out."

George and everyone else began moving back the way they had come. As they reached the beginning of the ridge, they encountered much of their company returning back to camp. Grouchy field artillery gunners, who had just hauled their guns all the way across, were not pleased about turning right around and hauling them all the way back.

"Ivy!" George said, finding his platoon. He and the rest of his squad ran over.

"Really, George, again?" she said. "Do I need to tether you guys to us so we don't get separated?"

"Uh, you left us behind."

"You were supposed to be following us!"

"And get shot by heavy pinning fire, right," commented a veteran sarcastically. "They got stuck. I saw them."

"Well, what're we doing?" George asked.

"Going back," replied Ivy. "We're a mess, they're a mess, and they're not chasing us. This whole attack was ill-advised. Bad idea. Our battalion is gonna spend a day preparing to advance."

"Did this attack accomplish anything at all?"

Ivy shrugged. "Made the Ogre happy."

"No," Bernie corrected her, "winning makes him happy. We didn't win anything."

"Ooh, but I bet you he won't tell the colonel that!" said Jack.

"Nope," added Ella. "He'll say, 'Colonel, I in all my ingenious gloriness defeatedes de enemyes.'"

"What?" said Jack.

Ella grinned. "Hoi, Oi Cap'n Oguh an' Oi sooch a smat guy. Oi win da bat'le!" She and Jack pealed off into shrieks of laughter. Ivy merely walked away, holding her head in her hands.

"If he catches you..." Bernie warned.

"What?" said Jack. "Who'll turn her in? We all hate him."

"Well, I don't think anyone *hates* him," George said.

"I do!" shouted a sergeant nearby.

"Hi Liam," Ivy waved. "Don't say that so loudly."

A shell sailed right over their heads.

Suddenly, an explosion burst nearby. "Ak!" she exclaimed, "we're still in range of those mortars. Everybody go!"

Another girl chuckled. "They're mortars, not flak guns, Ivy."

"See ya, suckers!" Jack called back at the Stanislausi.

"We'll come and whip your tushies tomorrow!" Ella added.

"You know they can't hear you, right?" Bernie commented.

"Yeah, so?"

"Okay then."

"You guys are freaks," someone said.

Jack grinned. "That should be our motto. Hey, Ivy, can we be the Freak Platoon?"

"Hell no," Ivy said. "Over my dead body."

"Aw," he and Ella chorused together. "That sucks."

"Not really," Ivy replied.

George quickly found that B Company's camp was being pulled forward to this hill instead of remaining on the other hill across the ridge. This was very close to the enemy positions.

"Lemme guess," he said, "Ogden had to advance and show everyone up."

"Precisely," said Ivy. "You're starting to learn him."

"Oh, but I bet they won't be far behind," said Jack.

"And hopefully Ogden won't feel it necessary to then show them up again," said George.

Ivy snorted. "Hopefully."

George spent the next two hours helping set up camp. Trucks were parked and unloaded, tents were pitched, and the usual rudimentary dugout defenses were hacked out of the ground before them. George spent much of that hour digging.

"Hey, Bernie," he asked.

Bernie stopped and leaned on his entrenching tool. It was very short, which made him look funny leaning on it. "Yeah?"

"Don't you think it would be a good idea to dig more dugouts all the way around our camp? When they attacked us this morning you said that they tried to encircle us in a pincer move."

"Yes, that would be smart."

"Great, let's tell Ogden."

"Ogden will hate you, a private, for giving him advice."

"Yeah," said a boy working near them, "forget that bastard. Let's just get some of the others together and dig them anyways."

"Alright," George said, looking around for his sergeant. Spotting her, he ran over, followed by Bernie and two other kids. "Ivy!"

She paused and looked up. "Yeah?"

"I think we should go around behind our camp and dig some more fortifications in case they try to circle around us again."

Ivy cocked an eyebrow. "Without asking permission?"

"Yes, let's just do it." He wanted to take the initiative and do the job that needed doing.

"Alright," she said. "It's a good idea. Go ahead and round up a few people. I think Jack and Ella would be more than happy to come with you." George chuckled and hurried off to look for them.

After several minutes of searching, however, the two of them were not to be found. Normally finding them was fairly easy, but this time they had disappeared completely.

"That's troubling," Bernie commented.

"More than troubling," Ivy said. "Ogden'll have my head if my platoon runs off and gets into trouble without his orders."

"I'm sure they won't get into trouble," another girl said. "They always seem to scrape by somehow."

"They always get into trouble," Bernie corrected. "They just make more trouble for the enemy than they get into."

Everyone gave up looking and went back to their previous work, digging and digging. George heaved another shovelful of dirt onto the rampart in front of the dugout he was working on, glanced over it, and bent over for another scoop.

Immediately, he darted back up with an empty shovel just in time to see Jack and Ella, crawling through the bushes, get to their feet and scurry into the camp. Their uniforms were covered with dirt.

"Jack, Ella, where were you?" George asked.

"Oh, we just went for a walk," Jack said.

"Just a little walk," Ella said innocently.

"Yes, I'm sure you did," added Ivy, walking up. "Just a little walk that required crawling through the dirt."

"Well, crawling is fun, you know," Jack replied.

"And there's fresh paint on your helmet."

"Oh, just a splotch," said Ella. "But lemme tell ya, there's a helluva lot more on that Stanislausi guy than there is on me."

"Yeah," Jack said, "it was great! We found some scouting patrol or something like that, and Ella snuck around behind them, and then I yelled and pretended like I had a lot more guys with me, so they all turned and retreated, and then Ella cut them down with her BAR rifle from where she had snuck around behind them!"

"Uh-huh," added Ella, "I suppose you could say they got *snookered*." She and Jack pealed off into laughter as Ivy held her head in her hands.

"That was just bad," George said.

"Actually it was very clever," Bernie said. "But *snuck* technically isn't a word."

"Who cares," Jack said with a wave of his hand.

"I told them we would come and whip their tushies," said Ella.

"You said you would do that tomorrow," George reminded her.

"Eh, tomorrow, give or take a few hours, you know."

"And they probably weren't even the same ones."

"Ah, the Stanislausi are all a bunch of doofuses, what difference does it make."

"That's what the Japanese thought of the Americans in World War II," Bernie reminded her. "Don't assume your enemy is a doofus."

Ella went on, ignoring him: "That's a fun word, *doofus*."

"Yeah," Jack agreed.

"Doofus, doofus," Ella said.

"Okay, guys," Ivy tried to interrupt.

"Doofus, doofus, doofus," Jack and Ella chorused together. "Doofus, doofus—"

"Guys!" Ivy said. "Listen, you're going to go with George to dig some fortifications behind our camp, okay?"

"Sounds great," they replied.

"And next time you decide to go on a solo ambush mission, can you at least tell me what you're doing?"

"But you would have said no," complained Ella.

"You're right, I would have."

"Well what's the fun in that?!"

"Ugh, just, go, with George. And don't go anywhere without George. George, I'm giving you the job of babysitting these two. They need it."

"Oh, bully," George said dryly.

"Hey, what about poopus?" Jack asked.

"Come on guys," George said, and they followed, giggling.

On the way, they passed Sally working on a dugout. Instead of getting down inside in the hole and digging, however, she was perched on the edge, trying to reach down inside with her entrenching tool, which was too short for that. Every time she got dirt on her clothes, she fussed at it, looking frustrated.

George shook his head as he watched. The army was definitely not where she belonged.

"Hey! Why don't we go give her a boot in the booty and help her get down in there to dig that hole?" Ella suggested.

"Guys, that's enough, please," George said. "At some point we do get a little tired of your antics."

"Sorry," Ella said, quieter than she usually spoke.

George skirted around behind the camp and looked at the landscape, pondering. Jack and Ella stood quietly for once. Bernie was always quiet.

"Okay, let's just dig some holes there, there, and— there," George said, pointing to spots. "I mean, wherever you want, I guess."

"Well..." Bernie began.

"Yeah?"

"You see that clump of trees and brush on that mound of dirt? Put a dugout that can shoot behind it so it doesn't provide cover for enemy soldiers. Same thing over there, too.

"And over there you should dig a dugout farther back so they have to cross more open ground to get to you. And there's another good spot for a dugout because it can cover the others well."

George listened intently, understanding why Bernie had selected those spots, and proceeded to mark out the rest of the holes they were going to dig himself. He was learning. Then they got to work.

Pretty soon the backside of their camp had decent positions that the infantry could man in case of an attack. George stood back and surveyed what they had accomplished in a pretty decent amount of time. It felt good to be prepared.

"Alright, that looks good," George said, brushing the dirt off of his hands.

"I'm hungry," Jack complained.

"It's not dinnertime yet, and Ogden will never let you eat early or get a snack he doesn't normally give out."

"We could bribe the cook," Jack suggested, the gleam back in his eye.

"Yeah, I'm not so sure of that."

"If you offered to do his sentry duty for him next time I bet that'd work," suggested Bernie.

"Yeah, not worth it," replied Ella.

"Just wait until dinner," said another girl. "It'll be all the more worth it when it comes."

"Stool on a shingle," Jack said with relish.

They all walked back over to the main part of camp where troops were being selected to go on a reconnaissance mission. Ogden was bellowing away and blaming earlier shortcomings on the poor behavior of his previous scouts.

"You privates can't get anything right unless I am there to babysit you!" he fumed.

"George!" Ivy called. "You're going this time. He wants different scouts."

"But I've never been scouting before," George replied.

"Don't worry, just follow Bernie and do whatever he does, and report back what you see, and you'll be fine. And leave as much stuff as you can behind. Go light."

George nodded and quickly prepared himself. He chucked his backpack, bringing only his pod pack and a few grenades, plus his bandoleer, of course. He probably wouldn't need the grenades, but he felt better having them.

"I'm ready," he said.

George joined a small handful of kids that were to go in one direction. He and the others let Bernie do the leading. Tiptoeing through the woods, Bernie was barely audible. George, on the other hand, made considerably more noise, even as he tried to be stealthy.

The sun was low in the sky, and it would be dark soon. They'd have to be quick. George wondered if he'd ever fight a night battle. So far every night had been spent peacefully in camp. Maybe someday he would even spend a night sitting in a foxhole like he often read of soldiers in World War II. Easy Company, for instance.

George followed Bernie through the trees, keeping his eyes peeled for the Stanislausi soldiers. Their camp was not very far away from his own, or so he thought.

Bernie came to a small clearing in the trees and turned right, skirting around it. George followed. With them were two girls and another boy, all of whom seemed to be more-or-less veterans.

Several minutes later, Bernie paused. George, who had gotten slightly bored and because of this wasn't paying very good attention, nearly ran into him. Bernie held up his hand and pointed.

There, not ten yards off, was a similarly-sized Stanislausi patrol pointing back at them. The enemy scouting parties stared at each other for a moment.

Then one of the Stanislausi girls raised her rifle and took a potshot at Bernie. Immediately, everyone scattered and a firefight began.

"Go around," Bernie quietly told the two girls, who just as quietly began maneuvering to get on the enemy's flank.

George crawled all the way into a bush rather ungracefully, scratching himself up a good bit but getting a decent firing position. They could see him and try to shoot him, but the bush stopped the paintballs. He fired rapidly through gaps in the foliage, forcing several enemies to duck.

Then suddenly, to his surprise, it was over. George saw a couple enemy soldiers wearing their casualty shawls, but the others were nowhere to be seen. Climbing out of the bush while being careful of the paint on its branches, he regrouped with the rest of his patrol. They were all present.

Bernie led them forward again at an oblique angle this time. George thought he saw one or two figures in the brush, but it was also getting dark and spooky, and he couldn't really be sure.

They circled around towards their camp, eventually returning a ways down the hill from it and having to climb back up. George could barely see beyond where the lights lit the area of their camp.

"We're done now?" George asked.

"Nope," said Bernie, "that was the easy part. Now for the debrief."

"Oh."

Bernie led them over to the circle of large tents that made up Captain Ogden's company headquarters where the other reconnaissance patrols were gathered.

In a minute, one of the patrols came out of the main tent, and George's patrol was called in. Ogden was standing in the middle of his tent surrounded by his staff and looking irate. "What'd you see?" he barked.

"We circled about half a mile in front of the camp—" Bernie began.

"What?!" Ogden cut him off. "You only went half a mile? Why the hell didn't you go farther?"

"It was getting dark."

"You could have used a flashlight! I mean, how incompetent are you?!"

"I didn't want to get us lost. We came close to being as it was."

"You guys would be hopeless without my leadership."

"Maybe next time we go scouting you can bring your leadership with us," Bernie suggested meekly.

"Shut up." Ogden glared at him. "What'd you see?"

"We got in a firefight with a Stanislausi patrol, killed two of them, and the others fled." There was a moment's pause.

"*And?*" Ogden demanded. "What else did you see?"

"Nothing," Bernie replied.

"No, you must have seen something else, a picket, their base, something."

"We only went half a mile."

"I want to know where the enemy is camped. There were others that went a *whole* mile and saw nothing either."

"Bully for them," one of the girls in George's patrol muttered under her breath.

"What are you not telling me?" Ogden demanded.

"Nothing," Bernie said.

"I bet it was right there and you were just completely oblivious to it." Ogden turned to the others in the patrol. "Tell me what you saw."

"Nothing," George said, "except for maybe some movements in the bushes, and I'm not sure if my eyes were playing tricks on me or not." This was just ridiculous.

"Blast it!" Ogden said. "Where the hell are they?"

"Um, sir," one of his staff members spoke up timidly, "maybe they withdrew a ways?"

For just a moment Ogden looked foolish. "Are you sure?" he asked.

"Yes."

"Alright, fine," Ogden replied. "Radio the colonel and tell him I cannot find the enemy and so I have concluded that I have defeated them and forced them to withdraw." The girl behind George choked for a moment while Ogden paused. "Ask him if he can get some aerial reconnaissance," the captain continued. "And ask him if he'll let me have Sanders' mortar platoon."

Looking a little weary, the radio operator put on his headset and got to work. Meanwhile, Ogden turned back to the patrol.

"Are you *sure* you didn't see anything else?" he insisted. George clenched his teeth. This was ridiculous. What a peach.

"No, sir," Bernie replied.

"Fine. Go," he said with a dismissive wave of his hand.

As George eagerly left the tent, the radioman gave his report, and George lingered to listen. "Colonel Hoffman says good job. We might get some spotter planes tomorrow. And he already gave the mortar platoon to Fred and that's final."

"Well ask him if he can get higher command to send us another mortar platoon that I can have."

"He says no."

"Ask him if Sanders will trade my machine guns for his mortars."

"Sir, that's a terrible idea," one of his advisors exclaimed, "we need those!"

"Shut up! I make the decisions around here!"

"He says you need your machine guns and may not trade them," the radioman affirmed.

"Blast it!"

The shouting inside the tent faded as George and his companions walked away.

"Boy, I would hate to be one of his staff," said a boy. "He can be so anal about stuff."

"Ditto," the girl replied.

"Why exactly is he a captain?" George asked. No one had anything to say. Clearly the army had its issues.

As George's patrol dispersed back to their individual units, they were mobbed by questions from the other kids who had just finished interrogating the other patrols and were unsatisfied with the lack of information they had received.

"Did you see anything?" "Where are they?" "What are they do-ing?"

"All we saw were a few kids out on patrol," George said.

"That's it?" "What about their camp?" "Yeah, where is it?"

"We assume they withdrew from us, but we don't know where," Bernie explained.

"No," said a girl, "they didn't retreat from us. They retreated from *Ogden*." There were snickers all around.

George and Bernie got cold leftovers from dinner, but since they were so hungry, they didn't care. George was also very tired from the day's activity and began nodding off before the flickering of the firelight. It danced soothingly, as if trying to hypnotize him.

When the Tattoo sounded, he groped his way into his tent and into his sleeping bag. When Taps sounded shortly afterward, he never even heard it.

The next morning George was awakened by Reveille and lay in bed for another few minutes, longing for more sleep. Finally, he dragged himself up after Bernie's quiet example and went outside where the cold morning air shocked the last tiredness out of him and felt good on his face.

Breakfast was served briskly and the troops were organized to move forward yet again. B Company's casualties were now very evident but not yet enough to seriously diminish her performance in battle.

"The Stanislausi are making an orderly retreat," Ivy informed her platoon. "We'll be marching forward briskly, but expect rear guard ambushes."

"Why are they retreating?" someone asked. "Did someone break through their lines somewhere?"

"Well, no," Ivy replied. "I think they are just really running short on manpower to span this entire front. They are smaller than us and we are overwhelming them."

"That means high command will be driving hard," a veteran spoke up, "to finish them off before their casualties start coming back."

Small talk continued as various kids shared bits of intel that they had come across. Conditions on the other fronts were pretty much the same as they had been before.

"Alright, get ready to go," Ivy told her platoon none too soon. "We'll be in the vanguard. The rest of the camp will follow behind."

George put on his backpack, leaving his bedroll and tent behind, and checked that he had enough pods, cartridges, grenades, and that his rifle was ready for action.

"And remember, George," Jack teased him, "no borrowing ammunition from the enemy." George chuckled while Ivy gave Jack a look.

"And remember, Jack," she said, "you're not the sergeant or the corporal."

"Aw, c'mon," he replied, "we actually had success."

"Get going!" Ogden ordered the vanguard. Turning to the others he yelled, "Get packing!"

"You know," Ella said, "he means to pack up the camp to move it, but that could be taken two ways."

"Would you all stop blabbering!" Sally snapped. "Just be quiet for once!" She seemed very upset this morning.

Ivy led them forward and they were accompanied by other platoons. This advance was less battle-like than the previous days and much more march-like. They walked briskly for half an hour without seeing anything. The terrain was much flatter and gently sloping, but was still woody.

After a while, George began getting bored and his thoughts drifted to home. It had been nearly a week since he had heard from his family. Cell phones were forbidden in the Alamedan Army since they were a distraction to the kids and a security risk. This meant communication was limited to snail mail, and B Company had not received any postal deliveries. The army had troops specially devoted to this job.

Suddenly, George pulled up abruptly. For the second time in twenty-four hours he had nearly run into Bernie. Bernie had stopped and was gesturing.

"What is it?" Ivy asked.

"In the bushes, just to the right of that ridge crest." The flat ground rose into a ridge running straight along their path as the hillside fell steeply away from it to their left and right.

"I don't see anything," she said after a moment.

"Neither do I," agreed George and the others.

"That yellow speck, right there," Bernie explained. Everyone peered hard and Ivy pulled out her binoculars. "It's the front sight on a field artillery gun," he clarified.

"Oh, I see it," Ivy said. "How in the world did you spot that thing?"

"I was looking for it," was his simple explanation.

"Okay, Hawkeye," Jack teased.

"It's gone now," Ivy said. "Maybe they've spotted us."

"They would be shooting if they had," George spoke up.

"Not if they wanted to lure us closer."

"But why would they use an artillery gun for an ambush instead of a machine gun?"

"Maybe we can sneak up on them and throw a grenade," Jack suggested.

"Great idea," said Ella, and cackled evilly.

"No, you two are not going anywhere," Ivy ordered.

"I'll go," volunteered Bernie.

"I think we should attack the position like normal," said Ivy. "You guys, go over there. BAR gunners in front. Spread out."

"I'll be fine," Bernie said.

"There may be more that we can't see." Bernie silently agreed with her.

"What we need are rifle grenades," said a boy.

"That's what the PIAT is for," someone replied.

"But a PIAT is so big and obnoxious to carry. Rifle grenades would be easy. Besides, we don't have any PIATs."

"That's 'cause they're big and obnoxious to carry."

"Exactly."

"Let's go!" Ivy said, and George got moving, sticking with his squad.

"Please stay with the group this time," Ivy said.

"Uh-huh," they replied.

Scurrying up the hill, they encountered no enemies, but the approximate location of the field artillery gun received plenty of paintballs. When they got close enough, Bernie got to use his grenade. Then the most eager of the kids pounced upon its hiding place and stopped.

George caught up. Sure enough there was a field artillery gun hidden in the bushes with ammunition dumped nearby, but there was not a single Stanislausi to be seen.

"It's been abandoned in the retreat," someone stated the obvious.

"They must not be far ahead."

"Forward, briskly," Ivy said, "but be on the alert."

George moved among the trees, trying not to expose himself, but in no way as stealthy as Bernie. He kept his rifle ready in case he needed to use it.

Suddenly up ahead, Alamedans began shooting and George's head whirled to process the situation before him. Apparently, they had encountered enemy soldiers and begun pushing forward, so George pushed forward too and hurried to keep up.

Then suddenly the enemy was pushing back and he found himself engaged in the firefight. He shot at whomever he saw and wherever he saw paintballs coming from. The action was beginning to become familiar again. He scored one good kill on another boy his age.

A few minutes later, the resistance softened and George moved forward through the paint-splattered woods, passing up several casualties. He shot one again by accident.

"Hey!" the boy protested.

"Oh, sorry," George apologized, "I didn't realize you were already dead."

"Pay more attention," the boy snapped and stomped off. "Idiot."

"Sally, don't walk in the open," Ivy said.

"I'm tired of walking through the bushes. I've got scabs all over my face and they hurt."

Then a barrage of paintballs pummeled her in the chest and knocked her to a sitting position. She wiped her eyes and tried to stifle a sob. Getting up, Sally crept away. George paused and looked back. It was as if she didn't like being here, but she didn't want to go back where she came from. He felt a pang of sympathy for her.

No one else heard her, however, as they were all focused on the enemy machine gun nest. The gunner swept his weapon to his left, never letting up on the trigger, and George threw himself face down in the dirt as his platoon was blasted head-on. Sally's predicament vanished from his thoughts.

He crawled into a bush for more protection but could not shoot back and could barely see. Paintballs thudded around him and the sounds of shooting, shouting, and running were up ahead, but he had no idea what was going on. He looked around his position and saw that he and everyone with him were thoroughly trapped. They would just have to wait.

George analyzed where the enemy machine gunner's exact position could be and imagined the battle unfolding ahead of him. Meanwhile, he was stuck here and couldn't participate. It seemed like an age that the Stanislausi machine gunner remained fixated on their position.

Finally, the pinning fire stopped and George scrambled to his feet, only to duck left behind a tree and hit the dirt once more as it resumed. His glimpse of the battle had told him that there was a dense firefight going on. Meanwhile, he was stuck once again and could not do anything.

Then he remembered his training and what Sergeant had drilled into his head — dig foxholes. Twisting sideways and freeing his entrenching tool from his belt, he began scraping a depression in the ground. Other soldiers near him followed his example and began digging their own foxholes.

He hadn't been digging very long when the firing stopped. He waited a moment, then carefully stood up and saw that it was all clear. His platoon arose and crept forward. Coming to the enemy machine gun nest, which had been silenced multiple times until the enemy infantry were repelled, they smashed the weapon with their entrenching tools to ensure that it would be of no more use to the enemy.

"Can't we save it and use it?" George asked. It seemed a shame to destroy it.

"Wrong caliber," Bernie replied.

"Oh, yeah," George said, remembering what had happened when he tried to borrow that boy's ammunition.

They hurried to regroup with the rest of their platoon, and everyone walked forward quickly. Potshots were taken here and there. Enemy infantry would appear in front of them, let them get close, attack, and then stage a fighting retreat. Cavalry continued to harass them through the trees.

"Where are we?" someone asked.

"No idea," someone else replied.

Ivy kept them moving, so on they went. Suddenly, George heard shots behind him. He turned and saw enemy soldiers advancing on their rear. Looking around, confused, he saw them coming from everywhere, like moths to a light bulb. Hopefully, the deadly insect-zapper electrified type.

Returning their fire, he ran for the main body of the platoon. Their field radioman was talking into his headset while Ivy stood nearby.

"We've gotten too far ahead and are now surrounded," she said. By now a small but determined attack was coming from their rear. "I'm gonna try to keep punching through their lines," she decided. "Let's go, fast!"

With that, George ran forward. Wasn't this the mistake Ogden kept making?

Chapter X

Everything whirled around George and became more and more chaotic. He could barely keep track of who was friend and foe and did not get much of a chance to shoot either. It seemed that there were a lot of green trench coats running that way, whichever way it was, so that was the way he ran, too, following the crowd. Where they were going he had no idea, but the last thing he wanted was to be left behind.

A paintball flew past his face. He ducked but kept on going. Holding his rifle against his hip, he fired haphazardly sideways, spewing paintballs in the general direction of enemy soldiers.

Seeing movement in his peripheral vision, he glanced sideways to aim his fire. He had taken his eyes from his path for no more than a few seconds when he felt his foot snag and went sprawling headlong into some sharp branches.

He did not stop, but scrambled to his feet, clutching his rifle tightly, stumbling forward through the brush and the fallen tree and onward. He was cut and scratched and bleeding in several places, but with the adrenaline pulsing through his veins he didn't really notice it.

George ran by someone sitting on the ground, saw a flash of white, and moved on. Whether it was a Stanislausi or an Alamedan, he had no idea. The kid flashed by in a blur.

"This way! Follow me! Keep moving!" Ivy shouted, standing in the middle of a throng of green trench coats and helmets. George made in her direction.

Paintballs flew towards Ivy, striking her helmet. She darted aside, putting several trees between herself and the direction they had come from, miraculously unharmed.

George lifted his rifle and shot towards the enemy that were shooting at his sergeant. Shouts brought other kids' attention to the point, and a BAR rifle took another trooper off of his horse.

Then there was shouting in another direction. George whirled around and fired while he stepped backwards, stumbling but just barely keeping his feet. An Alamedan boy ran past him and was promptly shot in the back. Three Stanislausi girls pursued and received paintballs to the chest and stomach. An Alamedan BAR gunner let loose his entire hopper right in the face of an enemy charge, resulting in slaughter. A cavalry trooper galloped past and shot the BAR gunner. Everyone was shouting, and all around George was a cacophony of friend and foe.

"Run!"

"This way!"

"Enemy three o'clock!"

"Get 'em!"

"Attack, shoot them!"

"Jerry, look out!"

"Duffer, they're right there!"

"On your six! No, your other six!"

"There, you guys, charge!"

"Tally Ho!"

"A-a-h-h!"

"I'm hit!"

"Over there, right there! There! *Right there!*"

"Agh, look out!"

"Cavalry four o'clock, BAR gunner!"

"Get back, you idiot!"

"Sandra, over there!"

"Left flank! Watch out! Behind that tree!"

"I'm dead!"

"This is FUBAR!"

"No it ain't," Jack said emphatically.

"This is awesome!" he and Ella chorused at the same time. "Jinx-jinx—"

"Jinx!" Ella got it out faster. "Ha! Gotcha!"

"I'm in a forest, psyche," he replied.

"So am I, psyche."

"I'm holding a rifle."

"So'm—" Ella cut off, stopped briefly and let out several short bursts of her BAR rifle at the enemy soldiers, then dashed on to catch up with Jack, who was taking potshots himself, their banter forgotten.

"Stay together!" Ivy was screaming from somewhere nearby. "Stay together!"

For an indefinite amount of time George continued on like this until suddenly he heard Ivy frantically yelling and telling everyone to stop. He stopped, panting, and peered around.

The enemy before them seemed to have vanished. He was standing in a campsite. It was a small clearing in the trees with a small building, a fire pit with logs arranged in a circle around it, and a single large tent.

"Stop, regroup! We'll hold out here!" Ivy said. "Might as well, we've broken all the way through their line. You guys," she said, randomly selecting whoever was at hand, "secure the perimeter!" The selected soldiers quickly moved to do so, engaging the enemy soldiers still attacking them.

"Take stock of our ammunition!" Ivy ordered.

George clumsily slipped off his backpack. It hurt the cuts and scratches on his arms, but he shook it off. He found that he had only two more pods, plus a few bottles of paintballs, and several grenades in his pack and on his person. He looked up and saw Bernie calmly doing the same, almost as if this was slightly boring to him.

"Bernie," George asked, "what does FUBAR mean?"

"Fouled Up Beyond All Recognition," Bernie replied without looking up.

"Yeah," someone said, "but in World War Two the first word would've made your mom wig out and ground you for two *weeks*."

Another boy looked up from nearby, confused. "Yeah, maybe, I mean, if your mom had a habit of coming to the front lines with you."

Ivy came by at lightning speed, tallying the platoon's ammunition. "Conserve your ammo," she said to each kid as she passed.

"How much ammo— how long do you think we can last?" George asked Bernie.

"The rest of the day, maybe," he replied. "Not any longer."

"Hey, look," a girl shouted from the open door of the building, "a toilet!" There was a rush, mostly of girls, to the building.

"With toilet paper!" one of them squealed. A line formed at the bathroom.

"We could use it as a blockhouse," a boy suggested. "I think we could open that window enough to shoot through."

"That would be horrible, that place is rank. It's a pit toilet. I can smell it," someone replied.

"Don't fall down the toilet!" someone else shouted.

Jack took a deep breath of the fumes. "Ah, delicious," he said with relish. One of the girls punched him in response.

"Get out your tents, blankets, tarps, anything," Ivy was saying, "and set them up as shields that we can hide behind and shoot from. Dig foxholes." She went around repeating the direction.

George opened up his pack again. Although he was not carrying his tent with him, he did have a tarp. Gathering it up in his arms, he followed Bernie to the other end of the campground. On the way they passed a young couple standing by their tent and looking around at everyone, bewildered.

"The ranger said there wouldn't be anyone else up here," he overheard the woman say to the man.

Gathering and breaking sticks to support their defenses, the Alamedans pitched up what they had in such a way that they could hide behind and shoot around it. Any sort of heavier fire, however, even a machine gun, would most likely knock it down, but it would do for infantry rifles. To augment the tarps, they scraped depressions in the ground with their entrenching tools.

"Hey, look," someone said, pointing to an old wooden sign at the end of the dirt road that led into the camp. It was faded and scratched, but George could still read "SUGAR SPRING" with the triangle campground symbol underneath it.

"Thank you, we'll take good care of it, and if we don't we'll get you a new one to replace it," Ivy said from behind him. George turned and saw four soldiers picking up the young couple's tent and moving it over to where the campground clearing ended and the road began. They set it in place where someone could hide behind it and someone else could crawl inside it and shoot out the window flaps.

"Guys, drag some big logs into the road to block it in case they try and drive right through here if they have a vehicle," Ivy said, "the biggest logs you can."

George, determined to do the best job he could to help his team, hopped to with several other boys and chose a log. They pushed and pulled on the ends to rotate it so they could roll it where they needed it to go.

"One, two, three, *push!*" shouted one of the boys, and they heaved it forward. The log had lots of short branches that made rolling it all but impossible, so they had to resort to shoving it across the ground.

George ducked as enemy paintballs spattered around him. Several other kids confronted this threat while he and his assistants kept pushing and dragging the log.

"Okay, this way, guys," he said, "we need to slide it this way."

"Move that tarp! It's in the way," one of his companions called. Two girls scrambled to do so. As soon as the log was through, they set it back up even better than it had been before.

Finally, George helped heave his end of the log into place. It sat across the road, mostly blocking it. He was sweating.

"That oughtta stop most anything," said his assistant from his end of the log.

"Let's get back inside," a boy from the other end replied, and they all hurried back behind the tent barricade that faced the road.

Everyone was holding his rifle with one hand and eating a field ration with his other. A light firefight was still going on. The young couple were brewing coffee and offering it to the kids. They seemed resigned to the company for the rest of the day.

Some kids tried eating with one hand and shooting with the other but got reprimanded by Ivy for wasting ammo. "You can't hit anything like that!"

"Annie Oakley could."

"Are you Annie Oakley?"

"Well, no, but—"

"Knock it off and do what you're told."

Having done all they could to fortify the campsite, the Alamedans settled down to wait for reinforcements. Their radioman had miraculously survived and was in contact with company headquarters. From what little George overheard, it seemed like Captain Ogden was not happy. And that was probably an understatement.

The situation went on like this for an hour. The light firefight was punctuated by one massed assault on their north side. Everyone had rushed to that side, repelled it easily, then rushed back across to an even bigger assault on the other side, which almost broke through but was still repelled with only one casualty.

George had a lot of waiting to do, and he found a seat with a beautiful view looking through the trees across the canyon to the woody hillside of Amador County on the other side of the Mokelumne River. Birds floated serenely through the clear blue sky, oblivious of the strife down below. Other than the fact that they were in a war zone under siege, it was a lovely campsite, and George was quite enjoying himself and not counting the hours.

Suddenly, there was a sharp bang and a crash and the sounds of a shell exploding and kids shouting. George scrambled to his feet, readying his rifle. A small artillery round had nailed one of their crude fortifications and knocked it over, splattering paint. Thankfully the kid in the foxhole behind it had been covered by the tarp when it fell and protected from the paint.

Everyone rushed to see what was happening. The paint was covered with dirt and the tarp re-erected. It took another thirty seconds before the artillery piece fired again. Apparently, the Stanislausi only had the one cannon. George could hear its air compressor rumbling in the distance.

Shells landed in several different places throughout the campsite, but everyone had quickly gotten out of the gun's line of sight as best they could. For about half an hour an intermittent rate of fire was kept up. It caused only a few casualties, however, and eventually stopped.

"They must really be hurting for men and weapons," someone commented, "or we'd be toast."

It was now late in the day, and George took a turn at the defensive perimeter. He set a spare pod and a grenade in the foxhole with him, took off his backpack as well, and settled down. A tarp propped up with sticks provided a wall in front of the foxhole.

"Conserve your ammunition," Ivy was going around, quietly reminding her troops. "We're almost out. But buck up, we can last the day. I know we can. And then reinforcements will be here. We've not done badly at all."

"What reinforcements?" someone asked.

"Dunno. Didn't say."

By now there were no more attacks. They knew the enemy was still out there, though, all around them. George caught a glimpse of what looked like a helmet once or twice, those fancy ones the Stanislausi wore. There was no way they were going anywhere.

The sun sank low in the sky. Water was not an issue, but the troops had not carried more than one meal's worth of field rations, and that was long gone. The young couple camping there had food, but not enough for an army. Besides, what would they eat if they gave it all away? George had an empty, hollow feeling in his middle. He felt miserable. Poor George, starving in the woods.

As he sat in his foxhole pitying himself, he thought about home again. He had only been gone, what, not even a month, but that was longer than any other time he had ever been away from home, at least by himself. This was great and all that, in a way, but he also missed his family.

Then his thoughts turned to what this must have been like in World War II. He thought of Easy Company sitting in their foxholes as people literally tried to kill them, for real, not a paintball "death." Many of them never returned home. Now George was free to play paintball.

Suddenly, there was a commotion up ahead, the sounds of battle, and all these thoughts vanished from his mind. Peering through the dusky woods, rifle ready, he saw soldiers coming. A lot of soldiers.

Everyone scrambled, thinking this might be their end. George and many others opened fire as the enemy closed in for the kill. Then they heard shouting.

"Cease fire!" "*Pugna Ut Vincas*!" "B Company!"

He stopped shooting, realizing that these were Alamedans. Finally, the relief force was here! Dozens of kids, or so it seemed, in green trench coats swarmed into their campground. The enemy field artillery gun got off one shot at them and went silent again.

"It's A Company!" someone shouted.

"What duffers to come barging on us like that," another soldier griped.

The Stanislausi siege was broken and the enemy retreated away. A Company's arrival had routed a good deal of their manpower and caused several casualties.

"Good old Fred!" someone shouted.

"Three cheers for Captain Sanders! Hip, hip—"

"Hooray!" everybody cheered.

"Hip, hip—"

"Hooray!"

"Hip, hip—"

"Hooray!"

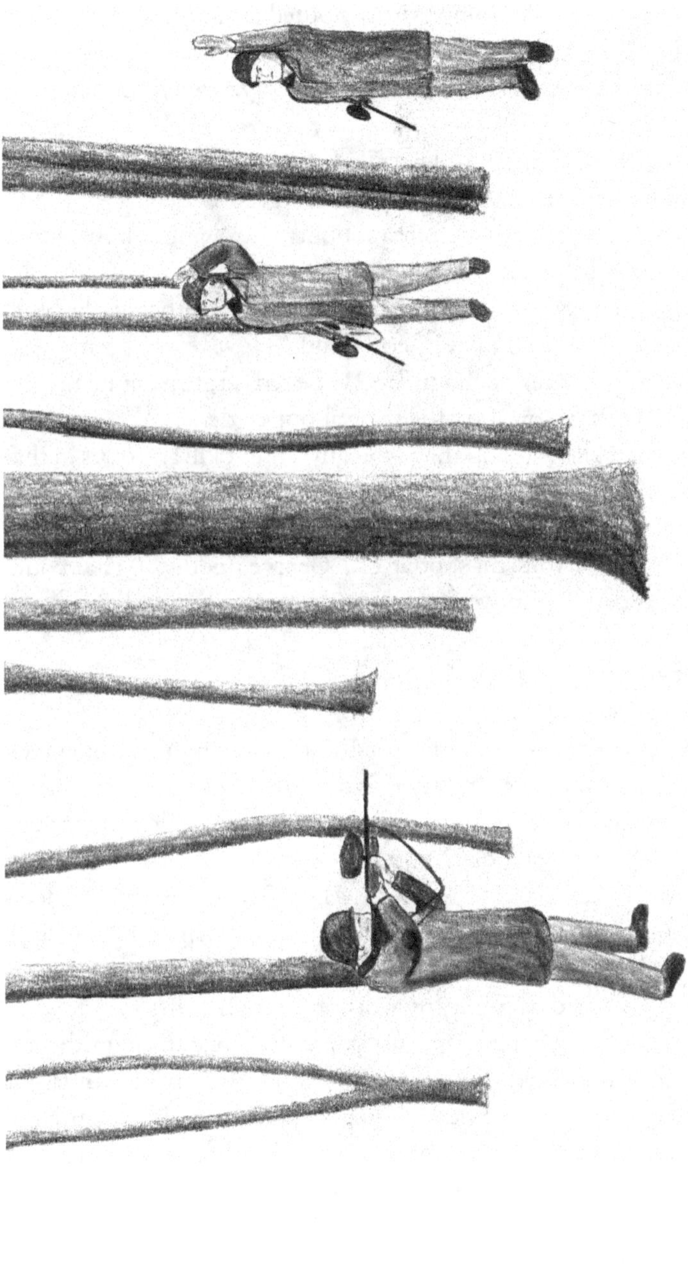

Arrival of A Company. *"Pugna Ut Vincas!"*

The soldiers of A Company distributed ammunition and food. They had very little of either to go around, but everyone got something. This morsel only served to make George even hungrier, however.

"George!" a familiar voice called. George started and looked around for the owner of that voice. "George, over here!"

George turned and saw a boy about his age waving at him, part of A Company. Instantly, he recognized him.

"John!" The two ran together and clapped each other on the back. "It's good to see you again," George said. "How've you been?"

"Great! This war is so much fun. And Fred is a great commander."

"Ugh, I wish I could say the same about Ogden."

John chuckled. "Good thing you guys didn't kill any of us in that friendly fire."

"Then it wasn't friendly fire."

"Yeah it was; you still shot at us." George nodded. "That could have been bad," John went on. "I still got shot in the leg by someone."

"Maybe the Stanislausi."

"No, it's our paint."

Suddenly, there was another commotion and more kids in green trench coats came traipsing in. This time, however, they were ragged and dirty and their shoulder patches indicated multiple different units. They also just looked a little different.

"It's the paratroopers!" someone yelled. George instantly remembered the paratroopers that had been dropped behind enemy lines quite a while ago.

"Wow," he said to John, "they broke through to us."

"Well, actually," John replied, "you guys broke through the enemy line and created this depression-hole. Their front kinda got skewed or crooked or something like that. We were able to outflank them some and then I think we shattered their line and they are in a pell-mell retreat or something like that."

George grinned, very pleased. "Maybe Ogden won't be quite so mad at us then."

"Fat chance," someone snorted. "He'll take all the credit, but Ivy'll be in for it."

"No, but, if he takes credit for Ivy's success and then punishes her for what she did, how does that even make any sense?"

"She screwed up, but he saved the day. Maybe she'll get off."

"I hope," Ivy muttered as she went by.

Bernie spoke up: "She did screw up, but we got lucky and it turned out well."

It was getting dark, so everyone gathered deadfall and built fires. Ivy ran around paranoid that they would start a forest fire with all of the trees around. Food and ammunition were stretched even farther so that the paratroopers could get a little sustenance. George, John, Bernie, Jack, and Ella all found themselves around a campfire with four of the paratroopers.

"Tell us your story," John insisted. The four boys were more than happy to oblige.

"Well," Jerry began, "we jumped out of our planes, floated down, and ended up scattered all in the wrong groups."

"You know, the usual," Bob interjected.

"Yeah."

"Didn't they shoot at you?" George asked.

"Oh, they shot at us with machine guns, but we threw grenades on them as we came down."

"Right." Bob took up the story. "Then—"

"I'm telling it," Jerry interrupted.

Bob rolled his eyes. "Fine."

"So we took them out, and then we landed and formed groups and went on a killing spree. We took out dozens and dozens of them. I must've shot fourteen myself. Maybe twenty."

"So we finished routing them, and then we decided to eat, so we ate, and—"

"Man, Jerry, pick it up or you'll be telling them all night long and all tomorrow, too."

"Okay fine, so, we fought and took our objectives, but then we ran out of food, so we had to go to some organic store or whatever where they charge a fortune for everything 'cause that was all they had.

"And... then the enemy sent some tanks, and we took them out with just rifles 'cause we'd used all our grenades taking a couple of forts. And we got a couple supply convoys, too."

"And how many casualties did all that cost?" John asked.

"Oh, just the dumb ones, so only a few. After we got rid of them we were even more successful 'cause they weren't screwing everything up and getting in my way. We rampaged around and ruined everything. That's why you guys were able to get this far. Oh, we killed a general too. Yeah, what other highlights..."

"Oh, the song," Bob suggested.

"Oh yeah, so it started to rain one night, so we decided to see if anyone'd let us sleep in their shed or something like that, so we found a good place and knocked on the door and this old couple opened it and Mickey sang. Mickey, show them the song."

Mickey cleared his throat and began singing while Bob and the fourth boy, Andrew, joined him in a slightly off-kilter blue-grass harmony:

> May I sleep in your barn tonight, mister?
> For it's cold lyin' out on the ground
> And the cold North wind, it is blowin',
> And I have no place to lie down.

Everyone clapped when they finished.

"Yup," Jerry resumed, "and so they let us sleep in their tool shed. Bit of a tight fit and awful' uncomfortable, but at least we stayed dry.

"So eventually we decided we'd better leave some of the war left for the rest of you guys to fight, and we were kinda running outta ammunition, so we started heading this way and we ran into you guys."

"Yup," Bob said, "that's about it."

George listened, amazed. He had always heard that the paratroopers were some of the choicest soldiers in the army. These guys were incredible. The fact that they had dropped out of the sky with no heavy equipment, done so much damage, and survived this far was amazing. They were like the D-Day heroes of the 101ˢᵗ Airborne, the Screaming Eagles.

Pretty soon Ivy demanded the extinguishing of every single campfire so that they would not burn the entire forest down.

"But that would be a great way to defeat the Stanislausi," Jack said.

"Yeah! Burn 'em and smoke 'em out and then we can just walk on in," Ella added. Ivy did not share their sense of humor, though, and hurried about establishing picket duties.

George had the first watch of the night with Bernie. They took up positions in foxholes outside the campground perimeter.

"Man, those paratroopers are awesome," George said.

"Oh, them?" Bernie replied.

"Yeah!"

"That might have been the tallest tale I ever heard."

George was dismayed. "Really?"

"Yup."

"Oh."

"Alright, bedtime," Ivy called.

"You have to sing us Taps," someone replied.

"What? Knock it off."

"No, sing us to sleep!"

"Yes, Taps!" everyone demanded.

"Ugh, *fine*. Are you guys kindergarteners?" Ivy began trying to sing Taps.

"Augh! You need to take singing lessons!" someone screeched.

Ivy cut off mid-song. "Just go to sleep!"

Being on picket duty with Bernie, George said very little. He saw even less and the hours passed without incident. Bernie kept him awake.

Finally, at midnight, they were relieved by the second shift. George bedded down in a foxhole with his backpack for a pillow and his trench coat to keep him warm. He was cold, but also excited for his first night in the field. On second thought, it was awfully cold. Like, freezing. He rolled himself up as snugly as possible and shivered to sleep.

The next morning, George was awakened by Ivy and Sergeant Alice Kimberley of the A Company platoon that had rescued them. Ivy could not sing, so she shouted, but Alice had a pleasant voice and sang:

> You've got to get up,
> You've got to get up,
> You've got to get up this morning;
> You've got to get up,
> You've got to get up,
> Get up with the bugler's call.
> > And if you don't get up,
> > I will come and kick your butt,
> > And your butt will be quite sore
> > If you do not heed the call.

"Technically," Jack informed her, "there is no bugler."

"I'm the bugler."

"Counterfeit bugler." Alice tossed her head and marched away. George had not heard those lyrics before. Interesting. Come to think of it, there were probably as many versions of lyrics to Reveille floating around out there as random people decided to invent.

The Stanislausi had completely vanished in the night. Everyone set to work putting the campground back the way it had been. The young couple's tent had been restored to them last night so they could sleep in it, and now the foxholes were filled in, the tarps packed away, and the log removed from the road. Meanwhile, Ivy and her radioman were in communication with company headquarters.

George finished his assigned work detail and packed up his stuff. He had a token amount of ammunition left that might not even be enough for one firefight. Hopefully, they were going to resupply soon.

At eight o'clock sharp the Alamedans moved out. The paratroopers headed for reserve where they would rest and be refitted, and the two platoons from A and B Companies set out to rejoin the rest of their units.

George and John marched together, enjoying the smell of the woods, the fresh mountain air, and the twittering of the birds. They even spotted a couple deer off in the distance.

They marched for an hour before the A Company platoon parted ways with B Company. Another hour of marching and George finally spotted the rest of B Company moving with their camp along a dirt road.

They hailed each other and B Company stopped while George's platoon greeted their comrades with a great shaking of hands, hugging, and thumping of backs. Then a cold, quick meal was served, much to George's relief, and they got going again.

George marched at the back of the unit. Ogden was nowhere to be seen, but Ivy had disappeared as well. The day wore on and George kept marching. There was no enemy in sight until B Company turned a corner and encountered a roadblock.

This roadblock had obviously been a hasty, last-minute idea. It was crudely built of rocks and logs and other local resources, including a broken-down military truck; and it was insufficiently defended. The Stanislausi manning the roadblock had no anti-tank guns, no artillery of any sort other than a single mortar tube, and only one light machine gun.

They had little cover to defend and the Alamedans cleared the roadblock with infantry and automatic suppressive fire support from the machine guns mounted on their trucks. In about five minutes, the survivors fled and were unpursued. They left everything behind to be captured.

The infantry then moved to clear the roadblock, but one of the kids pulled a large branch loose and detonated a booby trap that had been concealed in the pile, covering himself with paint. Ogden was impatient to be moving, but the veterans took an entire thirty minutes to clear the roadblock without further incident.

Attaching tow cables to pieces of the debris pile, they used their trucks to pull it apart and dismantle the trap. The booby traps that were not destroyed or detonated by this were now exposed and activated by throwing rocks. Then everything was swept away to the side of the road, and B Company was moving again. George had watched the entire proceeding from the back of the column, but his unit did not participate. Very interesting, nevertheless.

After another couple of hours, they stopped and began the routine of preparing camp — setting up tents, digging foxholes, and so forth. However, they were also ordered to prepare other positions.

"Are we doing this for reinforcements?" George asked.

"Yes," Bernie replied. "Probably."

Very soon George saw those reinforcements coming down the road. There were a few fighting vehicles, some tracked tanks, and a lot of heavy artillery just like the unit he had escorted after leaving boot camp. Some of them occupied the extra positions he had helped prepare, while others turned aside and drove on.

"We are organizing for the last big push," Ivy explained. "Up ahead the Stanislausi have prepared their last-ditch defensive line. Their military machine is broken, and they've put their last resources into two lines.

"The northern line above the Alpine State Highway is the Raymond Line, named for Mount Raymond. To the south on the other side of the highway is the Highland Line. They are the last thing that lies between us and what remains of the Stanislausi nation. It's their Seelow Heights and what's left of their army."

"So what will it be like?" George asked.

"Like, what do you mean?"

"Will it be bunkers and trenches?"

"Yes, bunkers, trenches, forts, barriers, any sort of obstacle. Tunnels, maybe. Our battalion is assaulting the Raymond Line. As I understand it the Highland Line will be the tougher nut to crack."

"They are nuts," Ella said.

"Well," someone commented, "it appears high command has managed to pry some support from Reno and send it over here." His tone indicated that he thought it was high time they had done so.

"Why don't we just wait until we can blast the snot out of them?" George asked.

"The longer we wait the more they can prepare, get their casualties back, and deepen their defense. So we're going in tomorrow."

"Is there a way around it?"

"I don't think so, but I don't really know either. I didn't make the decision."

"Not a very good decision," Bernie commented.

"How do you know?" Ivy replied. "Good soldiers follow orders."

"Good men know when to break them."

Ivy shrugged. "Well we're going in tomorrow. Anyhow, rest now. I don't think Ogden will let us do any resting tomorrow."

George now had some time off, but he didn't know what to do with it. Bernie made himself comfortable, pulled out one of his comic books, and quietly read.

"Hey wanna play cards?" Jack asked George.

"Sure," he agreed.

"Do you know how to play poker?"

"No."

"Okay, we'll teach you."

George sat down in a circle with Jack and Ella. Jack had a deck of cards and Ella had a pile of small rocks.

"Okay," Jack said, "we all start with a pile of rocks. Those'll be our currency. I'm gonna be the dealer first. But to play the game you have to ante, so put a rock in." George added his rock to the other two. "No, keep it in your own pile so we know how much you've put in.

"Now, I deal five cards to everybody. You keep them secret. Now starting with Ella we all bet."

George watched as Ella added three more rocks to her pile and then took one back. "Raise you by two," she said.

"George," Jack said, "you have to at least call, or match her bet. You can raise her, too."

"What happens if I don't want to call her?"

"Then you're out of the game and you lose what you've bet."

George added two more rocks to his pile. Okay, then, if that's how it works.

"When you do that say, 'Call.'"

"Call."

"Okay, and I'll call as well. Now we've all gone and we all have the same amount of money bet, so Ella gets to exchange as many of her cards as she wants for new ones."

"I'll take two," Ella said, putting two of hers on the ground. Jack drew two cards from the deck and handed them to her.

"So George, here are the hands and their ranks," Jack said, handing him a sheet of paper.

George studied the hands and his cards. He had an ace of diamonds, a two of diamonds, a jack of spades, a queen of hearts, and a two of clubs. Oof, it was so complicated sorting out what he could do with them. He set down the queen and the jack and said, "I'll take two."

Jack drew two cards and handed him a two of spades and a ten of hearts. Then he exchanged three of his own cards.

"Alright, now Ella gets to bet again," he said.

"I'll pass," she said.

George thought for a minute and said, "I'll raise it by one," and added a single rock to his pile. Why not.

"And I'll raise *you* by *two*," Jack said, tossing three rocks into his pile. "Now we're not all even, so we go around and bet again."

Ella looked at her rocks, then at her cards. "I fold," she said, and threw down her cards. "I ain't got nothin'."

George shrugged. "Call," he said, and bet two more rocks.

"And now we're done because we're even and we've all betted," Jack said. "Reveal your cards."

George set down his ten, ace, and three twos.

Jack set down a king, jack, and three sixes. "Oh, we both have three of a kind!" he exclaimed.

"Does that mean we tie?"

"No, because my sixes are higher than your twos, so I win the pot!" He happily scooped up all the rocks. "Good job. Now we play again."

George played until he lost all of his rocks, but he had a good time. He left Jack and Ella engaged in a furious poker war.

As George milled around, an army truck drove up. On its side, below the rose and laurels of Alameda, was a seal on which was written, "DEPARTMENT OF POSTAL SERVICES." Inside the seal was an emblem of crossed paintball rifles behind an envelope with wings, enclosed by laurels. The driver hopped down with his armed guards. Another soldier rode on top, manning a machine gun.

"B Company, 636th Infantry Battalion?" he asked.

"Yes, that's us," a boy near George replied.

The driver disappeared inside his truck and rummaged around. In a minute he came out with a bag of mail, which he delivered to the company headquarters. Then he climbed back on his truck and drove away.

There was a rush for company headquarters where Ogden assigned one of his aides to be the postwoman. George got in line, and when his turn came he showed her his ID card and received a letter.

It was his mother's loopy handwriting. She said that his family was well, they missed him and wished they didn't have to use the snail mail, Hannah wanted to know how he was, Greta wanted to know if he had died yet, and his dad had bought him a nice pocketknife on sale for when he came back. Also, his dad wanted his yard labor back. At the bottom, everyone had signed his or her own name. Gretel's and Hannah's sloppy middle school print, his mom's loopy cursive, and his dad's chicken scratch signature that he used with his credit card. There was never any fear that someone would be able to forge it.

George found the handwritten letter to be very special. It also impressed upon him how different life was in the army, and how different he was right now compared to his former life. Nothing had changed at home. Meanwhile, he was living in tents fighting a war. Well, a paintball war. But still a war. This was so much more exciting than school. Even so, he still missed home.

"When will the mailman be back?" he asked Bernie.

"Not for a while."

"Is there another way I could send a letter?"

"If we get to a town you could mail it."

"When will that be?"

"Not for a while."

"Oh." Bernie was so helpful sometimes. Not.

Nevertheless, George began writing a letter that night, determined to have a good long one ready the next time they reached a post office or the mailman came along. He had not gotten very far before the Tattoo sounded early. By now he knew what that meant, and put the letter aside. He was in bed before the sweet strains of Taps floated across the camp and coaxed him to sleep. Tomorrow would be a big day. They *were* going in tomorrow, right?

Chapter XI

THE BUGLER SOUNDED REVEILLE bright and early. George dragged himself out of bed. It was still dark, but light enough to see.

He dressed quickly and hurried outside. Breakfast was already being made. It was a quick, cold meal of food that had been prepared the night before.

Ivy rallied up her platoon and gave them a pep talk. "We're going forward under air support and a heavy artillery creeping barrage. This whole thing is carefully planned and must be carefully executed.

"We'll advance slowly until our field artillery and machine guns are within range of the line, and then the artillery will stop. When they stop, we charge."

"That's it?" George asked.

"Yes. Go very light. Take everything out of your packs that you don't absolutely need, or leave them behind if you want. And bring the PIATs this time.

"Alright, guys, we can do this! It's their Seelow Heights, and once we defeat them there is nothing left between us and the rest of Stanislaus."

"What remains of it," someone said.

George ate breakfast, and by now the sun had fully risen. There was a tense atmosphere in the air. He saw a few small vehicles armed with some light weaponry move out of sight.

"Where are they going?" he asked Bernie.

"Reconnaissance," Bernie replied.

George again went over his equipment. There was his bayonet, wet and ready in its sheath; his refill paint bottle; his ammunition pods in his pod pack; as many grenades as he could carry; his canteen and one field ration; his entrenching tool; and, of course, his rifle.

Hearing the drone of engines, he looked up and saw planes coming. Some of them were bombers that returned shortly, while others were spotters that periodically came in and out of his view as they flew their observation pattern.

Then the heavy artillery near them opened fire, and the noise was tremendous. The air compressors roared and the guns boomed and echoed as they discharged their shells.

"Get up!" Ogden roared to his troops. "Stand by!"

George pulled his backpack on and went to stand by Bernie. The rest of the soldiers were all forming up, ready to go, checking their equipment.

"Man, this is huge," George said.

"This battle?" Bernie asked.

"Yeah, with the artillery and the tanks and airplanes and every-thing."

"Tame to what's going on in Reno right now."

George thought about that. Over there was a massive army with most of their support resources clashing into a huge city against another massive army. Tens of thousands of kids. There would be street-by-street fighting, hemmed and boxed in, trapped by the buildings and channeled down killing zones. Paint everywhere.

"Can they get into the buildings?" he asked.

"No," Bernie replied, "the people in Reno lock 'em out."

Just then there were shouts as some of the other kids in B Company hailed some other soldiers walking towards them from the direction of the enemy. As they drew near, George could see two boys, one of whom was carrying a PIAT.

"What are you doing?" someone asked.

"We were in one of those patrol cars," the boy with the PIAT answered, "and we got shot out by an anti-tank gun we didn't see until it was too late. Jay and Aaron were both killed, but we made a break and ran for it."

"Where'd you get that PIAT?" a girl asked.

"Oh, we had it in the car," the boy replied.

"You have a *cannon* and machine guns on that thing, why did you need to bring a PIAT with you?"

"I dunno. But hey, I brought it back."

"Can we have it?" George asked.

"Sure, you guys probably need it." The boy handed it over to the nearest B Company soldier. "So long," he said, and they headed off to find their unit. "Good luck!"

"Alright, move out!" Captain Ogden barked. "We're going! Get in formation!"

Immediately, B Company's four platoons were arranged into a loose line. Ogden was coming with them, and he stood well in the back with the radioman where he could see, command his troops, and stay out of the thick of it.

A and C Companies were arrayed to their left and right while D Company followed behind as a reserve to be committed wherever it was needed. The machine guns and field artillery of the support companies were spread out behind the infantry. Finally, several tanks were driven out in front to lead the assault.

"Forward!" the captains cried to their troops, and they began moving.

The tanks led the infantry who walked slowly enough that the field artillery could keep up with them. They closed in upon the Alamedan heavy artillery barrage falling before them, and when they got close, the barrage began moving towards the enemy. They followed behind it.

George walked onward at this agonizingly slow pace. The minutes dragged by as the bombardment rained before them. Most of these shells were either smoke shells or specially designed to emit a blast of air that would send up a cloud of dust. This partially obscured the advancing infantry to the enemy but also made George feel like he was walking blindly towards a demise he couldn't see, which was somewhat unnerving. Up until now, he had always been able to see what was going on. Well, except for the times he was pinned by enemy fire. Then he saw nothing but dirt.

Everyone was getting antsy. They marched closer and closer, catching glimpses of the enemy positions ahead through the smoke and dust. The cloud dissipated fairly quickly, but not as quickly as they were moving. George coughed. He could taste the dirt in his mouth. It wasn't pleasant.

"Pick it up!" Ogden yelled. "Move it!"

"He wants to be the first, doesn't he?" George asked Bernie.

"Yup."

Then suddenly there was a concussion as an enemy round landed nearby. It was quickly followed by another round landing somewhere else. They were finally in range of the Stanislausi's biggest guns, which apparently weren't that big. Enemy artillery fire was scattered and erratic, however, and it did not worry George. Except, of course, it would be nice to actually see the gun that was shooting at him. Though that would mean they could see him, too, and they wouldn't be missing.

George felt like a soldier on D-Day as his landing craft inched towards the shore under enemy fire, the walls too high to see over, machine gun fire drumming against the door. He was stuck here, hemmed in on all sides, walking towards paintball hell.

"Go!" Ogden yelled. "Move it!" He shoved a soldier at the back of his unit, who stumbled and darted out of reach. George shielded his eyes from the dust with his hand, put his head down, and pushed on. They moved faster, he thought, but the tank in front of them stayed in front.

Suddenly, a shell went off right before George. It was a dust shell and spouted a plume of dirt that choked him. He closed his eyes and ran on harder. Then another shell landed nearby and he thought he saw a pinkish flash.

The air was filled with smoke and dirt, and George could not see, but there was artillery landing everywhere. Apparently, they were now in range of more guns? Wait, no, it was their own artillery! The enemy wouldn't be firing dust shells. What the hell had happened?!

Ogden was shouting, but George wasn't paying any attention. He could hardly see a thing, or breathe. Normally, George wasn't claustrophobic, but this was unlike anything he had ever experienced before. The air pressed in around him, isolating him in a blinding box. Where was Ivy? Where was Bernie?

Gradually, the artillery seemed to be ahead of them, but they were still sitting in a cloud of dust and smoke. George wasn't moving, but instead was coughing and looking around at the brown trench coats and helmets around him.

Then he saw Bernie walking back towards them, appearing out of the cloud of dust and smoke like a specter, with pink flashes all around him. He was as calm and unfazed as ever, and George made towards him, relaxing as he saw Bernie's confidence.

Gradually, he could see what was going on around him. Their advance had stalled, their line was uneven, and Ogden was furiously bellowing orders, trying to get moving again. They did, keeping pace now with the artillery shells creeping before them.

Then George noticed a sound like an airplane, but different from the bombers or spotters he was used to hearing. It was growing louder and coming nearer, and it sounded like it was very low. He looked around, trying to locate the plane though the obscuring haze.

He saw it, appearing through the cloud way down at the other end of their line where C Company was, and banking to its right. It was a single-engine propeller craft with something hanging underneath it, like a plane he saw on a farm once. At any rate, it was not Alamedan.

As it turned perpendicular to their line of advance, a pink cloud appeared beneath the plane and fell towards the ground, towards the soldiers below. And it was coming after him.

"Crop duster!" someone screamed, and George got it. That pink cloud was paint.

There was yelling and screaming that drowned Ogden out and instantly their already-harried formation descended into utter chaos.

Kids ran everywhere, tripping and falling; the tank driver gunned his engine to get away; and the crop duster was coming down their line towards him — very, very fast.

George forgot everything else and ran for cover as fast as he could. There was a copse of trees and brush behind them, and he dove into it, scratching and cutting himself again. Someone jostled him, and someone else stepped on his arm. He winced. That would leave a mark.

Peering up through the haze, George saw Bernie running for cover too, calm and collected, and not at all slow. He was running almost peacefully. Then pink liquid paint rained from the sky and fell over Bernie as the noise of the crop duster's engines climaxed overhead in a deafening roar that made George's ears ring. He stared. Bernie was gone.

The roar passed from George's right ear to his left and faded. The plane turned off and flew a wide circle, coming around and making a pass above a tank. Then it came around again and made another pass, but this time it did not come back. The crop duster flew back to Stanislaus and was gone.

George got to his feet as others did likewise. What he saw before him was carnage. Paint was everywhere. It was a mess. They were scattered, turned about, and disorganized. Casualties did not seem to be high enough for what had just happened, but still, they were there.

George realized he was not carrying his rifle anymore. He took one at random from those left lying on the ground. Then he looked around — and stared at Bernie walking towards him. There was not a speck of paint on him.

"Bernie, what? How, I saw— you were right in the middle of it!"

"Nope," Bernie replied, "I was on the other side."

George stared for a moment and asked, "Where's Ivy?"

"I saw her run away. She should be fine."

Hearing familiar laughter, George turned and saw Jack and Ella striding along like it was a grand day.

"Boy, that plane sure had a big bladder," Jack was saying.

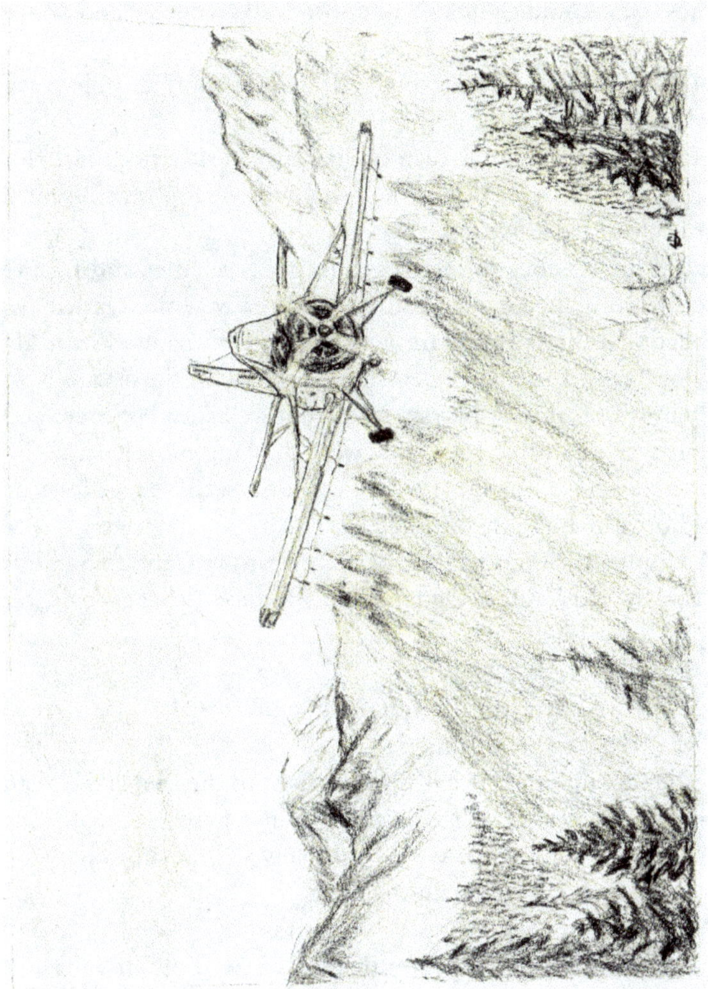

"Crop duster!"

"Yes but it couldn't hold it anymore," Ella replied, "and didn't make it to the potty."

"*We're* the potty," Jack explained, and they both doubled over laughing.

How those two could keep on like that in situations like this was beyond George, but even so he had to laugh at the joke. Bernie chuckled as well.

Everyone was beginning to group back together and restore a slight semblance of order to the company while Ogden demanded that they advance immediately. C Company was already moving again, and he was determined to stay in the lead.

By now the artillery barrage had crept well ahead of them and the air was clear, but they now were drawing more enemy fire from a defensive line George still couldn't see. Well, at least he could breathe now.

A Company began to turn back, retreating. Captain Sanders hurried over to Captain Ogden. "Phil," he said, "that crop duster will be back, we'd better get outta here. This is doomed to fail. We're already a mess."

"Maybe you are, but I'm not," Ogden retorted.

"Really? Look at your men."

"They are fine and we will take the fight to the enemy! You can be a blasted coward but I'm not going anywhere!"

"Philip, you and your entire company will be annihilated. I am not in a condition to support you."

"I don't need your support! Now scram!"

"Listen. You need to get your head screwed on straight and take responsibility for your soldiers," Sanders warned.

Just then a boy came running up to them, out of breath. "Captain Sanders, Sir," he panted, "Colonel Hoffman has ordered a withdrawal."

"See?" Sanders told Ogden. "Now you don't have a choice. Quit acting like an arrogant jerk and let's go! We're sitting here taking fire and you're acting like a five-year-old."

Ogden punched Sanders in the chest. Sanders stumbled back and brought his fists up, but did not return the blow.

"Fine, take the consequences of your stupidity," he said as he backed off from the fight. "I'm gonna do the best for my soldiers." With a final look, Captain Sanders marched back to his platoon.

Ogden was furious, but nevertheless he ordered that they advance to the rear.

"That's what the French say," a boy complained indignantly.

In a very short manner of time, they entered their camp much more quickly than they had left it. Their big assault had failed before it had hardly even begun. Many of the soldiers were angry.

"Ogden's a dumbass. Killing us with our own artillery," growled a veteran.

"Morons! They should have known about that blasted crop duster. Stupid!" another soldier raved.

"Can't we just shoot it down?" George asked Bernie.

"Nope. Not with paint."

"Well, what now?" George asked Ivy when he finally found her after getting back to camp.

"We'll have to wait and see," she replied.

Next morning George rolled out of bed to the sound of Reveille, wondering what would happen today. Also, he was filthy, and he couldn't bathe. It was a very uncomfortable feeling.

Breakfast was a proper meal of bacon and eggs on toast. For some reason the army didn't provide cereal or what might be considered normal breakfast foods.

George found Ivy after eating and asked her what the news was.

"I haven't heard anything. Ogden'll brief us eventually."

"What of our casualties?"

"What about them?"

"How many did we take?"

"Well... several."

"That's it? Just several?"

Ivy shrugged. "That's how I understand it. C Company had it the worst because they were attacked first. We had time to get outta the way. A Company fared the best."

George waited, but nothing happened. The day went by quietly, until he heard a familiar plane engine. This time everyone spotted the crop duster coming a long ways off and there was a scramble for cover.

A minute later when George peeked out the flaps of his tent, there was not a kid to be seen in the open. The crop duster made several passes over their camp, raining paint all over it, but everyone was safely holed up.

After it left, they all came out and surveyed the mess. Paint galore, everywhere, but fortunately no one had been hit. George got to work cleaning it up, mixing dirt in with the paint on the ground and throwing shovelfuls of dirt over the paint on their tents. The trucks were hosed off only as much as was needed. Water in a mobile army camp was not an infinite resource.

Everyone continued recovering from the previous day's engagement after cleaning up their camp, but it did not take long for the crop duster to reappear. It attacked another unit, however, and not B Company.

The plane made regular runs, although apparently the Stanislausi only had the one and were working it hard. George was aghast that there was literally nothing they could do about it. It was free to rampage about unopposed, slaughtering their soldiers, while they stood by idly and watched.

"Our bombers do the same to them," Bernie pointed out.

Eventually, it returned to attack their camp again. They scrambled for cover, it made a few passes, and when it flew off they all came out and started cleaning up again. George sighed. Time to do the job all over again because the enemy had just undone it. Though, that was the point, he knew.

Suddenly, the crop duster veered around and came bearing back down on them. There was screaming and yelling and George dived into the nearest tent. He did not come out until the plane was well away from them.

"Have you heard anything yet, Ivy?" George asked her later.

"Yes. We will be delayed two more days."

"We're not attacking tomorrow?"

"Nope. They need to bring in more smoke shells for the artillery."

"Why would that take so long?"

"It's a less-common round, not used so much, so it's not as readily available. We expended most of our stock yesterday."

The conversation ended there as the crop duster was seen returning, and everyone scattered to their tents. It attacked a different target, however, but still they remained undercover until it was gone.

Overnight George woke up to another crop duster attack, but he stayed in bed and went back to sleep. Only one more day of this, he hoped.

Next morning George's first activity after getting dressed was to clean up the paint the crop duster had sprayed overnight. It had now dried, which made it less dangerous but also a lot harder to clean. Water had to be used to dissolve it.

Breakfast was stew this time, consisting of rice, beans, canned vegetables, and dried beef. The cook had made it too spicy, eliciting many complaints from the kids. George tolerated the heat but didn't like it. At the same time, it was much more flavorful than the bland lunches at his school.

There were no more crop duster attacks on their camp. Apparently, the enemy had deemed this pointless because everyone had plenty of time to run for cover, so they had decided to let the Alamedans make the next move.

"They're hoping we'll renew the advance," said a veteran, "so they can catch us out in the open again."

"At least the colonel is smarter than that."

"I don't think Ogden would be if he were making the decisions."

"Oh, we'd all be dead a long time ago if he was colonel."

The Alamedan Air Force continued bombing the Raymond line. There were frequent flights of sometimes several aircraft passing by overhead. George took very little notice of them at this point. It was a familiar sight.

The troops had the day off and George played more poker with Jack and Ella, winning a few hands but losing the game. He still didn't mind, though.

Then there was activity around B Company. Supply trucks passed them and later returned going back, but there was no more news on the current situation. George was bored. It was getting late.

"George, you have sentry duty tonight," Ivy said. "The third shift." She showed him the dugout he would be sitting in.

George went to bed that night as Taps sounded, wondering what tomorrow would bring. He was also annoyed at having to do sentry duty. Why? He wanted to sleep. Why him? Why couldn't someone else do it? Why couldn't he do the first shift?

At three in the morning he was roused from his slumber by the sleepy-eyed, less-than-cheerful boy who had taken the second shift. Neither of them was in a good mood. George grumpily hauled himself over to the dugout and sat down by himself.

He wanted to sleep. Besides, this was boring. He made himself comfortable in the dugout where he could see the area he was supposed to be watching. The fresh dirt was actually quite comfortable. He yawned. Stupid sentry watch. The enemy was far away, anyhow. They wouldn't be coming this night.

"George!" Someone was calling his name. Groggily he came to consciousness and opened his eyes. There was Ivy glaring at him.

"What the hell do you think you're doing?!" she yelled. "Sleeping on the job!"

George stumbled to his feet, rubbing his eyes. "I'm— I'm, sorry. But nothing happened."

"Nothing happened this time! We could have all been murdered in our sleep and it would have been your fault!" She softened. "I have to take you to the captain."

George followed her glumly. Boy, he was really in for hell now. He had screwed up very badly this time. Finally, he followed Ivy into the command tent.

"Captain Ogden, he was caught sleeping on sentry duty," she said, and made her exit.

"You slept on sentry duty?!" Ogden roared. "Idiot! You're an incompetent moron! Were you trying to get me killed?"

"No, sir," George muttered, head down, hands in pockets. Oh, woe was he.

"I could court-martial you for this! But since I'm such a generous officer I will only make you go without meals until dinnertime. But don't *ever* do it again. And if I find out you ate anyway... You put me at risk with your stupidity. Now get outta here, I'm busy. Stupid private."

George needed no second warning and was gone. He slumped around, mopey. He had half-assed his job again. This time nothing had happened, but he had been caught. And something very bad could have happened, much worse than what had happened when he wasn't caught.

George made himself scarce that day as much as he could. He stayed around the perimeter, sitting in dugouts and just thinking when he wasn't busy. Ivy kept fetching him for various work details. It seemed like he was assigned to every menial task possible.

"George!" Ivy said with exasperation as she peered down into the dugout where he was crouched for the fourth time that day. "If you're going to hide and feel sorry for yourself every time you finish a job, at least do it in the same place so I can find you without walking around the whole perimeter."

George grunted. "Okay." His stomach gnawed at him. Why did Ogden have to choose no food of all possible punishments? He wasn't a ten-year-old who stood in the corner or skipped dinner anymore.

"Look," Ivy said, "just cooperate with me, and I'll tell the captain tonight that you've been amply punished and worked very hard."

"Alright."

George was ravenous for dinner when dinner finally came. Thankfully, no one said anything when all of a sudden he showed up for his first meal of the day. He avoided eye contact and everyone ignored him. That night he slipped off to bed before everyone else.

Early the next morning, George awoke to Reveille and knew that today was the day they finished what they had started. Breakfast was quick and simple, the company assembled, and they once more set off for the Raymond Line.

The advance under the creeping artillery barrage was another tense affair as the minutes dragged by agonizingly slow. They came in range of the Stanislausi's largest guns and another ineffective shelling began. George marched on.

More enemy guns opened fire, falling short of them. George envied the soldiers walking behind the tank. They had excellent cover. The problem was there weren't enough tanks for everyone.

A small shell landed close by and took out a girl. George gripped his rifle and marched on, one slow step after the next, everything in front of him obscured by a cloud of dust and smoke.

"Fix bayonets!" Ogden ordered. That meant they were getting close. Bayonets were never fixed until the last moment to keep the paint fresh. So they were already farther than last time. George pulled his bayonet from its sheath and firmly attached it to the socket on the front of his rifle as he walked.

Then he realized that the field artillery and machine guns had stopped advancing and were being left behind. The heavy artillery bombardment creeping before them jumped ahead. The tanks began firing. The field artillery began firing. This was it. Do or die.

There was a shriek as Ogden blew on his whistle as hard as he could blow. Knowing the signal, George joined everyone else in a pell-mell, head-on assault against the Raymond Line. He ran for everything he was worth blindly into the haze. Everyone else ran around him. Then the cloud of dust and smoke parted as he burst through it and all hell broke loose.

"*Pugna Ut Vincas!*" the Alamedans yelled. "*Pugna Ut Vincas!*"

Before George the ground sloped upward into a hill or a shallow ridge at the foot of the mountains. It was infested with Stanislausi positions. Machine guns sent paintballs whizzing past George and shells began falling. As the bombardment stopped, the enemy defenders rushed out of their cover to man their defenses.

The Alamedan tanks drove right on up into the fray, bringing their machine guns and cannons to point-blank range. An anti-tank shell struck the side of one of them with a bang and exploded, leaving paint dripping down the side but failing to take out any of the crew. The tank's cannon turned around to return fire while its machine guns engaged other targets.

George fired from the hip as he ran and his squad broke off, aiming for a smaller nest. He dodged paintballs behind trees as the enemy machine gunner fired and riflemen sniped. Bernie sought cover where he readied a grenade and lobbed it into the nest.

It went off with a bang, spraying paint, and he leapt up over into the nest, George right behind him. They shot a few kids at point blank, unsure who was and wasn't a casualty because no one had time to put on his casualty shawl, then charged with bayonets.

A boy in front of George fired multiple times, shooting the girl to George's left. George closed to contact in a single stride and jammed his bayonet into the boy's stomach. The liquid paint was squeezed out of the foam and smeared onto his shirt.

"Not so hard," he grunted, bent over and holding his stomach.

Just like that the machine gun nest was empty. Seeing another, they charged it from the side and emptied it with rifle fire and bayonets. Above that was a bunker made of plywood, logs, and tarps. It contained an artillery gun and two machine guns.

George followed Bernie as they maneuvered around its front, but ran into other nests and bunkers and dugouts that blocked their way. Some of them seemed to have tunnels that went back into the hillside.

The Stanislausi machine gunner cut down Alamedans trying to advance upon him. George shot him from the side and ran for his position, jumping in and shooting another boy.

A Stanislausi boy came at him with a rifle but George jumped in close and got him with his bayonet first. Then Bernie was there and they finished off two more boys with paintballs.

Their BAR gunner led them against a large, forbidding bunker, blasting its occupants with automatic fire. They fired back and shot him. Another Alamedan picked up his BAR rifle and emptied the rest of its hopper into the bunker. Then she sought cover to reload it.

Bernie took his bayonet off his rifle, slung his rifle on his back, and pulled a pistol from his backpack.

"Where'd you get that?" George asked.

"I had it."

George threw a grenade into the bunker, and upon its concussion, he and Bernie charged. Bernie entered first, using his pistol in one hand and his bayonet like a knife in his other hand.

George followed and came to with a boy. He dodged his fire and jabbed him with a bayonet. Then he blocked another attack with his rifle and swung hard, knocking the boy to the ground where Bernie shot him with his pistol.

Then something hit George hard in the helmet like an explosion in his head. He toppled over, dazed, stars flashing before his eyes. Ugh, ow. Good thing for his helmet. Grunting and stumbling to his feet and grimacing from the blow to the head, he saw Bernie grappling with his assailant. George grabbed the boy from behind and pulled him to the ground, limbs failing violently. Bernie quickly snatched up his pistol and shot the boy.

All around was savage hand-to-hand fighting. Pistols and rifles, bayonets, rifles used as clubs, sticks and branches. George grabbed his rifle and shot deeper into the bunker, rounded a corner, and encountered three more enemy soldiers.

He shot two as he ran forward and went to bayonet the third, but the boy shoved his rifle aside with one hand and grabbed him with the other. As George collided he turned, shoving his shoulder into the boy. They crashed into the wall and fell to the floor, rolling and shoving, jarring a fresh resurgence of pain in George's head again.

Then he took a foot to his stomach and gasped, the wind knocked out of him. Next his opponent pinched him hard in the nipple. George gasped and contorted. Oh, hell! Hell! That hurt! Angrily he lashed out and kicked himself free. The boy jumped at him again but met George's bayonet.

George paused, panting, and looked around at the three Stanislausi he had killed. One of them extended a hand.

"Nice job. I know this is the end for us. It's not because we were poor fighters."

George nodded and shook the hand offered to him, rubbing his left nipple. He took his bayonet off to wet it again in its sheath. "Why don't you surrender then?"

"It's paintball. Fight to the death!"

With a quick salute, George ran back around the corner. Bernie was reloading his pistol. Another girl was reloading her hopper. George ran to the mouth of the bunker and was shot at by a BAR gunner.

"Hey!" he yelled, ducking.

The BAR gunner realized he was an Alamedan and stopped shooting at him. "Sorry!" he yelled, and left to find another target.

George looked around and saw several Stanislausi reoccupying the machine gun nest below him. Grabbing the enemy machine gun still in the bunker, he cut them all down before they could fire a shot. He tried to engage another target, but the machine gun ran out of paintballs and he didn't know how to reload it.

Bernie was ready, so they climbed out and joined a random group of soldiers. Ahead was another bunker, firing vehemently. An artillery shell silenced its machine gunner, and everyone took the opportunity to charge. Another Stanislausi swiftly took over the weapon, however, and mowed down several Alamedans in the front of the charge. George and the rest of them dove for cover.

Another shell hit the bunker, silencing the machine gunner for a second time, and they charged again. George got there right as a third Stanislausi grabbed the machine gun. She blasted an Alamedan point-blank before Bernie shot her with his pistol.

He fired several shots to cover George as he climbed inside the bunker and finished off its last defender with his bayonet. Then another girl turned the corner from a tunnel in the back of the bunker. As she did, Bernie faced her and pulled the trigger. There was a click, and nothing happened.

Acting quickly, he dove to the ground as she fired, missing him and almost hitting George instead. Then Bernie sprang forward like a cat and was at her with his hand-held bayonet. She quietly put her casualty shawl on.

"That was close," George said.

"Yup," Bernie replied as he reloaded his pistol's magazine. George refilled his hopper, replaced his cartridge, and checked to make sure the recesses of the bunker were empty. They were.

Outside the bunker, he saw three Stanislausi charge two Alamedans. The five of them rolled down the hillside into trees and rocks, brawling furiously and bashing into everything in their path.

Everyone ready, they exited the bunker. Ahead of it was an Alamedan tank sitting dead where all of its crew had been knocked out. Using it as cover, George and Bernie advanced. A boy and a girl climbed aboard and manned its cannon and machine gun. The boy was shot by a Stanislausi rifleman.

George saw Jack and Ella running like madmen, grinning and whooping and hollering. They plowed into a bunker head on, crashing and thrashing into its occupants. There was a furious swinging and battering. A Stanislausi boy flipped headfirst out of the bunker and into a prickly bush with a yell. Then Jack and Ella jumped out and made for the next bunker.

Another enemy soldier came out from the depths of the bunker and fired after them. He missed and was hit by a paintball fired from somewhere else.

To his right, George saw Ivy, but he and Bernie turned left to engage a dugout. They took it and huddled there until other Alamedans silenced the machine gun that was pinning them.

Charging on, they grappled hand-to-hand, bitterly wresting the enemy's defenses one piece at a time. All around was chaotic, violent combat, but the Alamedans were triumphing and over-whelming the enemy.

Seeing that they were overrun, a platoon of Stanislausi soldiers came out of their cover. Screaming, "Banzai!" they charged the enemy with weapons blazing. "Tally Ho!"

Frantically, the Alamedans turned to face them, firing furi-ously. Some of the suicide chargers reached to bayonet range, but most were shot before that. George had never seen such an intense close-range deadly battle as that banzai charge. It had succeeded in killing several Alamedans. Cavalry troopers were now throwing themselves into the fray as well where they were vulnerable at close quarters among the rough terrain.

George fought on, helping to encircle existing enemy positions and laying fire on them from behind when possible, or getting stuck in with bayonets. He faced another banzai charge and slaughtered his attackers with another captured machine gun.

"Man, this is like the PTO in World War Two!" someone exclaimed.

"Hell no," George replied, "this is only paintball."

The fight went on, but the enemy was wearing down. So was the day, but as the sun sank low, the Alamedans held most of their objectives. George and Bernie found a dugout to spend the night in.

George devoured his field ration and found he was still very hun-gry. He had fought hard all day and burned a lot of calories. The unflappable Bernie had not gotten lunch and was hungry as well. Both of them were bruised and sore, and George's nipple was a purple lump. His head still throbbed from that blow. Man, what had hit him? Good thing for his helmet. This was one crazy battle.

"Hey, guys," said a girl with them, "food!" She had found a stash left by the Stanislausi in the depths of the bunker, which they feasted upon. Finally, George quenched the gnawing in his stomach.

It grew dark. From time to time they still heard the sounds of fighting, but the action had mostly died down. Then a boy stuck his rifle in their dugout. He lowered it when he saw who they were.

"This just in," he said excitedly, "breaking news: Stanislaus capitulates!"

"What?" George said, sitting up.

"Stanislaus has surrendered to join the Empire." Then the boy dashed away.

"Wait, but, I thought that didn't happen?"

An older girl spoke up. "It often doesn't," she said, "but since the Revolution there has been a change. Countries are more willing to join our Empire because they get representation and a say in the Parliament. Allies, now, not subjects."

"Members," Bernie corrected her.

"Revolution? There was a civil war?" George asked.

"Yes, Alameda used to have an emperor who was like a dictator," the girl explained. "There was a civil war that lasted for six months. The emperor was deposed."

"But we still have an emperor."

"They installed a new one with a constitution and a parliament. So now we have a republican empire that operates under a constitution."

"Huh," George said. "That's a strange government."

Several minutes later, three Stanislausi soldiers appeared at their bunker. The Alamedans scrambled to arms, but the enemy held up their hands.

"Our nation has surrendered," they said. "So, so do we. We want a comfortable place to sleep and something to eat."

"Then I'll shoot you and you can go home," George offered.

"No, we want to stay. We want to join Alameda."

George cocked his head. "Really?"

"If you can't beat 'em, join 'em."

"This isn't a trick?"

"On my word and honor, it isn't." The other two nodded.

George looked at Bernie. Bernie nodded. "For the night."

"Alright," George said, "come in. One at a time. I'll stand guard, you pat them down," he told his comrades.

"Just to let you know," one of the Stanislausi said as the Alamedans felt over him for any hidden surprises, "some of the others out there are still feeling very belligerent. You might want to set a guard."

It was agreed that they would rotate shifts of one standing watch at the entrance to the bunker, though it was also agreed that the Alamedans would do all the watching, and that watching would include keeping an eye on their new companions overnight. Drawing sticks, George got out of sentry duty entirely, much to his relief, and settled down to a restful night. Oh, how good sleep felt after such a long, hard day of intense physical combat.

Chapter XII

Next morning they awoke and breakfasted on the rations they had found in the bunker. Then George climbed out to see what was going on. His nipple was still tender, but felt better already. His head was still heavy and sore as well, but the throbbing pain was gone.

B Company was reorganizing and counting its losses. Casualties had been extremely heavy. Bruises, cuts, and scrapes were all being treated. Very few of the Stanislausi soldiers, however, had survived until morning. Most had given up their lost cause after having one good ferocious last stand to go down in history. Once they had lost, however, they gave in pretty easily.

Some die-hards, however, would not, and both Alamedans and ex-Stanislausi were shot during the hours spent combing the Raymond Line for remaining combatants.

George regrouped with Ivy and his platoon, which was quite small by now. Ogden was impatient to move on, however.

"Why?" George asked. "I thought we were done." Ivy just shrugged. "Also, she wants to come with us," George said, gesturing at the ex-Stanislausi girl with them.

"No way. She was just our enemy. You trust her?"

"They helped us comb the area," Bernie said.

"No," Ivy said. "They have to go report to an Alamedan office for reassignment where they'll be assigned safe jobs until they can be trusted in battle."

"That's boring," complained the girl. "We want to go on fighting."

"Sorry, but that's the way it works. We have to be cautious. For all we know you'll turn on us in the first battle. I don't want to ruin our company like that."

"You've taken heavy casualties," the girl persisted. "You need us to augment your numbers or your unit will be recalled eventually." Ivy stood silent, thinking.

"She has a point," Bernie said.

"Do you trust her?" Ivy looked him in the eye.

"Yup." He looked right back.

After a long minute of silence, Ivy dipped her head in consent. "Alright. I will see what I can do. At the very least you'll need Alamedan coats."

"I'll do it," the girl volunteered. "Where's your officer?"

"No, no, don't talk to Ogden," Ivy said quickly, "bad idea. I'll go speak to his staff. How many of you are there?"

"About forty of us." Ivy nodded and left. "Are you guys not allowed to talk to your officers?" the girl asked.

"No, no," George said. "Just, Captain Ogden is..."

"Difficult," Bernie finished for him.

"Yeah."

"Is that normal?"

"Nope."

"Yeah, he'd probably think it was a trick to assassinate him," George added.

Ivy returned in a few minutes. "All done," she said. "They'll send some uniforms up. Oh, also, apparently there are some Alpine rebels that refuse to surrender, and that's why Ogden is in a hurry to move on."

"That doesn't surprise me," said the girl.

"Why not?" George asked.

"They were always very... independent. By the way, I'm Cindy." She shook hands with the others.

"Bernie."

"George."

"Sergeant Ivy."

Pretty soon they got moving. B Company marched for hours. George was still tired after exerting himself in yesterday's battle. Finally, they stopped.

"Okay, this is where the rebels are," Ivy informed everyone.

George looked around. "Like, where? I don't see anyone."

"We have to find them." She gestured vaguely. "They're somewhere around here."

George shrugged and jettisoned his heavy backpack. Prepared for another battle, everyone spread out and began cautiously combing through the woods. They were now in mountainous terrain, and the trees were a lot thinner.

"Does it feel weird that you're attacking your own rebels?" George asked Cindy.

She chuckled. "Not the Alpines."

After twenty minutes of not seeing anything, George started to get bored. He was staring absently at a tree in front of him as he walked forward when, in his peripheral vision, he saw Bernie stop, raise his rifle, and fire a shot.

George snapped back into reality and peeled his eyes for the enemy soldiers. He saw them coming through the woods. Instead of being Stanislausi infantry, they had more variant, nondescript uniforms. In some cases, "uniform" seemed like a generous word. One boy didn't even have a helmet! Many of them were dressed in local vegetation, which made good camouflage, except for the fact that bushes didn't walk.

Occasionally, there was a rebel on horseback, but as soon as one got close, he became everybody's target. It reminded George of a submarine in World of Warships that snuck into the middle of the enemy fleet and then got detected. Instant death.

The Alamedans aggressively drove forward against these rebels, who offered little resistance, conducting a fighting retreat. They would dart in, fire a few shots, and dart out, skirmish style.

"Ha-ha! Gotcha!" Cindy yelled as one of the rebels put on his casualty shawl. He gave her a dirty look and disappeared.

"*Pine* for your lost glory, Al*pines*," Ella jeered.

Jack laughed. "Your Alpine shall soon be *mine*-mine!" Ivy shook her head.

"Are they normally like that?" Cindy asked.

"This is mild," George replied.

Skirmishing continued as they pursued the rebels until George saw a series of fortifications. It was their own defensive line, complete with a few scattered dugouts and nests for whatever equipment the rebels could get. George was ready. This would be easy compared to what he had done yesterday.

"*Pugna Ut Vincas!*" He charged into a crude bunker with Bernie. It was made of sticks and tarps and collapsed on its occupants as they tried to enter.

"Seriously?" George said. "We just knocked this thing down charging into it."

"Stops the paintballs," Bernie replied.

"Hey, you under there!" George yelled at the rebels struggling under the tarp. "Surrender!"

"No!" "Never!" "Death to Alameda!" "To hell with you!" they shouted back from underneath.

"Come on, guys," Cindy said. "I was at the Raymond Line, but I joined them. They're very nice, actually."

The tarp convulsed violently. "Traitor!" "Coward!" "I'll kill you!" "To hell with you too!"

"I think there are four people in there," Bernie said.

"Fine then." George prepared a grenade, lifted the corner of the tarp, and chucked it under. It went off and was accompanied by screams and shouting as the rebels flung the tarp aside and staggered out of what had been their bunker, splattered with paint. There were four of them.

"Blast it!" one of the boys spat. "Alamedan dogs, imperialist colonizers! I will never fight for you! I will go on fighting for your enemies until you are destroyed!"

"I told you these bunkers were a stupid idea!" one of the girls yelled at him. "We should have stuck to guerrilla warfare!"

"Shut up!"

"You're an idiot!"

The Alpines continued to throw their temper tantrums and bicker as George walked away. Man, these kids were a piece of work. He could tell why Cindy wasn't very fond of them. A few more bunkers were quickly neutralized, and the remaining rebels abandoned the defense and fled.

As they moved on, George encountered more guerrilla warriors. They climbed trees and sniped at the Alamedans and ex-Stanislausi from above, or charged in a quick attack before retreating just as quickly. They seemed to know the terrain like the back of their hands and had a small ambush waiting for B Company over every ridge, in every valley, around every corner.

The Alamedans quickly adapted to using their BAR rifles to pummel the surprise attacks wherever they appeared. This was effective in countering the rebels, who had little more than regular guns and never attacked with more than a handful of troops at a time.

Try as they might, however, they could not bring the rebels to a pitched battle and destroy them. Sure, they could go anywhere they wanted to, but they were constantly being harassed. The BAR gunners, used as point defense, had a low survival rate during those hours. Eventually, as they moved forward, they seemed to leave the rebels behind.

"Occupation forces will deal with them," Ivy said.

As the rebels disappeared, B Company picked up the pace. George marched on for hours. He had perfected the marching technique out of necessity and vastly increased his endurance. They encountered no more enemy soldiers, however.

"Where are we going?" Cindy asked.

"I'll bet you anything," Ivy replied, "that Ogden wants to be the first to cross the state line."

"I mean, that's pretty cool," Cindy replied.

"Well... you don't know Ogden," George said.

"But you'll learn," Bernie added optimistically.

One brief break was taken, and they marched on. George was exhausted, and hungry again; but, if the truth was told, he did want to be one of the first across the state line. Quite the bragging rights.

"How far do we have to go before we get to Nevada?" George asked.

"We just have to cross the Sierra Nevada," Bernie replied.

George stared at him. "We're crossing the Sierra Nevada?"

"Yup."

"Like, we're just going to march across the mountains?"

"Nope."

Ivy joined the conversation. "We're going to cross the mountains to Route 89, and then take the road into Nevada. But keep an eye out for any more belligerents."

George slung his rifle over his shoulder and ate a field ration as he marched. Mount Raymond faded into the distance behind them and the snow-covered peaks of the Sierra Nevada rose above them. They stuck to walking in the valleys where green fields interspersed pine forests.

B Company wound its way onward through the mountains. To George they seemed to be going random directions, but he knew Ogden was guiding them with some sort of GPS device. At least he hoped he was.

Eventually, they came down out of the mountains and George saw the interchange between Routes 4 and 89. There they stopped for a lunch break, but Ogden didn't wait long before rallying the company to keep marching.

This time they stuck to the road, marching along the shoulder through the pass in the mountains. The sun marched on above them and George's feet grew very sore. He felt like Ogden was trying to do another Truscott Trot. How much longer did they have to go? From Route 89 they turned on to Interstate 395 and kept marching.

Finally, as they marched along the edge of Topaz Lake that bordered the road, George saw a sign that read, "Welcome to NEVADA." Finally! There was the border! At the sight of it, everyone perked up and began to move a little quicker.

"Halt!" Ogden shouted, jumping down from his HQ truck. "I said *halt*!" he roared. Slowly, the infantry came to a stop and Ogden ran on ahead.

"Cheater!" Jack said.

"Sh-h!" Ivy hissed.

Ogden became the first of George's unit to set foot past the sign. He stopped, and everyone stood there and watched as Ogden stood still and did nothing. Then, slowly, he turned around, and for once in his life he was smiling.

"Welcome to Nevada, boys!" he yelled and threw his helmet in the air. George cheered and sent his helmet airborne with all the others. With cries of "*Pugna Ut Vincas*!" everyone dashed forward across the line.

"Hey, what about the girls?" Cindy complained.

George retrieved his helmet, which now had a dent in it. Wasn't it hard plastic? Anyhow, good, it would make a nice souvenir of this day. Finally, after days and days, Stanislaus was defeated and George stood with both feet on Nevadan soil. He had made it. He had screwed up the whole way, but he had made it.

Jack ran on twenty more yards and shouted, "I'm the first across the border!"

"No, *I* was!" shouted back Ogden, the smile vanishing from his face. "I passed the sign first!"

"The sign is in the wrong place!" Jack yelled back. "The pavement changes here, so the border is actually over here!"

"Shut up!" Ogden roared back. "You're wrong! Stupid private," he muttered, his cheerfulness gone. He remounted his truck and began the march again. George was in too good of spirits to really care and marched with a new spring in his step. They must be close to their camp, anyway. It was getting very late.

Finally, they arrived at the town of Gardnerville and set up a camp in a field opposite the Best Western Topaz Lake Inn, on the other side of Interstate 395. George longed for a nice hotel room and soft comfy bed, but at best he would have to pay for it himself, which was well beyond his finances.

"Welcome to Nevada, boys!"

"Ivy, can we go swim in the lake?" Jack asked.

"Yeah, that'd be fun!" said Ella. "Please?"

"No, it's getting dark. Besides, you don't have bathing suits."

"Actually I brought my swimming trunks," Jack said.

"So did I," Ella added.

Ivy stared at them. "Seriously? Who does that?"

"We do," Ella said.

"I like swimming," added Jack.

"Me too," said Ella.

Ivy sighed. "Maybe tomorrow if we don't rush off right away. As for tonight, get some firewood. Ogden ordered the cooks to prepare a special celebration meal."

George grinned. He didn't know what it was going to be, but it sure sounded good. A real feast to break up the monotony of the army diet — stew, stew, stew. Not that he didn't like stew, but once he got home he didn't want to eat stew for a month! Yeah, home. Wouldn't it be nice if his family was here to celebrate with him.

Pretty soon dinner was served out. To George's disappointment, it turned out to be more stew. But upon taking his first bite, he found that it was a rich tomato soup full of meat. It was delicious. There was also rice to go with it, and poached eggs, and bread, as usual. Ogden had also acquired plenty of soda to go around from the supermarket in Gardnerville.

Cindy raised a bottle of root beer. "To Alameda!"

"To Alameda!" they all chorused, raising their drinks.

"To B Company and the 636th!" Ivy added.

"Bottoms up!" called Ella, setting the example with a hearty draught.

Jack took a slice of bread and heaped his tomato stew on it. "You know what this is?" he asked. Ivy rolled her eyes. "Celebratory stool on a shingle!" Jack answered his own question. "Mm-mm. This party poop is the best-tasting poop I've ever had."

"You know, Jack," Ivy said, "it stopped being funny a long time ago."

"*I* think it's funny," Jack replied.

"But we don't."

"It's kinda funny," Cindy said.

"You haven't had time to get tired of it yet," Ivy explained.

"You're just bad-tasting party poop, you party pooper," Ella retorted. Everyone busted up laughing, and even Ivy failed to smother a smile.

The banter was interrupted when someone hailed them from afar off. George looked around for the origin of the voice and saw approximately a dozen kids walking towards them, well armed. They were hard to see in the dark because they were dressed all in black. They even had black hair.

All that seemed suspicious to George. They looked like ninja assassins with their black uniforms and black weapons and black everything. He picked up his rifle and looked around to see what the others thought.

"Who's that?" asked Cindy.

"Dunno," Ivy said, "but if they were going to attack us they wouldn't hail us like that."

"Could be a trick," George said. The black-clad ninjas came closer as he watched.

"Pretty daft trick," Ivy replied.

Then one of the ninjas raised an arm and shouted, "*Pugna Ut Vincas!*" Immediately Ivy got to her feet, raised an arm, and return the salute. Everyone else stood up as well.

"Don't get trigger happy," Ivy said.

The ninjas walked right up to them, and a girl in an officer's uniform stepped up to Ivy and extended a hand. "Captain Zara Fowler, 8th FANTOM Company."

Ivy broke into a grin and shook the hand. "I thought you might be. Just wasn't sure."

"Can't blame you," Zara said. "We're starving."

"Here, we've got room for a few," Ivy said.

Three of the ninjas sat down and received generous portions of food. The rest of them dispersed among other campfires to get their meals. George was very confused. What was a phantom company? Scare-tactic soldiers who dressed up as ghosts for infiltration? They certainly looked like phantoms. Ninja phantoms. Ghosts in the night. He shivered, glanced around at the darkness, and scooted closer to the fire.

No one said much while dinner was being eaten, but when the bowls had been licked clean and everyone was reclining before the fire and sipping on a can of soda, Cindy voiced his thoughts.

"What did you say your rank was?" she asked Zara.

"Captain in the 8th FANTOM Company."

"What's that?" George asked.

Zara looked at him. "You haven't heard of us?"

"He probably slept through Alamedan history at boot camp like I did," Jack said.

"I did not!" George replied. "I like history. They never talked about any ghost companies."

"Really?" Ivy said. "They should have."

"Well they didn't."

"Or you slept through it," Jack persisted.

Zara chuckled. "That's okay; I get to make a first impression. We're the special forces branch of the army and the brainchild of General Halsted. He wanted his own Army Rangers, so he created the FANTOM Corp."

"But why phantoms?" George asked.

"It's spelled F-A-N-T-O-M and it's an acronym."

"What does it stand for?" George asked.

Zara grinned sheepishly. "I don't remember. The general loves his acronyms. That and annoying Latin mottoes. Doesn't matter anyway."

"And dairy cows," said the girl next to Zara." All three of them giggled.

"What?" George asked.

"N-never mind," Zara chuckled.

"What's your motto?" Cindy asked.

"*Celeres Silentes Funesti*. But we pronounce it different every time." Everyone laughed.

"What does it mean?" George asked.

"Swift, Silent, and Deadly."

"Technically there's no *and*," the other FANTOM girl pointed out.

"How many FANTOMs are there?" Cindy asked.

"Around two thousand," Zara said with pride. "There was only one batch of recruits ever taken, and we've stayed pretty consistent in numbers ever since. But the commander told me he was planning on expanding the corp."

"You're training new FANTOMs?" Bernie asked keenly.

"Yup. Not me specifically, but we're going to grow our numbers."

"You've met Commander Cooper?" Jack asked excitedly.

"I have!" Zara said with a smile. "I know him personally. He's..."

"Intense?" suggested the FANTOM next to Zara.

"He's driven and a patriot—" Zara continued.

"That's an understatement," the other girl interrupted.

"—And he looks out for the rest of us," Zara finished. "Once he sets his mind on something, he doesn't stop."

"Is it true that he once pulled a gun on General Halsted?" Jack asked.

Zara burst out laughing. "He got into a disagreement with the general on... on a matter of some import. Frankly it's a miracle he didn't have him court-martialed. That was in Aldemont, where we first saw action. Our trial by fire."

"I thought Aldemont was Alameda's navy," Cindy said.

"That's... not... how it works," said Ivy, "but they weren't always our ally. General Halsted invaded the island and tried to conquer it, but King Adrian fought him to a standstill. Then a large Russian fleet arrived from across the ocean, first taking the Aleutians, so they allied to defeat it, and they became great friends. Aldemont has been our ally ever since. And we have our *own* navy, thank you very much. Theirs is just, better."

"They really need to fix this deficiency in history," Zara said.

George felt a tap on his shoulder and looked over to see Bernie offering black licorice from a tub. He took a piece. It had been a while since he had last had any candy. "Where'd you get that?" he asked.

"I had it," Bernie replied as the tub went around the campfire. George shook his head. Bernie always surprised him.

"Black licorice, my favorite!" Zara nearly squealed. For a few minutes there was silence as everyone sucked on their licorice. Jack and Ella gobbled theirs down and generously helped themselves to more.

"Why are you here?" Bernie asked Zara.

"We were returning from a mission elsewhere when high command sent out an urgent request for an assault on Alpine County Airport to disable Stanislaus' crop dusters. We volunteered."

"Oh, that was you?" Cindy said. "I wondered what happened to our air force. Those planes were our secret weapon."

Zara raised an eyebrow and squinted at Cindy. "'Our'?"

"She was a Stanislausi at the Raymond Line," Ivy said. "Somehow we let a bunch of them replace all of our soldiers that *they* killed."

Cindy shrugged. "You guys won. What else was I gonna do?"

"Banzai like the rest of your buddies," Jack said.

"Or join the Alpine rebels," Ella added.

"No thanks," said Cindy.

Zara chuckled. "Well, welcome aboard. I should have noticed that under your coat your uniform was different."

"It's dark," Cindy said.

"Stanislaus surrendered the day we took their Seelow Heights," Ivy said.

"Really?" Zara was surprised. "That's news to me."

"You took out the crop dusters?" Bernie regrouped the conversation.

"Yeah, so, we parachuted in near the airport, then infiltrated and sabotaged the three crop dusters. We're Ravens; we specialize in paradrops."

"There were *three*?" George asked. "I thought there was just one."

"Yes. You probably only saw one at a time. Sledge jumped in with a ten-pound maul and went to town on those planes."

The third FANTOM, a big burly boy, beamed with pride and malicious mischief. "They won't be flying anytime soon," he said with relish.

"Our job was to ground the planes long enough for the army to take the defensive lines. Once we had done that we abandoned the airport, but we took pretty bad casualties. Actually, we might have all been caught, but Mary sacrificed herself to save us. She bapped those Purple Ponies real good! A great loss to our squad, though." All three quietly dipped their heads in respect.

"She what?" George asked.

"Bapped them," Ivy replied. "You know, got 'em with her B— oh, that's right. You guys call it the BAR rifle. Well you know, it's technically the B-A-P-R, so we just call in the BAP. So she bapped 'em"

"That's awesome," George said, laughing.

"Thanks to her sacrifice, we were able to escape the airport. It's just a single runway on the side of a mountain. From there we're to link up with Alamedan troops, but we weren't in a position to do any fighting, so we escaped east over the mountains and came this way."

"Over the mountains?" Cindy asked, surprised.

"Uh-huh. It was rough going."

"You came pretty far. Didn't think you flatlanders could do it."

Zara smiled and raised an eyebrow. "We're FANTOMs," she said as if nothing else mattered.

"What was your other mission?" Bernie asked.

"Sorry, unfortunately I can't tell you. Classified, you know," she said regretfully. Bernie nodded.

"What's it like parachuting out of a plane?" George asked.

Zara chuckled. "It's kinda fun, and a bit scary. Exciting."

Hearing footsteps, George turned to see another FANTOM walk up to their campfire. "Captain Fowler, our transports are ready."

Zara blew out a breath. "No rest for the righteous." She and the other two got to their feet. "Well it was nice meeting you guys, and thanks for the food. And the licorice." Bernie got up and handed her the rest of the tub. Zara's eyes lit up. "Thanks! I owe you one some day. Alright, time to go. Bye!"

Everyone waved goodbye, and just like that, the FANTOMs were gone. George sat thinking about everything he had just heard. If the army paratroopers were something, these elite paratroopers were incredible. *They* must be the best of the best.

With the absence of Zara and her FANTOMs, their campfire lost much of its liveliness. Mostly everyone sat and stared into the fire, nibbling on leftovers and sipping soda. Jack and Ella played cards. Bernie read a comic book.

George's thoughts drifted back to home. It was great out here, camping in the field with his soldier buddies. He wasn't just here for fun; he was here to do a job. But at the same time, it reminded him of evenings with his family when everyone gathered together and set aside their distractions with good spirits. That didn't happen terribly often. He kinda wished they were here now.

It was late in the night before the Tattoo announced that it was time to go to bed. George helped put the campfire out and crawled into his sleeping bag. He lay there, listening to the night sounds, the crickets, and the sounds of the camp.

Finally, the clear notes of Taps sounded, slowly and soothingly. Lights went out, and George drifted off to sleep.

Next morning George automatically awoke to Reveille, but just lay there and listened to the tune, and then the sounds of the camp as it came to life. Finally, he got up and stepped outside into the cold morning air.

Bernie had had the morning watch that night. He would still be at his post somewhere on the perimeter until breakfast was served, when new picket duties would be established.

Jack came running up to Ivy. "Can we go swimming now?"

Ella was right behind him. "Yes, please! Before breakfast."

"Guys, it's freezing," Ivy said.

"So?" Jack replied.

"You'll die of hypothermia."

"You'll die of poopothermia if you keep being a party pooper," Ella said.

Ivy threw her hands up. "Fine, go swimming. But only if George babysits you."

"It's *friend*-sitting. We're not babies," Jack corrected her.

"Ooh, big difference," Ivy said sarcastically.

"C'mon, George," Ella said. "Bring your swimsuit."

"I don't have one," George said.

"Then go in your clothes."

"Go in your underwear," Jack suggested.

"No," Ivy interrupted, "there will be none of either."

"Thank you," said George.

"Okay, well, let's go," said Jack. He and Ella disappeared off to their tents to change and shortly reappeared ready to go swimming. George could not understand how they seemed oblivious to the cold despite what little they were wearing. And why did *he* have to be their "friend-sitter"?

"We're going back as soon as breakfast is ready," he told them.

"Did you think I would skip breakfast?" Jack asked.

"On second thought, no, you wouldn't. Why're you bringing your rifle?"

"To shoot the fish with," Jack replied.

"Oh, no you don't," said Ivy quickly. "That's a waste of ammunition and you'll ruin the gun. Leave your weapons with George."

"Aw, man," Jack said.

"Those poor fish," Ivy said. "What'd they ever do to you?"

"They were born," Jack said ominously.

"Yeah, he has a fish complex," Ella commented.

"I do not!"

"Just go," Ivy said, shooing them all away. "Leave me be. Your worse than my little brothers."

George paced up and down the shore of Topaz Lake enjoying the scenery while Jack and Ella dove off what looked like a man-made peninsula and raced each other to the boat dock. They splashed about and fought each other and seemed to be having a grand old time. Had it been warmer and had he had his swimming trunks, George might have wanted to join them. At any rate, a boat ride would have been fun.

Pretty soon George faintly heard the company bugler sounding mess call from some distance away. Jack and Ella had apparently missed it, however, as they went right on splashing.

"Guys!" George called. No answer.

"Hey! Jack, Ella! *Guys!*"

Their heads popped up and they treaded water. "Yeah?" Jack called.

"Mess Call!"

"Stool on a shingle!" Jack cheered.

Seconds later, he and Ella were clambering up the bank. The three of them wasted no time in getting back to camp. George had to run to keep up.

"Cold-cold-cold," Ella chattered in her bare feet.

They were some of the last to get their meal, but there was plenty to go around. George saw Bernie was back from sentry duty, eating his breakfast and reading a comic book.

George was pleased to find that breakfast this morning was bacon and eggs on toast with cheese. He still didn't care for eggs, but they were okay, after he had picked the cheese off and eaten it separately. Cheese and egg did not go well together.

"Heathen," said the horrified veteran sitting next to him.

Jack held up his egg on toast. "Know what this is?" he asked.

"Yes, Jack," Ivy said, "stool on a shingle."

"No. Eyeball on a shingle!"

B Company spent a relaxing morning in camp before Ogden ordered them to pack up. The break had been nice, but once more George was on the march again, always the life of an infantry soldier.

B Company continued down Interstate 395 before turning off onto Route 208, which they followed northeast for most of the day until arriving on the edge of Smith Valley that evening. Again, the evening was taken easy. Dinner was back to the old stool on a shingle, much to Jack's delight.

That night, George went to bed thinking about the last few days. They had really blown through Stanislaus, and driven right on into Nevada. He wondered how the siege of Reno was going. There had been no news lately. George's mind persisted in keeping him awake, until finally he fell asleep wondering when he would next see action. It had been awfully peaceful as of late.

Chapter XIII

George awoke late in the morning. It was nice to sleep in again. He wondered what was happening back in California. The remaining rebels were probably being mopped up by occupation forces. They would be having a time of catching all those kids.

Breakfast was a fine meal of more stool on a shingle. This one had a lot of steak chunks, which George liked very much.

"Whoever made this needs to chew their food better," Jack said.

George finished breakfast and wandered away, wondering what would happen next. He was already getting restless since they had wrapped up the Stanislaus campaign. So far he had helped contribute to a great success and he was eager to keep going.

The attitude in camp seemed very lax. At least Ogden wasn't around. Nor were any of his sergeants, come to think of it. Amazingly, not a single one of them had been killed in action at the Raymond Line. Was that really just three days ago?

Then Sergeant Liam stomped past him looking very angry.

"What is it?" George asked.

Liam turned around, glaring. "It's this blasted rivalry between Ogden and Spotorno and Westfall."

"What about it?"

"He's gone and left us in the lurch, that's what."

"What do you mean he's 'gone and left us in the lurch'?" George asked.

"The Ogre has taken most of his staff and gone traipsing off to battalion headquarters to play politics!"

"What politics?"

"Court-martial Sanders, gimme those mortars, oh look at me I'm such a great officer I should get a medal." Liam spoke in a scathing, mocking tone. "The usual. When we're attacking."

"We're going to attack the Lyonese now?" George asked, getting excited. Finally, some action!

Liam snorted. "Not anymore, *apparently*, 'cause *Ogden* has *more important things to do*. Arrogant know-it-all. Let the others fight themselves." He thrust his hands into his pockets and stomped away.

"The others are going to fight by themselves? Wait, Liam, so we were going to attack, but then Ogden just decided not to and so— Liam!" But Liam either didn't hear him or didn't care.

Troubled by what he had heard, George headed back towards the group. So Ogden was bailing on the other companies, apparently? Wouldn't he have, like, canceled their plans over the radio first or something? Or did he want to do that in-person with the colonel? Agh, it didn't make sense.

"George, what's going on?" Jack asked. "You look like the cat that *didn't* catch the canary."

"Oh, it's just Liam said we're supposed to be attacking today. And we are, except just not us, because Ogden has gone to see the colonel for politics." With these words, George drew the attention of several people nearby.

"Do you mean," someone asked, "that the rest of the battalion is going to be attacking while we, don't?"

"I think so."

"Blast it!" another soldier declared. "I bet this is all a scheme for Ogden to get a private audience with the colonel."

"And piss the colonel off at the same time?" a veteran replied.

"Nah, because Hoffman doesn't have a backbone. He won't do anything to Ogden. And Ogden's super pushy."

"Borderline manipulative sometimes."

"That's..." George struggled for words.

"Messed up," Bernie supplied him.

"Yeah. We should just go ahead without him if he's gonna be like that."

"Yup."

"You really think so?"

"Yup."

"Then someone should go tell the sergeants that."

"Go ahead, "Bernie replied.

"Me, why me?" George protested.

"Your idea."

"Yeah good idea," another soldier said.

"Then you come with me."

"Hell no, you think I want to get involved in this?"

"You said it was a good idea."

"Good idea for *you* to go. But don't tell the Ogre I said that."

George sighed and shrugged. "Fine." He turned around and walked all the way over to Ogden's HQ tent and paused outside. Ivy would understand, and she'd know what to do.

He pulled back the flap and stepped inside. Liam looked like he had gotten in trouble and been told to stand in the corner, which is where he was, facing the wall and by all appearances no happier than he had been the last time he spoke to George. He seemed to be slowly fermenting his resentment for the current situation. And Ogden. Probably just Ogden.

The other three sergeants were sitting or standing around quietly with Ogden's staff, except for the few he had brought with him, like his driver. Ivy glanced up. "Hi George," she said.

"Is it true?"

"Is what true?"

"You know, that Ogden is off, well, trying to get Captain Sanders court-martialed and—"

"Yeah it's true."

"Court-martialed my eye," Jackson muttered.

"It's Ogden who should be court-martialed!" Liam exploded, turning around. "Constantly trying to show everyone up, advance the farthest, get there first. Always trying to get the glory for himself.

I mean, he pushed us into our own artillery barrage and we lost kids because of it, but he gets on your back for sleeping on sentry duty." That last remark was said to George. Apparently, they hadn't forgotten it yet, but Liam had a point. That did seem rather hypocritical of Ogden.

"Woah, Liam, what set you off?" Ivy said.

"*Ogden* should be court-martialed!" Liam finished.

"And then he also just wants to commend himself to the colonel," Emma said.

"We're at a critical time in the campaign and he just *bails* on us!" Liam yelled.

"Liam, calm down," Ivy said. "Every time in a campaign is critical and I think this is probably one of the lesser ones."

"We should be invading Smith Valley right now!"

"Then let's do it," said George.

"But please, Liam, calm down," Ivy was saying. "You're all worked up, and if we all started acting like you we'd never get anything done." Liam calmed down a bit.

"Smith Valley can wait a day," Jackson pointed out.

"The longer we wait," Liam said, "the more Lyon County gets to dig in around the Methodist church and call in reinforcements. We should be moving *now*. Besides, that was the *plan*."

"Guys, guys," George said. "Then let's just go anyway without Ogden."

Ivy raised her eyebrows. "That is *strictly* against orders. He made it very clear that we were to sit put until he got back."

"Don't we have a job to do?" George said.

"Well," said Emma, "to control Smith Valley we need to take that, like, 'hamlet' around the Methodist church, the Catholic church, and then some farm buildings, right?"

"I don't remember where all that is," Ivy said.

"Use the maps, genius," Liam snapped.

"You're such a peach," Ivy retorted.

Jackson walked over. "They're in this drawer, I think." He opened it. "Okay, maybe that drawer." He opened it too. "Um-m..." Without a word, one of Ogden's staff walked over, pulled open a third drawer, and placed a stack of paper on the desk. "Ah, thanks," Jackson said.

"Ogden isn't gonna like you going through his stuff," Ivy warned.

"He's not here. If we don't end up doing anything he doesn't even ever have to know."

"I don't even care," Liam declared. "Ogden can go 'die' in a hole."

"Liam, be nice," Ivy said.

"Why should I? He's never nice to me. Butthead."

Jackson spread their documentation of the local area on the desk. Sent down from high command were maps, satellite images, and intelligence reports of enemy strengths and positions.

Curious, George came over to look. "Did these literally come from Google Maps?" he asked, examining the familiar graphics.

"Uh-huh," Ivy said with a chuckle.

"Okay," Jackson said, pointing at the maps, "A Company is flanking out to the north. C and D Companies are marching through Renner Farm, here. D Company heads more to the east for the Catholic church, and then the two jointly attack Hillcrest Cemetery here."

"With practically all of the heavy weapons support," grumbled Emma.

"Well," said Ivy, "Ogden said we were going to have some heavy artillery from brigade headquarters."

"It's not here yet, is it?"

"And we're supposed to be taking the Methodist church?" George asked.

"Which is critical to the success of the pincer move on the cemetery and taking the valley," Jackson replied "We can't afford to lose too much manpower."

"Don't we have some vehicles?" George asked.

"Yeah, but they're way out around here scouting," Ivy said. "Patrolling the southeast."

"Why do we need that?"

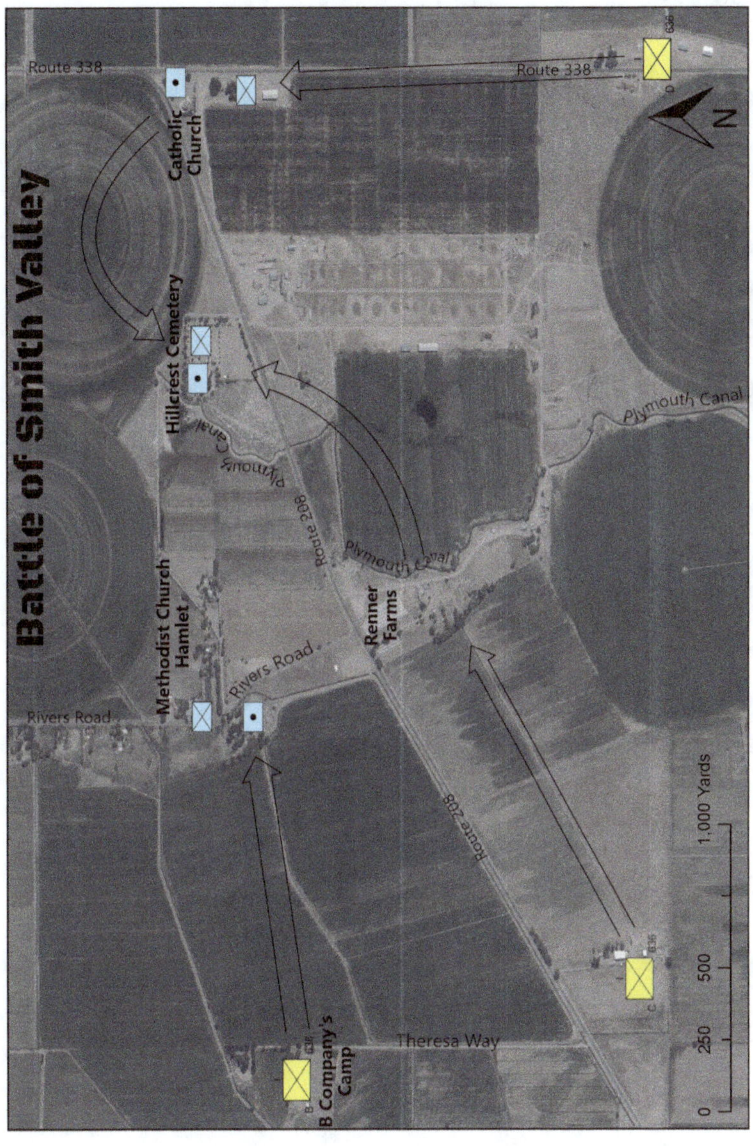
Battle of Smith Valley
Route 338
Route 338
636
N
Catholic Church
Hillcrest Cemetery
Plymouth Canal
Plymouth Canal
Plymouth Canal
Route 208
Methodist Church Hamlet
Renner Farms
Rivers Road
Rivers Road
Route 208
Theresa Way
B Company's Camp
1,000 Yards
500
250
0

"We're kinda isolated out here. Recon. They're all equipped with radios."

"So, when are we supposed to be attacking?" asked George.

"In a couple hours," Jackson replied.

"And C and D companies are gonna move on without us?"

"Unless Ogden gets the colonel to stop the offensive," Ivy said. "I don't think he'd want them winning a battle without him. He wouldn't get any of the credit."

"Hey," Jackson said to their radioman, "confirm with Westfall and Spotorno that the attack today is going ahead."

"Affirmative," the response came back a couple minutes later.

"Then if they haven't canceled yet," George said, "I say we just ignore Ogden and go ahead without him."

"Yes!" Liam declared. "I'm not gonna wait for that loser to get back from his career-building escapade."

"You're saying we should disobey orders," Ivy said severely.

"Ogden's being a fool," said George. "Why take orders from a fool."

"Well said," said Jackson.

"Thank you," said Liam.

"But," Emma countered, "our support is poor. Our manpower is low. We need reinforcements, better weaponry. I say we wait for that heavy artillery unit."

"And look," Ivy pointed out, "what about 49 Rivers Road right here? We're gonna bypass that to deal with later, but there could be enemy there. I think we need to send out scouts to reconnoiter the entire area and bring back more information before we do anything. And wait for support. Get the other companies to cancel the attack."

"Yes," said Emma. "Let's send some scouts to look around." The girls bent over the map and began pointing out objectives.

"Guys," George said, "it's not gonna be perfect, but we already made plans. There are two other companies that are depending on us to do our part. They could end up in a bad spot if we bail on them like Ogden bailed on us."

"George, we're not going to do anything," Ivy replied.

"But you have to, we need to."

"Ogden said not to."

"Who *cares* what Ogden said. Everyone else is counting on us. Like Jackson said, the pincer movement."

"We're not actually part of that pincer."

"No," Jackson said, "but we are attacking a sizeable force to prevent it from interfering with the pincer, so we might as well be."

"Except Ogden's being stupid," Ivy sighed.

"You agree with us," George pointed out, "but you're just gonna follow in his stupidity?"

"I'm doing my job."

"Your job is to lead your troops."

"My job is to follow orders."

"You have to lead the company because it's the right thing to do."

"I'm supposed to follow orders."

"You're worse than Ogden," Liam muttered.

"Excuse me?" Ivy said, suddenly riled up. "You think I'm worse than Ogden for doing my job, for not making his mess even bigger? Seriously? And George, if you're so set on us going anyway, then why don't *you* lead the company?"

"Yeah, you are the one that keeps suggesting we go ahead without Ogden," Jackson said.

"Guys, that's ridiculous," George retorted. "He could court-martial me. He's already threatened to once. And seriously, I'd be jumping like three ranks over you guys."

"You think *we're* safe from court-martials?" Ivy pointed out.

"A brevet captain," Emma suggested.

"Uh-uh," George said. "That's not my job, it's Ivy's job."

"I already told you what my job was," Ivy replied. "It's no more my job than it is yours, so why don't you do it."

George scowled. Seriously, what was up with her? *They* were the sergeants. "If Ogden's not here it's your responsibility," George said.

"In that case, I'm going to stay put."

"Jackson, Emma, Liam? You guys do it then."

"I agree with Ivy," Emma said.

"Jackson, Liam?"

"Eh... I dunno," Jackson said.

"Not if we can't all agree," Liam muttered.

"Why won't you go?" George was getting frustrated. This was ridiculous. They all *knew* what needed to be done, but they didn't want to do it. They were afraid to get in trouble.

"Why won't you?" Ivy shot back at him.

"It's not, my, *job*. It's *your* job. And Ogden's orders are stupid!"

"Not that stupid apparently if you're gonna follow them."

"I'm *not*, I'm trying to get *you* to not!"

"By following them yourself and insisting I be the scapegoat," Ivy said. She was getting punchy.

"I can't do it, you're my sergeant."

"And Ogden's my captain!"

"But it's not my job!"

"You said it was our job to support the other companies."

"Our job, as a company, with the officers leading."

"Why can't *you* lead?"

"It's your job! I've told you this like four times now. Do your job!" George snapped.

"I am. My job is to follow orders."

"So is mine!"

"So you want me to *not* do my job and get fired so you can say that *actually* you *were* doing your job and *you're* innocent. Hypocrite."

George glared at her. "Whatever." If that was how she's gonna be, then she could just enjoy being Ogden Junior. He turned to leave the tent and found Bernie blocking the doorway. "Move," George snapped at him.

"Nope," Bernie replied nonchalantly. George tried to shove by, but Bernie blocked his way.

"What is it?" George asked, exasperated. "Why won't you let me go?"

"Do it," Bernie replied.

"Do what?"

"Lead the company."

George stared at him. He had to be kidding. Seriously. "Bernie, I can't lead the company and you know that."

"Yes you can."

"Why?"

"Because you should."

"That's so helpful."

"It's the right thing to do."

"I know," George said, waving an arm in exasperation, "but Ivy's stubborn as a mule."

"So are you," she interjected.

George turned around to face her. "Except *I'm* right, so there. You're acting just like Ogden." Bernie tapped George on the shoulder to get his attention again. "What," George growled between his teeth.

"They need our help. She's not gonna do it, so you have to. Don't be like her."

George looked at him. Bernie had a point. Ivy would never take the lead in blatantly disobeying her commanding officer. It went against what she believed. And come to think of it, here George was, wanting *to* do it, but only going halfway — again. It was like the time he didn't finish that dugout, and it cost the lives of three soldiers. Or the time he didn't finish sentry duty, and something very bad could have happened because of that. Come to think of it, he never really did finish anything he started. Not unless it was a video game. Or he had someone breathing down his neck to get it done. But nothing bad had happened. Er, the second time. Of the two army incidents, that was.

He stared at the tent wall. He had come here to do something, to accomplish something, to be a success. He couldn't accomplish something if he didn't finish it — if he knew what needed to be done, but waited for someone else to do it for him. Maybe he didn't want to do it, but it wouldn't do itself.

He sighed. So this was the price of success. The bigger the success, the bigger the effort. Just like Jim had said, ages ago at boot camp. Ivy didn't want to take the lead in disobeying her commander. It wasn't her way. And it was his idea. And it was the right thing to do. If no one else was going to follow through with it, then it was going to have to be him who took responsibility — for himself.

His eyes returned to Bernie. Bernie looked back. "Do it," he said quietly.

"Are you sure?"

"Yup."

George hesitated. What if he failed? Then he would be a fool. If he never tried, he would never be able to be a fool because he couldn't fail. Or was he a fool for not trying? If he actually needed to do something, but he never tried, did he automatically fail? But if he did try and failed, he would be in *so* much trouble.

George thought of Lieutenant Diver Derrick who saved the Battle of Sattelberg in New Guinea, defying orders and single-handedly clearing ten Japanese machine gun nests and forcing them to give up the heights. Or Major General Daniel Sickles who disobeyed orders at Gettysburg and enabled the Union to completely rout the Confederate army. But then again, there were probably more stories of soldiers who got sacked for disobeying orders and screwing everything up.

George looked at Bernie again. Then his eyes drifted over everyone else in the room. They were all staring at him, waiting. Expecting. And the other companies who had no idea what was happening, who were expecting B Company to support them, who were counting — on him. Soldiers, counties. Alameda.

He looked back at Bernie, silently encouraging. George drew in a deep breath and slowly exhaled. He nodded at Bernie, then walked back into the tent and confronted Ivy. "Alright," he said, "I'll do it."

Liam looked at him. "You know, I think you could do it. Let's go."

"Well, at least we can all blame him when Ogden comes back," Emma said.

Jackson laughed. "You're a private, he can't demote you any more. Okay, I'm in. What's the plan, Captain Owens?"

Ivy jumped out of her chair. "Guys, are you kidding me?! This is a joke, right?"

"I'm serious," Liam declared. "To hell with Ogden. Let's get this job done."

"Emma, you agree with me, right?" Ivy asked.

"Ah-h, I mean, if he's willing to take the fall for it, then eh, sure, why not."

"That doesn't work," Ivy said, "you *outrank* him."

"Whatever," Emma said. "I also agree with him."

"Ivy, you're outvoted, okay," Jackson said. "Just be a good soldier now and shut up and follow orders."

Ivy held her head in her hands and sighed. "I can't believe were doing this."

"Great, then let's go," George said.

"Ogden's gonna hate you," Bernie commented.

"Thanks," George muttered. He paused. "Now what?"

"We go brief the troops," said Ivy dryly. "I take it you already know what the plan is."

"Okay." George picked up one of the maps and walked outside the tent. Now it was time to follow through with what he had just said he would do. He thought of the Green Berets: "Men who mean just what they say."

"Hey, guys," Bernie was casually mentioning to the privates, "George is taking over for Captain Ogden today."

This caused quite a stir. "Hey, isn't that the guy who slept on sentry duty?" "Why is he taking over?" "Who even is he?"

"The Ogre has abdicated his leadership over us when we need a leader," Jackson said, "so we've picked a new leader."

"One of our sergeants," the soldiers said.

"Your sergeants have made a decision. If you follow us, you follow George."

"I'm not sure about this." "I don't know." "Why the hell would you pick some random private to replace your captain?" "That is not how succession works."

"It's not like he could be any worse than Ogden," Jackson said cheerfully. George grimaced. The mode of confidence was overwhelming.

"You have a point." "Okay, fine, give him a shot." "Eh, it can't get worse than worse." "Alright, fine." "Whatever."

"George," Ivy whispered, "this is the part where you start leading."

George thought for a while of what to say. The whole company was gathered around, waiting impatiently. "Well?" "We're waiting." "Show us what you got."

Finally, George began in the most obvious way. "We need to take the hamlet around the Methodist church ASAP," he said, "to support the other companies and defeat Lyon before they can dig in and better prepare a defense.

"Across Theresa Way right there is eight hundred yards of a hay field to Rivers Road. Across that road is the 'hamlet' of buildings near the Methodist church that we need to take.

"We won't have artillery support because none of our field artillery guns have range to support such an attack. Right?" he asked their sergeant. Melvin nodded.

"We'll be under fire for much of that crossing," George continued, "but fortunately those big round hay bales are all over the field with the large flat side facing the direction of our attack."

George paused for a moment, looking around him and thinking. "How many of you have heard of the famous Easy Company of the 101st Airborne Division, the Screaming Eagles?" he asked. Many of the soldiers nodded their heads in recognition.

"They're a personal favorite of mine," he said. "During the Siege of Bastogne in the Battle of the Bulge in 1944, Easy Company was tasked with taking the town of Foy, which was held by the Germans. Easy Company was sitting in foxholes in a forest near the town. The foxholes are actually still there, and you can go see them.

"Anyhow, in order to attack Foy, there was this open field they had to cross, and their only cover was haystacks. They were successful and defeated the German force opposing them.

Methodist Church Hamlet
49 Rivers Road
Rivers Road
Smith Valley United Methodist Church
Rivers Road
31 Rivers Road
N
500 Yards
250
125
0

"Our battle will be much like that of Easy Company's attack on Foy, I think. We'll cross that farm field using the hay bales for cover and kick Lyon out of the Methodist church. If we're successful, which I think we will be."

"Don't say *think* so much," Ivy whispered. "It makes you sound unsure."

As many of the soldiers recalled the famous stories of Easy Company's exploits, enthusiasm for George and his plan began to grow.

"Now," George went on, "Take the PIATs. They'll be the best we have since our light field guns can't shoot eight hundred yards."

"Excuse me, Captain Owens," asked Sergeant Melvin. George did a doubletake and hesitated a few moments before acknowledging him. Those two words did not sound like they should go together. "Since my guns will not be able to fire in support of the attack," Melvin said, "I would like to offer my gunners to join your infantry in the charge."

"Great!" George said. "That will help bolster our numbers. How much do we have?" The sergeants quickly tallied up and gave him the figures for their platoons. "Yeah, that's enough, I th— I guess," George said. "Wait, what about your guns?"

"Leave 'em here. They'll be alright, I think," sergeant Melvin replied. "No enemy threat. We'll come back and pull 'em forward after we take the hamlet."

"Alright, if you're good with that then I think— er, it's fine." George looked around. "Machine gun platoon, I want you to follow behind and come up to support the attack if possible. "And," he paused. "Remember to pick up the BAR rifle or PIAT if the guy holding it is shot." That was common knowledge, but everyone was staring at him and he couldn't think of anything else to say.

"Okay," George said, "get ready," he finished lamely.

Weapons were handed out, the troops packed up and prepared for combat, and the sergeants rallied their platoons. George parlayed with them and they decided on each platoon's general route and target. Fifteen minutes later, B Company was ready. They stood around and looked at their commander.

George eyed the clock. It was ten minutes to ten, when they were scheduled to go forward. C and D Companies would be going forward, too, and depending on them. On *him*.

He looked around at the expectant faces underneath the brims of their helmets and felt the weight of his responsibility. Then he took a deep breath and gave the order. "Alright. Let's go!"

With steady, determined doggedness, B Company set off. One of the troops raised a fist and shouted their motto, and promptly everyone took up the cry as they poured across Theresa Way and into the hay field on its other side:

"*Pugna Ut Vincas!*" "*Pugna Ut Vincas!*"

Captain George went with Sergeant Liam. It had been decided that his line of advance would be the best place for the company commander to be.

B Company moved forward at a quick pace. The greener soldiers just kinda hurried forward, but the veterans deftly slipped from bale to bale. They knew all too well how a seemingly peaceful setting could suddenly turn into hellfire and brimstone in the blink of an eye. George had learned this himself.

But that was just the thing. A few hundred yards across the field, no sign of life stirred from the enemy positions. No booming of cannons or roaring of air compressors punctuated the silence.

George stopped behind a bale, peering around it across the rest of the field. "Shouldn't they be shooting at us by now?" he asked Liam.

"I guess they don't have any guns that can shoot this far."

"Or maybe they haven't seen us."

Liam snorted. "All these kids sneaking from hay bale to hay bale across an eight-hundred-yard field? I mean, I don't think we're that stealthy."

"Hm," George replied. Liam was much calmer now that Ogden's having bailed on them didn't matter so much anymore.

B Company moved forward a little farther. Still there was nothing. George was concerned. He gestured at Sergeant Melvin, who hurried over to him. "Hey, what's the range?"

Melvin pulled out his small black rangefinder and pointed it towards the church. He held his position intently for several seconds.

"Three hundred yards, Captain." George frowned, but motioned his group onward. Intently looking for signs of the enemy, they hurried forward to the next bale.

And the next one.

And the next.

"Are you sure they're still there?" Liam asked. "Maybe they abandoned the position."

"I highly doubt that," replied George as they ran to the next bale. Around them, the advance had grown more cautious as the distance closed.

"Maybe they only have small arms—"

Liam was cut off by the sound of a volley of cannon fire and the roar of air compressors as they kicked into life. A group of Alamedans and one ex-Stanislausi advancing across the field was caught by surprise and unceremoniously cut down by canister fire.

Across the field, there was an instantaneous dive for cover. The opening barrage was an unnerving surprise, but now George knew the enemy was there and that they were fighting, which was better than walking blindly into who-knew-what like he had at the Raymond Line.

"Keep moving, keep moving!" George shouted, waving his arm. "Put the pressure on!" He was getting into his role now.

B Company firmed up and moved forward as more guns joined the battle. The air buzzed thick with shells and canister shot as guns roared ahead of them. George could see that the shooting was coming from the copse of trees and buildings that formed the small residential area at 31 Rivers Road, on their side of the street.

George and Liam picked their way forward, dashing across the field from bale to bale. The bales were a good many yards apart. Liam looked out from their current position and scowled.

"What?" asked George.

"I hate seeing my own guys hit."

George looked around him at the advance. They were taking casualties. He knew not how many, but it seemed to be more than he liked.

"Keep moving!" he yelled. "Close the distance! All we gotta do is close the distance!" He had already seen that in close-quarters hand-to-hand fighting, Alamedan infantry triumphed. Against Stanislaus, at least. But this wasn't Stanislaus... He shook these thoughts from his head and focused on the battle. Having dispensed with attempts at stealth, sergeants and corporals shouted at their troops. The field was abuzz with the noise of enemy fire and the shouting of the army.

Suddenly, the noise was augmented as the Lyonese forces decided the Alamedans had closed to machine gun range. The fury of flying paintballs increased, and George and Liam were pinned behind their bale. Around them, other soldiers tried to make a break for the next bale through the pinning fire. One of them didn't make it.

Then the machine gunner shifted his aim, drifting across the field and giving George and Liam a break. They sprang forward, shouting at their troops.

"Keep going! We're almost there!"

B Company was a mere hundred yards from the enemy position now, but the battle was intense and they could not return the heavy fire they were receiving. The advance was taking heavy casualties.

Liam looked at George, concerned. "It's getting tough," he said. "Should we call it off?"

"No!" George said firmly. "'When the going gets tough, the tough get going.' And any attempt at withdrawal will take even more casualties, and then it will all have been for nothing."

Or his idea could have all been for nothing anyway if they failed this attack. Boy, then he'd *so* be in trouble. Liam made no reply, but led a handful of his men running across open space for their next cover.

B Company was now close enough that George could finally see the enemy gunners secreted in the buildings and foliage. Human bucket brigades fed a steady supply of fresh rounds to the artillery, while around them a heap of spent casings was being carted off by other kids.

George put his head down and led the next dash for cover. He felt stray paintballs strike his helmet, but none found the casualty area. Behind him, two of Liam's soldiers were not so lucky, catching a thick canister round full-on. These Lyonese apparently liked to use canister shot for their artillery.

The remainder of the group dived for the next bale and cowered behind it, peering ahead and waiting for a break to rush forward again. By now, most of the over-eager chargers were either subdued or casualties.

Suddenly, a small shell plummeted straight down and obliterated a squad sheltering behind the bale next to George.

"Hell, they have mortars!" Liam shouted.

George froze. Mortars. The one weapon against which their cover offered absolutely no protection.

"How come we never get mortars?!" Liam continued shouting. "If you ask me, they're more useful in an infantry action than machine guns and light field artillery combined! But we never have any of 'em! It's the one thing Ogden did get right!" Then he stopped and looked around. "George, do you think we can make it?"

"I dunno," said George. "But we have to try. Soldiers, keep moving! Push forward, put the pressure on! Go! Go!"

A few more minutes and B Company had finally come to the last rows of bales and were looking the enemy directly in the face. Finally, after all this time just to close the range. Now was time for the big push.

He looked around, and saw that like him the rest of B Company had stopped moving. They simply cowered behind their cover and looked out. Shot flew thick around them, and mortars were dropping from the sky every several seconds.

"Ready, Captain George?" Liam asked.

George checked his gun and gripped it tight. Then he nodded, slowly. "Ready," he said, withdrawing a whistle from his pocket and putting it in his mouth.

A moment of nothing passed. Then George shrieked on the whistle as loud as he could and left his bale as Liam shouted at his troops. B Company arose and charged the enemy. Having just blown his lungs out, George stumbled while catching his breath, but was running furiously a moment later.

A short killing zone was the last obstacle between them and 31 Rivers Road, the enemy battery position. PIAT gunners sent a dozen small shells into the position as their comrades were cut down in the open.

Then, shouting and shooting, the Alamedan infantry plunged through the trees and all chaos ensued. They went right for the gunners, first using rifle volleys as they ran and then getting stuck in with bayonets. The enemy bucket brigades scattered to arms. Officers shouted orders at their men.

In a mere few minutes, the forward gun position of the Lyonese forces had been routed and cleared, although, very annoyingly, they had managed to take some of their mortars with them. They were sure to have more ammunition somewhere else around here. Stupid mortars. The right wing of B Company stopped in the excellent cover available.

"Sergeant Melvin!" George shouted at the field artillery officer and his remaining gunners. "Get these guns turned back on the enemy! Somebody call our machine guns up from the back and tell them to set up here!"

Down at the end of the property, a few soldiers rousted the last Lyonese infantry from a storage shed. As they set up positions at 31 Rivers Road, they began drawing fire from across the street. However, the Alamedans no longer had long, open death-traps to cross.

George and Liam rounded up two squads' worth of their troops. "Alright, cross the street!" George shouted. "Get to those trees!"

A mad dash followed for the end of a line of trees going down the side of a dirt crossroad that turned out from Rivers Road and ran along the side of the hamlet. Reaching it, they filtered down the line of trees, jumping a couple of gaps in their cover.

Then the Lyonese launched a counterattack to try to take back 31 Rivers Road. The surprise charge and an intense firefight resulted in fifty-fifty control of the position for each side. George ordered his half platoon to move down the line of trees they were in and keep attacking the hamlet.

From a good position, he stopped and looked out across the battlefield. On the left flank, his soldiers had passed up the gun battery and occupied a vacant row of trees overlooking a house and a few buildings.

The actual church was even farther to the left, but as only bare field opposed it, its garrison had driven off the Alamedan vanguard with machine-gun fire. Apparently, the Lyonese had gotten into the building and turned it into a fortress.

Currently, the strategy involved flanking the church and taking the hamlet to its right, where the buildings remained locked up except for the storage sheds. A group of Alamedans with a machine gun had come around to the far side of 31 Rivers Road, and now the counterattacking Lyonese force was caught in an enfilade of small-arms rapid fire and some canister shot from their own capture guns.

Three concentrations of buildings formed the hamlet by the Methodist church, and now George was engaged in a heated firefight for the center group. He had lost several of the soldiers in his group, but gained a few reinforcements, including a PIAT and machine gun. BAR gunners darted around buildings and blasted the enemy with short bursts of rapid fire.

One of them was Cindy. She had taken the weapon off of a fallen Alamedan and was slowly getting the hang of it, using it to great effect. However, the gun jammed on her, and while she was struggling to figure out how to clear it, a Lyonese boy charged her, shot her, and made off with the BAR rifle to deprive Alameda of its use.

George frowned at the loss of a good soldier and a valuable weapon. Cindy had proved true to her word. She and her friends had done their part. He hoped he'd meet up with her again some-time. But there was no time to worry about that now.

Looking around, he saw Ivy bring up her platoon to take the left-most cluster of buildings nearest the church. Behind his position, the Lyonese counterattack against 31 Rivers Road had been fended off, and the guns were being dragged forward to support the rest of the company.

He ordered Liam to take a body of troops and attack the third and last concentration of buildings all the way at the end of the hamlet. Meanwhile, he began directing the encirclement and siege of the church fortress. Shells fired from the windows made this a hazardous job, and the open space behind the church offered no cover to approach it from that direction.

The Alamedans took up positions on the north and south sides of the building. The east and west were bare field, and anyone who ventured through them had to run a gauntlet of machine-gun fire.

"Man, those guys in the church have an awful lot of firepower holed up in there," George commented to no one in particular. "The yard is starting to turn pink."

Meanwhile, to the east, Sergeant Liam was encountering stiff resistance. A runner arrived from him requesting support, and George directed a machine gun and two PIATs to support him. Then George himself hurried off to the church.

"Alright, close in!" he shouted. "Get those machine guns firing on the windows!"

Next he began organizing the troops into an assault force to storm the building. As machine guns and light field artillery suppressed the hailstorm coming from the church, a dozen soldiers rushed the front door while a dozen more went for a couple of side doors. Ferocious struggles ensued, but finally the Alamedans bashed their way inside. George winced. The church doors would probably bear witness to the events of this day.

Surprisingly, the garrison in the church was not quite equal to the number of paintballs coming out of it. There were plenty of guns, but a lot of soldiers were multi-tasking and firing a machine gun with each hand.

At bayonet point the Alamedans wrested control of the church. It took some ten or fifteen minutes of fighting to clear every room, but they were ultimately successful. It appeared they still had the upper hand at this sort of combat.

From there they discovered that the surviving Lyonese in their sector of the hamlet had fled to 49 Rivers Road back across the street.

"Alright," George said, "flank wide around and surround that place. I don't want them escaping back the way we've come and spiking the guns we left behind or anything like that."

After seeing that operation set going under Ivy and Emma, George hurried back to the east end of the hamlet to check on Liam. He found a few pockets of enemy resistance that were gradually drawn into a noose and eliminated with grenades, PIATs, and rifle fire, especially from the BARs.

The whole operation had been successful so far, and B Company was now sweeping the area and securing it. They were running short of manpower, but they could still set up a good position here.

Returning to the other end of the hamlet, George found 49 Rivers Road under siege but still holding out. A few minutes of searching the area and he finally found Sergeant Melvin.

"Melvin, take your platoon and a squad of infantry and drag your artillery guns up here." Sergeant Melvin quickly rounded up his party and set off.

"Ivy, Emma!" George called. "Just keep 'em there until we get artillery support! Don't try and storm their position yet!"

It took more than twenty minutes to move the field artillery guns by hand across eight hundred yards of hay field and get them into position, but the wait was worth the casualties saved.

Shortly after getting into range and line of sight, the field artillery laid down a bombardment on the enemy position at 49 Rivers Road that included a few smoke shells they had in their arsenal. After about ten minutes, the infantry went in under cover of these shells. The ensuing fight was brief and highly successful.

George returned from overseeing this engagement to find that Liam had patrolled the entire hamlet and set up guards. George assisted him in laying out a defense with places for their weaponry. He ordered some nests dug for the machine and artillery guns to cover the open fields to their north.

To the east he could see at a distance C Company attacking the cemetery, but D Company was nowhere in sight. They must have been held up at the Catholic church. C Company was supposed to be half of a pincer move against the cemetery, but as it was they were on their own.

"Liam, I want a tally of our current troop count," he ordered.

"Yessir." Liam scurried off to complete his instructions.

Several minutes later, Liam returned. "George, the company is a little less than sixty strong, with eleven remaining artillery gunners." George contemplated this information. That meant at least forty percent casualties just today.

"Wait, where's Jackson?" he suddenly asked. "I haven't seen him since we charged."

"He was killed trying to encircle the church. His platoon is currently electing a new sergeant."

"Hm. That's too bad. Well, we're secured here. We need to bring our tents over and set up camp. And don't make it obvious who we are, just in case any reinforcements come for the enemy. And see if the radioman can call up the other companies and ask how the battle is going elsewhere."

"Will do," said Liam. "I think the prospects here are looking good. We're in a strong position and we've won a strong victory."

"Yes, well, it's not over yet. I think we might need to support C Company since D seems to be held up. And Captain Ogden still has to come back. He *better* bring some support with him."

"Yep. Alright." Liam turned to go, but stopped. "Hey, George," he said.

"Yeah?"

"You did it. You got us to do what we needed to do. When you first joined us, I never would have thought you capable of it. Well fought, well lead."

As Liam walked away, George contemplated his words. He had come a long way. And he was actually doing something. Something real, something tangible. He was accomplishing the job he needed to do. He was winning, and it felt good.

But this battle was not over. He hadn't won quite yet.

Chapter XIV

After watching the situation for several more minutes, George decided that something needed to be done about D Company's absence. Rounding up an ad-hoc platoon, he led them over to complete the pincer move on the cemetery.

They circled around to the north since C Company was attacking the cemetery from the south. The enemy were divided fifty-fifty between the actual cemetery itself and a cluster of buildings across the road.

The Lyonese spotted George's platoon going around their flank, but apart from a few shots in their direction they could not do anything about it. George went racing to go past the buildings and pulled up short.

"Blast it!" he said. "This way, go around!" There was a road between the cemetery and buildings, and an irrigation canal ran along the cemetery side of the road. It was too wide to jump and there was no bridge nearby.

Fortunately, a small detour brought them to the end of the canal where that road intersected another road. Swinging around it, they ran down the other side.

Unfortunately, this meant that they had to cross much more open ground than they had planned on crossing, and it did not take long for the Lyonese to see them coming. They were using the headstones as cover against the Alamedans as well as the ring of trees that ran around the cemetery.

"So disrespectful to the dead," said one of the Alamedans, shaking her head.

C Company was currently sitting back and using artillery against the enemy, waiting for D Company's other half of the pincer. Mortars would have been best in this situation, but only A Company had any.

Between George and the edge of the cemetery was roughly forty yards of bare ground. There was one single tree in the middle of it, but that was not enough cover.

The Lyonese turned a couple of artillery guns around on them and let loose with canister shot. Clusters of paintballs flew across the field, striking a few soldiers. Machine guns were being repositioned as well.

"Get back!" George yelled at the kids with him. "Fall back!"

Turning around, they ran back all the way they'd come as the Lyonese sent paintballs flying after them. They looped around the end of the canal and took one more round of canister shot, then the Lyonese turned their guns back against C Company.

George stopped for breath and looked around.

"Blast that canal!" someone declared.

"What now?"

"Well," George said, "we should go look at D Company."

Following George, the soldiers went well around the end of the canal and crossed the hay field where they had more round hay bales for cover. Another six hundred yards, and they got to the Catholic church.

Peering out and trying to not be seen, they could tell that D Company was not even at the church yet. D Company was farther south fighting its way up towards the church, trying to take a few buildings and clumps of trees. The Lyonese around the church were firing their artillery in support of that defense.

"I don't think we have enough manpower to do anything here," George said.

"Uh-uh," a veteran agreed. "We'll just get slaughtered. And we have no heavy weapons support."

"Okay," George said. "Let's go back around this way." He led them as they crossed through the middle of the first round field and then crossed the second one, trying to get a better look to their north.

"Captain Owens," a girl shouted, "look!"

George looked where she was pointing and saw, very small in the distance, a military force coming their way. There were vehicles and infantry, but he could not tell how many.

"It looks like they're going towards the Methodist church," he said. "Hurry!"

They ran all the way back to the Methodist church hamlet where B Company was sitting put. Ivy and Liam came running up to George.

"George!" said Ivy. "Where were you?"

"I was trying to support C Company."

"But if you're gonna be the captain then you can't just run off and not tell us where you're going. At least Ogden didn't disappear on us all."

"Oh. Sorry."

"What of C Company?" Liam asked.

"No good. I tried to support them by attacking from the other side, but there's a canal in the way. We had to go all the way around it 'cause there isn't a bridge and that meant we had to cross a bunch of open ground to get to the cemetery, but they had more artillery and we had to retreat. And D Company is not making very much progress at the Catholic church."

"Well, let's get some heavier weaponry and go support them," Liam said.

"No, wait," said George. "There's also reinforcements coming from that way." He pointed north.

"Reinforcements for us?" Ivy asked.

"No, Lyon. They're coming this way. We should prepare."

"How many?" she asked.

"Vehicles, infantry. I couldn't tell."

"They have vehicles?"

"Yes."

"Great," Liam said, "'cause we don't have any anti-tank guns."

"That's what PIATs are for," Ivy replied.

"But guys," George explained, "maybe they don't know we are here. I think we could ambush them."

Ivy shrugged. "Worth a try."

"Alright, get ready," George said.

Everyone scrambled to prepare a defense against the Lyonese counterattack. Their goal was to trick the enemy reinforcements into thinking that they were the original Lyonese garrison and that the position had not been taken by Alameda. George continued to direct B Company as their camp was hurriedly shifted out of sight behind the buildings and trees and left mostly unpacked.

The Lyonese force was hurrying closer, but did not seem to be expecting to engage in combat. Both vehicles turned out to be supply trucks and not tanks. The infantry was only roughly two platoon's worth and marched in a close group alongside the trucks.

The Alamedans waited until they drew closer and closer, but the Lyonese were slowing down. They seemed confused, and stopped, looking around as if something wasn't right.

"Fire!" George yelled, and the field artillery gunners let go with their first salvo.

The stationary, exposed enemy infantry made perfect targets and were hit in droves. Immediately, they scattered as the machine guns joined in. Lyon routed and rushed to get away, leaving one of their supply trucks behind.

"Charge, get that truck!" George yelled, and his troops leapt yelling and cheering from their positions. The Lyonese, apparently thinking they were being pursued, ran like hell in all directions to escape.

B Company stopped at the truck and looked around. There were a good many Lyonese soldiers wearing white shawls. The truck itself had paint in the driver's seat that made it unusable.

George came up and joined them. "Let the air out of the tires since we can't drive it back right now," he ordered. Quickly, they unscrewed the valve stems and the air slowly began to whistle out of the tires.

They turned around and headed back to the hamlet. George ordered camp set up properly now, and the area was further fortified with more dugouts and foxholes.

Then there was shouting as a truck drove up, parked, and a very angry Captain Ogden jumped down. George gulped. Ogden was back, and they definitely had done something he would know about.

"What the *hell*!" Ogden yelled. "I gave strict orders not to do anything, but you couldn't even follow my simplest instructions! I couldn't have been more clear! You guys can't do jack!"

"Actually, sir," said Ivy, "we took our objectives."

"Shut up! I am your captain and you disobeyed my orders!" Ogden raved. "I'll have you all court-martialed for this! Blast it! Hell, blast it!"

George turned around and saw where the company HQ tent was being set up. "Hey, guys," he said, "There's a better spot over there."

"What the *hell* do you think you're doing?!" Ogden screamed, storming up to him. "I am the captain. Are you the idiot who did this, this treason?!"

George gulped again. A bead of sweat dripped from under his helmet. Was this actually treason? Uh-oh. If only he had kept his mouth shut. He was in for it now. But it was done now, and he couldn't hide it either. "Yes, sir, you bailed on us. All we did was go ahead with the planned attack."

"Against *my* orders! And look at the casualties you took! If I had been commanding we would have taken *half* the casualties!" George was not so sure of that, but the Lyonese garrison had done very well for being outnumbered. "I'll be speaking to the colonel about you, and you're stripped of your rank, *private*!" Ogden finished.

"Um, sir," George said, pointing to the single chevron on his left shoulder, "I am a private."

Ogden glared at him. "Wait, you're that private who slept on sentry duty!" George sighed. Would they ever forget that? Or would his irresponsibility taint him for the rest of his life? "You're out to get me. It's a conspiracy. I'm not done with you. I could have you shot," Ogden finished sadistically. He walked away.

"Um, that's a thing?" George asked apprehensively, but received no answer. He had had his morning of glory, but now the company commander was back. It was somewhat of a relief, actually. Ogden bore a lot of responsibility, and in that sense he was admirable. But George dreaded what would happen to him now. Treason, a firing squad? Seriously, in paintball?

Ogden rearranged the camp a little bit. Some of it were his preferences, of course, but George was sure that some more of it was just to undo what George himself had done.

B Company remained inactive. George could still see the cemetery, and C Company was still at a standoff with the Lyonese holding it.

Finally, after what seemed like an age, he saw D Company coming from the Catholic church. They dragged their field artillery up and began firing on the Lyonese from behind. The infantry had even more open ground to cross than George had, but they had the heavy weapons support and the numbers to do it.

Gravestones only provide cover from one direction, and once D Company arrived C Company finally sprang forward into action. Between these two jaws of the pincer, the Lyonese that had held the cemetery for hours that day were quickly overrun.

The survivors dashed and made a break wherever they could. Some of them ran in the direction of the Methodist church where B Company's field artillery gunners fired at them.

The destruction of the Lyonese garrison holding the middle of Smith Valley was now complete. While the survivors had escaped to join other groups of soldiers at other farms around them, the Alamedans held the important ground. These other positions would be cleaned up when a general offensive began.

In order for that to happen, they would have to wait for support. Ogden had brought word that a heavy artillery battery was indeed on its way to their battalion. More supplies would be arriving, and eventually reinforcements.

The 636th Battalion was battle-worn and very low on numbers, but still effective enough for the role it was tasked with. They were just on the fringe of Lyon's domain, and for whatever reason this frontier part was hardly defended. Lyon must have been surprised by how quickly they overran Stanislaus and crossed the mountains. The main garrison had already been defeated. Of course the Lyonese would be sending an army to fend off the Alamedans soon enough, but by then they would be prepared for it.

The rest of the day was spent doing more digging, and when Ogden decided his troops were too idle he found more places for them to dig defenses. In the evening they were all given time off until bedtime. Everyone but George, who had to skip dinner and keep laboring. Ugh, again.

The next day, Reveille sounded late. George had already woken up feeling refreshed by the time he heard the bugler and was one of the first outside.

Breakfast was back to stool on a shingle. George was hoping for some good meals after the next supply delivery arrived. Maybe some fresh fruit. That sounded good.

"Hey, George, wanna play poker?" Jack asked.

"Again?"

"Yeah!"

"What about another game?"

"Uh... a different kind of poker?"

George shook his head. "Oh, fine."

He joined them and decided he could play a little bit and then go out quickly when he got a bad hand. Things didn't go as planned, however. First he got good hands and won the pot. Then, when he tried to go out on a bad hand, he raised the bet so high that eventually Jack and Ella folded, and he won the pot again.

Pretty soon he was in the lead and decided to try playing competitively. But as soon as he started trying to win, he began losing everything he had accumulated, and now the game was dragging on too long.

Fortunately, he had a good excuse to end it when the first supply convoy arrived. A few dozen trucks bearing their expected heavy artillery drove up and came to a stop in a column. Everyone jumped up to see, and Ogden began assigning work details.

The artillery were positioned along with their air compressors and ammunition a little ways behind the Methodist church hamlet. The infantry were set to work digging emplacements for them. Since they were expected to be here for a while, time was invested in substantial defenses that thoroughly secured their entire position.

These were large dugouts with fairly high ramparts that took about an hour of hard work each to complete, but eventually were finished. George rested on the ground and wiped the sweat from his brow as he watched the gun crews manhandling their equipment into position in the dugout he had just made. He knew that this dugout was not going to collapse on them because he had made it right.

Before they were even finished setting up, a fast supply convoy arrived escorted by a single patrol car. Two of these trucks needed unloading, and George found himself tasked with another job. He cheerfully pitched in. Working helped take his mind off what Ogden had told him and what consequences he feared were coming for him.

Once the trucks were unloaded, they needed to be reloaded with used supplies — the battalion's trash as well as spent shells and packaging, broken equipment needing repair, and casualties who wanted a ride back home. They would all be separated and processed at different points.

That complete, George wandered back over to the camp to see what was going on. Jack and Ella were playing another card game. Bernie was reading a comic book.

"When is the mail truck gonna be back?" George asked no one in particular.

"Right now," Bernie said.

George turned and saw a couple trucks driving up. One of them was another Alamedan postal truck. Weird how that timing worked, especially with Bernie. Like something in a book and not reality. He dashed into his tent and pulled out his letter, quickly closing what he had written so far. It wasn't as much as he liked. He hastily tagged on a postscript apologizing for that.

Running outside, he joined the line at the postal truck. The driver was accepting letters in a basket and handing out deliveries. One of them was a decently-sized package that a boy seemed very excited to get.

George took an envelope, quickly addressed it, and put it in the mailbox. The driver was in a hurry to leave and did so as soon as he could.

The other truck had disembarked infantry. Immediately, the newcomers were besieged by B Company kids wanting to know who they were and what news they had.

What they learned was that these soldiers were an ad-hock group of volunteers from depleted units who, rather than being sent back to rest, wanted to head to Nevada as some early reinforcements. The Southern Front was stalled again and had even lost ground, and Interstate 80 was still funneling supplies into Reno as X Corp had yet been unable to cut it off again. The Northern Front was going well.

"You know what we need," a boy declared, "is we need our own radio station where they report everything that's going on. We could listen to the news in the evenings. The Alamedan Evening News."

"Fireside Chat," someone suggested.

"You think I would believe a word of that propaganda?" said a skeptical boy. "No sirree."

The next day began like the previous one. George wondered how long his letter would take to get home and when he would get home himself. Would his battalion retire to rest, or would he become a casualty? He had survived this far, though, and there wouldn't be any more fighting for a few more days at least. He was only, oh, a third of the way through his service period.

In the morning, a plane arrived and landed in a nearby field where there were no hay bales. The bored kids of the battalion wandered over to go look at it. George was one of them. It was a small spotter aircraft equipped with a camera in the nose for taking pictures. It had one pilot and a copilot who also operated the camera.

After the crew got something to eat, they took off to reconnoiter the area. George wandered back to camp, still bored. Next time he needed to bring a book or something for days like this. That gave him an idea.

"Hey, Bernie," George asked, "can I read one of your comic books?"

"Sure," Bernie replied and showed George a dozen in a stack. George sifted through them: *Captain America*, *Axis Grinder*, *The Triple Terror*, and other titles, many of which he was not familiar with. Some of them looked old; not like they had been printed a long time ago, but like they had been written and published long ago.

Choosing *Axis Grinder*, George settled down and lost himself in the amusing story pretty quickly. The heroes lassoed a torpedo from their biplane, saving an unsuspecting merchant ship from the U-boat peril.

He was interrupted by a bugle call, but he couldn't quite remember what it was. The one he hadn't learned at boot camp. Bernie dropped his comic book and got to his feet.

"What is it?" George asked.

"Attack," Bernie replied and was gone. George remembered that one morning their camp was attacked by the Stanislausi with tanks, and scrambled to follow him.

Outside the tent, kids were running everywhere in a panicked frenzy, trying to pack everything up. George ran around until he found Ivy.

"What is going on?" he asked.

"We're getting out of here. The Lyonese have an army and it'll be here in less than an hour."

"What the hell?!" George yelled. "A whole army and they'll be here in an hour? How the hell did we not notice that?"

"The spotter plane just did."

"Oh boy. Looks like they're evening out the score."

"Yes. So now the goal is to save our supplies. Get the artillery out of here, then our equipment, and then save however much of the battalion we can."

George understood. Casualties would come back in two months. It was much harder to replace trucks, supplies, and their priceless heavy artillery should they be captured by the enemy.

"Get everything in the trucks!" Ogden yelled at his soldiers. "Move it! Never mind being neat! Blasted get going!"

George rushed to tear down his tent. It was clumsily stuffed aboard a truck, and he went back to help load other supplies. Ammunition was left piled haphazardly on the ground. It would be needed.

"Faster!" Ogden yelled. "Move it!" He too began to pitch in, getting everything loaded up, piled, and crammed messily into their trucks so they wouldn't lose it all to the enemy.

The heavy artillery gunners were moving as fast as they could. Most importantly they had to save the guns and air compressors. Ammunition and other sundry supplies would come after if there was time.

The fresh food was thrown out of its supply truck to make room, and everyone helped themselves as they ran around. Better to eat it than let it go to waste. George got to have his fresh fruit, but he didn't get to enjoy it very much.

In half an hour, they were almost ready to move. The area was a mess, but all of the very valuable equipment, such as tents, weapons, and the company headquarters had been stowed aboard the trucks.

Ogden addressed the troops. "I will be staying to command a rearguard action. We will make sure everyone else can escape."

George looked at Bernie. "I don't imagine they're expecting us to catch up with them once they escape?" he asked.

"Nope."

The soldiers of B Company began to prepare with silent grit. Already there were plenty of positions to man, but not enough kids to man them. George contemplated this job. It was not like any of his others.

About a third of B Company's remaining strength plus the ad-hoc volunteers dashed across the field to Smith Gage Road to assemble a roadblock, another third blocked Route 208, and the final third spread thinly across the Methodist church hamlet and B Company's former camp at Theresa Way. It was bare bones, but it would have to do.

Truck engines roared to life and they began to pull out. The infantry ran behind, and the heavy artillery lumbered onto the road. The retreat had begun.

George looked up from the Smith Gage Road roadblock and saw them coming in the distance, coming fast. He was ready to do what he had to do. If they could just buy fifteen, maybe only ten minutes for the others, it would be enough. He was ready to see this job through to the bitter end.

B Company had been left with very little support. A few machine guns to go around, a few field artillery guns, and a few PIATs. Colonel Hoffman wouldn't sacrifice any more equipment. They would have to make do.

A column of vehicles roared down the road. Had it not been for the hay bales obstructing the fields, the Alamedans would have never had a chance. As it was, vehicle traffic had to stick to the roads.

To George's right, much farther behind the mechanized column, the Lyonese infantry were crossing those fields. The Methodist church hamlet and Theresa Way were right in their path. Behind him, the slow convoy trundled onward. If they could just get on Route 208 and over the mountains, back into California, back to Alameda, they would be safe.

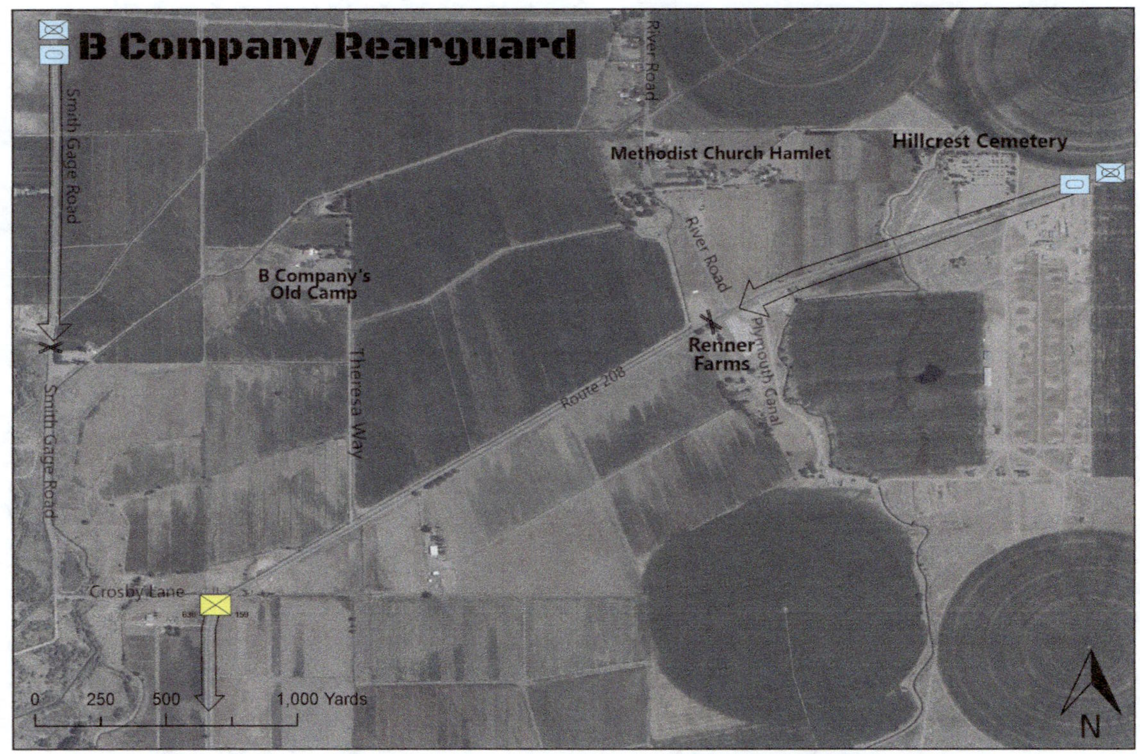
B Company Rearguard
Smith Gage Road
Smith Gage Road
River Road
Methodist Church Hamlet
Hillcrest Cemetery
River Road
B Company's Old Camp
Theresa Way
Route 208
Renner Farms
Plymouth Canal
Crosby Lane
0   250   500   1,000 Yards
N

George turned back to look at the oncoming vehicles. Their roadblock wasn't much — just some rocks, debris, and a hay bale they had rolled into the road — but it would stop a car. A local farmer had yelled at them for it to no avail before driving away on his tractor, still irritated.

The two field artillery guns with them were dug in on both sides of the road with a pile of shells stacked nearby. These gunners had volunteered to stay and fight in the rearguard action.

Ogden was over on Route 208 commanding the roadblock. Ivy was left in charge here. George looked over at Bernie. He was calm and cool as usual, sitting comfortably on the ground, focused.

Boom! The leading enemy vehicle fired at them from the cannon mounted on top. Boom! The one next to it fired as well. Two canister rounds swept through their roadblock, one hitting a field artillery gun position and killing two of its crew. Immediately, others scrambled to replace them.

Then they closed to machine gun range and opened up with a hail of paintballs. The Alamedan gunners, who had held their fire until now, sent two of their own canister rounds at the exposed enemy gunners, taking them out, and scrambled to reload.

George leapt back as the leading vehicle rammed into their roadblock, turning sideways and half rolling over. The impact sent debris flying, knocking over two Alamedans. Immediately, the Alamedan infantry attacked with rifles and grenades, liberally painting the vehicle and hoping to make it a temporary piece of their roadblock.

The attacking column stopped and soldiers jumped down from their transports and charged the roadblock. They were met with a hail of canister rounds, rifle volleys, BAR rifle automatic fire, and bayonets while their own vehicles turned every gun that could draw line of sight and even some that couldn't to support them.

There were no orders given. Ivy said nothing. There was nothing to say. They all knew that they had to hold off the mechanized column for as long as possible. It was desperate.

George shot his rifle rapidly at the enemy infantry. He was pretty sure he scored at least two kills, but with all the paint flying around he couldn't really tell.

Suddenly, he was struck in the chest repeatedly by several hard thumps. They stung and hurt like hell. He stopped firing, dazed for a minute. Then he looked down at his chest.

All down his front, on his chest, stomach, and legs, were pink blotches marking all the places where his skin stung. He watched several more paintballs strike him and distinctly felt their harsh impact. Then he looked up and saw the Lyonese machine gunner blazing away indiscriminately at everyone in front of him. The next moment a grenade went off right in the boy's face, and he stopped firing.

But George was already dead. He shook his head to clear the daze and put down his rifle. Then he scrambled to get back out of everyone's way. George had watched other kids go through this more times than he could count, but he still couldn't believe it was now happening to him. Well, it had to come sometime.

He struggled to put on the white casualty shawl he drew from the pouch on his belt. He had never even taken it out, largely forgotten it was even there. It was weird and slightly embarrassing to be wearing this thing. He felt like an old grandma.

"What do I do?" he asked no one in particular.

"Catch up with them," Bernie replied mechanically without looking back as he shoved a shell into the breech of the one field artillery gun they still had firing. "Get a ride home. Hurry." Boom! The gunner fired the shell as Bernie readied another.

Taking one look at his doomed comrades' valiant last stand, George took off running. He was not the only one. Some of the other casualties had chucked their packs, but George had personal belongings with him. He hoped that he would get the rest of his stuff back, which was all aboard one of the trucks he was trying to catch up to.

He could see the fleeing convoy, but it was very far ahead. He ran down the road and got farther than most of the kids, but eventually his legs failed him and he collapsed, panting.

A casualty. Finally, he was now a casualty. How ironic his thoughts this morning had been. It had happened so quickly: one moment he was shooting, and the next moment he was covered in paint. At least he would get to go home now, though. That was a good thing.

The Alamedan convoy was out of sight now. Hopefully, it was far enough ahead. Hearing engines, George looked back and saw the Lyonese column once more racing down the road. So his roadblock had finally fallen. Most likely everyone at it had been killed, too. Yes, they never could have cleared it if even one Alamedan was left to shoot them.

The mechanized column raced by in pursuit of the battalion. Once they had passed, George got up and joined the other casualties. The other dead kids. It would be a long walk. Fortunately, he still had his canteen and a field ration.

They walked in silence, resting independently but generally sticking together in groups. He chuckled. They were the Walking Dead.

Hours later, George finally reached Route 208. There was no way he was walking down a busy highway.

"Guys, what are we gonna do?" he asked. "We've just been abandoned in the wrong state."

"Wait for the Society," a boy replied.

"Huh?"

"The Society, you know, the umpires who run the Paintball Wars."

"Oh, yeah, right. They'll come and get us, really?"

"Probably. Like in a helicopter."

"A helicopter? Really? How will they even know we're here?" The boy shrugged and said nothing.

George sat down to eat his field ration and think. It was much too far to walk home. He could hitch rides on military vehicles, only there weren't any going his direction, and he didn't have any money to take a bus even if he could get to one. At least he was with a group.

"Look!" someone yelled around a mouthful of food. "It's the Society!"

George looked and saw a white helicopter coming their direction. He stared for a moment. Seriously, a helicopter, for real? Sure enough, though, it landed nearby and they all ran over. Inside was a boy piloting the craft and with him a girl, both wearing white uniforms.

"I can take fifteen of you," the pilot said. "There'll be another chopper in thirty."

George was one of the lucky fifteen to get aboard. "How'd you know we were here?" he asked.

The girl smiled sweetly at him. "We know everything," she said.

The door closed and the chopper lifted off the ground with a roar of its engines. George looked down on Smith Valley below and traced his path there over the last few days. He could now appreciate the size of the Lyonese army that had almost caught them. Spread all over the countryside were soldiers that looked like ants, accompanied by plenty of vehicles. They would have been toast, for sure.

The casualties landed at a sort of military base, disembarked, and were told to go check in at the office over there. Then the chopper lifted off to pick up more casualties.

When George's turn came, a girl in a white uniform sitting at a desk asked him for his ID card. He showed it to her and she did something on her computer. Then a ticket printed out and she handed it to him.

"Get on bus CA33K," she said. "That will take you to another base like this where you will get on bus CA14D, and that bus will drop you off at your home."

"Thank you," George said. "What do I do with my uniform?"

"Keep it. You'll want it when you come back. Just don't take off your casualty shawl as long as you're wearing it.

"Thanks," he replied and walked away. This whole system of returning casualties back home was impressively organized.

George found a white bus with CA33K written in big blue letters on its side. He showed the boy standing at the door his ticket and was let aboard.

When the bus filled up, it pulled out. George sat in silence for several hours, thinking about the rearguard. All this time he had missed home, but now he missed the army too. He missed Bernie, the camaraderie. Jack and Ella and their jokes. Ivy's leadership. Everything he had grown attached to since boot camp. Around the time his stomach started to growl, the bus arrived at another base.

George took a quick bathroom break and looked for his next bus. He would have to get home to eat anything. The bus wasn't there, so he sat down to wait. Fifteen minutes later it arrived, empty. He got in line and showed his ticket to the boy at the door, who took it and put it in a box.

"George!" a voice called to him.

He looked to the back of the bus. "Cassie! Hello!"

"How are you?"

"I'm good, you?"

"Yes. So you got killed too?" he asked.

"Uh-huh. I was up in Reno. It was crazy."

"Wow, really I've heard a bit about that. Were you trying to encircle the city and cut off Interstate 80 or were you invading the city?"

"I was invading the city. I died only the second day my unit was sent in. We were trapped in the streets. There wasn't anywhere to go."

They chatted intermittently for a couple more hours until the bus stopped and the driver called, "Cassandra Lewis!"

"Bye!" she said, and hopped off the bus. George rode in silence again through a couple more stops, then the bus pulled over where he could see his house out the window. His own house. He hadn't seen it in weeks.

"George Owens!" the driver called, and George exited. He walked up and looked around at the yard. It was just as he had left it, except the lawn had been mowed. He had always hated that job. Walking up the steps, he knocked on the door.

The door opened. It was his mom. "George, you're back!" she exclaimed, and hugged him. "I'm glad to see you. How was it?"

"It was great," George said. "It really was."

"Really?"

"Yeah!"

"Well then I'm glad you went. How come you're back so soon?"

"I got shot."

"Oh, I'm sorry. Did you get any of them?"

He grinned. "A few."

Mrs. Owens wanted to hear all about his adventures, but also wanted to cook dinner at the same time. George had not gotten very far before Hannah and Gretel got home from school and barged through the door.

"George, you're back!"

"And look, he's all pink. He got shot. I told you he wouldn't last long."

"He lasted longer than you said he would. George, why're you wearing a white shawl?"

"It means I'm a casualty."

His sisters giggled. "You look like an old grandma!"

George frowned. "Very funny."

"Well why don't you go get out of that dirty uniform," Mrs. Owens suggested. George ran upstairs to change. Finally, fresh, clean clothes. He put on comfortable stuff, too. Oh, how nice his bedroom smelt. There was no dirt and body odor. Everything was clean.

The girls were followed fifteen minutes later by George's dad coming home from work. There was a joyous family reunion, and George was made to start his account all over again, for the third time. Almost immediately dinner was called and they forgot about his adventures.

Finally, good old home cooking. He hadn't realized how good it was until he'd come back from eating army food. He was the young man come home, returned from fighting in a faraway land, the war hero. He was just like his dad. And boy was it good to be home.

Chapter XV

Bri-i-ing!

George listened to the school bell as it warned him of the next item on the schedule. It reminded him of the army camp bugler, but he was back in school now.

His chemistry teacher came down the aisle collecting assignments. When she got to George, she gave him the hairy eyeball and picked up his worksheet. She looked it over for a rather long time, making George nervous. Then she gave him a confused look and hurried on.

Finally, she said, "Class, you may be dismissed." George calmly got up and exited the classroom.

Instead of getting in line at the cafeteria, he sat down at one of the empty tables at the side and opened his lunchbox. Cassie got her meal and came to join him.

"That looks really good," she said, watching George eat his sandwich. "You brought that?"

"Yeah, I got up this morning and made myself lunch. I didn't want to eat that," he said, looking at the freezer pizza on her plate.

"It's okay," she said.

George enjoyed his lunch, but he also wanted to use the bathroom before his next class. So he ate quickly enough to do that and was just leaving the bathroom when the school bell rang.

George sighed. Back in prison again. Once more he was subject to the servitude of the classroom. Once more he was spending his days learning a lot of stuff. Once more he didn't really see the point of it all.

But on the other hand, it was a job he had to do. Maybe he didn't agree with doing it, but he didn't have much of a choice, either, and that was life.

So he sat at his desk and listened as his teacher listed off the numerous small countries of Africa and their capitals. The map was a nightmare with scores of border lines and capitals marked across the sprawling continent. Knowing any of this was of no importance in life, it seemed to him. They were just impressive but unuseful facts. Brain exercises.

Nevertheless, here he was, and if he didn't learn them he would do poorly on his test. Then his grades would stay bad. George knew that, years down the road when he got to the education that really was important to his career, his grades would mean something. Maybe not these grades, but his grades overall would impact his future success to an extent. How good of a job he did preparing defenses on the battlefield directly impacted whether or not they won and how many people died. Also, people tended to judge you based on your grades. At least some did. Employers, maybe.

So George got out his school notebook, which had until now been used mostly for doodling, and tried to write down what his teacher said he was supposed to memorize.

Finally, he stamped his feet on the doormat and stepped into his home, the home where he had slept last night in his warm, comfy bed after taking a shower. It wasn't a tent cramped with other kids who hadn't showered in a week, and it wasn't a foxhole, not that either of those were terrible. It was just home.

"Hello, Honey, how was school?" his mom asked.

George grinned. "Well..." he said, "it was school. But it could have been worse."

"Like how?"

"It could have been a foxhole in a thunderstorm under artillery fire."

"Did that happen to you?" she asked, concerned.

"No, but, if I had had to sit in the mud all night like that, I might have wished I was just back in school."

"I see. There are worse things than school after all. Well, dinner will be ready in an hour. I'm glad you're home, George. It wasn't quite the same without you."

"Yes, it was a lot less depressing," his dad commented as he shut the door behind him.

Suddenly, Hannah and Gretel came dashing down the hallway into the living room. As they entered, they turned and coasted sideways in their socks on the hardwood floor. Gretel came to a smooth stop, but Hannah slipped and nearly knocked the lamp off of its table by the couch.

"Whoa!" his mom yelled. "You almost broke my lamp! That was expensive, and the last thing we need is to take you to the ER to remove glass shards from your feet."

"Sorry," Hannah replied.

"No more of that."

"Okay."

"George!" Hannah said. "Tell us more about the battles you were in."

"Yes, I didn't get a very thorough account," Mr. Owens said, sitting down on the couch.

"That's because Gretel wouldn't stop talking," Hannah complained.

"Alright," George agreed and took a seat in an armchair. His mom and sisters all found seats as well.

"Well, what do you wanna hear?" George asked. "I mean, there's a lot."

"What was your first battle?" Hannah asked.

"Yes, the one where he died!" Gretel interjected.

"That was much later than my first battle," George said. "But my first battle, well, I didn't fight it, but the first one I saw, our artillery had stopped and they were firing. So we went forward out front to cover them, and the Stanislausi—"

"Who's that?" his dad asked.

"Stanislaus County."

"Oh, I get it, that's what you call them."

"Yeah. So, the Stanislausi were ahead of us, and they were being defeated."

"By you?" Hannah asked.

"No, by the Alamedans who were ahead of us who were fighting the battle. We were just guarding the artillery, who were firing in support of the battle."

"Oh, okay," Hannah replied.

"Well, my squad sneaked off."

"Were you supposed to do that?" his dad interrupted.

"Er, no, but I was following my corporal."

"What's that, corporal leads your squad, right?"

"Right."

"You know, that's what the Nazis said in World War Two about all the disgusting things they did. They were just following orders."

"Uh-huh," George said dryly. "So, as I was saying, we sneaked off, and we came across this anti-tank gun hiding in the bushes."

"You mean the anti-tank gun was hiding all by itself?" his dad interrupted again.

"No it had crew. There were two boys."

"Only two crew to an anti-tank gun?"

"It's a small gun. So they were hiding in the bush, and an enemy vehicle came along—"

"Like a tank?" Hannah asked.

"Uh, no, it was more like a truck. It came around a bend, and they fired a few shots at it and took out the driver and the gunner on top."

"How were they able to hit the driver?" his dad asked.

"Through the hole in the side."

"Why was there a hole in the side so they could get shot?"

"'Cause there has to be one, those're the rules."

"What," Gretel exploded, "there's *rules*? That's stupid!"

"Gretel, it's paintball, there has to be rules or it wouldn't work."

"That's still stupid."

"Let me finish telling the story! So they took out the driver and gunner but a few other soldiers jumped out and ran away."

"Did you get 'em?" Gretel asked.

"No, they got away."

"You shoulda got them!"

"We weren't expecting that."

"You should have been! A good soldier is prepared for anything his enemy does and wouldn't let them get away."

"Right, 'cause you definitely have a lot of experience in that."

"Okay, guys, that's enough," Mr. Owens interjected. "Let George tell his story."

"So after that we made sure it was safe for the anti-tank gunners to move their gun to a better spot around the corner of the road."

"How'd you do that?" his dad asked.

"We went and looked."

"You looked around the corner?"

"Yes, we went and scouted around the corner to make sure it was safe."

"That's it?"

"Uh, yeah, what were you expecting we did?"

"I dunno, something... more exciting. Like the time I—"

"Cody," his wife interrupted, "you just told Gretel to let George tell his story."

George's dad grinned. "Go on." He gestured to his son.

"Well, they moved their gun, and then we went back, and that was the end of the battle. We were just walking and guarding the artillery again."

"Tell us how you died," Gretel asked.

"You really love that part," George observed.

"Yes, because she missed you so much and that's why you finally got to come home," his dad said.

Gretel made a face. "Who killed you?" she asked.

George grinned. "A Lyonese machine gunner on a tank."

"When was that?" his dad asked.

"When I died," George said cheekily.

"Yeah, duh, I know that, but what battle?"

"We were fighting a rearguard to give everyone else time to escape."

"Why were you doing that?"

"'Cause there was an army we didn't know about that was about to destroy us."

"How did you *not* know about it?" his mother asked.

"Because we didn't think there was an army there, and then a plane spotted it and we all scrambled to get away."

"Well why didn't you see it before?"

"Mom, I don't know, I'm just a private."

"That was dumb."

"Yes, but. Anyhow, I died defending a roadblock to stop the tanks so our artillery could get away. They're very slow."

"Why are they slow?"

"Because they are. They have to tow these big guns and everything."

"So were you successful?" his dad asked.

"Huh?"

"Did you hold them off long enough, or did you fail and get them destroyed?"

"I... don't know."

"Why not?"

"I was a casualty. I left and never saw what happened." George thought quietly for a minute. Did the heavy artillery get away? Was his battalion destroyed? Had he done a good enough job? But what else could he have done, honestly? Too bad casualties had to wait two whole months to find out. There ought to be a news outlet for the Paintball Wars so he could keep up with Alameda from home.

"Well, I'm sure you have homework to do," his mom said.

"Ugh, yes," he replied, but it was work that needed doing, so he got up and went to his room. There was a lot of overdue work that had piled up while he was gone. It was agonizing to be stuck here doing school all over again, and he fought the mental urge to just push it aside and do something easy.

But it was work that had to be done. If he did the easy thing, there would be consequences, just like that time three soldiers died because he couldn't be bothered to dig that foxhole properly. So he bit his lip and got it done. He should apologize to those girls if he ever saw them again. But would he even know them?

The next day at school, he sought an audience with one of the academic advisors. George was hoping to get into advanced classes and move to online asynchronous classes so he could control his day more. That would really help when he went back to the army. He could tap into school remotely and not fall behind. Maybe he could even do dual-enrollment and take classes that would count towards college as well.

Unfortunately, he found that he would have to wait until the next semester to start doing any of that, and he had to wait until high school to do dual-enrollment, but he went ahead and got on the waitlist for a few classes. If he actually put the effort in, he could get through school quicker and even be better off. He would talk with the advisor again tomorrow.

That evening, FedEx delivered a package to his house addressed to "Pvt. George Owens." Upon opening it, he discovered it was his personal belongings that he had been separated from during the retreat. His "personal effects," as they had worded it, like he had died. Oh, wait, he had. Well, it was nice to have his stuff back.

A few weeks passed, and George got his report card from school. He glanced it over. There were no A's, but there were no C's either. He had straight B's. B was not a bad grade. Cool.

When he got home from school and walked into the kitchen, he saw that the trash can was about to overflow. Instinctively, he turned around to escape before someone could tell him to take the trash out.

But then he stopped. First of all, he was the only one in the room. Secondly, this was a job that needed doing. If he didn't do it, somebody else would have to do it, and technically it *was* his chore. And if someone else had to do it, he was stealing from that person, just like Captain Hughes had said. And letting everyone down, and— oh, never mind all the rest of it.

George set his report card down on the counter, lifted the bag up and tied the strings, and carried it outside to the trash can. Whew, there was something rotting in there that smelled pretty rank. He came back in and turned to go upstairs.

But he stopped. He wasn't finished with the job yet. He hadn't put in a new trash bag. Remembering the time he had fallen asleep on sentry duty when something bad could have happened but luckily didn't, he turned around and headed for the kitchen. It was so annoying going to throw something away and finding that someone had not bothered to replace the garbage bag in the trash can.

"George," his mom said as he walked back into the kitchen, "is this your report card?"

"Yeah, it has my name on it."

"You got all B's."

"Yeah?" he replied as he put the trash bag in the can.

"I'm impressed! What brought this about?"

"I dunno. I just decided to do it."

"Well good job. Keep doing it. And thank you for taking the trash out. It's a big help."

"Uh-huh," he replied.

When Mr. Owens got home from work, he came and found George. "Hey, George, why don't you come help me in the yard?"

George grimaced. He had always hated yard work. Crossy Road was so much, well, easier. But for one, his dad's "suggestion" was, in fact, an instruction from his commanding officer; and two, it was another job that needed to be done.

So he went outside and offered to run the weed eater while his dad mowed the lawn. It almost reminded him of the BAR rifle a bit, except the vibrations made his hands hurt. Then they built another raised garden bed and filled it with soil under the supervision of Mrs. Owens.

"George," she said, "you've really developed some muscle tone. You're looking ripped." George shrugged, slightly embarrassed, silently willing his mom to not start talking about girls swooning at his physique.

"I bet the girls'll like that," his dad supplied with a grin. Ugh, great. Never fear, Dad to the rescue.

"Dad..." George muttered.

"The army put you to a lot of work?" his dad asked.

"Uh-huh. Lots of digging, lots of marching. It was tiring, but I've gotten used to it."

"Well it's good for you. You should keep it up. You'd be surprised at how quickly you can lose that endurance and get all flabby again. I'm assuming you want to go back?"

George nodded. "Yeah, I do." But not to attract girls. No thank you. Uh-uh.

"Are you going to take your school more seriously?"

"Yes. I'm planning on taking some AP classes and switching to online."

"Online learning requires self-discipline. You have to be your own teacher. Are you gonna do that?"

"Yes. I don't want to drag it out anymore. I'll be able to work when I want, too. No more class schedules."

"You'll still have due dates just like regular school."

"Yeah, I know, but, it'll be more convenient when I'm away in the army."

"Good. That's what I want to hear. It looks like this experiment paid off. I'm liking what I see. Keep it up. I wish I had taken my youth more seriously. In hindsight I can see that I wasted so much time accomplishing nothing. I want better for you than that. A better career." George nodded. "It took the Marines to straighten me out. So learn from your old dad and don't be a slouch like I was." George grinned. He had good parents; he really did.

That night after dinner, George did the dishes. No one asked him to. No one even brought it up. He had seen that it needed to be done, so he did it and he did it well. He didn't leave any dirty pots on the stove, and none of the dishes he washed had to be rewashed. The rest of his family was probably watching Netflix in the living room, but that was okay. His sisters could take a turn tomorrow night.

An hour later, when George finished putting the last clean dish away, he stepped back to look at the clean kitchen. He wiped down a section of the counter he had missed, then stepped back again to survey his handiwork. There was a satisfaction in what he had accomplished.

Finally, George's two-month casualty leave had expired and he could return to the army. He'd come back to life! He packed up eagerly, dressed in his clean, washed uniform, and his mom dropped him off at the same place where his journey had first begun with his trip to boot camp.

He signed in at the desk, received his ticket, and stood around, waiting. There were other kids in city clothes and others in Alamedan uniforms, like him, returning from their casualty period. He didn't recognize any of them.

George struck up a conversation with one of the boys. "So where were you deployed?" he asked.

"Up north, with Halsted's First Army," he replied.

"Wow, cool! Did you meet the general?"

"No. I saw him, but I've never stood face-to-face with him. Where were you?"

"I was on Eastern Front. Calaveras County, all the way to Nevada where I died manning a roadblock in Smith Valley."

"What was going on?"

"We were surprised and had to make a quick retreat before they destroyed us. I was the rearguard."

"Wow. Did you escape?"

"Well, I think *they* did, but I really have no idea. I'll find out. My unit definitely died." They both chuckled. "How did you die?" George asked.

"I was in a tank and we were trying to take Red Bluff. There are some important freeway interchanges there that we wanted to gain control of."

"You're a tanker?"

"Yup. I was the main gunner."

George grinned. "So naturally a prime target."

"Yeah. We were also the platoon leader, so I was like right up in the front." They both laughed.

That was when several army trucks with canopy-covered beds drove up, parked, and soldiers holding clipboards opened the tailgates and hopped out.

"Load up!" they barked.

"Good luck!" the tanker told George.

"Thanks, you too!" George replied. He gave his ticket to the soldier with the clipboard and was admitted into the "cattle truck" as they jokingly called it. Its crude interior didn't bother him as much, though. The army had toughened him up. He remembered his first journey, bouncing along on these rough benches while Sally whined about Jack and his lack of deodorant. Whatever had happened to Sally? He hoped she was happier at home than she had been in the army.

George grinned. Jack and Ella, the company goofs. He missed their antics. He was looking forward to seeing Bernie, too. Bernie was probably the one person who had escaped their roadblock alive. He would be lounging on his bunk, reading a comic book when George walked into the barrack, just like when he first met him. George laughed inwardly at the thought.

When the journey was over, he climbed out of the truck and stretched. Instead of boot camp, he was back at the same military base where he had first joined B Company and met the Ogre. He retraced his steps from that day to the office where he presented himself to the boy at the desk.

"ID card," the boy asked. George handed it over. The officer consulted his computer and tossed the card in the trash.

"Hey, what're you doing?!" George exclaimed.

"You're being issued a new ID," the officer replied.

"Oh." George calmed down, but he was confused.

"Here you go," the officer said and handed it over.

"Do you replace IDs every time someone comes back from being a casualty?"

"No," the boy looked at him funny, "only when we have to." He printed out some papers, stapled them together, and handed them to George.

"I'm not with B Company anymore?" he asked, concerned.

"No, you are. Now go down that hallway and they'll fit you out. Come on, you're holding up the line."

George got out of the office. This was very confusing. He pulled out his ID and glanced it over as he walked. Then he abruptly stopped short and carefully read it again. Sure enough, he had seen correctly: "CAPTAIN; OWENS, GEORGE; B/636."

In wonder, he walked into the large gym-like area and showed his ID to the officer. It was "Gramps," the same boy who had told him how great Alameda's backpacks were. He didn't seem to recognize George, though. A lot of kids probably passed through here.

George's private's coat was replaced with an officer's coat. The only difference was that instead of a single chevron on his shoulder, there were three chevrons and a rocker, but it still made him feel important. He also received a dress uniform with a fancy coat that had epaulets to be worn on formal occasions such as parades, trousers with pinstripes down the sides, and a fancy hat.

George found his old barracks, but they were closed and locked. He banged on the door. No answer. What was going on? Oh, it was probably in his packet of papers. He frowned. Now for an awful lot of reading.

Finally, after wading through miles of text, he saw that he needed to go to Barrack B8, which he found quickly enough. Apparently, the barrack assignment wasn't always the same. Hesitantly, he took his seat at the desk where Ogden had insulted him on his first day. Finally, he would get to tell Ogden what to do instead of having to put up with him. That would be fun! Serve him right.

Being a company commander clearly came with more paperwork. He would learn that in time, though, despite all the reading. Hopefully, there were classes he could take. He knew the army had books he could read. He would read them, too. And he would probably get to dine with the officers and get better food as well.

George got up and went into the barrack. Sure enough, Bernie was on his bunk reading a comic book as if he had never become a casualty at all. With him was James Alcott, George's old corporal. Funny, what a surprise. They never had gotten around to replacing him, had they.

"Seriously, Bernie, come on," he was saying, "enough with the games. I want to know who our new captain is. I'm tired of waiting and I know you know, so just tell me already."

"You'll see," Bernie replied casually without looking up from his comic book.

"At least tell me what they did with that blasted Ogden. Oh, he'd better not be my sergeant. If he's my sergeant I'm gonna be pissed. Bernie, come on, you're getting on my nerves!"

"Hi Bernie!" George said.

Bernie set his comic book down, sat up, and saluted George. "Hello, Captain Owens," he said.

"Wait, what?" James started. "Did you just call him captain?"

"Uh-huh," Bernie replied, reclining back and returning to his comic book.

James stared skeptically at George, who beamed back. Sure enough, he had three chevrons and a rocker on his left shoulder. "Is this a prank?" James asked.

"Nope," Bernie replied.

George handed his ID card to James. "I can't wait to command my troops in battle," he said. "When do we go back to the front?"

"Not for a while," Bernie replied.

"Ah, man," George replied. "Well, time for me to train first."

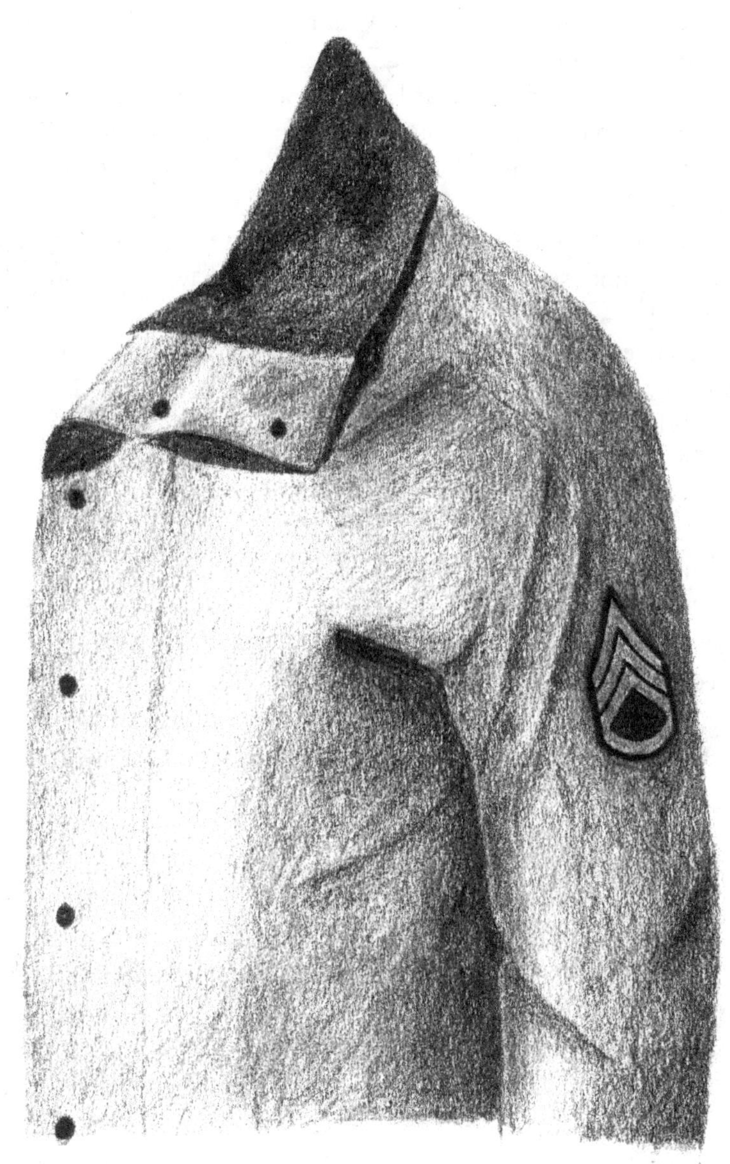

Captain Owens.

James looked at his ID for several long seconds, then handed it back. He scrutinized George. "What happened while I was dead? I seem to have missed something."

George laughed. "Well at least you won't have to put up with Ogden anymore. I can't wait to order him around for once. Don't worry, I'll make him be nice to you. Could I move you to another platoon?"

"You could pull a Uriah the Hittite on him and get him killed in battle," James suggested. "Then we wouldn't have to put up with him."

George laughed. "That would be funny. Maybe I should. I should see if I can get Cindy in my unit, too."

"Who's Cindy," James asked, "you're girlfriend?"

"No," George said indignantly, "she's a Stanislausi that joined us after we beat them."

"What? You just, trusted her and let her join you?"

"Her and forty others. They earned it."

"Forty others?! That's against regulations. Even though it's often ignored. Which is stupid. And they didn't murder you in your sleep?"

"Nope. Ogden allowed it. Them joining us, that is; not our being murdered in our sleep. But yeah, Bernie, what'd they do with him? Fire him? Demote him to a private?"

"Nope," said Bernie. "They promoted him to colonel."

"What the hell?!" George exploded. "Are you kidding me?"

"Nope," Bernie replied.

"Uh-oh," James said.

"Blast it!" George went on. "I'm gonna be right underneath that bastard. You've got to be kidding me. Who the hell did Ogden bribe to make him a colonel? We'll be worse off than before! Ogden competing with his peers at the battalion level. It'll be a nightmare! Blast it!"

Bernie cocked an eyebrow at him. "George," he said, "you've come a long way from where you started, but life isn't fair nor is it easy. Don't ruin your success."

"You know," George asked, "why is it that you are still a private? You should be like a colonel or something."

"I'm a soldier," Bernie replied, "not a leader."

"Rubbish, that's a lie. You make a great leader, I know."

"Mentor would be a better word. I have my ambitions, but now is not my time."

"Okay," George said slowly and shook his head. Bernie always was an enigma.

Bernie looked at him. "But you have a long career ahead of you," he said. "Make the best of it."

George nodded. "And hey, what happened to the battalion? Did they make it?" he asked apprehensively. Did he even want to know the answer?

"We made it," Bernie replied.

Oh, phew. They had done it. "Wait, 'We'? Are you saying — you survived?"

"Yup."

"Like, seriously, you actually survived?"

"I hid in a foxhole."

George stared at him. Only Bernie could pull off something like that. Magic force field for sure, and invisibility to boot. "What of B Company?"

"B Company doesn't exist right now."

"Yes it does," James said, "just we're the only ones here yet."

George breathed a sigh of relief. They had held back Lyon long enough. He had seen his job through to the bitter end and saved the battalion. He had achieved success. And now he was the captain of his own company! When they all came back to life, that was.

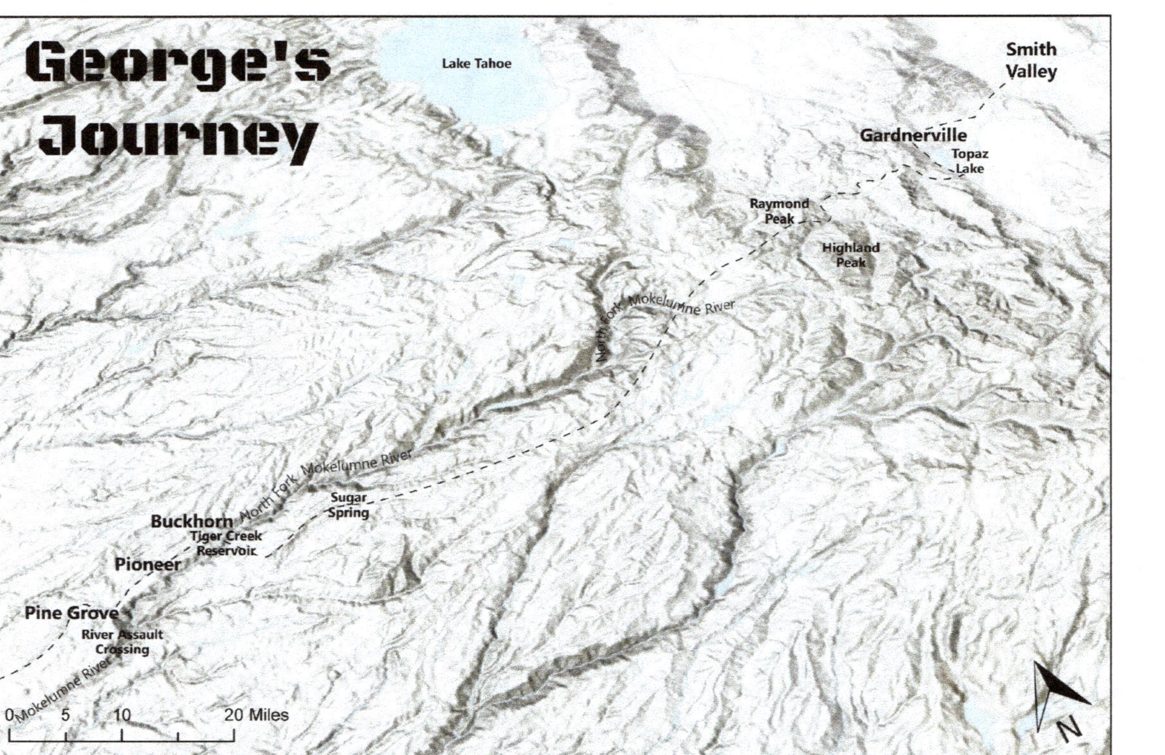

George's Journey
Lake Tahoe
Smith Valley
Gardnerville
Topaz Lake
Raymond Peak
Highland Peak
North Fork Mokelumne River
North Fork Mokelumne River
Sugar Spring
Buckhorn
Tiger Creek Reservoir
Pioneer
Pine Grove
River Assault Crossing
Mokelumne River
0   5   10   20 Miles
N

Acknowledgments

Thank you most of all to my family for supporting me in this, my first novel, and for beta reading my book. Thank you to my sister Emeline for pitching in whenever I got stuck trying to name a character, and to my brother Matthew for your advice on making the story more interesting and believable. The two of you together spared no criticism when you identified something about this book that could be improved to make it a better story. Thank you especially to my mother for being my copy editor. You spent a great many hours pouring over my manuscript, phone in hand, marking everything just in case. Any remaining errors are probably my fault.

Thank you to Joshua, my Paintball Wars partner, for helping me get the story right. Your grammar proficiency may cause me to cringe, but you have a sharp eye for storytelling, plot, and world-building. There are several scenes in this book that would still be subpar or illogical for various reasons had you not taken the time to explain to my stubborn self how they could be more effective.

Thank you to Becca for your story structure and plotting advice as a fellow aspiring author. Your feedback helped shape the earliest stages of writing, and your pointed questions and opinions helped me to identify where I wanted this book to go and keep it on the straight path of my plot when the story began to wander.

Thank you to Mrs. Leonard for beta-reading and editing my book and sharing your decades of experience in English. In discussing this book with you, your comments on theme and character development proved to be of invaluable help in clarifying George's character arc and his internal lesson to me so I could more effectively implement them in the book.

Thank you to Mrs. Boyle for beta-reading my book and advising me as someone who has already been through the self-publishing process several times. She writes the *Off the Itinerary* young adult fiction series under the author name M. Liz Boyle. Visit her website at mlizboyle.com.

Thank you to my Great Aunt Nancy for beta-reading my book and providing unique feedback from an audience I couldn't have easily accessed otherwise.

Notes

Book cover art and illustrations by Matthew Halsted.

Illustrations by Emeline Halsted.

Map imagery by Nick Budros (nickbudros.com, nick@nickbud ros.com) using ArcGIS, and edited in GIMP by the author.

Unit symbols created with Spatial Illusions Unit Symbol Generator (spatialillusions.com) and edited in GIMP by the author.

Book cover designed in GIMP (gimp.org) by the author.

Book formatted in Atticus (atticus.io) by the author.

Chapter I. George plays World of Warships, a free-to-play MMO naval wargame that is designed for serious, engaging battles over historically-accurate ships. Crossy Road should need no introduction. George watches two YouTube channels: *Yarnhub* does non-gory cinematic 3D "movies" of military history, and *Half as Interesting* does short infotainment videos on literally any random subject that strikes their fancy.

Chapter II. The song sung by the boot camp aides to tease the new recruits is an excerpt from "The Cruel Wars" by The Dreadnoughts. The Alamedan flag was designed by Joshua using the free software Paint.net (getpaint.net).

Chapter III. Reveille and Taps are both traditional military bugle calls. The West Point Band has a good album of common bugle calls on YouTube. Both calls have many variations of lyrics. The song sung by the boot camp aides about wanting to murder the bugler is an excerpt from "Oh, How I Hate to Get Up in the Morning" by Irving Berlin.

Chapter IV. Drill Sergeant Hayes mentions *The Art of the Rifle* by Jeff Cooper, which is a fabulous book on the principles of riflery and marksmanship. One of the trainees mentions War Thunder, a free-to-play MMO vehicular combat game with historically-accurate ships, planes, and tanks that uses realistic damage modeling instead of arbitrary HP for an "authentic" battle experience.

Chapter V. The artillery gunners sing a compilation of lines from "Praise the Lord and Pass the Ammunition" by Frank Loesser.

Chapter VI. The "River Assault Crossing" 3D map utilizes data with service credits to: NAIP Images, Airbus, USGS, NGA, NASA, CGIAR, NLS, OS, NMA, Geodatastyrelsen, GSA, GSI, and the GIS User Community."

Chapter VII. The "Crossing at Tiger Creek Reservoir" 3D map utilizes data with service credits to: NAIP Images, Airbus, USGS, NGA, NASA, CGIAR, NLS, OS, NMA, Geodatastyrelsen, GSA, GSI, and the GIS User Community."

Chapter X. The paratroopers sing an excerpt from "May I Sleep in Your Barn Tonight, Mister?" a traditional American song. Hank Thompson sings a good version.

Chapter XIII. The "Battle of Smith Valley" and the "Methodist Church Hamlet" maps both utilize data with service credits to: NAIP Images.

Chapter XIV. The "B Company Rearguard Action" map utilizes data with service credits to: NAIP Images.

Back Matter. The "George's Journey" map utilizes data with service credits to: California State Parks, Esri, HERE, Garmin, SafeGraph, FAO, METI/NASA, USGS, Bureau of Land Management, EPA, NPS, Esri, CGIAR, USGS, Source: Airbus, USGS, NGA, NASA, CGIAR, NLS, OS, NMA, Geodatastyrelsen, GSA, GSI, and the GIS User Community. The author portrait was photographed by Sandy Halsted.

About the Author

William DeForest Halsted IV is the mastermind and creator of the world of the Paintball Wars. He wrote his first novel, *Private Owens*, at age seventeen. Besides writing, William enjoys reading, especially history, especially military history, and especially World War II history, which has greatly impacted the creation of the Paintball Wars Chronicles. He is slowly amassing his own mini library of military nonfiction, as well as old war movies from the '60s and '70s. William also enjoys playing board games with his family and video games with his remote friends. Additionally, he founded Halifico Motion Picture Productions YouTube channel with family and friends to pursue another hobby, filmmaking. As a musician, he plays the violin, piano, concertina, and sings. He lives with his family in California on a 200-acre ranch, where he is currently pursuing a bachelors in English with the intention of going to law school.

William can be contacted at paintballwarschronicles@gmail.com. He would love to hear from his readers.

Review Request

If you liked this book, please leave a review on Amazon. Customer reviews are the single most important metric Amazon uses to rank products in search results and will do wonders to help my book. You can also post reviews on other online sellers or book review websites like Goodreads. Please also share word of this book with anyone you think might be interested. The more readership I get, the more it will help me to continue telling the stories of the Paintball Wars.